W9-BXW-143

"Gripping."

"By the time I finished the book, I was riding an incredible book high that was making me want to start the series over again."

"Hands down the best of the series yet! I devoured this book."

More acclaim for the bestselling series

HEART OF VENOM

"Amazing . . . Estep is one of those rare authors who excels at both action set pieces and layered character development. This one-two punch makes *Heart of Venom* and all of Estep's Gin Blanco books unmatched entertainment!"

"Action-packed with tons of character growth . . . One of the best books in the series, which says a lot because Estep's writing rarely, if ever, disappoints."

"Wonderfully intense and graphic fight scenes, a plot that doesn't slow down, and bad guys that bring new meaning to the word *sadistic*."

DEADLY STING

"Classic Estep with breathtaking thrills, coolly executed fights, and a punch of humor, which all add up to unbeatable entertainment!"

"This book is brimming with suspense and fast-paced action. The pacing and plotting are absolute perfection! There's never a dull moment!"

—*Under the Covers Book Blog*

WIDOW'S WEB

"Estep has found the perfect recipe for combining kick-butt action and high-stakes danger with emotional resonance."

—*RT Book Reviews* (Top Pick!)

"Filled with such emotional and physical intensity that it leaves you happily exhausted by the end."

—*All Things Urban Fantasy*

BY A THREAD

"Filled with butt-kicking action, insidious danger, and a heroine with her own unique moral code, this thrilling story is top-notch. Brava!"

—*RT Book Reviews* (Top Pick!)

"Gin is stronger than ever, and this series shows no signs of losing steam."

—*Fiction Vixen*

SPIDER'S REVENGE

"Explosive . . . Hang on, this is one smackdown you won't want to miss!"

—*RT Book Reviews* (Top Pick!)

"A whirlwind of tension, intrigue, and mind-blowing action that leaves your heart pounding."

—*Smexy Books*

JENNIFER ESTEP

Black WID⚙W

AN ELEMENTAL ASSASSIN BOOK

POCKET BOOKS

New York London Toronto Sydney New Delhi

Pocket Books
A Division of Simon & Schuster, Inc.
1230 Avenue of the Americas
New York, NY 10020

This book is a work of fiction. Any references to historical events, real people, or real places are used fictitiously. Other names, characters, places, and events are products of the author's imagination, and any resemblance to actual events or places or persons, living or dead, is entirely coincidental.

First Pocket Books paperback edition December 2014

POCKET and colophon are registered trademarks of Simon & Schuster, Inc.

For information about special discounts for bulk purchases, please contact Simon & Schuster Special Sales at 1-866-506-1949 or business@simonandschuster.com.

The Simon & Schuster Speakers Bureau can bring authors to your live event. For more information or to book an event contact the Simon & Schuster Speakers Bureau at 1-866-248-3049 or visit our website at www.simonspeakers.com.

Cover design © Tony Mauro

Manufactured in the United States of America

10 9 8 7 6 5 4 3 2 1

ISBN 978-1-4767-7454-1
ISBN 978-1-4767-7338-4 (ebook)

To my mom, my grandma, and Andre—for your love, patience, and everything else that you've given me over the years.

To my grandma (again)—who is never everyday old stuff.

To my papaw—you will be missed.

ACKNOWLEDGMENTS

Once again, my heartfelt thanks go out to all the folks who help turn my words into a book.

Thanks go to my agent, Annelise Robey, and editors, Adam Wilson and Lauren McKenna, for all their helpful advice, support, and encouragement. Thanks also to Trey Bidinger.

Thanks to Tony Mauro for designing another terrific cover, and thanks to Louise Burke, Lisa Litwack, and everyone else at Pocket Books and Simon & Schuster for their work on the cover, the book, and the series.

And finally, a big thanks to all the readers. Knowing that folks read and enjoy my books is truly humbling, and I'm glad that you are all enjoying Gin and her adventures.

I appreciate you all more than you will ever know.

Happy reading!

* 1 *

It was torture.

Watching your mortal enemy get everything she'd ever wanted was torture, pure and simple.

Madeline Magda Monroe stood off to one side of a wooden podium, her hands clasped in front of her strong, slender body and a serious, thoughtful expression on her beautiful face. Next to her, a city official sporting a brown plaid jacket and a gray handlebar mustache droned on and on and *on* about all the good things that her mother, Mab Monroe, had done for Ashland.

Please. The only good thing Mab had ever done in her entire life was die. Something that I'd been all too happy to help her with.

Then again, that's what assassins did, and I was the Spider, one of the best.

Madeline's crimson lips quirked, revealing a hint of her dazzling white teeth, as though she found the same irony in the speaker's words that I did. She knew precisely what a sadistic bitch her mother had been, especially since she was cut from the exact same bloodstained cloth.

Still, even I had to admit that Madeline made an angelic figure, standing there so calmly, so serenely, in her tailored white pantsuit, as though she was truly enjoying listening to all of the prattle about Mab's supposed charitable works. It was high noon, and the bright sun brought out the coppery streaks in Madeline's thick auburn hair, making it seem as if her long, flowing locks were strings of glowing embers about to burst into flames. But Madeline didn't have her mama's famed elemental Fire power. She had something much rarer and far more dangerous: acid magic.

Madeline shifted on her white stilettos, making the sun shimmer on the silverstone necklace circling her throat—a crown with a flame-shaped emerald set in the center of it. A ring on her right hand featured the same design. Madeline's personal rune, the symbol for raw, destructive power, eerily similar to the ruby sunburst necklace that Mab had worn before I'd destroyed it—and her.

Just staring at Madeline's rune was enough to make my hands curl into fists, my fingers digging into the scars embedded deep in my palms—each a small circle surrounded by eight thin rays. A spider rune, the symbol for patience.

Mab had given me the scars years ago, when she'd melted my spider rune necklace into my palms, forever marking me. I just wondered how many more scars her daughter would add to my collection before our family feud was settled.

"I'd say that she looks like the cat who ate the canary, but we both know that she'd just use her acid magic to obliterate the poor thing." The suave, drawling voice somehow made the words that much snarkier.

I looked to my right at the man who was leaning against the maple tree that shaded us both, his shoulders relaxed, his hands stuffed in his pants pockets, his long legs crossed at the ankles. His hair was a dark walnut, blending into the trunk of the tree behind him, but amusement glinted in his green eyes, making them stand out despite the dappled shadows that danced over his handsome face. His ash-gray Fiona Fine suit draped perfectly over his muscular figure, giving him a casual elegance that was the complete opposite of my tense, rigid, watchful stance. Then again, Finnegan Lane, my foster brother, always looked as cool as an ice-cream sundae, whether he was out for a seemingly simple stroll in the park, wheeling and dealing as an investment banker, or peering through a sniper's scope, ready to put a bullet through someone's skull.

Finn arched an eyebrow at me. "Well, Gin? What do you say?"

I snorted. "Oh, Madeline wouldn't use her acid magic herself. She'd manipulate someone else into killing the bird *and* the cat for her—and have the poor fool convinced that it had been his idea all the while."

He let out a low chuckle. "Well, you have to admire that about her."

I snorted again. "That she's a master manipulator who likes to make people dance to the strings that she so gleefully wraps around them before they even realize what's happening? Please. The only thing I admire about her is that she's managed to keep a mostly straight face through this entire farce of a dedication."

Finn and I were standing at the back of a crowd that had gathered in a park in Northtown, the rich, fancy, highfalutin part of Ashland that was home to the wealthy, powerful, and extremely dangerous. The park was exactly what you'd expect to find in this part of Northtown: lots of perfectly landscaped lawns and towering trees with thick tangles of branches, along with an enormous playground that featured seesaws, swing sets, a sandbox, and a merry-go-round. It was a picturesque scene, especially given the beautiful blue-sky October afternoon and the rich, deep, earthy scent of autumn that swirled through the air on the faint breeze. But the pleasantly warm temperature and cheery rays streaming through the burnt-orange leaves over my head did absolutely nothing to improve my mood.

At my harsh words, a couple of people turned to give me annoyed looks, but a cold glare from me had them easing away and facing the podium again.

Finn let out another low chuckle. "You and your people skills never cease to amaze me."

"Shut up," I muttered.

As the speaker droned on, my wintry gray gaze swept over the park, and I thought about the last time I'd been here—and the men I'd killed. A vampire and a couple of giants, some of Mab's minions, who were torturing and about to murder an innocent bartender before I'd intervened. The swing sets, the merry-go-round, one of the lawns. Men had died all over this park, and I'd even drawn my rune in the sandbox in a dare to Mab to come find me, the Spider, the elusive assassin who was causing her such consternation.

And now here I was again, months later, confronted with the next Monroe who wanted to do me in.

Sometimes I wondered if I could ever really escape the past and all the consequences of it. Mab murdering my mother and my older sister, then trying to kill me and my younger sister, Bria, leaving me alone, injured, and homeless. Fletcher Lane, Finn's dad, taking me in and training me to be an assassin. My finally killing Mab earlier this year. All the underworld bosses who'd been trying to murder me ever since then.

The city official finally wrapped up his tediously long speech and gestured at Madeline. She stepped forward, reached up, and took hold of a black rope attached to an enormous white cloth that had been draped over the wrought-iron gate that arched over the park entrance. Madeline smiled at the crowd, pausing a moment for dramatic effect, before she yanked on the rope, ripping away the cloth, while giving an elaborate flourish with her free hand.

Fancy, curlicued letters spelled out the new name in the black metal arch: *Monroe Memorial Park.*

I glared up at the sign, wishing I had one of the blacksmith hammers that my lover, Owen Grayson, used in his forge, so I could kneecap the gate, send it crashing to the ground, and then knock out each and every one of those damn letters in the toothy smile of the arch. Especially the ones in *Monroe*. But, of course, I couldn't do that. Not now. Maybe late tonight, when the park was nice and deserted, and no one was around to see me vent my pent-up rage on an innocent sign.

This wasn't the first dedication I'd attended in the past few weeks. After finally making her grand appearance in Ashland back in September, Madeline had wasted no time in claiming her millions in inheritance as M.M. Monroe, moving into Mab's mansion, and letting everyone know that she intended to pick up all of her mother's business interests, legitimate and otherwise.

I didn't know exactly what her master plan was, but Madeline had set about ingratiating herself with all sorts of civic, charitable, and municipal groups, saying she wanted to continue all of the good works her mother had funded while she was alive. Of course, she was lying through her perfect teeth, since Madeline was no more charitable than her mama had been. But if there was one thing that folks in Ashland responded to, it was cold, hard cash—or at least the promise of it.

And so the dedications had begun. A wing at the Briartop art museum, the train station, several bridges, a good chunk of the interstate that wrapped around the downtown loop, and now this park. Every few days, it seemed like someone was engraving, chiseling, painting, broadcasting, or proclaiming something else in Mab's name at dear, dutiful daughter Madeline's teary and oh-so-grateful requests.

And I'd been to every single breakfast, luncheon, dinner, tea party, cocktail hour, coffee klatch, barbecue, and fish fry, trying to figure out what my new enemy was up to. But Madeline was an excellent actress; all she did was grin and make small talk and preen for the cameras. Every once in a while, I would catch her staring at me, a small smile playing across her lips, as though my obvious stake-outs were amusing her. Well, that made one of us.

Of course, I had Finn digging into Madeline, trying to find out everything he could about her past, her personal life, and her finances, in hopes of finding a clue to what she was planning for me and the rest of the Ashland underworld. But so far, Finn hadn't been able to find anything out of the ordinary. Neither had Silvio Sanchez, my new self-proclaimed personal assistant.

She had no criminal history. No massive debt load. No large cash withdrawals from her bank accounts. No sudden, hostile takeovers of any businesses—legal or otherwise—that Mab had once owned. And perhaps most telling of all, no late-night, hush-hush meetings with the underworld bosses.

Yet.

Still, I knew that Madeline had some sort of scheme in mind for me. Impending evil always made my spider rune scars itch in warning—and anticipation of turning the tables on my enemies.

Usually, Madeline ignored me at the dedications, but apparently, she wanted to chitchat today, because she shook hands with the official, then strolled in my direction. And she wasn't alone.

Two people followed her. One was a giant bodyguard dressed in a white silk shirt and a black pantsuit, around seven feet tall, with light hazel eyes and a sleek bob of golden hair that curled under at the ends. The sun had reddened her milky cheeks, giving her skin a bit of hot, ruddy color and darkening the faint freckles that dotted her face. The other was a much shorter man, clutching a silverstone briefcase in front of him and dressed in a light gray suit that was even slicker and more expensive than Finn's. A lion's mane of hair wrapped around his head, the arches, dips, and waves as pretty and perfect as icing decorating a cake. His elegant silver coif hinted at his sixty-something age, despite the tight, tan, unlined skin of his face.

Emery Slater and Jonah McAllister. Emery was the niece of Elliot Slater, who'd been Mab's number one giant enforcer before I'd taken credit for killing him, while Jonah had been Mab's personal lawyer and someone whose many crimes I'd taken great pleasure in exposing back during the summer. Needless to say, there was plenty of hate to go around among the three of us.

"Incoming," Finn murmured, straightening up, pushing away from the tree, and moving to stand beside me.

Madeline stopped in front of me, with Emery and Jonah flanking her. The giant and the lawyer both shot me icy glares, but Madeline's features were warm and welcoming as she sidled a little closer to me, and a serene smile stretched across her face.

"Why, Gin Blanco," she purred. "How good of you to come out to my dedication today. And looking so . . . spiffy."

I wore what I always wore: black boots, dark jeans, and a long-sleeved black T-shirt. Next to Madeline and her crisp white suit, I resembled one of the hoboes who sometimes slept in this park. Madeline might seem all sweetness and light on the outside, but on the inside, I knew that her heart was full of venom and as vicious as mine.

"Why, Madeline," I drawled right back at her, "you know that I wouldn't have missed it for the world."

"Yes," she murmured. "You do seem rather fond of popping up everywhere I go."

"Well, you can hardly blame me for that. It's always so very lovely to see someone of Mab's stature honored in such small but touching ways."

Madeline's lips quirked again, as if she was having trouble holding back her laughter at my blatant lie. Yeah. Me too.

"Funny thing, though," I said. "You know was I've noticed? That Mab's name isn't actually *on* anything. It's always just 'Monroe Memorial this' and 'Monroe Memorial that.' Why, if I didn't know better, I'd almost think that *you* were going around town putting *your* name on everything. Instead of your dearly departed mama's."

Finn chuckled. Emery and Jonah shifted their cold stares to him, but Finn kept laughing, completely immune to their dirty looks. He was rather incorrigible that way.

Madeline's green eyes crinkled a bit at the corners, as if she was having to work to maintain her sunny smile. "I think that you're mistaken, Gin. I'm honoring my mother exactly the way that she would have wanted me to."

"And I think that you have as little love for your dead mama as I do. You couldn't care less about what she would have wanted."

Anger flashed in Madeline's eyes, making them flare an even brighter, more vibrant green, the same intense, wicked color as the acid that she could summon with just a wave of her French-manicured hand. She didn't like me calling her out on her true feelings for her mother, and she especially didn't like that I'd pointed out that the dedications were all about her ego, not Mab.

Good. I wanted to make her angry. I wanted to piss her off. I wanted to rile her up so much that she couldn't even see straight, much less think straight, especially when it came to me. Because that's when she would make a mistake, and I could finally figure out what her endgame was and how I could stop it before she destroyed everything and everyone I cared about.

"But who am I to judge?" I drawled on. "I wouldn't care either, not if she had been my mother. I guess it's one of those little things that we'll just have to agree to disagree on."

Madeline blinked, and she forced her crimson lips to lift a little higher. "You know, I think that you're right. We are just destined to agree to disagree—about a great many things."

We stared each other down, our stances casual and our features perfectly pleasant but with a deadly, dangerous coldness lurking just below the smooth surfaces.

"Anyway, I'm afraid I must be going," Madeline said, breaking the silence. "I have another dedication to prepare for tomorrow. This one's at the library downtown."

"I'll be there with bells on."

"No," she said in a pleased voice. "I don't think you will. But I do thank you for coming out here today, Gin. As you said, it's always so very lovely to see you."

Madeline smirked at me, then pivoted on her stiletto and moved back toward the podium, shaking hands and thanking all for their support and well wishes. Emery and

Jonah each gave me one more hostile glare before they trailed after her. Soon the three of them were in the heart of the crowd, with Finn and me standing by ourselves underneath the maple.

"She really is something," Finn said in an admiring tone, his eyes locked onto Madeline's lithe, gorgeous figure.

Despite his being involved with Bria, Finn was still a shameless flirt who loved to charm every woman who crossed his path. He would never do that with Madeline, for obvious reasons, but that didn't keep him from ogling her for all he was worth. I scoffed and rolled my eyes.

"What?" he protested. "She's like a black widow spider. I can admire the beauty of such a creature, even if I know exactly how deadly it is."

"Only you would think that being eaten during your postcoital bliss would be worth it."

Finn shrugged, then flashed me a mischievous grin. "But what a way to go."

He stared at Madeline another moment before looking over the rest of the crowd. He must have spotted someone he knew, perhaps one of the clients at his bank, because he waved, murmured an excuse to me, and headed in the direction of a wizened old dwarf who was wearing a large pink sun hat and an even larger diamond solitaire that could have had its own zip code. Finn never missed an opportunity to mix business with pleasure, and a moment later, he was attached to the dwarf's side, having winked and wiggled his way past her female giant bodyguard. Finn gave the elderly woman a charming smile as he bent down and pressed a dainty kiss to her brown, wrinkled hand. Well, at least he was an equal-opportunity flirt.

But I continued to watch Madeline, who was still shaking hands and was now standing directly below the arch that bore her family's name. Maybe it was the way the sun was hitting the metal, but the word *Monroe* seemed to flicker and gleam with a particularly intense, sinister light, as though it were made out of some sort of black fire, instead of just sturdy old iron.

Madeline noticed me staring at her and gave me another haughty, pleased smirk before turning her back and ignoring me completely. Emery and Jonah did the same, moving to flank their boss again.

All I could do was stand there and watch my enemy have a grand old time, basking in the warm glow of everyone's collective, attentive goodwill.

Maybe I'd been wrong when I told Finn that being eaten was the worst part.

Maybe waiting for the black widow to kill you was the real torture.

☀ 2 ☀

The dedication wrapped up soon after that, and Madeline, Emery, and Jonah got into a black Audi and drove away from the park, probably off to the Monroe family mansion to plot and scheme the rest of the day away.

I stood beneath the maple, alternating between glaring at the Audi as it zoomed away and that metal arch that was now a permanent reminder of Mab, Madeline, and all the horrible things they'd done to me and the people I loved. My hands clenched into fists again, my fingers digging even deeper into my spider rune scars, and cold anger seared my chest from my heart all the way down into the pit of my stomach.

Finn finished flirting with the elderly dwarf and her bodyguard and wandered back over to me.

"I need a drink," I growled.

He perked up. "Now you're talking."

We left the newly crowned Monroe Memorial Park

behind and walked about half a mile until we came to a gray, featureless building that looked like it might house corporate offices. A large sign of a heart with an arrow through it was mounted over the front doors, the only clue that there was more to this gin joint than met the eye. Northern Aggression, Ashland's most decadent nightclub, was run by Roslyn Phillips, a vampire friend of ours.

It was barely past one in the afternoon now, so the neon sign was dark, although it would light up as soon as the sun set, a glowing red, orange, and yellow beacon that would invite folks from near and far to step right on inside and indulge themselves in all the hedonistic pleasures the club offered—blood, liquor, sex, smokes. You could get all that and more inside, in as small or large quantities as you desired, as long as you had enough money to pay to play.

Roslyn knew that Finn and I were going to the dedication, so she'd invited us to swing by afterward. I knocked on one of the doors, but there was no answer. I rang the buzzer too, in case Roslyn hadn't heard my sharp, loud raps. Still, no answer.

"You think something's wrong?" I asked, worry replacing my earlier anger. "That someone's holding Roslyn inside?"

That's exactly what had happened a few weeks ago when Beauregard Benson, a vampire drug dealer, held Roslyn hostage and forced her to lure me over to the nightclub.

"I'm sure that Roslyn is fine," Finn said. "Not everything in life is part of a dastardly plot against you, Gin."

I gave him a flat look.

He sighed. "But, given your past experiences, I suppose that it wouldn't hurt to check and make sure that everything's kosher." He held out his hand. "If you will be so kind?"

Just like Madeline, I was an elemental with powerful magic. And, just like Madeline, I had a rare talent—being gifted in not one, but two of the main areas, Ice and Stone, in my case. So I held out my own hand and reached for the cool power running through my veins. A silver light flared, centered in the spider rune scar in my palm, before fading away. A second later, I handed over two long, slender Ice picks to Finn.

He bent over and inserted the picks into the lock. Ten seconds later, the tumblers *click-click-click*ed into place, and the door *snick*ed open. Finn tossed the Ice picks onto the asphalt to melt away.

He grinned. "Child's play."

I shook my head and followed him inside.

The interior of Northern Aggression was dim, with only a few low lights on here and there, and the VIP section off to one side was completely dark. Finn strolled forward, walking out onto the springy bamboo dance floor in the center of the club, but I took a more circumspect route, hugging the thick, red velvet curtains that covered the walls and scanning the shadows, looking for any hint of danger. I also palmed a silverstone knife, one of five that I always carried on me—one up either sleeve, one against the small of my back, and one tucked into the side of either boot.

Just because I didn't think that Madeline would strike

out at me somewhere like Northern Aggression made it all the more likely that she would. That was just the way my perpetual bad luck went. I was fully expecting some sort of sneak attack from her, a proverbial knife erupting from out of nowhere and stabbing into my back again and again until I was down for the count and bleeding out. That she'd been in town for more than a month and hadn't made an obvious move yet only set me that much more on edge.

Oh, yeah, waiting for the black widow to strike was *definitely* the worst sort of torture.

"What do you mean there's a problem?" a loud, angry voice sounded.

Finn and I both stopped as a door set into the back wall burst open, causing the curtains to swirl in surprise, and Roslyn Phillips came striding through, holding a cell phone up to her right ear. She was wearing a fitted, pale green pantsuit that brought out the rich, toffee color of her eyes and skin, as well as highlighting her gorgeous, curvy figure. A thin headband dotted with clear, square crystals held her black hair back from her face, although the displeased pucker of her glossy pink lips distracted from the symmetrical beauty of her flawless features.

Roslyn spotted Finn and pointed her finger at the elemental Ice bar that lined one wall, telling him to make himself comfortable. Finn headed in that direction, but I took one more look around before sliding my knife back up my sleeve, going over, and settling myself on the stool next to his. Still holding her phone, Roslyn marched around the Ice bar and started stalking back and forth behind it, making the bamboo floor creak with her hurried steps.

"Understand you? Of course I understand *you*. More important, I understand *this*—we have a contract," Roslyn snapped to her caller. "And if you don't honor it, then I will sue you for every drop of liquor and cash that I can squeeze out of you. Understand *that*."

She slammed her phone down onto the bar, causing a few chips of elemental Ice to fly up from the frosty surface. Roslyn glared at the device before pinching the bridge of her nose. She grimaced, revealing the small fangs in her mouth, before letting out a long, tired sigh and dropping her hand from her face.

"Sorry, guys," she said. "As you can tell, I'm having a bit of a problem. I heard the buzzer and was coming to get you, although I see that Finn went ahead and let you in anyway."

He winked at her. "I never let a little thing like a locked door stand between me and a free drink."

Roslyn laughed, but a cold finger of unease crawled up my spine.

"What sort of problem?" I asked.

She shook her head. "Despite the fact that we have an iron-clad contract and have been working together for years, my liquor distributor has suddenly decided to triple his prices. He's threatening to stop delivering to the club altogether unless I give in to his demands. Greedy bastard."

Roslyn reached under the bar and pulled out a pen and notepad. She flipped over to a new sheet on the pad, then turned around and started counting the bottles of colorful liquor sitting on the mirrored-glass shelves behind her.

"Why do you think he did that?" I asked. "Why now?"

She shrugged and kept on counting. "He probably realizes how much money I make just on liquor sales alone, and he wants a bigger piece of the pie."

"You don't think that it's something else?" I persisted. "That someone put him up to it?"

Beside me, Finn snorted, slid off his stool, and went around behind the bar.

Roslyn stopped taking inventory and looked over her shoulder at me, her eyebrows knitting together into a puzzled expression. "Who would put him up to something like that?"

Finn grabbed an expensive bottle of gin off one of the shelves and gave it an admiring glance. "Oh, no doubt Gin thinks that it's some sort of elaborate plot on the part of one Madeline Magda Monroe."

"Madeline Monroe?" Roslyn said. "Why would she care about my liquor distributor?"

I sighed. "Because you're my friend. Because she hates me. Because she's evil that way. Because she delights in being petty and cruel and watching others suffer, no matter how small and trivial the problems are that she creates."

Roslyn gave Finn a look that clearly said she thought I was off my paranoid rocker, although she was too polite to come right out and say so to my face.

Finn shrugged back, silently agreeing with her, then set about fixing a gin and tonic with a fat wedge of lime, which he slid across the Ice bar to me. "Here. Drink this.

It's a double. Maybe it will drown out some of your delusions."

I glared at him, but he merely wagged his eyebrows in response, before making another gin and tonic for Roslyn and then a final one for himself.

The vampire waved her hand. "Finn's right. These things happen from time to time. My supplier's been making noises for a while now about trying to renegotiate our contract. It's nothing. Just the cost of doing business, especially in Ashland."

"Don't I know it," Finn agreed. "I'll drink to that."

The two of them clinked glasses, then started chatting about all of the crooked businesspeople they both knew and all the fast ones that those folks had tried to pull on them over the years. But I just sat there, letting their cheery conversation wash over me, my elbows propped up on the cold surface of the bar while I cradled my glass in my hands and brooded into my gin. Normally, I would have enjoyed shooting the breeze with Finn and Roslyn, but right now, I couldn't even muster up enough enthusiasm to down my drink.

Maybe Roslyn's problems with her distributor were a coincidence. Maybe it was a complete fluke that the guy had decided to raise his prices today. Maybe it was just the cost of doing business in our corrupt Southern city, like my friends had said.

The only problem with all of that was that I didn't believe in coincidences. Not really, and especially not now, with Madeline in town. Not when there was a chance, however small, that Madeline was pulling someone's strings, even if it was to make trouble for Roslyn instead of me.

Then there was Madeline's not-so-veiled threat at the dedication earlier, when she'd said that I wouldn't be able to follow her to that library event tomorrow. Had she meant that I wouldn't be there because I'd be trying to help Roslyn? But Finn was right. That seemed patently absurd, even for my exceedingly high level of paranoia. Roslyn didn't need my help with her distributor. She could easily take care of something like that herself, just as she had for all the years she'd been running her club. Really, the guy would be a fool to deliberately lose her business, given how much liquor she ordered from him weekly.

Finn and Roslyn kept chatting, and I chimed in when necessary, but mostly I sat at the bar, trying to puzzle out what Madeline would get out of messing with Roslyn, other than the satisfaction of making the vampire's life difficult. That would be more than enough motivation for Madeline, but maybe my friends were right. Maybe I was being overly paranoid and crying wolf, when there wasn't really anything to be worried about.

But the thing about crying wolf was that the danger was always real and always waiting to gobble you up.

So despite Finn and Roslyn's assurances that everything was fine, I couldn't help but feel that Madeline had finally fired the opening salvo, shattering the delicate détente of our previously cold war.

Finn and I chatted with Roslyn for about an hour before her workers started showing up to get the club ready to open for the night. The two of us walked back to our cars, which we'd left in the Northern Aggression parking lot, and went our separate ways.

Finn headed downtown to his bank to put in the appearance of actually working today, but I'd taken the afternoon off from the Pork Pit, my barbecue restaurant, to attend the park dedication. Since I didn't have to report in anywhere, I drove over to the Monroe family estate.

Yes, I was probably being paranoid, but it had kept me alive this long. No reason to stop now.

Actually, I didn't drive over to the Monroe estate so much as I parked near it, steering my latest Aston Martin onto the side of the road at the next house over, a six-story mansion that belonged to Charlotte Vaughn. I stopped my car about a quarter mile down the road from the open iron gates that led into the Vaughn estate and stuck a white plastic bag in the driver's-side window, as though something was wrong with the car, and I'd gone to get help.

I couldn't exactly cruise down the street past the Monroe mansion, not without being spotted by one of the giant guards manning the closed gate there. But I'd trespassed on the Vaughn grounds many times before, and it was easy enough for me to scale the stone wall, drop down to the other side, and disappear into the thicket of trees that ringed the lawn. After that, it was just a matter of moving through the afternoon shadows until I could step into the dense woods that connected the Vaughn estate to the Monroe one.

Just before I entered the woods, I stopped and looked up at the Vaughn mansion. The white lace curtains were drawn back from the windows on the third-floor library, revealing a woman with black hair sitting at a desk, a phone cradled in between her ear and shoulder as she typed on a keyboard. Charlotte Vaughn, someone I'd helped and hurt in equal measures years ago. But I wasn't here to see Charlotte, so I slipped into the woods and continued on.

Charlotte might be Madeline's closest neighbor, but their respective mansions were still a couple miles apart, so it took me the better part of an hour to reach my destination—a couple of old, gray, weathered boards that had been nailed about thirty feet up in a sturdy maple and covered with a ragged, tattered camouflage cloth that had seen better days.

At first glance, it looked like a deer stand that some enterprising hunter had erected and then forgotten about long ago, but just a couple of weeks ago I had come out here in the dead of night and put together my makeshift tree house. Madeline had any number of anonymous, disposable minions whom she could send to the Pork Pit to spy on me anytime she desired, and I'd wanted my own way of keeping tabs on her.

I checked the ground around the tree house, looking for footprints, broken branches, and disturbed earth, but the bunches of leaves, twigs, and pebbles that I'd piled in strategic spots were undisturbed. As a final precaution, I reached out with my magic—my Stone power this time—and listened to the emotional vibrations and actions that had sunk into the rocks hidden in the leaves.

But the stones only whispered of the growing chill of the longer nights and the slow, steady approach of the winter they knew was coming. I probed a little deeper with my magic, but no dark, devious mutters, notes of worry, or trills of fear sounded back to me. Nothing bigger than a rabbit had been near my tree house since I'd been out here three nights ago.

Satisfied, I shimmied up the tree, hoisted myself up onto the boards, and checked the black duffel bag full of supplies that I'd left here a few days earlier. Binoculars, bottles of water, chocolate granola bars, a digital camera, a directional microphone, some sniper scopes. All the tools an assassin would need to do some serious recon on a target.

And Madeline was definitely my target, just the way that I was hers.

I seated myself in a comfortable position, picked up the binoculars, and peered through them. This particular tree stood on a rise, and my little house was situated high enough in it to give me a clear view of the back of the Monroe mansion, which featured an Olympic-size swimming pool surrounded by a patio. Despite its being October, the pool hadn't been covered up for the season yet, and the rippling blue water provided a colorful contrast in the heart of all that gleaming gray granite.

The only things that ruined the elegant scene were the wooden planks, orange extension cords, piles of power tools, and burly dwarves shouting to each other as they moved into, out of, and around the sides of the mansion. Even though I was more than five hundred feet away from the patio, I could still see the thick clouds of saw-dust that puffed out of the open doors and windows and lazily swirled through the air, bringing the harsh scent of paint fumes along with them.

Madeline was doing some extensive remodeling, both inside and out, and construction crews had been roaming the grounds every time I'd come over here to spy on her these past few weeks. I'd thought about disguising myself as one of the workers to see exactly what she was doing inside the mansion, but it wasn't worth the risk. I didn't care if Madeline was remodeling. I just wanted to know what her plans were for me and my family.

Still, as I watched and listened to the crews shout updates and directions to each other, I couldn't help but think back to the last time I'd been so close to the mansion, the night that I'd tried to assassinate Mab by sneaking onto the grounds, climbing onto one of the mansion roofs, and sniping her with a crossbow through a dining room window. What I hadn't known was that Mab had been hosting a dinner party for the group of bounty hunters she'd hired to track me down. Instead of killing Mab that night, I'd ended up getting shot and running through the woods for my life.

Then again, that's how a lot of my nights ended.

So I wasn't eager to risk another assassination attempt at the mansion. Not yet, anyway. Knowing my bad luck, I'd get spotted before I even got close enough to try to kill Madeline. Also deterring me were the giants who patrolled around the mansion, keeping an eye on the construction workers. All of them were armed with cell phones and guns, along with their massive fists.

More gun-toting giants marched back and forth across the lawn, coming all the way down to the edge of the grass. But they didn't venture into the woods beyond, much less come close to where I was perched. There was no point to it, not during daylight hours anyway, since they would have a crystal-clear view of anyone slipping out of the tree line and trying to cross the lawn to get to the mansion—and be able to shoot her down before she got halfway across the grass.

Still, I thought it was a bit sloppy of Madeline, not extending the security net farther out. When Mab was alive, giants had roamed deep into the woods at all hours of the day and night, and nasty things like sunburst rune traps had been carved into the tree trunks, ready to spew elemental Fire in your face if you were unlucky enough to trigger them. Not to mention the trip-wires, bombs, and other deadly surprises that awaited anyone stupid enough to try to breach Mab's outer defenses.

But Madeline seemed content to just secure the mansion itself, along with the landscaped grounds surrounding it. I wondered if she was really that confident in Emery Slater and the giant's ability to protect her. Or perhaps Madeline was that confident in her own acid magic, along with the giant blood running through her veins, courtesy of her father, Elliot Slater.

So I leaned back against the tree trunk, peered through my binoculars, and munched on a chocolate granola bar, since I'd only had a liquid lunch at Northern Aggression. Truth be told, keeping watch in the woods was a pleasant enough way to spend an afternoon. It reminded me of many a hike that I'd taken with Fletcher. And at least I felt like I was actually doing *something* to figure out what Madeline was up to, instead of just twiddling my thumbs and waiting for her to crush me under the sharp, pointed heel of her white stiletto.

Still, while I kept my tree house lookout, I texted all my friends, checking in and making sure that they weren't dealing with any sudden, suspicious problems like Roslyn was.

Owen was going into a meeting, while Eva Grayson, his baby sister, and Violet Fox, her best friend, were at their usual classes at the community college. Violet's grandfather, Warren T. Fox, was running his store, Country Daze, up in the mountains above the city.

Jolene "Jo-Jo" Deveraux was busy perming, cutting, teasing, dyeing, and styling her clients' hair at her beauty salon, while her sister, Sophia, was manning the Pork Pit for me, along with Catalina Vasquez, my best waitress. Catalina's uncle, Silvio Sanchez, was off doing whatever personal assistants to assassins like me did.

Phillip Kincaid and Cooper Stills, respectively Owen's best friend and mentor, were playing poker on Phillip's *Delta Queen* riverboat. And Detective Bria Coolidge, my sister, and her partner, Xavier, were dealing with the never-ending paperwork that came with being some of the few good cops in Ashland.

So everyone was busy and distracted with their own lives, and I was the only one obsessing about Madeline and what she might have planned.

Then again, that's the way it usually was.

Finally, an hour, two granola bars, and a bottle of water into my vigil, I was rewarded when the back doors of the mansion opened, and Madeline strolled out onto the patio, followed by Emery and Jonah. Madeline looked like she'd been working out, given her tight, white yoga pants and matching tank top. Her auburn hair was pulled back into a ponytail, while a white towel was draped around her neck, obscuring her silverstone crown-and-flame necklace. Emery and Jonah both still had on their suits from the dedication.

Madeline tossed her towel aside and settled herself in an oversize, white wicker chair that overlooked the pool. A maid wearing a white shirt and black pants with a bright red bun of hair brought out a silver tray with a pitcher of lemonade and several glasses. Emery and Jonah both waited until Madeline had a tall, frosty glass of lemonade in her hand before sitting down in matching chairs across from her.

I was pleased to note that Jonah didn't look particularly comfortable, his briefcase sitting square and upright in his lap as if it would shield him from Madeline's acid magic should she decide to unleash it on him. Jonah also tugged at his tie as if it were strangling him and eyed Emery with open suspicion, as if he expected her to try to beat him to death at any second.

It would serve the weaselly lawyer right if Madeline killed him. After all, he'd tried to steal her inheritance and had embezzled from Mab for years before that. Madeline had as many reasons to want him dead as I did, if not more. I doubted that she would do the deed for me, though. Not while she thought that McAllister could still be of some use to her.

Madeline and Emery sipped their lemonade, so I put down my binoculars, picked up the directional microphone, and flipped it on. Silvio had purchased the toy for me a few weeks ago. I'd told him what I wanted, and he'd shown up with it at the Pork Pit the very next day, with only a mild, chiding raise of his eyebrows as he handed me the bill. I would never admit it to him, but I kind of liked having an assistant, especially one as quiet, discreet, and efficient as Silvio.

Once I turned the microphone on, I started fiddling with the knobs, trying to maximize the range and clarity of sound. Mostly, what I heard was the steady, high-pitched *whine-whine-whine* of the power saws that the dwarven workers were using, along with the heavy *thwack-thwack-thwack*s of nails being hammered into boards. Whatever the crews were doing inside the mansion, it sounded big, loud, and impressive. Exactly what I would expect, given what a splash Madeline had made when she came back to Ashland.

After about ten minutes, some of the workers took a water break, and the sounds of the sawing and hammering died down to more muted, manageable levels. I leaned forward and adjusted the microphone a bit more, trying to get the most out of it that I could, before I pointed it at the patio again. It took me another thirty seconds, but I finally found a sweet spot that let me hear their conversation. I also raised my binoculars back up to my eyes and peered through them.

". . . how are things progressing?" Madeline asked.

Emery chugged down her lemonade, set the glass on the table, pulled out her phone, and started texting on it. "Everything's set."

Madeline turned her gaze to Jonah. "And you?"

He cleared his throat and adjusted his tie again. "Everything's ready on my end. I've reached out to all the right people. Dobson, in particular, is ready and eager to get started."

I frowned. Dobson? Who was that? And what was he so ready and eager to do? I pulled out my own phone and texted myself a note with that name so I would remember it later.

Then the wind picked up, bringing more paint-and-sawdust fumes along with it. I moved the directional mike from one side of my makeshift tree house to the other, but the breezy gusts kept me from hearing much more than sharp, staticky crackles of air.

But it didn't matter because Madeline drained the rest of her lemonade, then rose to her feet. She gave Emery a conspiratorial smile, not even bothering to glance at Jonah, who was clutching his still-full glass of lemonade with one hand and his briefcase with the other.

"Good," she purred. "I'm glad that everything's finally in order. It's been a long wait, but now it's time to really make my presence known—to everyone in Ashland."

Madeline beamed at Emery for another moment before turning and sweeping into the mansion.

Jonah got up and started to follow her, but Emery moved in front of him, giving the lawyer the same cold gaze that she regarded everyone else with.

"Don't fuck this up," she growled. "Or you'll be wishing that Blanco had killed you when she had the chance."

Jonah smiled, trying to defuse the tension between them, but the expression didn't even come close to reaching his brown eyes, and his tan skin seemed even tighter than normal, as though he was clenching his teeth together to keep them from chattering in fear. I wondered how he liked his new masters. I was willing to bet that Madeline was more of a nightmare than Mab had ever been, given her propensity for playing games with people.

Emery gave Jonah one more hard look before she too disappeared into the mansion.

The lawyer stayed where he was, swaying back and forth on his feet, as though he were about to topple over in a dead faint. He glanced around, making sure that no one was paying any attention to him, then put his lemonade down, opened his briefcase, reached inside, and drew out a not-so-small silver flask. He threw his head all the way back and drained the flask's contents, whatever they were.

I chuckled. Poor Jonah. Just a month in and drinking on the job already. Aw, I just hated that for him.

After he drained his flask, McAllister stuffed it back into his briefcase, snapped it shut, squared his shoulders, and headed back into the mansion to suffer through whatever else Madeline and Emery had planned for him for the rest of the day—

Crack.

I froze at the sharp, staccato, unexpected sound. But what was even worse were the voices that accompanied it a second later—low, gruff voices that were getting louder and louder the closer they got to my location.

❊ 3 ❊

I remained as still as death, scarcely daring to breathe, as I waited and listened, trying to determine if I'd been spotted.

"Do you really think there's someone out here?" a giant rumbled, his low, deep voice much closer than before.

"I don't know," another one muttered back to him. "But Emery thought she saw the sun reflecting off something in the woods. She texted and told me to come check it out."

Since they hadn't spied me yet, I slowly, carefully, quietly turned off the directional microphone, so the *crackle-crackle* of static wouldn't give me away, and then set it down, along with my binoculars. I dropped down onto my belly, ignoring the splinters that pricked through my T-shirt and into my stomach, and eased over to the edge of my makeshift tree house, peering out through a rip in the camouflage fabric at the forest floor below.

Sure enough, about ten feet ahead, a large clump of rhododendron bushes rustled, and two giants stepped around it.

Sloppy, sloppy, Gin! I silently cursed myself. I'd been so focused on fiddling with the microphone and trying to hear what Madeline and the others were saying that I'd neglected to keep an eye on the guards patrolling the lawn. Two of them had slipped away from their posts and were now creeping through the woods toward my position, heads swiveling left and right, guns drawn, fingers curled around the triggers, scanning their surroundings for the smallest sign of movement so they could blast the danger into oblivion.

Emery must have seen the sun winking off my binocular lenses as I was watching their little lemonade party. But instead of sounding the alarm and sending a platoon of giants after me, she'd been discreet about things, slyly dispatching her men to my position, and hoping to catch me in the act—and then murder me.

I remained absolutely still and silent as the giants swept the woods below. I could have palmed a knife, leaped down from my perch onto their backs, and killed both of them, but I doubted that I could do it quietly enough to keep all the other guards from running in this direction. And if the giants swarmed on my position all at once, well, I'd have a hard time escaping, especially since Emery would no doubt come and lead the charge. She wouldn't be satisfied until I was trapped—or dead.

But even more than that, I didn't want to tip my hand that I'd been watching the mansion. I might need to come back out here again, and I wanted my hidey-hole to be intact if I did. So killing the giants was out, unless absolutely necessary to save my skin.

But I also couldn't slip away while they were right below me. All I could do was lie still, wait, and hope that they wouldn't have the bright idea to look up and see if someone was hiding in the branches above their heads.

"This is pointless," one of the giants finally muttered, holstering his gun and leaning against the very tree that I was perched in. "There's nobody out here. Emery is being paranoid, like always."

The other giant stopped as well, but he didn't put away his weapon. "Well, you know they're worried about Blanco and what she might do when things start happening. They definitely expect her to retaliate. Or to try to, anyway. Not that she should have much of a chance to, if things go according to Madeline's plan."

My eyes narrowed. What specific *things* could he be talking about? Madeline could set into motion any number of horrible scenarios that would piss me off enough to break our stalemate and finally come after her.

But this . . . this sounded like something *big*. My worry cranked up another notch.

"And then there's the party," he continued. "Everyone's on edge about that. If things go the way Madeline expects them to with Blanco, it will be fine. If they don't, well . . ."

He trailed off, and the two men exchanged a tense, knowing look.

My eyes narrowed even more. Madeline was throwing a party? When? And what for? Was she trying to get the Monroe mansion designated as some sort of historic landmark? That would fit in with all the construction going on, and it was just the sort of bizarre, egocentric thing I would expect, given everything else she'd done over the past few weeks.

"Anyway, you're right," the second man said, finally holstering his weapon as well. "There's nothing out here but trees and squirrels. Let's go back."

For once, my luck held, and the giants turned around and returned to the mansion without looking up and spotting me.

As soon as they were out of earshot, I slithered down the tree, landing in a low crouch. I palmed a knife and scanned the surrounding foliage, in case another team was lurking around, but everything was quiet. Those had been the only giants Emery had sent into the woods.

I left my gear where it was, hidden beneath the camouflage tarp up in the tree house, since it was all anonymous and nothing that could be traced back to me. Besides, I might still have use for it.

When I was satisfied that the woods were deserted, I slid my knife up my sleeve, got to my feet, and hiked back to the Vaughn estate to retrieve my car and drive home.

As I walked, I thought about everything the giants had said, but their cryptic words only raised more questions than answers. I'd have to get Finn and Silvio to nose around and see if they could find out who the mysterious Dobson was and if they could pick up any rumors about this party that Madeline was planning, who was invited, and what it was for.

I'd learned an important lesson today, though. No matter how careful and clever I thought I was, Madeline and Emery were even more so, and I'd have to be at my very best to weather whatever storm they had planned for me.

I made it back to my car and home to Fletcher's house without incident. I checked in with all my friends again, trying to be casual about things, but everyone was still fine. Whatever Madeline was plotting, it wasn't happening tonight.

I went to bed early, trying to put my worries out of my mind, but I tossed and turned for most of the night. Even in the small, fitful bouts I did sleep, I dreamed of Madeline, still looking angelic in her white suit, although the emerald in her crown-and-flame rune necklace flashed brighter and faster than a strobe light in warning. Her crimson lips lifted into a cruel smile, even as her eyes started burning neon green, and two balls of elemental acid formed in the palms of her hands. Then she reared back and threw her magic at me. The acid exploded like twin bombs against my skin, melting, melting every part of me it touched, eating through my muscles and tendons until even my bones began to bubble and dissolve. . . .

I woke up with a scream stuck in my throat, and I didn't even try to go back to sleep after that.

Instead, I sat up, snapped on a light by my bed, and reached for the black velvet box sitting on the nightstand. I cracked open the top of the box, revealing a beautiful necklace. A pendant shaped like my spider rune was the centerpiece of the design, with each delicate link in the chain also shaped like my symbol. A birthday present from Owen, who had crafted the piece in his forge.

Other than its sentimental value, the most important thing about the necklace was that it was made out of silverstone, just like the ring on my right index finger, which was also stamped with my spider rune. Silverstone could absorb and store all forms of magic, and many elementals had jewelry made out of it so they could have an extra reserve of power in case they needed it for something important, like an elemental duel.

More than once, I'd thought about going over to the Monroe mansion, knocking on the front door, and challenging Madeline to a duel. That would be one way to settle our differences and end our family feud once and for all. But I didn't know if I had more raw magic than she did, and it would be suicidal to fight her like that if I didn't even have a chance of winning. Besides, she would never accept such a challenge. Madeline liked her machinations more than anything else.

Still, ever since Owen had given me the necklace, I'd been feeding my Ice and Stone magic into the spider rune pendant and links, along with my ring. Just in case Madeline did the unexpected and decided to attack me head-on.

I might not be able to stop my nightmares, but I could plan for the coming battle. Besides, Fletcher had always said that preparation was one of the keys to victory.

So I reached for my magic, watching the cool silver light flare to life in my palms, centered in my spider rune scars. Then I placed my necklace in one hand and my ring in the other, watching as the metal slowly soaked up all the light, all the power, like a dry sponge absorbing water. When the last of the light vanished, I knew that the silverstone had stored that first wave of magic, and I summoned up another one, then another.

I stayed in bed, funneling more and more of my power into my jewelry, until it was time to get up, take a shower, and head to the Pork Pit.

I got to my restaurant early, right after nine o'clock. After checking the front door and surrounding windows for rune traps and other explosives, I went inside and flipped on the lights. I stood by the entrance and looked out over the booths clustered by the windows, the chairs and tables beyond that, the long counter with padded stools that ran along the back wall, and the faded, peeling, blue and pink pig tracks that curled through all of it.

Normally, the sight of the restaurant with its simple, well-worn furnishings and cozy atmosphere was enough to lift even my darkest mood. Not today. Not given my nightmares. And especially not when I still had no idea what Madeline was up to.

But there was nothing to be done about my growing unease and dread, so I closed the door behind me and got to work. Turned on the appliances, wiped down the tables and counter, washed the pots and pans, mopped the floor, refilled all the ketchup bottles. I even whipped up a pot of Fletcher's secret barbecue sauce, going a little heavy on the cumin and black pepper to give it an extra-smoky, spicy kick, and put that on one of the stovetops to simmer away.

By the time I finished with my morning chores, I felt much calmer. Madeline might be plotting against me, but I could handle whatever she dished out, just like I'd taken care of Mab all those months ago—by shoving my knife through her black heart. Like mother, like daughter would be just fine with me in that regard.

Finally, the only thing left to do was to take out the trash, a far more dangerous endeavor than it should have been. I swung the plastic bag over my shoulder and cautiously opened the back door of the restaurant.

More than one person had tried to kill me in the alley that ran behind the Pork Pit. All of the crime bosses wanted me dead because whoever accomplished my murder would have a clear claim on Mab's vacant throne as the head of the Ashland underworld. Hence all the minions they'd sent to jump me these past several months.

But things had been quiet ever since I dispatched Beauregard Benson a few weeks ago on the street right in front of his Southtown mansion. I'd only had to drop two bodies back here since then. The quiet was another thing that worried me. Because if the underworld bosses weren't sending folks to attack me, that meant they were scheming other ways to mess with me. I had enough problems with Madeline already. I didn't need any more.

But no one was clenching his fists and lying in wait for me beyond the back door, clutching a gun and crouching down beside a Dumpster, or cupping a ball of elemental Fire in his hand, eager to rush forward from the far end of the corridor and roast me alive.

I lingered in the alley, looking left and right, but it was deserted, and I didn't even hear the usual rats, cats, and stray dogs scurrying across the pavement, looking for whatever garbage they could eat that had oozed out of the overflowing trash cans.

So I dumped my bag of garbage, went back inside the restaurant, and pushed through the double doors, stepping back out into the storefront—

A cast-iron skillet zoomed toward my head.

I ducked, and the skillet slammed into the wall behind me instead of plowing straight into my skull. I whirled up and around, turning to face my attacker. It was a woman, about my size, five-seven or so, with murder in her eyes and bright red hair that was pulled back into a bun.

I looked past her and realized that the front door was partially open. I'd been so worried about Madeline that I'd forgotten to lock it behind me when I came in to work this morning, giving my would-be killer easy access to the restaurant. I cursed my own sloppiness for a moment before focusing on my attacker again.

Her white, button-up shirt, black pants, and black sneakers were as anonymous as her plain features were. My gaze kept going back to her copper-colored hair, her only distinguishing trait. I'd seen that hair, that sleek, tight bun, somewhere before, sometime very recently, although I couldn't quite remember where. But it didn't much matter who the woman was, whom she worked for, or why they both wanted me dead. She'd come in here intent on killing me, and she was only going out one way—bloody.

"Die, bitch!" the woman screamed.

"You first!" I hissed back.

She'd been rifling through the cookware while I'd been dumping the garbage because she'd dragged out all of the pots and pans and had lined them up on the counter in a neat row. She grabbed the closest one to her—an old cast-iron skillet of Jo-Jo's that I baked corn bread in—and came at me again.

It was one thing to be attacked in my own restaurant. I expected that these days. But using my favorite skillet against me? That was just plain *rude*.

I sidestepped the woman's second blow, but instead of whirling around for a third one, she kept going all the way over to the end of the counter where a butcher's block full of knives sat. She grabbed the biggest blade out of the block, then whipped back around and waggled the utensil at me.

"I'm going to carve you up with one of your own knives," she growled.

I rolled my eyes. Like I hadn't heard that one a hundred times before. Folks really needed to be more creative with their death threats.

The woman let out a loud battle cry and darted forward, brandishing both the blade and the pan at me this time. No one had ever attacked me with my own cookware before, so it was a bit of a new experience to be dodging knives and skillets, instead of bullets and magic. But I managed it.

With one hand, I blocked her overhead blow with the skillet. With my other hand, I chopped down on the woman's wrist, making her lose her grip on the knife. For an extra punch, I grabbed hold of my Stone magic at the last second, using it to harden my hand so that it was as heavy as a concrete block slamming into her wrist. Her bones snapped like carrot sticks. The woman howled with pain and staggered back, giving me the chance to dart forward and kick the dropped knife away, sending it flying up under the counter.

She swung the skillet at me again with her uninjured arm, but this time, I stepped up, turned my hip into her body, and jerked the heavy iron from her hand as she stumbled past me. But I didn't let her go too far. I darted forward, grabbed her shoulder, and yanked her back toward me, even as I brought the pan forward as hard as I could.

CRACK!

You could do a lot more than just cook with a cast-iron skillet, and that one blow was more than enough to cave in the back of the woman's skull. All of the movement in her body just *stopped*, and she dropped to the floor like a brick someone had tossed out a window.

Thud.

Blood poured out from the deep, ugly wound I'd opened up in her skull, like water spewing out of a freshly cracked coconut. Gravity lolled her head to the side, turning her empty hazel eyes toward the front door, almost as if she were still seeing it and wishing that she'd stayed on the other side, instead of venturing in here and meeting her death so bright and early in the morning.

I let the pan slip to the floor, then put my hands on my knees, trying to get my breath back. The fight hadn't been all that long, but the cast-iron skillet was heavier than it looked, and it had taken quite a bit of muscle to use it so viciously.

But even as I bent over, my gaze flicked to the windows, and I wondered if anyone had seen my fight to the death with the woman. But the commuters were already at work, and it was still too early for most folks to be thinking about lunch yet. The few people who did pass by on the street had their heads down, more interested in checking their phones than paying attention to their surroundings.

So I straightened up, went over, and shut and locked the front door before closing the blinds on all the windows. Then I turned my attention back to the woman. Blood continued to ooze out of her skull, painting the blue and pink pig tracks on the floor a glossy, garish crimson. More blood had spattered all over the skillet too, along with the woman's hair, skin, and bits of bone and brain matter.

I sighed. Damn. Why couldn't she have just jumped me in the alley like usual? Now I'd have to wash all the skillets and knives and mop the floor—*again*.

Sometimes, it just didn't pay to come in early.

· 4 ·

Normally, I would have hauled the woman's body out to the alley, piled some garbage bags on top of it, and waited for Sophia to come in so she could dispose of it during one of her breaks. But I didn't want to leave a corpse lying outside the restaurant, not now, with all my worries about Madeline. It would be just my luck that today would be the day that she finally put her grand scheme into motion. So I needed a better hiding place for the body. At the very least, it would be one less thing to worry about. Out of sight, out of mind, and all that.

So I grabbed the dead woman under the arms and dragged her into the rear of the restaurant, all the way over to the freezer against the back wall. Then I dropped to my knees and patted her down, but she wasn't carrying a wallet or any sort of ID, and no rune tattoos were on her hands, arms, or neck to tell me what gang she might have belonged to, if any. She didn't even have a cell phone stuffed into one of her pants pockets.

I frowned. Weird. No one went anywhere without her phone these days. So I had no idea who she was or whom she might have been working for. But on the bright side, no ID and no phone meant that there wasn't anything else for me to get rid of.

So I opened the freezer lid, then hoisted the dead woman up and over the side into the frosty depths below. I even went the extra step of piling several bags of ice and a couple dozen boxes of frozen peas on top of her, to further hide the body. I absolutely *hated* peas, and I never, ever served them in the restaurant, but I kept the boxes around for just these sorts of occasions. Because, really, who would ever want to see what was underneath piles of frozen peas?

After the body was stowed away, I retrieved the knife that had slid under the counter and washed it, along with all the pots, pans, and skillets that the dead woman had dragged out.

I wiped down everything with bleach to destroy any minute traces of blood and was mopping the floor again when a key turned in the front-door lock, and Sophia Deveraux stepped inside.

I might be somewhat grungy and anonymous with my jeans-and-T-shirt ensembles, but Sophia always stood out in a crowd. She had on the same sort of black boots I did, although her jeans were actually white today, and paired with a black T-shirt with a pair of fuchsia puckered lips in the center of it. The words *Kiss off, fool!* arched over the lips in silver sequins. Matching fuchsia streaks shimmered in Sophia's black hair, along with silver glitter, while pale pink shadow and silver mascara made her eyes seem even blacker than usual. Silver cuffs adorned her wrists, and a black leather collar studded with silver hearts circled her neck, completing her chic Goth look.

At the sight of me mopping the floor, Sophia stopped and eyed the pink water sloshing around in my bucket.

"Problem?" she rasped in her low, eerie, broken voice.

I shrugged. "Not anymore. She's in the freezer with the peas."

Sophia nodded, knowing exactly what I was talking about. After she got rid of the body, I'd have to defrost the freezer and scrub all of the bloodstains and smears out of it, as well as order some more frozen peas. I sighed. Sometimes, killing people just wasn't worth cleaning up the mess afterward.

While I finished mopping, Sophia started cooking, and we opened up the restaurant. Catalina Vasquez came in to wait tables and help with the lunch rush, followed by her uncle.

Silvio Sanchez was a short, lean, quiet man who tended to blend into the background with his subdued gray suits and ties. Unlike Jonah McAllister, Silvio's silvery hair was cut short and neatly brushed, and he didn't try to erase the faint lines that had grooved into his middle-aged bronze skin. I thought that the vampire was still a bit too thin, given how much of his blood and emotions Beauregard Benson had drained out of him a few weeks ago, but so far Silvio was resisting all of my attempts to fatten him up with the Pork Pit's home cooking.

As was his custom now, Silvio perched on a stool three spots down from the cash register, opened his silverstone briefcase, and pulled out his cell phone and tablet. He was always texting, typing, and making notes about something, although I couldn't imagine what he found so interesting about the comings and goings at the restaurant to so thoroughly record them all daily.

"Hello, Gin. I'm here for the morning briefing," Silvio said, swiping through several screens on his tablet.

I bent down and grabbed a dish towel from a slot under the counter so he wouldn't hear me sigh. I didn't think that my life was busy or complicated enough for a morning briefing, much less the afternoon briefings that Silvio had been making noises about adding to our so-called *schedule*, but I perched on my stool and listened as he told me about all the various information he'd gleaned from his contacts. Who was looking to expand into running drugs, guns, and other illegal products; who was trying to muscle in on a rival's territory; who had threatened to kill the competition in retaliation for some perceived slight.

When he finished, I shared the information I'd overheard in the woods yesterday about the name Dobson and the party Madeline was throwing.

"See what you can find out about it please," I said. "Especially when it is and who's been invited. I want to know if it's another flower-themed tea for the society ladies or something more important."

He gave me a sharp look. "And where did this information come from? I haven't heard a peep about Madeline hosting or attending any kind of party, not counting that library dedication later today."

I waved my hand. "Oh, a little bird told me."

Silvio frowned, his gray eyes narrowing in accusation.

"You haven't taken it upon yourself to spy on Madeline, have you? Because that would be a very foolish thing to do, Gin, directional microphone or not. I believe we addressed this during last Friday's morning briefing."

He might have found that microphone for me, but he'd also realized exactly what I wanted it for. Last Friday before the restaurant opened, Silvio had made me turn off the lights so he could set up a projector and give me a presentation, listing bullet point by bloody bullet point all the ways I could get captured and killed if Madeline caught me spying on her.

I'd smiled and nodded through the whole thing, but I hadn't told him about my tree house in the woods outside the Monroe mansion. I didn't want to add to his lecture about what a foolish risk I was taking—and how he should be the one doing the spying instead. Silvio took his self-assigned duties rather seriously that way. He'd even offered to help Sophia get rid of bodies, although the Goth dwarf had just snickered and gone on about her business solo as usual.

Apparently, Silvio didn't want to have to find a new boss because he was always chiding me about spying, proper body disposal, and other things like that, as if I hadn't spent my entire adult life being an assassin and careening from one dangerous situation to the next. His concern was touching, really, it was, but I'd been on my own for so much of my life that it also felt a bit . . . *smothering*. Most of the time, I felt like a wayward baby duck that Mother Silvio was trying to wrangle back in line.

"Of course I wouldn't spy on Madeline," I chirped in a bright voice. "Like you said, it's far too big a risk to take."

The vamp kept eyeing me, so I escaped his steady, suspicious stare by going over to a table Catalina was clearing.

"Did he tell you to be careful again?" she asked in a soft, amused voice, having overheard more than one of my conversations with her uncle.

I sighed and took a stack of dirty dishes from her. "Something like that."

She chuckled. "Well, I'm glad that he finally has someone else to worry about besides me. Takes some of the pressure off."

I stuck my tongue out at her, but Catalina just laughed again.

The lunch rush came and went with no problems, although I had to stop one of my waiters from opening the freezer with the dead body in it. He mistakenly thought something else was in there besides blood, ice, and frozen peas.

A little after one o'clock, the front door opened, and the bell chimed, signaling a new and most welcome customer—Owen Grayson.

I focused on him, taking in the rough, rugged beauty of his black hair, violet eyes, and slightly crooked nose, as he strolled over to me. Owen leaned across the counter, brushing his lips against mine. I returned his kiss and inhaled, drawing his rich, metallic scent deep down into my lungs, before he drew back.

"It's good to see you," I murmured.

He grinned. "It's good to be seen."

Owen had been busy with some big business deal the past week, so we hadn't spent a lot of time together. On one hand, I didn't mind the separation, as it gave me more time to spy on Madeline. But I always missed Owen when he wasn't around. Of course, we'd talked on the phone a couple of times a day, but it wasn't the same as being with him, watching him smile, hearing him laugh, feeling his arms around me. So it was good to see him, and it meant more to me than he knew. Because when he was here with me in the restaurant, I knew that he was safe.

"What about me?" another, far whinier voice called out.

Finn stepped up next to Owen. Their offices were close to each other, so the two of them must have met up and walked over here together to grab lunch.

"Well?" Finn demanded, crossing his arms over his chest, a petulant look on his handsome face. "Don't I merit some sort of greeting?"

I waved my hand at him, just to annoy him. "You? I saw you yesterday. Why, you're just everyday old stuff."

Fletcher would always say that whenever he wanted to rein in his son's ego a bit. Not that it ever worked for long, though.

Finn huffed and slapped his hands on his hips. "Everyday old stuff? *Everyday old stuff?* I am *insulted*, Gin. *Deeply* insulted."

Owen winked at me, amused by Finn's exaggerated histrionics. I ignored my foster brother, leaned across the counter, and kissed Owen again.

Finn might have been *deeply* insulted, but his wounded feelings didn't keep him from plopping down on the stool next to Silvio, with Owen taking the one that was the closest to my seat behind the cash register. Owen and Finn said their helloes to the vamp, who was texting on his phone, working his sources to try to find out about Dobson as well as Madeline's mysterious party. Silvio murmured a polite response, but his eyes never left the small screen.

Sophia and Catalina took care of the rest of the customers while I fixed up my friends' food—a grilled-cheese sandwich and sweet-potato fries for Silvio, a fried-chicken salad slathered with honey-mustard dressing for Finn, and a double-bacon cheeseburger and onion rings for Owen, with triple-chocolate milkshakes all around.

I had just set the guys' food on the counter in front of them when something entirely expected happened. The front door opened, and Madeline strolled inside, with Emery trailing along behind her.

Madeline looked the same as always—auburn hair, green eyes, crimson lips, white suit. Her silverstone crown-and-flame necklace glittered like a ring of ice around her throat, while the matching ring flashed on her finger. Emery wore her usual black suit with a white shirt, almost as if she were playing opposites with her boss's clothes.

Catalina seated them in a booth by the storefront windows that was almost directly across from my position at the cash register. Madeline gave me a cheery little wave as she settled herself in her seat, then leaned forward and started talking to Emery in a low voice the second that Catalina had taken their drink order and moved away from them.

It didn't surprise me that Madeline was here. She'd come to the restaurant at least once a week to eat—and usually more—since she'd been in Ashland. In her own way, I supposed that Madeline was keeping as close an eye on me as I was on her with my tree house outside her mansion.

Still, her smile seemed particularly smug, and her mood particularly perky today. I glanced at the clock on the wall. It was creeping up on one thirty, and the library dedication was at three, the event she said that I wouldn't be attending for some mysterious reason.

Dread tickled my stomach, and I reached up and touched the spider rune pendant resting in the hollow of my throat, hidden under my T-shirt and apron. I was wearing my necklace and ring today, just as Madeline was, and the feel of my Ice and Stone magic pulsing through the silverstone soothed me.

Owen, Finn, and Silvio had all noticed my newest customers, and the three of them stared at Madeline and Emery for several seconds before turning to face me. Silvio started texting on his phone again, his fingers moving even faster than before.

"What's her game?" Owen murmured.

"Other than torturing Gin with her mere presence?" Finn replied in a snide tone. "That's probably enough for her."

I shook my head. "Oh, I doubt that."

But there was nothing I could do about Madeline, short of demanding that she leave and making a commotion that would disturb my other customers. Which might be exactly what she wanted. So I resisted the urge to tell her to get out of my restaurant and fixed their food in silence. Both she and Emery had ordered barbecue-beef sandwiches with sides of baked beans, fried green tomatoes, and potato salad.

I thought about poisoning their food, just like I did every time they ate here, but I resisted the urge. While highly entertaining, Madeline's dropping dead in a plate of barbecue would be just a little too suspicious and bring far too much attention to me. Besides, I'd noticed that

Emery always tasted their food first anyway, on the lookout for poison, like a good bodyguard should be.

So I handed the hot plates and poison-free food off to Catalina, who served them, then sat back down on my stool. I looked at the copy of *On Her Majesty's Secret Service* by Ian Fleming that I was supposed to be reading for the spy-literature course I was taking over at Ashland Community College, but I didn't pick up the book. I wouldn't be able to concentrate on it. Not while Madeline and Emery were here.

Owen's phone beeped, and he pulled it out of his pocket, frowning at the message on the screen.

Once again, that cold finger of unease slithered up my spine. "Something wrong?"

He sighed. "It's this deal I'm trying to get done. Two weeks ago, all we had to do was sign on the dotted line, and everything was finished. But ever since then, the guy has been balking at every little thing. Now he's telling me that he's gotten a better offer from someone else, when yesterday he was in my office saying that he was finally ready to sign the contracts. Excuse me, but I need to try to talk him down—again."

Owen slid off his stool, moved over to the wall next to the cash register, and started texting on his phone.

"Don't even think it," Finn warned, noticing the tense look on my face.

"What?"

"That this is some sort of plot on Madeline's part. Deals fall through all the time. Trust me. I know."

Silvio looked up from his phone and shook his head. "I don't know. I'm with Gin on this one. Madeline comes into the restaurant, and Owen suddenly gets bad news? It seems a bit suspicious to me."

Finn clapped the thin man on the shoulder, almost sending him spinning off his stool. "That's because you spent most of your life working for a psychotic vampire who enjoyed sucking the emotions out of people at the drop of a hat. Relax, Silvio. You and Gin are paranoid enough for *everyone*."

Silvio and I both gave Finn a sour look, but neither of us said a word. Maybe he was right, and we were too paranoid, but that was one of the reasons we'd both survived this long. In fact, Silvio's paranoia was one of the things I admired most about him, along with his attention to detail. The vampire sniffed and smoothed down his tie, making the small silverstone spider rune pin in the center of the gray silk flash underneath the lights.

Now that he'd teased Silvio a sufficient amount, Finn slurped down the rest of his milkshake while he checked his own phone and messages.

"Don't worry," I said in a low voice, handing Silvio a plate of chocolate chip cookies that I'd baked earlier. "You'll get used to Finn . . . eventually."

"I rather doubt that," Silvio responded in a dry tone.

I hid a smile.

Despite my growing unease, Madeline and Emery remained in their booth, eating their food, while I chatted with my friends. Things were fine, if a bit tense, for the next ten minutes, until the front door opened again, and a gorgeous woman strolled inside.

She was as perfect as perfect could be—sleek black hair,

light hazel eyes, porcelain skin. Her plum-colored skirt was barely legal, and the matching four-inch stilettos on her feet made her toned legs seem even longer than they were. Smoky gray shadow and fuchsia lipstick highlighted her features, while a thin gold chain glinted around her neck.

Every head—male and female—turned to stare at her as she sashayed over to the counter. But as pretty as she was, I didn't like the look of her, and I glanced down, making sure I had an extra knife within easy reach in one of the slots in the counter underneath the cash register.

But the woman wasn't interested in me. She didn't even glance at me as she sidled up next to Finn, sliding onto the stool that Owen had vacated, since he was still leaning against the wall, texting his skittish businessman.

Silvio shot the woman a wary look as well, but Finn was all smiles as she leaned over and propped one elbow up on the counter, giving him an excellent view of the impressive cleavage spilling out of the top of her tight suit jacket.

"Are you Finnegan Lane?" she purred in a low, sultry voice.

Finn immediately brought out the big guns and favored her with his most dazzling, charming, aw-shucks grin, the one that had turned more than one woman into a pile of blubbering mush and made her panties pop off like a bottle top. "Why, I most *certainly* am Mr. Finnegan Lane. What can I have the pleasure of doing for you?"

The woman gave Finn a sexy smile. She leaned in a little closer, and so did he, until he was practically sitting in her lap. The woman let out a breathy sigh, making her cleavage emphatically rise and fall under Finn's appreciative gaze. Then she reached into her suit jacket, drew a folded piece of paper out from inside her lace bra, and slapped it into his hand.

"You've been served," she chirped, sliding off the stool and strutting away. "Have a nice day!"

Finn almost toppled off his own stool, but he managed to grab the counter at the last second and hoist himself back upright. He kept staring at the paper in his other hand, then the door that the woman had disappeared through, as if he couldn't believe what had happened.

Maybe it was wrong, but I laughed—loudly—at his obvious confusion. It was the first time in ages that I could remember anyone getting the better of him. I'd always thought that Finn's incessant flirting would get him into trouble, and it looked like today was finally that day.

Finn roused himself out of his stupor and unfolded the paper, scanning the document, his green eyes bulging wider and wider with every word he read.

"Problems?" I asked in a snide tone.

"I'm . . . I'm . . . I'm being *sued*!" he sputtered, whipping the paper back and forth in the air as if it were a flag in the middle of a tornado.

"For what?"

Finn stopped sputtering long enough to read through the document a little more carefully. "Mismanagement of funds at my bank."

I frowned. Of all the things that Finn could get sued for, that one should have been pretty far down on the list. He might have no qualms about tap-dancing around the IRS and their tax rules and regulations, but he did a great job investing, protecting, and growing money for his clients.

Finn's face grew darker and angrier the longer he scanned the paper. "Oh, it's from *this* schmuck. I should have guessed. He got all pissy with me last quarter because I only got him a ten percent return on his investment, when he wanted twelve. Doesn't he know how craptastic the market is right now? Mismanagement of funds, my ass. I've made this idiot a fortune this year alone. A fortune!"

Finn continued to rant and rave, but I tuned him out and stared at Madeline. She was still talking to Emery, although she had seen the commotion surrounding Finn, since everyone in the restaurant was now looking at him like he was a few bananas short of a fruit salad.

Roslyn and her greedy liquor distributor. Owen and his flip-flopping businessman. Finn and his impending lawsuit. Three seemingly separate things that had happened to my friends in twenty-four hours. A cold ball of worry formed in the pit of my stomach.

I dragged my gaze away from Madeline. I started to ask Finn another question, but I didn't get the chance. The door to the restaurant slammed open, jangling the bell so hard that it almost flew off the top of the wooden frame, and Eva Grayson stormed inside, a backpack and a crumpled piece of paper clutched in her fists and angry tears in her blue eyes.

"Owen!" she yelled. "Finally!"

Owen looked up from his phone. "Eva? What's wrong?"

She marched over to her big brother and thrust the piece of paper at him, the sharp, hurried motions making her long black ponytail slap against her shoulders. "I've been suspended from school."

"What? Why?" Owen took the paper from her and snapped it open.

"For cheating," Eva spat out. "Somebody told the dean that I was selling answers to a chemistry test. I got called over to the administrative office this morning. The chem professor and the campus police were there too, and they all totally blindsided me. I'd never seen that stupid test before, and I certainly didn't sell the answers to it. I don't even *know* the answers to it. But no matter what I said, or how much I denied it, they all just kept staring at me and saying that it really would be better if I admitted everything. I got so fed up that I told them all to go screw themselves. They said that they had to investigate the situation, and that I was suspended until they could figure things out."

Eva clamped her lips together, but she couldn't keep the tears from trickling down her flushed cheeks. Owen put his arm around her shoulder, murmuring into her ear as he tried to comfort her.

Eva's distress was enough to get Finn to put aside his own problems. He looked at her and Owen, then glanced over at Madeline, before finally turning back to me.

"Still think I'm being paranoid?" I sniped.

He never got the chance to answer me.

The front door opened yet again, and a giant with broad shoulders and a substantial potbelly waddled inside. His salt-and-pepper hair was cropped into a buzz cut that he had somehow spiked up even more with hair gel, while his cheeks had the ruddy look of someone who either drank a lot or was a cheeseburger away from having a heart attack. But what really caught my attention was the gold badge clipped to the pocket of his navy suit jacket, right over his heart.

A cop—one who was pretty high up on the food chain, judging from his expensive attire and the cocky way he walked.

And he wasn't alone.

Two uniformed officers, also giants, entered the restaurant behind him, along with a short woman wearing a pale pink pantsuit and holding an official-looking clipboard.

The cop marched over and stood in front of the cash register. Behind him, I could see Madeline staring at me and smiling.

That cold worry shot out through the rest of my body, freezing me from the inside out. This was it, this was the beginning, this was the start of Madeline's plan for me, whatever it was.

The cop gave me a hard, flat stare, his brown eyes as icy as my heart felt right now.

"You Gin Blanco?" he barked out, as if he didn't already know the answer.

"The one and only," I drawled back.

"I'm Captain Lou Dobson with the Ashland Police Department," he said, his gravelly voice booming through the restaurant. "And you're wanted for murder."

❊ 5 ❊

The last, loud echoes of Dobson's voice faded away, and an eerie, absolute quiet descended over the Pork Pit.

Everyone stopped what they were doing. The customers froze, their barbecue sandwiches, fries, and half-eaten onion rings clutched in their hands, while Catalina and the rest of the waitstaff hovered next to them, holding stacks of napkins and carrying pitchers of water, lemonade, and sweet iced tea. Owen hugged Eva a little closer, while Finn swiveled around on his stool to face Dobson. Silvio stopped texting, instead discreetly angling his phone and taking photos of the three cops and the woman standing with them. Sophia threw down the dish towel she'd been using to wipe off the counter and crossed her arms over her muscled chest.

But for the most part, everyone's wide eyes were focused on me, as they wondered how I would react to Dobson's accusation.

Well, really, it wasn't an accusation so much as it was the cold, hard truth. I had killed more than my share of folks over the years for a variety of reasons—money, revenge, survival. The police captain would have to be a lot more specific about whom he thought I'd murdered.

Still, I couldn't help but wonder if he was referring to Beauregard Benson. A few weeks ago, I'd gone to the vampire's Southtown mansion and bashed in his prize Bentley with one of Owen's blacksmith hammers before daring Benson himself to fight me. Our battle had ended with Benson bleeding out in the middle of the street after I'd plunged one of my knives into his rotten heart. Nothing special there, except that a group of gangbangers, vampire hookers, their pimps, homeless bums, and other folks who called Southtown home had gathered around to watch our fight. It was definitely the most public of my many crimes, but so far no one had squealed to the cops about it. But it looked like my luck had just run out on that count.

So no, this wasn't entirely unexpected, but it was still troublesome. As an assassin, as the Spider, I was used to attacking my enemies from the shadows and then slipping away into the darkness, leaving no trail behind for anyone to follow. But I hadn't done that with Benson, for many reasons, and now it seemed like it was coming back around to bite me in the ass.

I looked past Dobson at my real enemies. Emery seemed almost happy, or what I assumed passed for it with her, since her expression wasn't as dark and dour as usual. Why, that almost looked like the beginnings of a smile on her face. And Madeline was positively *beaming*, her green eyes sparkling with obvious delight at my impending misery and ultimate doom.

I stared at her a second longer, fixing her smug smile in my mind. I was going to enjoy slapping that smirk off her face when this was all said and done. But for now, there was nothing to do but face the music—and figure out how I could get myself out of this mess.

I slid off my stool and got to my feet.

"And why would I be wanted for murder?" I asked, answering the giant's accusation, careful to keep my voice calm and neutral. "I'm just a simple business owner, trying to get by, the same as everyone else."

Dobson smiled, revealing slightly crooked, too-white teeth. "Because you're the one who committed it, Ms. Blanco. Someone's missing, and you murdered her just as sure as I'm standing here."

A collective gasp rippled through the Pork Pit at his words, but I kept my features blank, as though nothing were out of the ordinary and I hadn't just been accused of murder in my own gin joint. But my mind churned and churned, focusing on the most important word the captain had said—*her*. Which indicated this wasn't about Benson at all, but rather a woman. But who?

"Really?" I said. "And who says that I murdered someone?"

Dobson waved his hand. "Oh, that's not important right now. But rest assured that we have a witness to your crime."

"Oh, I doubt that."

His cold brown eyes sharpened. "And what do you mean by that?"

I shrugged, then gave him my best, widest, most innocent and shit-eating grin. "Because nobody talks in Southtown."

More than a few chuckles rippled through the storefront, with Finn, of course, laughing the loudest and longest. Dobson glared at the customers who had dared to be amused by my quip, and the chuckles quickly died down. Suddenly, everyone was very interested in their food again, instead of the drama unfolding at the cash register.

Dobson unbuttoned his navy suit jacket and drew back the fabric, planting his hands on his hips. More than anything else, the gesture was meant to reveal the gun holstered to his black leather belt, a clear warning that he would shoot me at the slightest provocation, including any more mockery of him. But the motion also made his jacket sleeve ride up, revealing a platinum watch set with diamonds on his wrist. A cute little trinket. I wondered if that had been part of his payoff from Madeline for coming in here and accusing me of murder.

"Nice watch," Finn drawled, echoing my thoughts. "Especially on a captain's salary."

A flush swept up Dobson's thick neck, cranking up the color in his cheeks to fire-engine red. A few more titters of laughter sounded. Everyone in Ashland knew that the majority of the cops were even more crooked than the city's criminals. I looked past the giant at the two uniformed officers and the woman with the clipboard. None of them were wearing any obvious, expensive bling like their boss was, but all three of them started shifting on their feet. Guilt by association.

"I don't care for your insinuations, Ms. Blanco," Dobson snapped. "I work for the good people of Ashland. The ones that you've been menacing, terrorizing, and murdering for years."

Well, he had one out of three right.

"And you haven't been doing a very good job of it, now have you?" I said, my voice deceptively sweet and light. "If I've been doing all of that for all these years, like you claim. Seems like someone's been slacking off on his job, the one that the good people of Ashland pay him to do. Apparently very well, judging from that watch on your wrist, just like my foster brother said. Who knew that being a civil servant could be *so* very rewarding?"

More snickers sounded, making Dobson's face burn even redder than before. I half expected a whistle to sound and for steam to start shooting out of his ears, like it would with a cartoon character, but of course that didn't happen. After a few seconds, Dobson reined in his temper, and some of the angry flush faded from his face, although his brown eyes iced over that much more.

"Regardless of your charming opinions, you need to come with me," he barked. "I have a few questions to ask you down at the station."

He gestured at the uniformed officers. The two of them, a man and a woman, exchanged an uneasy look behind Dobson's back. They didn't want to get anywhere near me, not with my reputation. Smart folks. But they were more afraid of their captain than they were of me, because he turned and gave them a pointed glare, and they finally shuffled forward, the woman reaching for the handcuffs attached to her thick, black utility belt.

"Don't bother," I told her. "I'm not going anywhere

with you. I know my rights, and unless you have a warrant for my arrest, then I'm staying right here in my restaurant where I belong."

"That's not an option," Dobson growled. "You're coming with us, and that's final, Ms. Blanco."

"Forget it," I snapped right back at him. "Especially since you still haven't told me who I supposedly murdered."

His lips turned up into a smile. "Why, I thought you'd never ask. Her name is Shanna Bannister."

He reached into his jacket pocket, drew out his phone, and tapped on it. He turned the screen around so I could see the image he'd pulled up on it—a photo of the redheaded woman I'd killed in the storefront this morning.

In the image, Shanna Bannister was wearing a white shirt with black pants, and her hair was pulled back into a tight bun. It was the same sort of outfit she'd had on when she attacked me, but her clothes and the stiff way she was standing reminded me of something, some sort of uniform . . .

And I suddenly realized exactly who she was—the maid I'd seen serving lemonade to Madeline, Emery, and Jonah yesterday at the Monroe mansion.

For whatever reason, the redheaded maid had come in here and tried to kill me. No doubt Madeline had arranged the whole thing, either by threatening Shanna in some way or promising her a rich payday if she succeeded in murdering me. But Madeline had also realized that I would more than likely take out the other woman instead, and now the acid elemental was going to trap me with my own survival. Clever.

"Recognize her?" Dobson asked. "Her employer reported her missing when she didn't show up for work today."

Despite the gears grinding in my mind at this revelation, I kept my face calm, stared at him, and arched an eyebrow. "And you immediately jumped to the conclusion that I murdered her?"

"Shanna Bannister was seen entering your restaurant this morning. And she never came back out." A thin smile twisted Dobson's face. "Given your reputation, it wasn't hard to put two and two together."

A couple of the customers gasped, but most of them started nodding their heads and muttering to each other. Everyone in the underworld knew that I was the Spider, but they weren't the only ones. All of my staff had gotten wind of the rumors too, and the few customers who hadn't heard the whispers hadn't been paying attention.

"Now, don't make me call the rest of my men in here to cart you out," Dobson said. "Save yourself that much embarrassment."

He gestured at the windows. I hadn't noticed before, but four cop cars were parked on the street outside, with six more uniformed officers waiting on the sidewalk. All of the cops stared in through the glass at me, their hands on their guns, ready to storm inside and strong-arm me out of here, should I do something supremely satisfying but ultimately stupid, like cut Dobson's throat where he stood.

But if I went outside and got into one of those cop cars, I wouldn't ever get back out again. I knew it instinctively, the same way I knew Madeline had set this whole thing up. She hadn't cared an iota about her maid, and when the woman hadn't been able to kill me, Madeline had decided that having me arrested for murder would be a fun way to torture me before I died. If this hadn't been her plan all along.

If I went with the cops, no doubt good ole Captain Lou Dobson would put a clip full of bullets in my chest on the way to the police station, claiming that I'd tried to escape. Then I would be dead *and* disgraced, and Madeline could get on with her plans for the Ashland underworld, whatever they might be.

"Don't make this any harder on yourself, Blanco," Dobson barked. "You can come along quietly . . ."

He didn't add *or else*. He didn't have to.

"If you so much as flap your hand at me again, I'm calling my lawyer and suing your sorry ass for harassment," I snapped.

His eyes narrowed to slits. "Then you better start dialing because you are coming with me—one way or the other."

"Actually, Gin doesn't have to call anyone," Silvio piped up. "I'm her lawyer, and I'm right here."

The lean vampire hopped off his stool and moved to the end of the counter, so that he was standing beside me. With his gray suit and stiff posture, he did seem like a lawyer, right down to the superior look he shot Dobson. The giant loomed over Silvio, as though he wanted to punch the shorter man, but in the end he drew back, restraining himself, although I could see what an obvious effort it was.

Silvio glanced at me, and I raised my eyebrows in a silent question. He shrugged. I didn't know if he was a lawyer or not, but he was willing to play the part for Dobson. My new assistant was definitely getting a raise—should I live through this.

Out of the corner of my eye, I could see Madeline frowning. Apparently, she'd thought that Dobson could cart me off and murder me with no problems. She hadn't factored Silvio into her crafty calculations.

"Well, now that that's settled, I suggest you get the hell out of my restaurant," I said, my voice as cold as a winter night. "Before I sue you, the department, and anyone else who strikes my fancy right now."

Dobson turned his head, as though he was going to look over his shoulder at Madeline and Emery for guidance, but he noticed me watching and caught himself. He snapped back to face me, although he took several seconds to tuck his phone away, button his suit jacket, and calm down, thinking about how to handle the situation. But apparently, he had another ace up his sleeve, because a pleased smile spread across his face.

"I'm afraid that won't be possible, Ms. Blanco," Dobson said, a cheery note in his low, gravelly tone. "Because in addition to my questions, Ms. Winona Wright here is one of the chief inspectors with the Ashland Health Department, and she's had some disturbing complaints about your restaurant."

He gestured, and the woman with the clipboard slowly stepped forward, her eyes fixed on the pig tracks on the floor, instead of looking at me. Obviously she didn't want to be here. I wondered how Dobson had bribed or bullied her into making an appearance. Didn't much matter. She was about to cause problems.

"What sort of complaints?" I asked in an icy tone.

"Bugs in people's food, roaches in the storerooms, filthy restrooms, unsafe working conditions . . ." the inspector mumbled, her voice pitching lower and softer with each supposed infraction.

Finally, she finished, and Dobson fixed his gaze on me. "So, as you can see, Ms. Wright needs to do a full inspection in order to substantiate the validity of these claims," he crowed, knowing that he had outmaneuvered me.

Dobson brought his fingers to his lips and let out a sharp whistle that made even Sophia wince. "Come on in, boys!" he called out.

The cops outside on the street headed toward the front door, and the invasion of the Pork Pit officially began.

❋ 6 ❋

I might not have to go with Dobson to the station for questioning, but there was nothing I could do about the health inspector, who had the legal right to inspect every corner of my restaurant anytime she wanted to.

Including right now.

Given the tension, accusations, and hostility in the air, everyone was suddenly eager to push their plates away, pay up, and skedaddle, especially at the thought that there might be bugs in their food and cockroaches crawling around in the corners. Of course, the real roaches were out in the open where everyone could see them—Dobson, Madeline, and Emery—but I'd have a hard time convincing my customers of that.

So I gave the waitstaff the rest of the day off with pay, stationed Catalina at the cash register, and told her to charge everyone half price as they left, if they were even willing to pay that much for my supposedly tainted food.

I wasn't going to quibble about money today. No, I had far bigger problems to worry about.

"What do you want me to do?" Owen asked in a low voice, coming over to stand beside me. "Whatever you need, you know I'm here for you, Gin."

I shook my head. "There's nothing you can do. Go, take care of Eva's problem at school and the one with your business deal. That's the best thing you can do for me right now. Madeline's screwing with us, and I need to know that you guys are safe."

Besides, something could always go terribly wrong here, with all the cops with all their guns swarming all over everything, and I wanted the two of them out of the line of fire, should it come to that.

"Are you sure?" Owen asked. "I can stay. I *want* to stay."

His violet eyes glittered with anger, and he eyed Dobson with open hostility, Owen's fingers curling into fists over and over, as if he wished that he had one of his black-smith hammers handy so he could kneecap the giant for me. Owen's protective stance and obvious care and concern touched me the way it always did—and made me even more determined to get him and Eva out of here before something worse happened.

"I'm sure."

"I'll call you later," he promised. "Just as soon as we're done at the college."

I nodded. Owen wrapped his arms around me, giving me a soft, lingering kiss. I held on to him as tightly as I could, returning his kiss with an even deeper one of my own, trying to let him know how much he meant to me. Finally, we broke apart, and he rested his forehead on mine.

"Whatever happens, stay safe," he whispered.

"Always."

I stepped back. Eva came over and hugged me as well.

"I know you'll make that bitch pay for all of this," she whispered in my ear.

I drew back and winked at her. "Don't you know it," I said, sounding far more confident than I felt about actually making that happen.

But my bright, breezy tone and false bravado worked on Eva, who let out a soft laugh, her face a little less tense than before. Owen put his arm around her, and the two of them left the restaurant. The bell over the front door chimed with a mournful note as they stepped out onto the street and disappeared from sight.

"What about me?" Finn asked, taking Owen's place beside me.

"You need to leave too," I said. "Go to your bank, and get everything squared away there. Look into the lawsuit, and see what needs to be done about it. Like I said, Madeline's screwing with us. She wants us to react, she wants us to fight back, she wants us to be so pissed off that we do something stupid that gets us into even more trouble. So the best thing we can do right now is to stay calm, play it straight, and follow the rules."

Finn sniffed. "Rules are for *other* people."

I gave him a look.

"All right, all right," he said. "I'll see if I can figure out what else she might have up her sleeve. Or, at the very least, who else might be on her payroll."

"Check into Dobson for me too. I want to know why he's helping Madeline and exactly how much pull he has in the police department." A thought occurred to me, and more worry twisted my stomach. "And see if you can get a hold of Bria. There's no way she wouldn't have come down here if she knew what Dobson was up to. He must have gotten her out of the way somehow, and I want to make sure she's okay."

Finn nodded, promised to touch base with me later, and left the Pork Pit.

The cash register *ring-ring-ring*ed as Catalina calculated order tickets for the long line of customers. With the rest of the waitstaff having already gone out the back, that left me, Silvio, and Sophia with Dobson, Winona Wright, and the other cops in the restaurant.

Dobson looked at me as if he wanted me to put up more of a fight about the health inspection, probably so he could use my refusal to arrest me on some trumped-up charge. But all I did was give him a cold, flat stare in return. His face fell a little when he realized that I wasn't going to protest, but he got over his disappointment.

"Well, then," he said, rubbing his hands together in anticipation, "let's get started."

Dobson marched back to the men's restroom, yanked open the door, and looked inside. "Filthy," he pronounced. "Absolutely filthy."

I walked up behind him and peered around his broad body. The restroom wasn't filthy, since I had cleaned it this morning. In fact, nothing was out of place at all, unless you counted the lone, crumpled paper towel that someone had tossed at the trash can. The towel had missed the mark, since it was lying on the floor a foot short of the container.

Dobson shook his head. "I wouldn't take a piss in here with someone else's dick. Make sure you make a note of that, Ms. Wright."

The only dick here was him. I had to grind my teeth together to keep from kicking him in the back of his knee, pushing him forward through a stall door, and drowning him in one of the toilets.

The giant moved from the restrooms to the cooking area, which ran along the back wall. Sophia stood in front of the ovens. She hadn't moved a muscle since Dobson entered the restaurant, and her arms were still crossed over her chest, so that all you could see were the words *Kiss off* on her T-shirt. Yeah, that about summed up my mood right now.

Dobson did a double take at the Goth dwarf, but he was wise enough to skirt around her, instead of ordering her to get out of the way or using his enormous body to shove past her. He wouldn't have been able to move her, not even with his giant strength, not when she was glowering at him like that. But what the good captain did do was purposefully shove his elbow into a full pitcher of sweet iced tea, making it tip over and spilling the sticky concoction all over the floor.

"Whoops," Dobson said with obvious, malicious glee. "But, hey, isn't a wet floor an unsafe working condition? And treacherous for customers? What do you think, Ms. Wright?"

The health inspector sighed and closed her eyes for a moment, as if she was ashamed to be part of this obvious charade and witch hunt, but she dutifully checked off something on her clipboard.

After deliberately spilling a pitcher of lemonade, Dobson stormed into the back of the restaurant, where he found fault with everything from the temperature of the walk-in freezers (too warm), to the ketchup bottles lining some metal shelves (too cluttered), to the unopened boxes of flour and cornmeal in one of the cabinets (too full of invisible roaches). And he did the bull-in-a-china-shop routine the whole time, knocking over, spilling, and breaking everything he could shove his giant elbows, hips, and knees into.

The health inspector followed him, ducking out of the way of the flying bits of shattered dishes and fat puddles of spilled beverages as best she could, all the while adding more and more supposed infractions to the list on her clipboard. Silvio, Sophia, and I were right behind her, with the rest of the cops bringing up the rear, making sure I didn't attack their boss for supposedly doing his job.

Still, Dobson's tirade was more annoying than anything else, until he went over to the far side of the restaurant.

"Hey," he called out. "What's in these?"

He pointed to the freezers that lined the walls, including the one in the very back—where my skillet-wielding attacker's body was currently resting in peas.

I finally realized why Dobson had dragged the health inspector along with him. After Madeline had sent her maid in here to attack me, and she hadn't come back out again, the acid elemental would have known that I'd killed her maid and that her body was around here somewhere. So she'd sent Dobson in to find it.

If the health inspector opened that freezer, then Dobson would get to do exactly what he'd come here for in the first place. Arrest me for murder, cart me off to jail, and kill me on the way there—just like Madeline wanted.

But there was no way I could stop him from opening the freezer. Any sort of protest on my part would only make him that much more eager to see what was inside it. I was well and truly stuck in Madeline's black widow's web, and there was nothing I could do but start figuring out how many of the cops I could keep busy while I yelled at Silvio and Sophia to run to safety.

Still, I shrugged, trying to be as nonchalant as possible, hoping against hope that I could bluff my way out of this. "Nothing special. Just some ice, frozen food, things like that."

"Well, let's open them up," Dobson crowed. "I want to see it for myself. It's probably all rotten, like everything else in here."

I kept my face blank as he went over to the first freezer. Dobson gave me a knowing smirk, lifted the lid, peered inside, and found . . . several bags of ice, just like I'd said.

The giant didn't make any derogatory comments this time, but he gave me an angry glare. He let the heavy lid drop and slam shut with an audible *whomp* and moved on to the next freezer, almost as if he was looking for something specific.

Like, say, a body.

The one that he knew was here somewhere.

Dobson headed over to the second freezer, and I leaned over and put my lips close to Silvio's ear. "Are you really a lawyer?" I whispered.

"Of course I am," he whispered back. "Who do you think bailed out all of Beau's drug dealers when they got swept up by the cops? It was easier and more efficient for me to get my license and take care of things like that myself rather than wait for some lawyer to show up. Why do you ask?"

"Because I'm going to need one," I muttered.

Sophia heard the last part of our conversation. She gave me a thoughtful look. She knew what was in that last freezer as well as I did.

Dobson snorted in disgust and let the second freezer lid fall and *whomp* back into place, since it was full of innocent things like frozen packets of corn, bags of cranberries, and tubs of summer strawberries that Jo-Jo had added sugar to and frozen to eat during the winter months. His gaze locked onto the final freezer, and an excited grin split his face. He knew he was about to hit the jackpot, and he hurried in that direction—

At the last second, just before Dobson could grab the freezer handle, Sophia sidled forward, stuck out her boot, and tripped him. The giant stumbled forward, his skull *crack*ing against the side of the freezer, before his legs slid out from under him, and he did a header onto the floor.

Dobson let out a low groan, and I had to press my lips together to hold back my snickers. Sophia winked at me, her black eyes sparkling with merriment and revenge.

A couple of officers rushed over, trying to help their boss, but Dobson shoved them away and got to his feet. A large purple bruise had already started to form around the jagged cut over his right eye, but the growing goose egg on his face didn't keep him from glaring at Sophia.

"You did that on purpose," Dobson muttered.

Sophia grinned, although the look was more feral than pleasant. "Whoops," she rasped.

That angry red flush exploded in Dobson's cheeks again. It matched the blood dribbling down the side of his face.

"Arrest her!" he screamed. "For assaulting an officer of the law!"

One of the uniformed cops stepped forward. "I'm sure it was just an accident, sir," he said in a timid tone. "It is a little cramped, what with all of us standing around back here—"

"Cuff that bitch!" Dobson roared. "Now!"

The officers didn't like it, but they didn't have a choice. They cautiously approached Sophia, who held her hands out in front of her, as meek as a kitten, and let the cops cuff her, even though she could have snapped their necks like breadsticks if she wanted to. But Sophia wasn't above raising her cuffed hands to her lips and blowing the captain an exaggerated kiss.

"Get her out of here!" Dobson roared again.

Silvio looked at me, and I jerked my head, telling him to go with Sophia. The officers led her into the front of the restaurant, with Silvio trailing along behind them.

Dobson stopped the phony inspection long enough to grab some napkins off a metal rack and use them to wipe the blood off his face.

"Now," he growled, crushing the dirty napkins in his hand and tossing them aside. "Let's see what's in that freezer—"

But Ms. Wright had already beaten him to it, lifting the freezer lid and taking a quick peek inside. "Nothing interesting. Just some frozen peas." She let the lid slam shut and made a note on her clipboard.

"Are you sure?" Dobson asked, giving me a suspicious look.

"I can actually see to do my job, Captain," Ms. Wright snarked, the first bit of bite that she'd dished out the entire time she'd been here.

He looked at the freezer again, as if he wanted to shove past her, grab the lid, and open it up himself, but in the end he gave her a curt nod. After all, she was the one supposedly conducting the inspection.

I stared at Wright. She didn't so much as glance at me, but her hand trembled as she scribbled another note on her clipboard. I didn't know if she really hadn't seen the maid's body underneath all the frozen food and bags of ice or if she just wanted to piss off Dobson by not letting him look inside. Either way, I wasn't about to question my small bit of good luck.

With the so-called inspection complete, Dobson whipped around and shoved back through the double doors, with the uniformed officers following him. Wright headed in that direction as well, although she stopped a few feet away from me and dropped her head, as though studying the ketchup bottles that Dobson had strewn all over the floor.

"Tell Bria thanks again for helping me out with my ex-husband," she said in a whisper-soft voice. "He's never getting out, and he'll never hit me again, because of her."

So it wasn't luck that had saved me—it was Bria's kindness to this woman. I wondered what kind of nightmare my sister had saved her from. It must have been bad, for Wright to return the favor here and now and risk Dobson's wrath.

She hurried after the cops. I waited several seconds, then followed her into the storefront.

By this point, Catalina had cashed out all of the customers except for two—Madeline and Emery, who were still seated in their booth, calmly eating the rest of their food. Of course they were. They knew that nothing was wrong with it and that the only things dirty and rotten in here were the two of them, along with their flunky Dobson.

If it had just been the three of us in the restaurant, I would have palmed one of my knives and attacked them, consequences be damned. But I knew that's exactly what Madeline wanted—for me to lose control, fly into a rage, and assault her and Emery in front of the cops.

So I focused on remaining calm and pressed my fingertips against the scars in my palms, letting the feel of the runes center me. I was the Spider, and Fletcher had taught me to be patient above all else.

"So what's the verdict?" Dobson asked Ms. Wright, as if he didn't already know what he'd bullied or bribed her into saying.

The health inspector sighed, tore the top piece of paper off her clipboard, and passed it over to him. Dobson made a pretense of reading the paper, even though everyone knew that he was the one in charge here—not Wright.

"Well, I'm afraid that our tips were right," he said in a smug voice that told everyone that he wasn't sorry at all. "I'm sad to say that your restaurant has totally failed inspection on all counts, Ms. Blanco."

"So how much will the fine be?" I asked.

I expected him to quote some ridiculous figure upward of a hundred thousand dollars, most of which would no doubt end up in his own pocket. But instead, he gave me a cruel, calculating smile that made that cold unease surge through my body again.

"Oh, there's no fine," Dobson crowed. "I'm afraid the violations are far too severe for that."

I knew what he was going to say next, but that still didn't lessen the impact of his booming voice and harsh words.

"The Pork Pit is closed."

* 7 *

His words hit me like a shot to the heart—hard, brutal, and utterly ruthless.

It was one thing to accuse me of murder in front of my customers. Really, it wasn't anything at all, given all the folks I'd helped move on from this life to the next over the years. It wasn't an accusation so much as it was a fact. Many, many times over.

But shutting down the Pork Pit, closing my gin joint, that was like carving out a piece of my *soul*—one that I didn't know how to live without.

And Madeline knew it, given the smirk on her face as she sipped her sweet iced tea.

But I kept my own face blank and my mouth shut as the health inspector handed over several notices to the cops, which Dobson took great delight in ordering his men to post all over the windows. They were just thin sheets of yellow paper, but somehow the notices seemed to shut out the afternoon sun completely and cast the interior of the restaurant in dark, murky shadows. A uniformed officer taped one of the notices up on the window across from the cash register, blocking the warm rays of sunlight that had been touching my face. I felt like someone had doused me with a bucket of ice water.

No, not someone—Madeline Magda fucking Monroe.

When the notices were all taped up, Dobson swaggered back over to the cash register, which I was standing behind.

"Aw, don't look so glum, Ms. Blanco. You can always try to fix your violations and have another inspection." He smirked.

He didn't tell me that I wouldn't pass, no matter how much I scrubbed and cleaned or how many bribes I doled out. His meaning was obvious.

So I pushed my sick heartache aside and smirked back at him. "I don't know what Madeline is paying you, but I can tell you this. It's not going to be enough."

Dobson's brown eyes narrowed. "Is that a threat, Blanco?"

"Oh, sugar," I drawled. "I don't make *threats*. Just promises."

For the first time since he'd swaggered into the restaurant, the giant looked a bit rattled, so rattled that he did finally glance over at Emery, as if seeking her reassurance that she wouldn't let me kill him for his arrogant stupidity. She nodded, which made Dobson relax. Fool. He was going to pay for this, the same as Emery and Madeline were.

Dobson reached into his jacket pocket, drew out a business card, and threw it at me. I snapped my fingers forward and snatched the card out of midair, making him blink in surprise.

"Call me when you're ready to talk about the missing woman," he said. "But be warned. The longer you wait, the less likely you are to cut a deal for her murder."

Instead of responding to his taunt, I crumpled his business card in my fist and tossed it into the trash can behind the counter. Score one for me.

Dobson's cheeks burned tomato red with rage, but he whirled around and left the restaurant, yanking the front door open and stepping out onto the sidewalk. Ms. Wright and the other officers followed him.

Through the notices covering the windows, I could see Sophia standing beside one of the cop cars, her hands cuffed in front of her, waiting to be taken to the station. Catalina was talking to her, and Sophia kept nodding her head in response. Silvio lurked a few feet away from them, chatting up one of the officers about something. Probably what a crooked asshole Dobson was.

With her minion gone and his mission complete, Madeline finally deigned to sop up the last smear of barbecue sauce on her plate with a bit of bread, pop the whole thing into her mouth, and push her empty plate away. After taking one more slow, slurping sip of her iced tea, she slid out of her booth, got to her feet, and strolled over to me, her stilettos *crack-crack-crack*ing against the floor. Emery left the booth as well, stepped outside, and stationed herself by the front door, staring over at Sophia, who glared right back at her.

Madeline set their white order ticket down on the counter, along with a hundred-dollar bill, which was more than enough to pay for the food she and Emery had eaten.

"I'm so sorry to hear that the restaurant's been shut

down, Gin. I didn't think there was anything wrong with the food. Other than it being a bit too salty." She shrugged. "But you know the system. You do one little thing wrong, and everything just seems to snowball from there."

I stared right back at her, not showing any emotion, and not saying a word. This was her moment to crow, and I was going to let her have it.

Every condemned person deserved one last meal, and monologue.

Madeline leaned forward. "See? I told you that you wouldn't make it to the library dedication. Next time, you really should listen to me. Now, I'm afraid that you're going to have to spend the afternoon bailing your friend out of jail. Better try to get her out of there before tonight. I'd hate for something . . . unfortunate to happen to her while she was locked up."

Maybe that had been Madeline's plan for me. Maybe Dobson wouldn't have shot me to death on the way to the station after all. Maybe he would have put me in lockup with the worst of the worst and let nature take its course. Even I could only battle so many enemies at a time, especially in a small, confined space like a jail cell.

Madeline kept staring at me, that smug, satisfied smile on her face stretching her crimson lips higher and wider than ever before. I dropped my gaze to her order ticket and money lying on the counter. Cold rage surged through me, and I reached down and picked them both up, one in either hand.

A sharp, painful, burning sensation scorched my fingers the second they touched the papers, as though my hands were about to burst into flames, even though my skin remained perfectly smooth. But it wasn't any kind of elemental Fire power at work, and no runes flared to life on either the order ticket or the money. Since Madeline had touched them both, invisible waves of her acid magic had soaked into the papers, since she was one of those elementals who constantly leaked magic, even when she wasn't actively using her power. Although I thought that in this case she had put a small bit of effort into coating the papers with her magic, knowing that I would reach for them, if only to put her money into the cash register. It would have been one more fun little way for her to fuck with me today.

Madeline's smile widened a smidge more, as she fully expected me to start screaming as soon as I touched the papers and felt her power. But I didn't scream. Didn't yell. Didn't holler, curse, and fling the papers away in surprise, pain, and anger. Instead, I ignored the horrid, searing sensation of her acid magic as best I could, and I didn't reach for my own Ice magic to numb my hands to block the agonizing sensation.

I raised my gaze to hers, my gray eyes colder than the coldest winter night. Then I slowly crumpled her order ticket into a tight wad, until my knuckles whitened from the strain. I held on to it for several seconds longer than necessary, just to show her that I could, even though every nerve ending in my hand was screaming at me to let go. Finally, I threw the smushed wad into the trash can, just like I had Dobson's business card. Another point for me.

I was still clenching the hundred-dollar bill in my other fist, and I deliberately held it up in the air, right in front of her smug face, and then tore it in two. The sound of the paper ripping was as loud as a gunshot in the hushed quiet of the restaurant.

But I didn't stop there. I put the two halves of the bill together and then ripped them apart, until I had four pieces.

Rip-rip-rip-rip.

I did that over and over again, until I had reduced the hundred-dollar bill to tiny pieces. Then I dusted them all off my hands, watching the green and white bits float down to the counter like confetti.

By this point, my fingers felt like they were nothing more than brittle bones about to dissolve from the searing strength of Madeline's acid magic, even though my skin remained unblistered and unblemished. But the scorching pain was nothing compared to the cold rage beating in perfect sync with my heart.

For the first time since I'd met her, a bit of uncertainty flickered in Madeline's eyes. She'd deliberately coated the money and order ticket with her acid magic, another of her little traps, but I wasn't reacting the way she had expected. She might play games, but so could I.

"You made a mistake," I said in a calm tone. "Several, actually."

Madeline arched a dark, delicate eyebrow. "Really? And what would those be?"

"You dragged my friends and family into this. Roslyn. Finn. Owen. Eva. You shouldn't have done that."

She shrugged, unconcerned by the ice in my voice. "It's not my fault that your friends are having such . . . difficulties."

"Of course not. You would never stoop to actually getting your hands dirty yourself unless you absolutely had to. That's why it took you so long to come at me. You had to set all your little cogs and wheels into motion to screw with me and the people I care about. Like getting Dobson in your pocket, and having him browbeat that poor health inspector into going along with this sham here today."

"You give me far too much credit, Gin. I might have made some new friends since I've been in town, but what you're talking about sounds like a grand conspiracy. I'm just an employer who was concerned about a worker. That's why I reported my maid missing this morning, nothing more. Emery was nice enough to contact Captain Dobson for me, since he was an old friend of her uncle Elliot's. Dobson promised to look into things, and he drew his own conclusions from the information I gave him."

"Sure he did."

But Madeline didn't miss a beat. "I hate to point this out, darling, but you sound a bit . . . paranoid. As if the whole world is arrayed against you. Perhaps you should take some time off while the restaurant is closed. Talk to someone about these feelings of persecution you have."

"You're right," I said, disdain dripping from each and every one of my words. "I have given you far too much credit. I thought that you would do something grander, more impressive. But this"—I waved my hand out at the restaurant—"this is *nothing*. Rather disappointing, actually. Mab would have been so much more direct about things. Why, your mama would have burned this place to the ground with her bare hands already. Not spent all her time and energy bribing, wheedling, and batting her eyes to get my restaurant shut down by a crooked cop."

"I am *nothing* like my mother," Madeline snapped, her calm façade finally cracking at the mention of Mab. "She was a grand fool."

"Mab was many things, but she was never, *ever* a fool. Not when it came to me. She once hired a whole squad of bounty hunters to come to Ashland just to hunt me down. And when she finally figured out who I was, well, she called me out herself, face-to-face, elemental to elemental, villain to villain. You could have done the same. You *should* have done the same. Challenged me to a duel and tried to kill me yourself with your acid magic."

I snorted and gave another dismissive wave of my hand. "But you? With your sly little schemes? You're just a pale, weak imitation of her, sugar."

Madeline couldn't stop herself from sucking in a ragged breath at my insult, but I wasn't done yet.

I leaned over the counter so that our faces were inches apart. "You should have killed me the second you had the chance. That's the other mistake you made, and that's the one that's going to cost you—*everything.*"

Madeline's green eyes burned with anger, and I could almost see the gears grinding in her mind as she debated whether to reach for her acid magic and try to take me out, right here, right now, all her elaborate schemes be damned. But after a moment, she blinked, then blinked again, and the hot rage in her gaze cooled, congealed, and crystallized into icy, calculating hate. Yeah. Mine too.

I stayed up in her face a few seconds longer to let her know that I'd seen her hesitation, then drew back behind the cash register. "You should have come at me head-on, but you just had to play a little game with me instead."

"Perhaps I like my *games*," Madeline replied, her voice and features mild and unruffled again.

"Oh, I know you do. But there's one problem with playing games."

She arched her eyebrow at me again. "Oh, really? What's that?"

I smiled, showing her my teeth and all the cold, cold venom in my heart. "There's always a chance that you can lose."

Another flash of uncertainty darkened her eyes before she was able to hide it. "I never lose, Gin. And I don't intend to now."

"Intentions are for fools. You do, or you don't. Or in your case, you just *die*."

Her crimson lips pulled back, and she returned my smile with an even wider, toothier one of her own. "Oh, I think that you're talking about yourself in this case, Gin. After all, you're the one in trouble with the law, not me."

"We'll see."

"Yes, we will," she murmured. "Yes, we *will*."

We stared at each other a few more seconds before Madeline tilted her head at me.

"As much as I enjoy our little chats, I'm afraid I must be going. I've still got that dedication to attend. And you . . ." She stared around the deserted restaurant. "Well, you've got a lot of problems to take care of, don't you?"

I didn't respond.

"But don't let this little bit of unpleasantness get you down. I do hope that you enjoy the rest of your day, Gin. I know I certainly will."

Madeline gave me one more arrogant smirk before she pivoted on her white stiletto and sashayed out of the Pork Pit.

* 8 *

I would have liked nothing more than to palm a knife, run around the counter, and bury the blade up to the hilt in Madeline's back. But I couldn't do that. Not without getting even more stuck in her web than I already was.

Besides, Emery and Dobson were peering in through the windows, waiting for me to attack Madeline. Attempted murder would land me in a jail cell lickety-split, and if that happened, then the acid elemental would get exactly what she wanted.

I wasn't about to fall into that trap, so I let her walk away—for now.

A few seconds later, the front door opened, and Silvio stepped inside.

I untied my apron, pulled it off, and tossed it onto the counter. "Now what?"

He came over to me, grabbed his silverstone briefcase from where he'd left it on the counter, and opened it, sliding his tablet inside. "They're taking Sophia down to the main police station to book her for assaulting Dobson. Given the situation, I suggest that we follow them and be waiting when they process her so we can bail her out as quickly as possible."

I nodded, scanning the storefront, but Catalina was nothing if not efficient. In addition to cashing out the customers, she'd also gone ahead and turned off the appliances, put the extra food away, and stacked the dirty dishes into plastic tubs. All I had to do was walk out the front door, lock it behind me, and the restaurant would be closed.

The only loose end was the dead woman in the freezer, but it wasn't like I could move her body to a better location right now. Not with Dobson and the cops milling around outside and peering in through the windows. I didn't even dare to leave the storefront and go stack some boxes on top of the freezer. The cops might notice, come back in, and search the restaurant again.

But instead of leaving, I settled my gaze on the framed, blood-spattered copy of *Where the Red Fern Grows* that hung on the wall close to the cash register. My own little tribute to Fletcher, since that was the book he'd been reading the night he was tortured to death in the Pork Pit.

I hadn't been able to save Fletcher, but I wouldn't lose his restaurant too. I would find a way to beat Madeline at her own game, as dark, dangerous, and twisted as it was. I wasn't going to leave anything to chance, not anymore, so I went over and took the framed book off the wall, along with a photo of Fletcher and his friend Warren T. Fox, taken back when they were young.

"Gin?" Silvio asked, wondering what I was doing.

I came around the end of the counter and handed him the frames. "Here. Keep these safe for me. Please."

Most folks would have thought it strange that I was so concerned about a battered book and an old photo, but Silvio nodded and took them without a word, slipping them both into his briefcase.

"My car is down the block," he said. "I'll wait for you there."

He nodded, then turned and left the restaurant, opening and closing the door so carefully that the bell barely made a whisper at his passing.

I walked over to the door and started to follow him, but something made me stop and turn around.

My gaze swept over the storefront, so familiar with its booths and tables and the pig tracks curling across the floor, but yet so very different right now, with its empty seats and dirty dishes and crushed napkins that littered everything. Even though the sun was shining brightly outside, beating in through the yellow notices taped up to the windows, the interior still seemed dim and dull and sad.

Hollow, just like my heart.

But there was nothing I could do to fix it right now, and Sophia needed my help.

So I clicked off the lights, turned the sign on the door over to *Closed*, and left the Pork Pit.

I locked the front door behind me, hurried down the sidewalk, and slipped into the passenger's seat of Silvio's navy-blue Audi. A blue-and-pink pin shaped like the neon pig sign outside the restaurant dangled from the car's rearview mirror. Of course, the real sign above the front door was dark now, since I'd turned off all the lights, but the crystals in the pin sparkled in the afternoon sun, as bright, colorful, and vibrant as ever. It comforted me.

Silvio cranked the engine and pulled away from the curb. While he drove toward the station, I pulled my phone out of my jeans pocket and hit one of the numbers in the speed dial.

She answered on the third ring. "Yes, darling?"

Jolene "Jo-Jo" Deveraux's voice filled my ear, but it wasn't the soft, sweet, Southern drawl I expected. Instead, Jo-Jo's voice was harsh, clipped, and angry. I opened my mouth to answer her, but a loud *screech-screech-screech* cut me off, followed by a series of *bang-bang-bang-bang*s.

I frowned. "Jo-Jo? What's that noise? What's wrong?"

She huffed in my ear. "Apparently, someone didn't like the perm I gave her last week and is claiming that I burned her scalp and made all her hair fall out. A bunch of folks from the health inspector's office are here, plowing through the salon, scraping paint off the walls, and making a mess of everything. Now they're saying that I've got black mold everywhere, even though I just remodeled the entire salon a few months ago."

My hand tightened around my phone. So Madeline had sicced the health department on Jo-Jo too, and from the sound of things, they were demolishing the dwarf's beauty salon in the back of her antebellum home. I'd wondered why Madeline had spent so much time ingratiating herself with all the civic and other groups in town. Now she was making all those connections and all that money she'd spread around work for her.

"And, to top it off, I've got a bunch of stuck-up snobs from the historical association here," Jo-Jo went on, her voice getting louder, sharper, and angrier with every word. "They're claiming that I haven't been taking proper care of *my* house—the house that's been in *my* family for more than a hundred and fifty years—and that there's some silly ordinance that says that unless I bring it up to code in thirty days, that the historical association can take ownership of it. Over my dead body, that's what *I* say."

"Jo-Jo, listen to me—" I started to warn her to just go along with them for now, but I didn't get the chance.

"Hey!" she snapped. "There's no mold on that wall. Don't you *dare* punch that sledgehammer through my brand-new paneling!"

Thump-thump-thump.

Crash-crash-crash.

Bang-bang-bang.

More and more demolition noises rang out, along with the sharp, distinctive *tinkle-tinkle-tinkle* of breaking glass.

"Great. Now there's a giant hole in my wall, and one of these idiots has managed to upend and break an entire tub of nail polish all over the floor. I'm sorry, Gin, but I have to go. I'll call you back when I get these morons out of my salon."

She hung up before I could tell her about the trouble Sophia was in—or how Madeline was screwing with all of us today, including her.

I thought about calling her back, but she probably wouldn't answer. Besides, Sophia was in more danger right now than Jo-Jo was. Still, I sent a text to Finn, asking him to check in with Jo-Jo when he got a chance. I waited, but the phone didn't beep back. Looked like Finn was busy dealing with his own problems. I sighed and put my phone down on the console in the center of the car.

Silvio cleared his throat. "I take it that Ms. Deveraux is having some trouble as well?"

"Another surprise visit from the health inspector," I muttered. "And the historical association. Madeline hit her with a double whammy."

"She has certainly been effective in planning her attacks to target all of you at once. A classic divide-and-conquer tactic."

"I know," I muttered again. "And I didn't even see it coming. I thought that she would send a swarm of giants into the restaurant or hire a passel of assassins to attack me. This is Ashland, after all. Instead, the bitch is trying to legalese me to death."

"The law can be as effective a weapon as anything else," Silvio pointed out in an annoyingly calm tone. "Sometimes, even more so than direct brute force or overwhelming numbers."

I slumped in the leather seat, put my head back, and closed my eyes, trying to rein in my temper and growing frustration. I didn't do *legal*. I did black-of-the-night, launch-myself-from-the-shadows, cut-your-throat attacks. Not this . . . this political *maneuvering*.

It disgusted me that Madeline wouldn't come right out and face me herself, elemental to elemental, but there was nothing I could do about it. Right now, she had the advantage, and my friends and I were scrambling to playing catch-up. No, scratch that. We weren't playing catch-up. We weren't even playing defense. Madeline had blindsided all of us, and we were sprawled every which way on the battlefield, flat on our backs, trying to find enough strength to shake off all the punishing, head-spinning blows she'd landed on us one after another.

I brooded the few blocks over to the station. Like many buildings in the downtown loop, the main head-quarters of the Ashland Police Department was located in a large, sprawling prewar building made of dark gray granite that took up an entire block. With its columns, crenellations, and curlicued carvings of leaves and vines, it was a lovely structure, despite the ugliness that passed through the doors daily.

Silvio pulled into the lot attached to one side of the building and parked. But instead of getting out and going into the station right away, I sat in the car.

Thinking.

If there was one thing I'd come to know about Madeline, it was that she always had a backup plan, usually two or three or four or more. Dobson hadn't been able to drag me away from the restaurant in handcuffs, but here I was at the police station all the same. If this was where she had planned to spring the next part of her trap for me, whatever it was, then I was sure that Madeline had already adjusted her scheme accordingly. Something bad was waiting for me inside the station—I just didn't know exactly what it might be.

So I went through various scenarios in my mind, most of which ended up with me either being trapped in a jail cell or shot to death in the middle of the station while the crooked cops of Ashland looked on and cheered. But one thing was certain. I couldn't go into the station armed.

Not with all the metal detectors and scanners. That would be a quick way to get arrested and carted off to that cell that was sure to be waiting for me.

So as much as it pained me, I palmed first one knife, then the other, setting them next to my phone on the center console. I leaned forward, removed the weapon from the small of my back, then reached down and plucked the two knives out of the sides of my boots.

"Here," I said, straightening back up and handing the three blades over to Silvio. "Take these, and keep them safe for me. Please."

He nodded and took the knives from me, careful of the sharp edges, then picked up the other two weapons from the console. "I have a hidden compartment built into the bottom of the trunk. I'll put them in there."

I nodded, then slipped the ring off my right index finger and passed that over to him too. Then came the final, most difficult thing—unhooking the necklace from around my throat.

I pulled the chain out from underneath my T-shirt and held it out, staring at the spider rune pendant—that small circle surrounded by eight thin rays. The symbol for patience. Something I needed right now more than ever before.

I wrapped my hand around the rune, pressing it against the matching scar embedded deep in my palm. The slight weight comforted me, as did the cold, solid sensation of my Ice and Stone magic rippling through the smooth surface of the metal, waiting to be used. But that was why I was leaving the ring and the necklace with Silvio. They contained far too much of my power to let them fall into the wrong hands should things go from bad to worse inside the station, the way I suspected they were going to. If the cops did arrest me, they'd take everything away from me. Madeline had already closed down the Pork Pit. She wasn't getting my jewelry too. It was far too precious to me, and not just for the power it contained.

"Would you like me to take that as well?" Silvio asked.

For a moment, I curled my hand even tighter around my rune. Then I forced myself to nod, let go, and hand the necklace over to him.

We got out of the car. I stood watch, scanning the parking lot for any sign of Madeline's spies, while Silvio opened the trunk and secured my weapons and jewelry. I felt naked, exposed, and vulnerable without the slight, comforting weight of my knives resting on my body and sad, empty, and lost without the feel of my ring and necklace and their reserves of Ice and Stone magic humming against my skin.

I was a strong elemental, but I didn't know if I could overcome Madeline's acid power without my knives or extra reserves of magic, all of which I'd just willingly stripped away. But Sophia was in trouble and needed my help, which she wouldn't get with my lollygagging around in the parking lot. So I drew in a breath and headed for the station, with Silvio shutting the trunk, locking the car, and falling in step beside me.

The inside of the police station was much nicer than what you would expect. Then again, the po-po could afford to keep everything in tip-top shape, given all the bribes they accepted. A narrow corridor ran for about fifty feet before opening up into the enormous room that was the bureaucratic heart of the station. The floor and walls were made out of beautiful gray marble with silver flecks running through it, while the diamond-shaped panes in the tall, wide windows were so clean they almost appeared transparent. Crystal and brass chandeliers dropped down from the vaulted ceiling, which soared a hundred feet overhead and also featured mosaic flowers carved out of pale rose quartz. The only things that ruined the elegance of the room were the security cameras mounted to the walls, their red lights winking on and off like devilish fireflies as they swiveled around in slow, steady circles.

A brass plaque embedded in one of the columns near the entrance boasted that the interior had been restored to its original grandeur with the help of the Ashland Historical Association. Captain Lou Dobson's name was on the plaque too; he was listed as the liaison between the department and the historical association. Well, I supposed that explained how he'd help Madeline sic the group on Jo-Jo. All he would have had to do was make a couple of phone calls and cash in some favors.

Silvio and I passed through a metal detector at the end of the corridor while a bored-looking uniformed officer ran Silvio's briefcase through the X-ray scanner. Dobson must not have had time to put the word out to be on the lookout for me because the officer waved us through without a second glance.

"Let's go over to booking," Silvio said after he'd retrieved his briefcase. "That's where Sophia will most likely be."

I nodded and followed him out into the main part of the station.

Silvio must have spent more time bailing out Benson's drug dealers than I'd thought because he moved through the station with ease, navigating around lines of people and roped off sections as though he'd long ago memorized where the clogged trouble spots were. Even more telling, several officers waved and called out friendly greetings to the slender vampire.

Silvio nodded back, stopping a few times to speak with those he knew well. I tagged along behind him, feeling like the proverbial third wheel, but I trusted Silvio enough to realize that if he was taking the time to talk to someone, then he was most likely trying to get more information about Dobson and what the captain's plans might be for Sophia—and me.

Finally, we reached the back of the room, where dozens of desks clustered in bunches, all of them sleek chrome contraptions covered with computers, monitors, and ringing phones. Detectives wearing suits and ties sprawled in their executive, leather chairs, gabbing on their phones, while others milled around the espresso machines that lined one section of the wall, along with wooden tables that boasted platters of fresh fruit, buttery croissants, and a dozen different kinds of Danishes. I snorted. No bad coffee and stale doughnuts here. The po-po had a better spread than most of the corporate climbers in the downtown skyscrapers.

Still, it wasn't all strawberries and shortcakes. Uniformed officers moved back and forth in front of the detectives' desks, carrying files, murmuring into their radios, and escorting some unhappy-looking individuals from one side of the station to the other. Three vampire hookers slumped on a wooden bench next to the espresso machines, their skirts riding up and their tops drooping down, showing inordinate amounts of leg and cleavage as they waited to be booked. An archway cut into the wall a few feet away led into another room that featured a fingerprint station, a camera, and a height chart for mug shots.

Sophia was sitting at the end of the bench, looking calm and unruffled, despite the handcuffs that were still cinched around her wrists. The same couldn't be said for the hookers, who eyed her with obvious curiosity.

"Boo," Sophia rasped, causing the hooker closest to her to shriek and almost fall off the bench.

One of the many knots of tension in my chest loosened at the knowledge that Sophia was okay. Silvio went over to the officer in charge to see what he could do to help her, but I scanned the room, looking for Dobson.

It didn't take me long to find the giant. The second I spotted him, my chest knotted right back up again because he was standing next to a pair of desks, along with two familiar figures. One of them was a woman, about my size, with shaggy blond hair and blue eyes. The other was a giant, around seven feet tall with thick muscles, ebony skin, and a pair of aviator sunglasses that had been propped up on top of his shaved head. My baby sister, Detective Bria Coolidge, and her partner, Xavier, who was also Roslyn's significant other.

Things were definitely going from bad to worse, just like I'd feared.

I looked over to find Silvio slipping a wad of hundred-dollar bills into the booking officer's hand. A second later, the officer was pulling out his keys and unlocking the cuffs on Sophia's wrists. Relieved that Silvio was taking care of her, I hurried over to Bria and Xavier.

Dobson looked over at the steady *smack-smack-smack* of my boots on the floor, and a wide grin spread over his face. My chest tightened even more. I'd been so busy with everything that had happened at the Pork Pit that I'd forgotten there was one person I hadn't heard from today—Bria.

But given the smug expression on Dobson's face, I was just in time to witness whatever Madeline had planned for my sister and Xavier too.

Bria turned to see who Dobson was staring at and did a double take when she realized it was me. Given my nocturnal activities as the Spider, I didn't spend a lot of time in the police station. In fact, it was the one place in Ashland that I studiously avoided, especially since Bria and I tried to keep our professional lives as separate as possible. But it seemed like Madeline had made sure that they were going to overlap today—in the worst way possible.

"Gin?" Bria asked, the shock apparent in her voice. "What are you doing here?"

"Haven't you heard?" I sniped. "I've been accused of murdering a missing woman, the Pork Pit has been shut down for health violations, and Silvio and I are here to bail out Sophia, who supposedly assaulted the cop who was conducting the health inspection. But really, the clumsy fool fell down all on his own. Isn't that right, Dobson?"

The captain glared at me, that angry flush creeping up his neck again. He opened his mouth, no doubt to deliver some cutting remark, but his cell phone rang, stopping him before he could get started. Dobson checked the number on the screen and gestured at two uniformed officers standing nearby, the same two who'd been with him when he first came into the Pork Pit earlier this afternoon.

"Watch them," he barked, then stepped away a few feet to answer his call.

Dollars to doughnuts, Madeline was on the other end of the line, giving him some last-minute instructions for this part of her plan.

"Gin?" Bria asked. "What's going on?"

"Finn didn't call you?"

She shook her head. "We've been up in the mountains all day. The cell reception up there is terrible, so we turned off our phones to save the batteries. We just got back a few minutes ago."

"Why did you go up into the mountains?"

"Supposedly, there was some sort of shooting at the Bone Mountain Nature Preserve," Xavier rumbled. "At least, that's what Dobson claimed when he sent us up there this morning. But there was no evidence of anything like that. It was all leaf-lookers and bird-watchers."

So Dobson had sent the two of them on a wild-goose chase to get them out of the way while everything else was going down. A bad feeling ballooned up in the pit of my stomach, bursting through the tension in my chest, and sticking in my throat, choking me from the inside out. Because Bria and Xavier were here now, and so was I— just in time to witness whatever horrible thing Dobson had planned for them. Another part of the grand scheme that Madeline had put him up to, and another bit of my friends' misery that she wanted me to see and experience firsthand.

"Gin?" Bria asked again. "What's wrong?"

I quickly, quietly filled them in on all the problems that Madeline had caused for everyone, including closing the restaurant.

"That's ridiculous!" Bria snapped when I finished. "The food is great, and you don't have any health violations."

"It's just Madeline spinning her webs and playing her games," I murmured. "And I don't think she's done yet."

"What do you think her endgame is?" Xavier asked. "I mean, closing down the Pork Pit is terrible, but it's nothing permanent."

I thought of the hate that had flared in Madeline's eyes when I faced her down at the restaurant. "Oh, I'm sure she's working on fixing that."

Dobson finished his call and stepped back over to us, his ruddy face full of excited expectation. While he'd been talking, more and more detectives and uniformed officers had gathered around, sipping their espressos and shoving croissants in their mouths as they waited to see what would happen next. Many of the cops had the same sort of sneer on their face that Dobson did, but more than a few seemed uncertain or outright hostile to the giant and his cronies.

"Is there anyone here you can trust?" I asked Bria. "Anyone higher up on the food chain than Dobson that can help you and Xavier?"

She glanced around, looking at first one face, then another, just like I had. Her expression became grimmer and grimmer the longer she looked. "A few people. Not many. Dobson's the third highest-ranking officer in the department, and he's the one in charge of all the detectives, including Xavier and me. Besides, most of the time everyone waits to see which way the wind is blowing before they take sides, no matter what their rank is."

Something that was perfectly normal in Ashland, which meant that Bria and Xavier were pretty much screwed. Yeah. That was definitely the theme of the day. But before I could tell them to brace themselves for the worst, it went ahead and happened.

"Step away from your desk, Coolidge," Dobson barked out.

Bria blinked. "What? Why?"

He held out his hand, and one of the officers stepped forward and passed him a piece of paper, which Dobson then slapped down on the edge of her desk. "So I can search it," he sneered. "Seems we've gotten a tip about some Burn pills disappearing from evidence lockup. Someone seems to think they've wound up in your desk. Imagine that. Your sister is a cold-blooded killer, and you're a dirty, pill-popping cop. Must run in the family."

Bria gasped, and all the color drained from her face at his harsh, jeering insults.

Dobson's brown gaze flicked to Xavier. "Unless you and your partner are in on it together. Might as well search them both, while we're at it. Clean out all the trash at once."

"The only trash here is you, Dobson," Xavier growled, stepping up so that he was nose-to-nose with the other giant. "Unlike the rest of you crooked bastards, Bria and I don't steal evidence, and we sure as hell don't take drugs."

Dobson smirked at Xavier, whose hands clenched into tight fists, as if he was thinking about punching the captain. I definitely knew *that* feeling.

But Bria stepped up and put her hand on her partner's shoulder, silently warning him against it. "It's okay, Xavier. Let them search. We both know they won't find anything."

"Oh, I wouldn't be so sure about that," Dobson crooned.

Bria and Xavier looked at each other, their faces tight, both of them realizing they were being set up. But the worst part was that they both knew there was absolutely nothing they could do to stop it since Dobson outranked them. So they had no choice but to reluctantly move away from their desks.

The captain made a big show of opening the top few drawers in Bria's desk and rifling through the pens and papers inside. He kept making faces the whole time, as if he were disappointed that he hadn't found anything incriminating yet. The tension in the air built and built, and a few of the cops started muttering with worry, probably hoping that he wouldn't start searching their desks and find all the illicit items hidden inside.

Finally, Dobson had gone through all the drawers except one. He paused a moment, that smirk flitting across his face again. He already knew exactly what was in that last drawer because he'd planted it in there earlier, while Bria and Xavier were up on Bone Mountain.

"Well, well, well," Dobson crowed, bending down and

sticking his beefy hand into the drawer, as if he'd discovered something completely unexpected. "What do we have here?"

He pulled a plastic bag filled with red and green Burn pills out of the drawer.

He held up the pills and let out a low whistle. "Forget about your own bad habit. Looks like you've decided to go into business for yourself. What do you say, Coolidge? How much were you planning on selling these babies for out on the street?"

Dobson tossed the Burn pills on top of Bria's desk and gave me another arrogant smirk. "Like sister, like sister, I suppose. Either way, Detective Coolidge, you are officially relieved of duty—effective immediately."

☼ 9 ☼

This time, Bria's hands were the ones that clenched into fists. "I don't know where those pills came from, but I didn't put them there."

"Right," Dobson drawled. "And I'm the tooth fairy."

He looked at the crowd of cops who had gathered around, but everyone's faces were cold and shuttered. Yep, everyone was waiting to see how the cookie would crumble in this situation. Bria knew as well as I did that Dobson had already won, this round at least, but she didn't want to believe it. She kept glancing from one detective, one officer, to another, hoping that someone would speak up and tell Dobson that he was full of shit, that she was a good, honest cop and that there was no way she would ever steal evidence, much less sell drugs.

But no one did.

Instead, silence descended over the crowd, spreading out to the folks in booking and beyond. Everyone stopped what they were doing and turned to watch the drama unfold.

"As of this moment, you are suspended without pay, Detective Coolidge," Dobson sneered, his loud, gravelly voice echoing through the entire station. "Of course, there will be a thorough investigation into your many crimes, but if I were you, I'd go ahead and clear out your desk. We both know that you won't be coming back—ever."

Bria's fists clenched tighter, her eyes burned brighter, and the set of her jaw hardened with every lie Dobson spouted. Being a cop was just as important to her as running the Pork Pit was to me, a way to honor and follow in her foster father's footsteps, and so much a part of who she was that she could never be or do anything else that would make her nearly as happy. For Dobson to take all of that away from her, especially on such an obvious, ridiculous, phony charge, well, it made her as angry as I had been at the restaurant earlier—and Bria's reaction was just as cold as mine had been.

She approached Dobson, and the two officers who'd been flanking the giant sidled away from him. So did all the other cops who'd gathered around. They all knew that Bria was a powerful Ice elemental, and they could all see the mix of magic and rage flashing in her frosty blue eyes. They didn't want to get caught in the cross fire should she decide to unleash her magic on Dobson. Even the good captain himself swallowed and took a step back.

Bria noticed them backing away, and she let out a loud, derisive snort. Like sister, like sister, after all.

"Cowards," she called out, her light, lilting voice

booming even louder than Dobson's had. "The whole sorry lot of you."

Once again, she looked from one face to another, even as her own features tightened with disgust. A few of the cops had enough guilt and shame to lower their heads, rather than meet her angry gaze.

Finally, Bria focused her attention on Dobson again. "You're not going to get away with this." She spat out the words as if each and every one were an icicle shooting out of her lips and stabbing into his smug smile.

"It seems to me like I already have, Coolidge," he sneered.

Bria stepped forward and tilted her head back so that she was staring directly into his face. "This is bullshit, and we all know it, Dobson. You've never liked me because I actually try to do my *job*, because I actually try to help people, protect them. Not hurt them like you do. You've been looking for an excuse to get rid of me for a long time now."

He bent down and smiled right in her face. "Well, it looks like I finally have one, doesn't it?"

Xavier stepped up beside my sister. "Bria's a good cop. Everybody knows that. And everybody knows that you're just a thug who likes to hide behind his badge and the power you think it gives you."

Dobson straightened up and gave Xavier a hostile look. "And you should be grateful that I'm going to let you keep working here. But, for the record, as of this moment, you're being busted back down to patrol, Xavier. The graveyard shift over in Southtown. Good luck with that."

A muscle twitched in Xavier's jaw as he ground his teeth together. That was the worst possible shift in the worst possible part of town. Xavier would be lucky if he made it a week without getting shot at—or worse. But even more than that, it was a proverbial slap in the face after all his years of working his way up through the ranks, especially when all he was guilty of was doing the right thing and standing up for his partner.

But Bria wasn't afraid of Dobson and his threats. She moved even closer to him, her eyes colder than I'd ever seen them before, even when she was fully embracing her magic.

"You're not going to get away with this," she said in a voice that was pure ice. "I don't know what Madeline Monroe paid, promised, or plied you with to set all this up, but I hope that you enjoyed it. Because she's going to burn you alive with her acid magic the second you are no longer useful to her. The next time you're in the station, they'll be carrying *you* in on a stretcher, with what's left of you stuffed into a black body bag."

Every part of Dobson bristled at her harsh words, even his already spiky, salt-and-pepper hair. "You know what? I've had enough of you two and your empty threats. Pack up your shit, get out, and don't ever come back. That's an order, Coolidge."

He whirled around to stomp away, but Bria reached out and latched onto his arm. Dobson shook her off as hard as he could. Given his giant strength, Bria went flying back five feet into her desk, bouncing off the side of the sleek, shiny chrome and falling on her ass. But my sister scrambled right back up onto her feet. She started to throw herself at Dobson, but Xavier held his hand out, stopping her.

But Dobson had had enough because he let out a low growl and drew back his massive fist. He was actually going to hit Bria in front of everyone. His murderous brown gaze locked onto my sister's face, and I knew that he was going to punch her as hard as he could—and that he could easily break her neck with that one blow.

I didn't think—I just acted.

I stepped in front of my sister and shoved her back toward Xavier, out of the way of Dobson and his killing strike. Even as I pushed Bria back, I whirled around to face the captain. I wasn't strong enough to catch his fist in my hand, so I ducked his punch, slammed my elbow into his potbelly, hooked my foot around his ankle, and used his own forward momentum to trip him and send his smug ass crashing down to the floor.

Loud, shocked gasps rang out, rippling through the crowd, but they vanished just as quickly, and silence fell over the entire station again.

One . . . two . . . three . . .

Five . . . ten . . . fifteen . . .

The seconds ticked by, but the only sound was Dobson's heavy rasps as he lay on the floor and tried to get his breath back.

Then a small *scrape-scrape* sounded, as one of the hookers got up off the bench, making it slide back. The hooker gave me two thumbs-ups, then started clapping her hands together.

"Woo!" she called out. "You go, girl! You put that free-loading bastard in his place!"

The second hooker got to her feet and joined in. So did the third one, until they were all clapping and cackling with glee, along with Sophia, who let out an earsplitting whistle of approval. Their chuckles were contagious, and they surged throughout the station, spreading from one cluster of people to the next until everyone was laughing at Dobson.

His face turned from red to purple to almost black with rage as he sprawled on the floor, and he had another goose egg on his forehead to match the one he'd gotten from the freezer at the Pork Pit. He tried to scramble to his feet, but his wing tips slipped on the slick marble, and he fell back down onto his knees again. His clumsy effort only made everyone laugh louder.

This time, Dobson grabbed hold of one of the drawer handles on Bria's desk and carefully hoisted himself upright. He turned first one way, then the other, and the chuckles stopped, the air thick and heavy with tension and silence again. Even the three hookers sank back down onto the bench and ducked their heads, although Sophia remained standing, her arms crossed over her chest, the words *Kiss off* showing on her T-shirt again.

Dobson stalked over to me and drew his fist back. I tilted my chin up and stood there, waiting for him to sock me in the jaw, or at least try to.

But at the last second, he thought better of it and stabbed his finger at me instead. "Arrest that bitch," he snarled. "For assaulting an officer."

"That seems to be a popular excuse with you," I drawled. "And that was hardly an assault. Trust me. If I assaulted you, then you would be crying to your mama about it."

"Take her away," he growled. "Right fucking *now*."

Rough hands grabbed me, pulling me away from Bria and Xavier. My sister reached for me, but Dobson stepped in front of her, blocking her path. Bria glared at him, her hand dropping to the gun holstered on her black leather belt, as if she was thinking about doing something violent and stupid, just like I had.

"It's okay, Bria," I called out. "He's not worth it. I'll be fine."

But we both knew it was a lie, and more and more worry pinched her face.

"I'll get you out of here," she promised.

"Of course you will," I replied in an easy voice.

Another lie, since we both knew the only way I was getting out of here now was in a pine box. I'd escaped Madeline's trap to sucker me into police custody back at the restaurant, but now here I was tangled up in it all the same. She'd probably told Dobson to assault Bria at some point during their confrontation, knowing that I would step in to stop him. Part of me had realized that I was giving Madeline exactly what she wanted by taking down Dobson and that he would use my intervention as an excuse to arrest me. But at least I'd saved my sister from his physical wrath.

The two officers holding on to me tightened their bruising grips on my upper arms, but I didn't move, I didn't resist, and I didn't fight back. That would just make things worse.

Silvio had been standing next to Sophia, and they both came striding over. The vampire planted himself in front of Dobson.

"Where are you taking my client?" Silvio demanded. "She didn't do anything wrong. She was simply defending her sister. What could you possibly be charging her with?"

Dobson looked down his nose at the other man. "Assaulting an officer, for starters. As for the rest, well, give me a few minutes. With all the bad things that bitch has done, it shouldn't be too hard to come up with something else." He glanced over at the men still holding on to me. "Take her away."

"Forget it," Silvio snapped. "She's right here. Let's get her processed and out on bail. *Immediately.*"

"Aw, I'm sorry, Mr. Lawyer Man, but I'm afraid that it's too late to do that now. There's just no way to process her in time for release before the end of business today. I'm afraid that your client will have to spend the night in jail." Dobson held his hands out to his sides as though he were helpless in all of this. "Them's the rules. I'm sure you understand."

It was just after three in the afternoon, plenty of time to get me processed and out on bail, but we all knew that wasn't going to happen. Now that Dobson had his hooks into me, he wasn't going to let go until one of us was dead.

Silvio's gray eyes glittered with anger, and he straightened up to his full height, which was still more than twelve inches shorter than Dobson's massive, seven-foot frame. "What *I* understand is that if Ms. Blanco gets so much as a hangnail while she is in your custody, then she will sue you, the department, and every other person in this station."

"So many empty threats," another voice called out. "It's a good thing that I happen to be an expert on legal matters like these."

Jonah McAllister wove his way through the crowd, his shiny black wing tips *tap-tap-tapp*ing out on the floor the drumbeat of my approaching doom.

"Oh, look," I drawled. "Another cockroach out in the middle of broad daylight. Will wonders never cease."

Jonah's jaw clenched, but the rest of his too-tight skin didn't move with the sour expression. "Oh, Gin." He let out a hearty, merry chuckle. "You don't know how happy it makes me to finally see you here, where you belong."

"Well," I drawled back, "I'm sure that you can give me some tips on how to navigate the big house. Especially when it comes to bending over for everyone. Tell me, how is that pesky court case against you progressing? You know, the one with all those disturbing counts of murder, robbery, and conspiracy? Hmm?"

Jonah's brown eyes narrowed, and his mouth flattened out as much as it could, but he didn't respond to my taunt. Didn't much matter. I knew the real reason he was here. In fact, I'd been waiting for him or even Madeline herself to show up ever since I entered the station. But I supposed that she was still too busy with the library dedication to her dead mama to come and see about me—yet.

Jonah looked over at Dobson. "Rest assured, Captain, that if this woman assaulted you, then you have every right to arrest her. The law will back you up on that, in my expert opinion."

"The only thing you're an expert at is being a weasel," I cut in, ignoring his flimsy justifications. "We all know that Madeline sent you here to be her eyes and ears. Glad to see she's found some use for you. It won't last, though. You know that better than anyone. As soon as she's done with you, Madeline will use her acid magic to dissolve that smooth face of yours into a puddle of melted skin. I bet it happens soon too. Like, say, right after that party she's planning?"

It was a calculated jab, and I had the satisfaction of seeing Jonah blink in surprise. "How do you know about the coronation—"

He clamped his lips shut, realizing that he'd already said too much. This time, my eyes were the ones that narrowed. Coronation? Perhaps it wasn't so much a party as it was Madeline asserting herself and taking control of the underworld, just like Mab had done so many years ago.

And I finally realized what Madeline's crowning achievement was going to be—my murder.

This was it. This was her endgame. This was what all the underworld bosses had been so desperately trying to accomplish these last several months. Madeline had just been smarter, slyer, and more motivated to make it happen than anyone else. She had realized that sending her minions after me head-on like all the other bosses had was a stupid waste of time and resources. So she'd waited, and she'd plotted and planned, and she'd decided to hit me where it would hurt the most—by going after my friends. Roslyn. Owen. Eva. Finn. Jo-Jo. And now Sophia, Bria, and Xavier were caught up in the mess too.

Silvio had once told me that Madeline wanted to burn my world to the ground before she killed me. Well, so far, she was doing a bang-up job of it, and all I saw were flames every which way I turned. Hurt my friends, murder me, and take control of the underworld all at the same time. Even I had to admit that it was a neat, ambitious hat trick, and she was pulling it off beautifully so far.

"Enough talk," Dobson growled. "She assaulted me, and she's been arrested. So put that bitch in a cell. *Now.*"

Silvio, Bria, Xavier, and Sophia protested, shouting in louder and louder voices that I was innocent, that I hadn't done anything wrong, that this was the worst sort of frame-up. But it was no use. Dobson was in charge, and all the other cops were either too crooked or too afraid of him to do anything but follow his barked orders.

So the fine boys in blue of the Ashland Police Department did what most of them had probably been dreaming about for a long time now—they carted my ass off to jail.

❊ 10 ❊

More and more cops surrounded me, creating an unbreakable ring, before the two officers still holding on to me shoved me forward.

I looked over my shoulder. Silvio, Bria, Xavier, and Sophia surged forward, but Dobson dropped his hand to his gun, a clear warning that he would start shooting if they tried to interfere or help me in any way. So my friends were forced to pull up short. Even if they'd gotten past Dobson, there was no way they could have fought their way through the rest of the cops flanking me.

"Gin! Gin!" Bria started yelling, standing on her tiptoes to see through the crowd that separated us.

"It's okay!" I yelled back. "I'll be all right!"

Her panicked gaze met mine for a split-second before the cops pushed me through an archway set into the back wall, and she disappeared from sight.

* * *

The archway opened up into a long hallway, with more wooden benches lining the walls, and rooms and jail cells branching off either side. But instead of stopping, opening one of the cells, and shoving me inside, the two cops tightened their hold on me and marched me to the far end of the hallway and through another archway.

Deeper and deeper we went into the station, twisting and turning through one corridor after another, with more and more members of the po-po coming out from their posts to join my parade. They didn't want to risk my making a break for it. Hence all the muscle. Couldn't blame them for that, since that's exactly what I was thinking about. Slamming my fist into the face of one of my handlers, grabbing somebody's gun, and shooting, fighting, and magicking my way out of here.

But it wouldn't work. There were too many cops with too many guns and far too many itchy trigger fingers. No, right now, I needed to bide my time and see exactly what sort of game this was. Because I had a sneaking suspicion that Madeline wasn't through playing with me yet. Otherwise, Dobson would have shot me in the middle of the station right after I'd tripped him, not ordered his men to cart me off to places unknown. So I would be patient and endure whatever torture was coming until I could figure out a way to turn the tables on Dobson and the rest of the cops.

Finally, we reached the end of this particular hallway, where a steel door was set into the wall. One of the officers plucked an old-fashioned skeleton key off a ring of them clipped to his belt, inserted it into the lock, and opened the door. The two officers pushed me forward, and I was forced through to the other side, where a short hallway opened up into a large room with one singular, striking feature—an enormous jail cell.

The cell itself was about twenty-five feet square, far larger than all the others we'd passed. Two long wooden benches squatted inside it, pushed up against the bars, while two dirty, grimy toilets were set into the back wall, jutting out from the gray marble. The rest of the room was completely bare and empty, except for dozens of wooden chairs that had been arranged outside the bars. Stairs led up to a second-floor balcony that wrapped around and overlooked the cell, almost as if it were a stage. But the most telling thing was that there were no security cameras anywhere. The cops didn't want anyone to see what went on in here.

Even though I'd never before been here, I knew exactly where I was.

The bull pen—a place that prisoners went into and never came out of again.

But all I could do was stand there and wait while the officer used that same skeleton key to open the cell door. The second guy patted me down, but I'd left my knives, jewelry, and cell phone in Silvio's car, so there was nothing for him to take away from me. When that was done, hands pressed on my back, shoving me forward into the middle of the empty space.

I righted myself and turned around. The officer quickly swung the cell door shut and locked it again, lest I try to make a break for it. Once I was secure, some of the tension eased, and the cops looked through the bars and smirked at me, as if I were a tiger caged in a zoo. But

I wasn't the animal here—they were, for what they did in this place.

"I wonder how long she'll last."

"The bitch is supposed to be tough."

"We'll see just how tough when she goes against the group that Dobson picked out."

"Who's got the book on it?"

"Osborne, I think . . ."

I tuned out their sly murmurs, instead studying their faces, and memorizing as many of their twisted smiles as I could. I wasn't dead yet, and if I lived through this, well, they were going to wish they hadn't.

I thought whatever cruel thing they had planned might start immediately, but after making sure that the cell door was locked, the cops trickled out of the room and shut the main door behind them, probably off to report to Dobson that I was all squared away. I wondered if the captain would come back here to gloat, or if Madeline herself would show up, now that I was finally, exactly, where she wanted me. I didn't know, but I had more important matters to think about right now.

Like escaping.

So I did what anyone stuck in a cell would do—I started trying to figure out how to get out of it.

But the thick, solid bars were all made of silverstone, and I couldn't so much as rattle them. I might be a powerful elemental, but even I didn't have enough juice to get through that much of the metal, and the bars would simply absorb any magic I threw at them. The floor was useless as well, since it was a solid slab of gray marble. Plus, we were on the ground level. Even if I cracked open the floor with my Stone magic, I had nowhere to go but down into the dirt. So I moved on to the back of the cell and splayed my hand across the cool wall.

The marble hummed with low notes of despair and desperation, the emotions of everyone who'd been locked in this cell. But mixed in with the somber chorus of doom were also high-pitched shrieks, the sharp, piercing, agonized cries of everyone who'd been forced in this cage before me and had left a bloody, tattered, broken mess.

If they'd been lucky enough to leave at all.

I shut the sound of the stone's cries out of my mind and examined it more closely. The marble was at least a foot thick, with silver flecks sparkling like diamond chips in the smooth, glossy surface. It was definitely a wall designed to keep people in, even elementals like me. Oh, I could blast through the marble, but it would take too long, make too much noise, and use up far too much of my magic. It wouldn't do me any good to bust out of the police station only to get shot in the parking lot because I didn't have enough energy left to run.

But it was an exterior wall and the only part of the cell not lined with silverstone bars, so I forced myself to look at it again. There had to be some way to get through it, even if there wasn't a window, and the only things attached to it were the two toilets—

My gaze locked onto the toilets. At one time, they might have been clean white porcelain. Now they were so filthy that they were grayer than the floor and spattered with blood and other things I didn't want to look at, much less smell. But I breathed in through my mouth to lessen the stench of vomit, urine, and blood, squatted down next to one of the toilets, and looked at how it was attached to the wall.

And I thought of something that might actually get me out of here.

It was a long shot, but it was the only chance I had. So I used the toe of my boot to flush the toilet, cocking my ear to the side and listening to the gurgle of water in the pipes. When I was satisfied, I did my lady business, flushed the toilet again, placed my hand on the cleanest spot of porcelain I could find, and reached for my magic. Elemental Ice crystals formed on my palm, then spread out, climbing up over the rim of the toilet and then down into the bowl of water below.

I kept my power at a low but steady level, feeding more and more Ice into the toilet, until I was satisfied that it would do what I wanted it to. When I finished, I waited three minutes, wondering if someone might have sensed me using my power and would storm into the room to check on me. But Dobson thought that he'd finally trapped me, and I didn't hear the slightest sound of movement beyond the bull pen. So I felt safe enough to repeat the process on the second toilet.

Once I'd set my plan into motion, there was nothing to do but wait until Dobson or someone else came back here. Besides, I needed to rest to help replenish the magic I'd used. I might still be breathing, but this was just a temporary respite, and I'd need every scrap of power to survive what was coming.

So I curled up on one of the hard wooden benches, made myself as comfortable as possible, and drifted off to sleep.

* * *

I wasn't really all that tired, since it was only about four in the afternoon, but the roller coaster of the day's events and emotions had taken its toll on me, and I quickly dozed off, especially given the unnatural silence in this part of the station. But it wasn't long before the blackness receded, and I started to dream of my past, the way that I had ever since Fletcher was murdered last year. . . .

We were in trouble.

Fletcher and I ran side by side, trying to get out of the warehouse. But no matter how hard we pumped our legs or how fast we sprinted, it didn't seem like we had moved at all. No wonder, since the enormous shell of a building covered the better part of three acres. Bare bulbs dropped down from the ceiling, casting out more shadows than light, while old, empty wooden crates covered the concrete floor, along with odd, loose bits of metal, long snakes of stripped wires, and rusted lengths of pipe.

Crack! Crack! Crack! Crack!

But what really concerned me were all the bullets zipping through the air in our direction.

Whoosh! Whoosh!

Along with the balls of elemental Fire.

Zing! Zing! Zing!

And the razor-sharp crossbow bolts that further splintered the wooden crates as we darted past them.

Oh, yeah. The old man and I were in serious trouble.

And to think that the evening had started out so well.

As the Tin Man, his assassin code name, Fletcher had been approached about taking out Liza Malone, a crooked cop who liked to strong-arm protection money out of small-

business owners over in Southtown . . . and then do absolutely nothing in return when some real danger came calling. Like, say, the three gangbangers who'd deliberately crashed their stolen car through the storefront windows of a mom-and-pop grocery and then stormed inside and shot up the place, including the owners' thirteen-year-old son.

The kid had died in his big brother's arms. A news photographer had captured that heartbreaking sight, and the image of the guy clutching his baby brother's bloody, lifeless body to his chest had run on the news for days.

According to Fletcher, the Colson family had demanded that Malone find the people responsible for killing their boy. She told them that she would—for another fifty thousand dollars. Up front, of course. The Colsons didn't have that kind of cash, but they'd scraped together what they could and given it to Malone. In return, the cop had done nothing but sit on her ass and jack up her prices for everyone else in the neighborhood who was paying her protection money.

Through his various cutouts, dead drops, and back channels, the Colsons had reached out to Fletcher to get what justice they could, and the old man had handed things off to me, since I was twenty-two now and far more spry than his aging bones. I had found and taken out the three gangbangers a week ago. The fools had been bragging all over Southtown about how tough they were, robbing a family and killing a kid. I didn't even have to bribe anyone to find them. Easiest job Fletcher had ever sent me on. One of the most satisfying too.

But the gangbangers had told me all sorts of interesting things before they died—like the fact that they'd been paying protection money to Liza Malone too. As long as they slipped the cop a cut of their take, she was perfectly happy to look the other way as they went about their reign of robbery in the neighborhood. Now, double- or even triple-dipping was nothing new in Ashland. More like a long-standing tradition and a favorite sport. But this time, it had cost an innocent boy his life. The Colsons wanted payback, and I'd been dispatched to get it for them.

So I'd started following Malone on the sly, tracking her movements, analyzing her habits, and learning every single thing I could about her. When I had a plan of attack I thought would work, I took the final step and talked things out with Fletcher, the way I always did now, even though I'd moved out into my own apartment and was doing most of the jobs solo. The old man had agreed with my assessment and plan, and he'd even tagged along with me on this one, since taking out a cop—even a crooked one—could be tricky.

I'd learned that Malone liked to host an after-hours poker game for cops, lawyers, and whoever else had enough coin to buy in at her ten-thousand-dollar, cash-only minimum. Fletcher and I had decided to do the hit here at the abandoned warehouse where the game was played every couple of weeks, since plenty of bad folks would be around who would be sure to blame each other for killing Malone. Besides, the warehouse was out in the sticks, miles away from anything, so there would be no one around to hear any gunfire, should things come down to that. So we'd locked and loaded up our supplies, driven out to the warehouse two hours before the game was supposed to start, and gotten into position, waiting for our target to arrive.

The hit itself had been easy enough.

I'd been waiting in one of the stalls in the grungy space that passed for a bathroom when Liza Malone finally got up *from the poker table to take a potty break. She was washing her hands in the cracked, stained sink when I slithered up behind her, clamped my hand over her mouth, and slit her throat. She was dead before I lowered her body to the dirty concrete floor.*

But what Fletcher and I hadn't counted on was not being the only ones interested in Malone.

Apparently, some other folks had found out about Malone's game and all the cash lying on the table and had decided to take it all for themselves. I'd just finished wiping my knife off when the steady crack-crack-crack *of gunfire sounded. I opened the bathroom door to see two men and two women shooting the five other cops sitting at the poker table.*

So I held my position, waiting for the right moment. When they finally stopped firing and moved toward the splintered table to see how much blood-spattered money was there, I slipped out of the bathroom and started tiptoeing across the warehouse. Fletcher had come inside with me, to provide backup should I need it, and the old man was hunkered down behind a battered crate, right where I'd left him more than two hours ago when I'd gone into the bathroom, waiting for the game to start.

"Gin?" Fletcher whispered. "You okay? Did you get Malone?"

"Yeah, right before those folks decided to jack the poker game. Come on. I think we can get out of here before they see us—"

I should have known better than to even think *such a thing, much less say it out loud. My bad luck would never let me get away that easy, and this time was no exception.*

Because, of course, one of the women chose that exact

moment to look in my direction. I'm not sure exactly what caught her eye, perhaps the gleam of my knife or the hand that I held out to help Fletcher up, but her eyes locked onto me, even though I was half-hidden behind the crate, and she started shouting to her friends.

"Hey! There's somebody else in here!"

That's when the bullets started flying. Naturally.

Still, I didn't think that we were in serious danger until one of the men started hurling balls of elemental Fire at us. I didn't know who he was, but he had some serious juice, and I could feel the power pulsing in the flaming balls that streaked past Fletcher and me. If one of those hit us in the back, we were done for, despite the silverstone vests we both wore.

And, of course, we were at the wrong end of the warehouse from where Fletcher had left his white van, since he hadn't wanted to risk anyone's coming to the game, seeing the vehicle, and wondering whom it belonged to.

But there were more of them than there were of us, so all we could do was run and hope that we could get away.

We might actually have made it—if the doors hadn't been barred.

I skidded to a stop, really, really hoping that my eyes were playing tricks on me, given the dim lights. But, of course, they weren't.

The double doors that Fletcher and I had snuck in through earlier now featured two large, heavy metal bars across them. I cursed. One of the giant cops who'd come to play poker must have put them there, trying to make sure that no one would enter the warehouse and interrupt their game.

"Cover me!" I yelled at Fletcher.

He nodded and took aim with his gun, firing at our pursuers and making them scatter and duck down behind the wooden crates.

Crack! Crack! Crack!

While Fletcher and the thieves exchanged shots, I surged forward, put my shoulder under one of the bars, and tried to lift it. But it was made out of solid iron, and I couldn't so much as budge it.

"It's no use!" I yelled. "I can't move it!"

We were trapped, so I whipped back around to face our attackers and tightened my grip on my bloody knife, determined to protect Fletcher and take down as many of them as I could before they killed us—

"Over here!" Fletcher hissed.

He waved me over. He'd spotted a door that led into another room about thirty feet away and had already taken up a position there. I ran in that direction while Fletcher let loose with another round of bullets, covering me. I hurried past him into the open space. He fired the remaining bullets in his gun, then darted inside the room, slammed the door shut behind us, and threw home a series of locks that had been set into the metal. The door wouldn't hold for long, not against the elemental's Fire, and I turned around to start running again—

And realized that we'd come to a dead end.

No doors, no windows, not even a skylight. Just bare concrete walls all around. Trapped—we were trapped with no way out and nothing but danger and death coming up fast behind us.

While Fletcher reloaded his gun, I prowled around the room, looking for something, anything that might give me an idea on how to get out of here. But the only things in the room were a couple of empty, graffiti-covered metal barrels, the kind that I always imagined Sophia used to dispose of bodies. One of them even had a crude white skull and crossbones painted on the side. The Goth dwarf would have approved of that, at least.

"Damn it," I snarled, kicking one of the containers, although it was so heavy that it barely moved. "We're stuck here, like fish in a barrel, waiting for them to come in and finish us off."

Fletcher shook his head and crooked his finger at me. I moved over to the door and pressed my ear up against the metal, like him. I could just make out the sounds of muffled conversation. Our pursuers had realized that they couldn't blast their way through the locks with their guns, and they were trying to figure out what to do, the same as us.

"We can't let them leave," one of the women said. "They saw us kill all those cops."

"Can you burn through the door with your Fire, Will?" a man asked.

The second man, Will, let out a disappointed breath. "Nah, it's too thick, and I've used up too much of my power already."

"Will doesn't have to burn through it with his Fire magic," another woman said. "I say we bury them in here, along with all these cops. Take the cash, blow up the building, hide the bodies. Just like we planned. Two more corpses won't matter, if they can even find them in the rubble. We've already got the warehouse rigged. I've got an extra charge in my bag. I'll plant it here in front of the door. Then we can blow them all at the same time and get out of here."

The others agreed that this was an excellent idea, and I heard several sets of footsteps scurrying back and forth on the other side of the door, no doubt pulling out and arming the explosives that would turn us and this whole place into pancake central.

"Now what?" I whispered.

Fletcher looked around and around the room, trying to come up with an idea, just like I had. But he was more successful because his green gaze locked onto the barrels.

"If we can't get out, we can't get out," he said. "Nothing's going to change that no matter how much we curse. So let's give them exactly what they want—us dead and buried."

Fletcher grabbed one of the barrels, tipped it over, and crawled inside. It was a tight fit, but he folded up his body well enough so that the metal shell completely covered him.

Good thing, since I heard a series of blasts at the other end of the warehouse, and the concrete started screaming about all the fire, heat, and explosives that were ripping through it and heading in this direction.

Boom . . . Boom . . . BOOM!

Every successive blast was louder and closer than the last, and the entire building started to shake.

"Come on, Gin!" Fletcher called out above the growing din. "Get a move on!"

I had no choice but to follow his lead, tip one of the other barrels onto its side, and crawl inside. The metal smelled dry and ashy, and I could feel soot covering every part of me, almost like it had been used to store coal to burn in a furnace.

I pulled my feet inside the container just in time to keep them from being crushed by a chunk of stone that broke free from the wall and crashed to the ground. A second later, the door blew in with a deafening, fiery roar. The shock wave sent spiderweb cracks thicker than my fingers zigzagging through *the floor and up the walls, and the room collapsed in on itself. A deadly shrapnel of concrete, cinder blocks, and thick lengths of rebar flew through the air, all of which clattered against and dented in the side of my barrel, as if I were in the middle of a terrible hailstorm. In a way, I suppose that I was.*

As the debris knocked more and more dents into the sides of my makeshift cocoon, I wondered if the metal would give up and cave in completely. All it would take would be one piece of rebar to skewer me to death. Fletcher too. But it was too late now to do anything but huddle inside and hope that the barrel would somehow hold up against the chunks of stone that were raining down all around us—

BANG.

For a moment, I was still in the warehouse, still trapped in that soot-coated barrel, still watching the ceiling collapse and starting to bury Fletcher and me alive—

BANG.

The noise sounded again, snapping me out of the last dregs of my dream, my memory. I opened my eyes and sat up, putting my back against the bars and looking toward the cell door.

Dobson stood on the other side, a long, thick, black nightstick in his hands.

BANG.

He smacked the wood against the bars a third time, but I didn't give him the satisfaction of flinching at the hard sound.

"Rise and shine, Blanco," he crowed. "You've got visitors."

* 11 *

Dobson stepped to one side so an officer could insert a key in the cell door and open it. Five people trooped inside the barred space, a mix of men and women, all wearing the charcoal-gray prison jumpsuits of the Ashland correctional system. The officer stepped inside as well, unlocking and removing the silverstone handcuffs that kept the prisoners' strength and elemental magic in check before scurrying back out with the cuffs and locking the door behind him.

I looked over the prisoners for a few seconds before turning my attention to the other people streaming into the room—all the ones outside the cell.

Uniformed officers, suited detectives, even the janitors and administrative staff gathered around the three sides of the cell. They stared through the bars at me, sizing me up, just as I was them. Then fat wads of cash started going from hand to hand to hand, and the conversation started, the chorus of voices getting louder and more excited as the money moved from one person to the next.

"Give me a thousand on whoever's fighting Blanco."

"Make it two thousand for me."

"Five thousand says that she doesn't even last five minutes in there."

So there was to be some serious gambling to go along with tonight's blood sport.

I expected nothing less from the bull pen.

I'd heard whispers about this place for years, and Fletcher had a file on it in his office, although I'd only skimmed the information. Still, I knew the gist of it. About this single cell hidden deep in the police station where the cops corralled particularly strong, sadistic, and troublesome prisoners, sicced them on each other late at night, and watched the resulting carnage for their own twisted amusement. From what I'd heard, the fight didn't end, and the cops didn't open the cell door, until at least one prisoner was dead.

And tonight, they wanted that prisoner to be me.

According to the rumors, most fights in the bull pen featured only two prisoners, not the five-on-one grudge match I was facing. But Dobson had obviously made some special arrangements for me, no doubt on Madeline's orders. Still, as the rolls of bills kept going from one person to another, I couldn't help but wonder how many folks were betting on me. Finn certainly would have, if he'd been here. But given the knowing smirks aimed in my direction, it didn't seem that many people were willing to take a chance on me, not when I'd been so clearly marked for death. Their loss.

Dobson moved through the crowd, shaking hands, slapping backs, and taking bets, just like the aw-shucks good ole boy that he portrayed himself to be. He was definitely the ringmaster of this little circus, and I wondered how long he'd been bringing prisoners back here just so he could watch them bleed out and pad his own pockets at the same time. Well, I hoped that he enjoyed the show because tonight was going to be the final performance, if I had my way.

A clock mounted on the wall across from the cell told me that it was a few minutes until midnight. No doubt that's when the action would officially get under way. So I used the remaining time to look beyond the cell and the cops, and I realized that people had also gathered on the second-floor balcony that overlooked the bull pen.

Three people, to be exact—Madeline, Emery, and Jonah.

Madeline relaxed in a padded seat behind the balcony railing, in the exact center of the room, directly across from the cell door, so that she could have the best view possible of my impending demise. Emery was seated at her right elbow, just like always, with Jonah standing a few feet away. All three of them were smiling with cold satisfaction, and a bottle of liquor was perched on the railing in front of them, as though they were going to toast my death. I wondered if they were going to smoke some cigars too.

I stared up at Madeline, my gray eyes locking with her green ones. Her smile widened, and she gave me a cheery wave, as though I were a knight going into battle to earn the favor of some fair maiden, instead of a prisoner who was about to be beaten within an inch of her life before she was summarily executed. I wondered if Madeline would come down here and do the deed herself with her acid magic, or if she'd let Dobson open the cell door and put a couple of bullets through my skull.

It didn't much matter what she had planned—it wasn't happening either way.

So I dropped my gaze from Madeline and focused on the people who were the most important right now—the five prisoners locked in the cell with me.

Two giants, two dwarves, and an elemental with a ball of Fire flickering in her hand. The giants were tall and wide, the dwarves short and stocky, and all four of them had thick, barrel chests and rock-hard muscles that bulged against the sleeves and legs of their gray jumpsuits. No doubt they'd augmented their natural strength by obsessively lifting weights, the way that so many prisoners did. Any one of them could easily beat or strangle me to death with his or her bare hands.

I studied the elemental for several seconds, watching the ebb and flow of the orange-red flames coating her palm. She had a decent amount of juice, but she wasn't in my league, and I could easily overcome her magic with my own Ice and Stone power. That's probably what Dobson was counting on. Having the Fire elemental keep me busy blocking her scorching power, while the giants and dwarves surrounded me, hammering on me with their fists until they cracked through the protective shell of my Stone magic. Then nature would take its course, and my face, skull, and ribs would cave in from the heavy blows. Once I was down on the floor, it would all be over except for the screaming, and Dobson or even Madeline could enter the cell and kill me at leisure.

My hands clenched into fists, my fingers pressing into

the spider rune scars embedded in my palms. Not going to happen. None of it. Not tonight.

Not to the Spider.

Finally, all the bets had been placed, and all the money had been collected. Dobson *bang-bang-bang*ed his nightstick on the cell bars and let out a couple of loud whistles to get everyone's attention. The crowd quieted, and folks sat down in the chairs around all three sides of the cell. The five prisoners inside the bull pen spread out in a single line in front of the door. I finally got to my feet, moved over in front of the toilets so that I was directly across from the prisoners, and stared them down, my face even colder and harder than all of theirs were combined.

"Well, as y'all can see, we have a new, shall we say, *challenger* in our humble arena tonight," Dobson crowed, his gravelly voice harsh with excitement.

Hoots and hollers filled the air at his words, but I tuned out the roars and stared at my enemies, trying to gauge their strengths and weaknesses and, most important, how I could beat them all. While everyone was busy cheering, I put my hand on the marble wall above one of the toilets, making sure that my plan, my Ice magic, was still in place. Everything was as it should be, and I dropped my hand before anyone noticed what I was doing.

Dobson droned on and on and *on*, psyching up the crowd for my death match. He really should have been a ringmaster the way he twirled his nightstick around and around in his hand like it was a baton. Apparently, the good captain thought that his prattle was supposed to scare me, because he finally wound down and peered through the bars at me.

"Well, Blanco? Any last words? Any begging for your life you want to do?"

"The only one who will be begging by the time this is over with is you, Dobson." My voice was as cold as death. "You'd better hope that Madeline or Emery kill you before I get my hands on you. Otherwise, there won't be enough left of you to slurp up with a straw."

Dobson's brown eyes narrowed, but he didn't respond to my taunt. He thought that he'd already won. So did Madeline. But they hadn't. Not by a long shot.

"And now," Dobson said, drawing out the words, "let the game begin!"

All around the perimeter of the cell, people yelled and cheered and clapped and whistled. For a moment, it was almost like I was back in Southtown, facing down Beauregard Benson in the middle of the street, while that crowd of gangbangers, hookers, and bums looked on. But those folks had been more or less on my side. The only thing the people here were cheering for was my bloody, brutal death.

Dobson dropped his hand, which must have been some sort of signal to the five prisoners inside the cell, because they all shouted and charged forward at once.

Five on one. Not bad odds. I'd figured that Dobson would pack so many inmates into the bull pen that they'd tear me apart on sight and I wouldn't even have a chance to fight back. But the giant had left me plenty of room to maneuver, a mistake that I planned to take full advantage of.

For my family, I thought. *For me.*

Then I screamed and charged forward as well.

✣ 12 ✣

Unlike the five folks coming at me, I had more of a plan in mind than just charging wildly at my enemy. When I'd built up enough speed, I dropped to my knees, sliding, sliding, sliding across the slick marble floor. Even as I zoomed forward, I reached for my magic, forming a thick, jagged dagger out of elemental Ice. I grinned. I always felt so much better with a knife in my hand.

I slid right into the middle of the oncoming group of prisoners and lashed out, driving the Ice dagger deep into the side of one of the giant's knees. She howled, her legs flying out from under her, and landed flat on her back. Her head cracked against the floor, and her eyes rolled up into the back of her head. But she was just stunned, not dead, and I wasn't done with her yet.

Even as the Fire elemental pulled up short and reared back to throw her ball of flames at me, I threw myself on top of the dazed giant, grabbed her shoulders, and then used my momentum to roll her heavy body over on top of me.

The flames punched into her back a second later.

The Fire elemental must have had orders to kill me as soon as she could because her first blast would have been plenty enough to do it, if I hadn't been using the giant as a human shield. The giant screamed and screamed as the flames scorched through the thin fabric of her jumpsuit and then her skin beneath. Her blond hair went up in a puff of smoke, and the stench of burning, charred meat filled the room. I was dimly aware of the cheers, jeers, and shouts of everyone watching, but I ignored the sounds and focused on the only thing that mattered right now—surviving.

I reached down and yanked the Ice dagger out of the giant's knee, making her howl that much louder. Then I buried the crude blade in her neck, puncturing her carotid artery and putting her out of her misery.

One down, four to go.

Blood arched up from the giant's wound, like water spewing from a fountain. The crowd hushed, and silence descended over the bull pen. They actually thought that I was already dead—until I wiggled out from underneath the giant's body and got back up onto my feet.

The Fire elemental let out an enraged shriek that she hadn't toasted me to death, and she reached for her power again, forming another ball of flames in the palm of her hand.

Viselike arms closed around me from behind, trapping my own arms down by my sides. The second giant had snuck up behind me, but that was okay, because I was going to use him just like I had the first one. With me seemingly pinned in place, one of the dwarves advanced on me, an evil grin stretching across her face. She held out her hand, and I saw the gleam of a shiv made out of a blue toothbrush handle that had been sharpened to a daggerlike point. So Dobson had outfitted at least one of the prisoners with a weapon, trying to give them that much more of an advantage. But really, he'd just made it that much easier for me to kill the dwarf, since I was going to bury that shiv in her throat.

Instead of rushing forward, the dwarf kept the shiv close by her side. She wasn't going to get suckered in as easily as the first giant had.

"You got her?" the dwarf growled.

I made a show of struggling against the giant, as if I were trying to break free of his rock-solid arms, even though I had no chance of doing that.

"I've got her," he growled back. "Hurry up and gut her already."

The dwarf grinned again and moved forward.

I waited until the last possible moment, then, using the giant as leverage, I lifted my feet off the ground and kicked the dwarf in the face. One of my boots hit her dead-on in the nose, breaking it and making blood spatter everywhere. My other foot caught her in her right cheek, glancing off the thick bone there, although the tread of my boot imprinted itself deep into her skin, making her look like she had some sort of bizarre, red road rash.

The dwarf yelped and clasped her hands to her face, more concerned with her busted nose than with me at the moment. As my feet fell, I used the downward arc to smash my right boot as hard as I could into the giant's instep. He grunted, but he didn't let go of me.

The dwarf wiped enough of the blood out of her eyes to raise the shiv and lash out with it at me. I slammed my boot onto the giant's instep again and again, and he finally wobbled, the tiniest bit off-balance. His arms loosened for a fraction of a second, and I let my legs slide out from under me, dropping to the floor like dead weight, and escaping his tight, bruising grip.

The dwarf realized what I was up to, but it was too late, and she was too committed to her strike to stop. She plunged the toothbrush shiv into the center of the giant's chest. She'd put all her strength behind the blow, punching the makeshift weapon right through his ribs and up into his chest cavity, where it had lots of vital things to hit, rupture, and tear through.

The giant screamed and screamed, blood streaming down his chest in warm, coppery spurts. He staggered back, ripped the shiv out of his body, and tossed the weapon aside. But his actions only made the sucking chest wound that much worse, and he teetered back and forth on his feet for a few seconds before his knees buckled. He curled up into a ball on the floor, both hands pressed tight against his chest, trying to stop the blood loss, even though it was already far too late for that.

Two down, three to go.

The dwarf's mouth gaped open, but I didn't give her the chance to shake off her surprise. I scrambled over, snatched up the bloody shiv from where it had clattered to the floor, and threw myself at her.

I went low, tackling her around the knees, since I was no match for her incredible upper-body strength. She'd been standing close to one of the cell walls, and I shoved her back far, fast, and hard enough to make her head smack up against the bars and rattle her brain around inside her skull.

I was half on the floor, hanging on to the dwarf's knees like a child clinging to her mother. The dwarf shook off her daze and put her arms on my shoulders, trying to push me off. Even as her fingers dug into my skin, I raised the bloody shiv and rammed it deep into the meaty part of her thigh, twisting and twisting and twisting the weapon in as deep as it would go, before ruthlessly yanking it back out again.

The dwarf yelped with pain, so I stabbed her again, trying to hit her femoral artery so she'd bleed out. I wasn't that lucky, but I'd put more than enough force behind the blow to make her feel it. The dwarf screamed, her feet scrabbling for purchase on the slick floor. Her worn-out sneakers slipped in a pool of her own blood, and her legs went out from under her. The dwarf slid down the bars, until she was on the floor with me.

I kept stabbing her the whole time.

Punch-punch-punch-punch.

Using the toothbrush shiv, I opened up wounds in her legs, chest, and arms. Whatever I could reach. I wasn't picky. Then, when she was down at eye level with me, I drove the shiv so far into her throat that there wasn't enough of the plastic sticking out for me to grab hold of and yank free again.

The dwarf died with a wheeze, pitching to one side, her body *scrape-scrape-scrap*ing against the bars almost like she was rattling a tin cup back and forth asking for more food. A second later, she landed on the floor, choking to death on her own blood.

Three down, two to go—

Fingers dug into my hair, yanking me away from the dead woman and making me yelp. The second dwarf had finally gotten in on the action, and he pulled me up and then shoved me forward, mashing my face against the silverstone bars, as if he were trying to push my whole head through them. With one hand, he held me up against the bars. With the other, he slammed his fist into my back and kidneys over and over.

Thwack-thwack-thwack-thwack.

The folks watching the fight hadn't had much to cheer about up until this point, but they hooted and hollered with delight and surged up out of their chairs as the dwarf pinned me against the bars. Dobson got right up in my face on the other side of the metal.

"How does it feel, Blanco?" he hissed, spittle spewing out of his lips. "Knowing that you're going to die here tonight?"

Instead of responding, I snaked one arm through the bars and grabbed his silk tie. Then I yanked him forward as hard as I could, making his head *bang* against the bars just like his nightstick had earlier and adding a third goose egg to the collection on his face. Dobson grunted and fell back on his ass, making the crowd howl even louder.

I would have liked to have reached through the bars, latched onto Dobson's ankle, and dragged him back in range so I could strangle him to death with his own tie, but there was the small matter of the dwarf and his continued pummeling of me.

So I flung my right hand out to the side and reached for my magic. A second later, I had another Ice dagger clutched in my fingers. I twirled the crude weapon around, brought it up, and then stabbed the dwarf in the thigh with it. He grunted, but he didn't stop his assault.

The dagger broke off in his leg, so I wrapped my hand around the jagged end and let loose with another round of Ice magic, this time blasting my cold, frosty power deep into the wound I'd opened up in his thigh—along with certain sensitive areas a bit higher up on his body.

That was enough to get the dwarf to yelp and finally let go of me, since I'd just given him the worst case of frostbite *ever*. I whipped around and gouged my fingers into his eyes, adding to the pain already racking his body. The dwarf slapped at me, but his blows were wild, and his hands clattered off the bars instead of hitting me. Behind him, I could see the Fire elemental drawing her hand back, another ball of flames crackling in her palm. So I grabbed hold of the dwarf's jumpsuit and pulled him close to me, ducking down behind his short body as best I could.

The elemental's Fire ball exploded against his back a second later.

The dwarf screamed, and so did the folks who'd gathered behind me, as they ducked to get out of the way of the flames shooting through the gaps in the cell bars.

The dwarf wasn't quite dead, but he was close enough to it, so when the flames died down, I shoved his charred body away and stepped toward the elemental.

Four down, one to go.

The Fire elemental's eyes narrowed as she stared at me, both of us moving step by step, going around the cell in a large circle. Finally, I stopped when I reached the back wall, standing right in front of the two toilets.

"You don't have anybody to hide behind now," she hissed.

"I don't need anybody else," I snarled back, throwing my hands out wide. "Take your best shot, bitch."

All around the cell, the crowd pressed forward on all sides, clutching the bars, sensing that this could finally be the end of me. Even Dobson had managed to get back on his feet, *bang-bang-bang*ing his nightstick on the bars in a steady drumbeat of encouragement. His screams for the Fire elemental to kill me *right fucking now* were among the loudest.

I looked up at the balcony. Madeline, Emery, and Jonah were all on their feet now, clutching the metal railing, and leaning forward in anticipation. The giant and the lawyer were both smiling wide, thinking that I was about to meet my maker at long last. But Madeline's expression was far more subdued, almost pensive, as if she realized that I was up to something.

But I pushed Madeline out of my mind and focused on the more pressing threat of the Fire elemental standing twenty feet from me. On the floor in between us, the shivved giant and the burned dwarf let out softer and softer moans of pain as they circled the drain toward death. The other giant and dwarf that I'd already killed lay where they had fallen, their sightless eyes fixed on me in ugly, silent accusations.

But the Fire elemental didn't have a scratch on her yet, and she still had plenty of magic left, given the hot glow of the orange-red flames pulsing in her hand.

Excellent.

Thick pools of blood covered the floor, adding even more shiny gloss to the slick gray surface as the crimson rings oozed out toward the barred edges of the cell. All around me, the stone muttered about the violence I had just dished out, adding more dark notes to the guttural chorus that had already sunk deep into the marble from all the fights that had taken place here before. The stone's cold, harsh song matched my mood perfectly.

But this was the end of this particular battle, and I was already thinking about how I could win the next one—my escape.

We stood there, elemental to elemental, and faced each other. That ball of Fire still crackled in her palm, but I didn't reach for any of my magic, not even my Stone power to harden my skin to withstand her heated assault.

I didn't need my magic. Not for this.

Finally, the Fire elemental got tired of waiting for me to do something. Urged on by the roaring crowd, who'd started *bang-bang-bang*ing on the bars in anticipation of my end, she gave me a cruel smile, then reared back and threw the ball of flames at me. She put everything she had into this last, final kill shot, and I could feel her trying to channel the last scraps of her magic into the roaring mass of Fire even as it left her hand and streaked through the cell toward me.

I waited and waited . . . everything slowing down as the flames grew closer and closer . . . the glow of them brighter and brighter . . . the feel of them hotter and hotter . . .

And then I simply stepped out of the way.

The flames roared past me and slammed dead center into the toilets, just the way I'd wanted them to. Normally, nothing much would have happened, except that the two porcelain thrones would have gotten a good scorching before the flames died down.

But earlier, when I was pouring my elemental Ice magic down into the toilets, I'd gone the extra step of freezing all the water in them—and in all the pipes that snaked through the marble wall behind them.

Given what I'd heard about the bull pen, I had figured that there would be some sort of death match in here, and that Dobson would send in at least one elemental to try to kill me. For once, I'd gotten lucky, and it had been a Fire elemental. Not only that, but she'd been the last prisoner standing, just as I'd wanted her to be.

Because if there is one fact that has dominated my entire life from the moment that Mab murdered my family, it was this: Fire and Ice never, *ever* mix.

Her scorching heat met my intense cold, and the toilets exploded.

I turned away and ducked down, putting my hands over my head and finally reaching for my Stone magic to harden my skin into an impenetrable shell so I wouldn't get sliced to ribbons by the porcelain shrapnel zipping through the air.

The explosion seemed to go on forever, although it couldn't have lasted more than a few seconds.

Everyone in the crowd screamed, scattered, and started stampeding toward the exit, probably thinking that I'd somehow set off a bomb inside the cell, but their hoarse shouts and the *smack*s of bodies hitting the floor were drowned out by the sound of the cold water gushing out of the busted pipes. I thought that the Fire elemental shrieked as well, but she didn't concern me anymore. I'd be surprised if she could muster up so much as a candle flame right now, as water-soaked as the area was.

I shut all the screams and shouts and *glug-glug-glug*s of water out of my mind. Because if I didn't get out of here now, I never would, and I wasn't about to waste this opportunity.

So I ran over to the back wall of the prison, placed both palms flat on it, and let loose with a torrent of my magic. The exploding toilets and busted pipes had knocked out large chunks of the wall, and I poured my Ice magic into all the gaping holes and jagged cracks left behind in the marble, driving it down into the stone as deep as it would go. Then, a second later, I sent out a blast of Stone magic, shattering all those pockets of Ice.

I did this over and over again, causing more and more water to rain down on me, until the entire wall started to crack and crumble. My eyes cut left and right, scanning what was left of the wall, and I reached out with my magic, looking for the one weak spot that would send the whole thing tumbling down. It was right . . . *there!*

I let loose with one sharp, final burst of magic, and my Ice and Stone power punched a gaping hole all the way through the wall. This time, dust choked the air, although it was quickly washed away by the continual gushes of water. But I only had eyes for the starry midnight sky and open space beyond the wall, and I sloshed through the puddles of water, determined to reach it.

"Get her!" Madeline screamed, her voice higher and more furious than I'd ever heard it before, the sound nothing at all like her usual soft, smug tone. "Kill Blanco!"

Grinning and laughing all the while, I scrambled over the busted pipes and broken stone and out into the night.

❋ 13 ❋

Crack!

Crack! Crack!

Crack! Crack! Crack!

Some of the cops recovered enough to send a hail of bullets in my direction, but the spewing water spoiled their aim and swept most of the projectiles away completely. I staggered outside, stepping away from the hole in the wall and out of the line of fire. It would be just my luck to escape from the bull pen only to have someone get in a lucky shot that blew out the back of my skull as I was running away.

As I darted forward, I took stock of my surroundings—the police impound yard.

Cars, vans, and SUVs of all shapes and sizes sat in neat rows in the smooth, wide lot, their clear windshields and chrome rims glinting underneath the tall lights planted in the asphalt. In the distance, spotlights studded a chain-link fence that gleamed a bright, molten silver, with the razor wire on top shimmering like pointed diamonds.

I swiveled back and forth, half-expecting to see some uniformed officers running in my direction, drawn by the sounds of the explosion and the continued *crack-crack-crack*s of gunfire. But no one appeared. Looked like the po-po thought that the fence was enough to keep the cars safe and secure in the lot. Well, it wasn't going to keep me penned in. Not for long.

I'd taken a beating during the bull-pen fight, but I made my legs churn as fast as they could as I raced through the rows of cars. I must have been in the junk section because all I saw were rusted-out rattletraps that should have been compacted years ago. I stopped at the first decent-looking ride I came to—a late-model Dodge Charger—grabbed a metal pipe that was sticking up out of a nearby trash can, and used it to shatter the driver's-side window. A second later, I was inside the vehicle, ripping into the wires under the dash.

It took me longer than I would have liked, since I wasn't as good with cars as Finn was, but the engine finally rumbled to life.

Good thing, since the cops had arrived.

They poured out of the hole in the wall, all of them drenched by the still-gushing water, but all of them still clutching guns. Dobson was leading the charge.

I snapped the seat belt into its buckle, then shoved the gearshift into reverse and slammed my foot down on the gas, peeling out of the parking space and steering straight for the wall.

The cops realized that I was zooming toward them, and they all yelled and scrambled to get out of the way. I was hoping to pancake Dobson against the stone, but he threw himself to one side just before the rear bumper of the Dodge Charger slammed into what was left of the back of the station.

The impact jarred me, but I threw the car into drive and stomped down on the gas. Directly across from me, five hundred feet away, lay the main gate that led out of the impound yard.

Crack! Crack! Crack!
Crack! Crack! Crack!

More and more bullets zipped in my direction as the cops got back onto their feet and fired at the vehicle. The back windshield busted out, the driver's mirror flew off the side of the car, and gray stuffing puffed out of the passenger's headrest, but I didn't care. I was only using this vehicle to get out of the impound yard and then as far away from the station as I could. After that, I needed somewhere to regroup, at least for a few minutes, and I needed to find some way to let my friends know what was going on. I had no doubt that they had been at the station all day long, trying to get me released, but the information coming out of there would be garbled—if the cops didn't cover up my escape completely.

But where to go? Madeline had done her homework on me, so she knew all of my friends and family. A fact that she'd demonstrated over the last two days as she'd screwed with their businesses, jobs, and more. She'd be expecting me anywhere I went, and she had enough men at her disposal to follow and track me all through Ashland.

The Pork Pit, I finally decided. I needed knives, fresh clothes, money, a burner cell phone, and some tins of

Jo-Jo's healing ointment, at the very least, if I was going to survive the rest of my escape, and that was the closest place to get them. It was a calculated risk, and I was sure that Madeline, Dobson, and the rest of the waterlogged cops would be right on my heels, since that would be the first place they would look for me.

But since the restaurant was closed, courtesy of Madeline and her machinations, none of my friends, family, or employees would be there. I didn't want any of them getting caught in the cross fire if Madeline and the others did catch up to me.

While I was mulling over my options, the impound gate zoomed up to meet me. A cop was stationed in a white guard shack to the left of the entrance, and I could see his mouth hanging wide open as he watched the car approach. He wasn't used to people driving out, only those going in.

I pressed my foot down on the gas as far as it would go and reached for a bit of my Stone magic, preparing myself for what was to come—

CRASH!

The Charger ripped through the metal gate as if it were paper, since it was just shut, instead of being padlocked. I lost control for a moment, the wheel whipping back and forth under my hands, and the vehicle careened out onto the street, sideswiping a parked patrol car.

I fought the wheel and wrenched it back into place. Above the roar of the engine, I could hear more *crack-crack-crack*s of gunfire, along with the wail of sirens. Dobson wasn't wasting any time dispatching his men to hunt me down.

So I put my foot back down on the gas, blew through the red light at the end of the block, and made the sharp turn toward the Pork Pit.

The restaurant was only a few blocks away, so it took me less than five minutes to get there. I didn't know if I had enough of a head start, but I didn't waste any time trying to hide my stolen car. Instead, I parked it right in front of the Pork Pit and left it running so I wouldn't have to hot-wire it again. Besides, if the cops found it before I was done inside and I had to ditch the car, I could always go out the back and disappear into the alley and the maze of side streets behind the restaurant.

I didn't have time to be subtle, so I put my hand against the panes of glass in the front door and then froze and shattered them with my Ice magic. I hated desecrating my own restaurant—Fletcher's restaurant—but I didn't have a choice. Time was the most important thing right now. Not feelings.

I reached through the opening, turned the lock, and stepped inside. Then I sprinted through the storefront and shoved through the double doors. The back of the restaurant was pitch-black, but I'd long ago memorized the layout, so I was able to slap on the lights with no problem.

I went over to the freezer in the back and dragged a black duffel bag out from behind it. I stopped long enough to open the top, feel around in the bag until my hand closed over a knife, and slide it up my sleeve. The second thing I rooted around for was the burner phone tucked away inside. It took the phone far too long to light up and even longer still for my bruised, bloody, damp hands to punch in his number, but I managed it. He answered on the first ring.

"Gin!" Owen's worried voice filled my ear. "Is that you?"

"It's me," I said, zipping the bag back up and slinging the strap over my head and across my chest.

"Where are you? What's going on? I'm at the police station. There's been some sort of explosion, and now the cops are yelling and running around everywhere."

"I'm at the Pork Pit," I said, opening one of the double doors and peering out into the storefront. "I busted my way out of the station, and the cops are searching for me."

I paused a moment to listen, and the wail of sirens got closer and closer and louder and louder. Too risky to go back for the car now, not with the cops so close. Besides, it would be too easy for them to track me from behind, shoot out the tires, and close in for the kill. Out to the alley it was, then.

"What do you need?" Owen asked. "Tell me how to help you. Whatever it is, I'll do it. Finn, Bria, Xavier, Silvio, and I are still at the station, but we're going to the parking lot right now. We'll get there as fast as we can."

His words warmed my heart and brought a smile to my face as I unlocked and opened the back door, ready to step out into the alley and make my escape—

Crack! Crack! Crack!

Bullets slammed into the doorframe, and I saw three cops standing in the alley, guns up, firing at my location.

I cursed, ducked back inside, and shut the door. The

cops had already blocked off the back of the building, but I didn't want them getting inside, so I threw the locks and toppled a metal shelf full of ketchup bottles in front of the door for good measure.

"Gin?" Owen asked, his voice sharpening with worry. "What's that noise? What's happening?"

I didn't have time to answer him as I shoved through the double doors and ran back out into the storefront. Looked like I'd have to risk using the car after all.

Outside, the street was still clear. My heart lifted. I was going to make it out of here after all—

Madeline Monroe stepped into sight.

I hesitated, just for a second, but that was long enough for Emery Slater to appear beside her, with Jonah McAllister and Captain Lou Dobson on the other side. Behind them, blue and white lights flashed, and several police cars *screech-screech-screech*ed to a halt at the intersections. Even if I could have taken out Madeline, Emery, Jonah, and Dobson, there was no way I could get past the cops at the ends of the blocks without getting pumped full of bullets.

Trapped—I was trapped inside the Pork Pit.

❊ 14 ❊

"Gin?" Owen asked again, his voice louder and more worried than ever before. "What's going on? What's happening?"

"Madeline's outside the restaurant," I said, my voice calm, even as my mind churned and churned, trying to think of a way out of this. "The cops have the Pork Pit surrounded."

Owen sucked in a ragged breath. "Gin"—his voice came out as a low, agonized whisper—"tell me that you can get out of there. Please, *please* tell me that."

More and more cops arrived, stopping their cars at both ends of the block and cordoning it off, the blue and white lights on their vehicles spinning around and around. Some of the cops took up positions behind their cars, using the open doors as shields, while others jogged down the street and out of sight, no doubt to further block off the alley behind the restaurant.

"I'm sorry, Owen."

He let out a choked cry, the anguished sound piercing my heart, but I forced myself to tune him out and to concentrate on the most important thing right now—staying alive.

Madeline stepped up to the front door of the Pork Pit. Still clutching the phone to my ear, I approached the door from my side until only about five feet separated us. We stared at each other through the empty space where the glass had been.

"I knew that you'd come straight here." Madeline shook her head as though I'd disappointed her. "So predictable, Gin. I expected more from you."

"Let's see, I took out five inmates all by my lonesome, escaped your bull pen of death, and busted out of the police station," I drawled back. "I think that I'm doing pretty well so far, considering that you and your proxies haven't been able to kill me yet."

She shrugged. "It's only a matter of time now. We both know that. The entire restaurant is surrounded. There's no escape for you, Gin. Not this time."

Through the phone, I could hear Owen cursing Madeline for all that he was worth. Yeah. Me too.

Still, I kept my face calm as I stared her down. "I might die here tonight, but you're not going to get off so easy. How are you going to explain this? I doubt that even your pet stool pigeon there can cover up all of this. Especially since I left such a glaring reminder of my presence back at the police station."

Madeline gave me a thoughtful look, then glanced at Dobson. "You know, Gin, I think you're right. Best to cut off any loose ends now."

"Don't listen to her," Dobson growled, glaring at me

through one of the windows. "I can handle everything, just like I promised, just like I have so far."

"Sure," I mocked. "If letting me kill four people, escape police custody, steal a car, and roar out of your own impound yard is your idea of *handling things*."

"You fucking bitch!" he yelled.

The giant drew his gun out of his holster and started firing at me.

Crack!

Crack! Crack!

Crack!

But instead of punching through the window and then my skull, the bullets snagged in the thick glass, with spiderweb cracks zigzagging out in all directions from the sharp impacts.

"Bulletproof glass," I said, leaning to one side of the cracks so that Dobson had a clear view of my smug smile. "A girl's best friend."

He growled and started to raise his gun again, but Madeline sidled over to him. "Here," she said, holding out her hand. "Let me."

He reluctantly handed over his weapon, and Madeline strode back to the door with its busted-out glass. She raised the gun, aiming it at me through the open space. I tensed, ready to dive out of the way and reach for my Stone magic to harden my body—

But Madeline whipped around and shot Dobson instead.

Crack! Crack! Crack! Crack!

Madeline was an excellent marksman, and three holes appeared in his chest, clustered right over his black heart, while the fourth bullet punched through the middle of his throat. Blood bubbled out of his lips, and he choked and choked, as if he could actually cough up the bullet lodged in his neck. Dobson teetered back and forth for a moment, staring at Madeline in disbelief, before dropping to the sidewalk.

I looked past the dead giant, expecting to see the cops leave their vehicles behind and sprint in this direction. But Dobson must have told them that he was taking care of things and to stay back, because the other officers held their positions at the ends of the block, although I could hear their hoarse shouts of *Shots fired! Shots fired!*

Madeline turned her attention to me again. "You're right, Gin. Dobson would never be able to explain all of this away. But now I can."

She stepped forward. I tensed again, wondering if she was going to shoot at me, but she only threw the gun in through the shattered door pane. The weapon tumbled end over end before clattering to a stop at my feet.

"You killed Dobson with his own gun, then holed up in your restaurant. The cops surrounded the place, but tragically, they weren't able to take you alive."

"And why is that?" I asked.

Instead of answering me, Madeline crooked her finger at Emery. The giant bent down, and Madeline whispered something into her ear. Emery nodded and stepped out of my line of sight. She reappeared less than a minute later holding a cigarette lighter and a bottle with a fat wad of white cotton stuffed into the top. Emery passed the bottle to Madeline, who turned it around so that I could see the label on the expensive liquor.

The irony almost made me laugh—almost.

"Gin to be the end of Gin. I think it's rather fitting, don't you?" Madeline purred. "I had Emery bring this and some other supplies along tonight just in case you survived the bull pen. If you had, I was going to toss this inside the cell and watch you burn. You actually gave me the idea, when you were talking about my mother earlier today and how she would have already dispatched you with her Fire magic. You made an excellent point. I was extremely disappointed that you didn't die in the bull pen, but this will be so much *better*. So much more *satisfying*. After all, my mother extinguished most of the Snow family with her elemental Fire. Rather fitting that I'm going to use a similar flame to finally kill you too. Good-bye, Gin."

She held out the bottle. Emery flicked on the cigarette lighter, bent down, and lit the cotton rag in the top of the gin. Madeline stared at the red flames, which were the same color as her smiling crimson lips, then tossed the Molotov cocktail in through the shattered door.

The bottle of gin exploded against the floor.

I'd backed out of the way of the bottle and the flames that spewed out from the shattered glass, but a few seconds later another Molotov cocktail sailed in through the open door, this one thrown by Emery, adding more fuel to the fire, so to speak.

I stared at Madeline through the growing flames.

"Cover all the exits," she told Emery. "Keep her inside. Nobody approaches the building until there's nothing left but cinders."

Emery nodded and moved off to do her boss's bidding. I thought about plowing through the door and taking my chances with Madeline, but she could still kill me with her acid magic. And by this point, the cops had actually started to approach the restaurant, no doubt with even more members of the po-po on the way. I wasn't getting out of here.

I was going to burn to death inside the Pork Pit.

For a moment, the helplessness, the despair, the absolute *certainty* of my impending, painful, fire-filled death threatened to overwhelm me. I wobbled on my feet, like Dobson had before he'd dropped to the ground and bled out. But I wasn't going to have the luxury of a quick death like that. I was going to go up in flames and die screaming, just like Madeline wanted me to—

A small explosion sounded, as the last bit of glass from the first bottle of gin shattered under the growing heat. The flames scorched along the floor, as if they were following the path of the pig tracks back to the restrooms. In an instant, the hungry swath of fire had obliterated the blue and pink marks, the ones I'd walked over a thousand times before.

Cold rage erupted in my heart, icing over my despair. Fletcher had already died in here, been hideously tortured in the very same spot where I was now standing. I hadn't been able to save him, but I'd be damned if I was going to just lie down and *die*, especially at the hands of Madeline Magda fucking Monroe.

"Gin! Gin!" Owen screamed in my ear. "What's happening? We're almost to the restaurant. Finn and Bria are with me, and Silvio and Xavier are on their way. Just hold on until we get there. Do you hear me? Hold on!"

"Whatever happens, I love you," I said, watching the flames snake across the floor and start crawling up the sides of the blue and pink booths. "And I love Finn and

Bria and everyone else too. Make sure they know that. And whatever you do, don't give up on me. No matter how bad things seem."

"Gin, wait—"

I ended the call and slid the phone into my jeans pocket. Owen and the others wouldn't get here in time, and I couldn't let their anguish distract me from the things I needed to do now.

A third Molotov cocktail, this one thrown by McAllister, sailed in through the empty door pane. It too exploded and sent even more heat scorching through the restaurant. It wouldn't be long before the storefront was completely engulfed. The fire would spread through the rest of the building quickly after that, leaving nothing behind but the foundation and the brick walls.

And me—if I was very smart and very, very lucky.

I was calmer now, more in control. I knew what needed to be done. It was the same feint that Fletcher and I had managed, all those years ago, during the hit at the poker game. The principle was the same now as it had been back then. I couldn't leave the restaurant, but no one could come in and get me either. Only one way to break this stalemate.

Madeline wanted me dead in the worst possible way. The restaurant was on fire, and even if I did stumble out of the building, the cops were waiting outside to shoot me. It was a troubling problem, but the answer was surprisingly simple.

I needed to stay in the Pork Pit.

I needed to surrender to the flames.

I needed to die.

✣ 15 ✣

Still keeping one eye on Madeline, Emery, Jonah, and the cops gathered outside, I hurried through the storefront, pushed through the double doors, and went into the back of the restaurant, as though I were trying to escape from the heat, smoke, and flames for as long as possible. That was partly true, but I also wanted to fortify my position. Just because Madeline wanted to burn me to death didn't mean that she wouldn't send Emery or the cops inside to try to pump me full of bullets first.

So I tipped over a heavy metal rack lined with containers full of sugar, flour, and cornmeal in front of the double doors to keep anyone from coming at me that way. When that was done, I hurried over to the back door. The locks had held, although every once in a while I would hear a *ping-ping-ping* against the metal. The cops were still outside and still shooting, to keep me trapped inside so the fire could do its work.

So instead of using my Stone magic to harden my skin, opening the door, and making a desperate attempt to escape out into the alley, I went over to the freezer in the back.

The one with all the frozen peas in it—and the body.

Madeline wanted me dead, but she was also smart enough to make very, very sure that her goal had finally been accomplished. She wouldn't be satisfied with just burning the Pork Pit to the ground. She would want concrete proof of my death.

She would want to see my ruined, ashy, burned body.

In fact, she would *demand* it, and she wouldn't be satisfied with anything less. If there was no body, then she would assume that I had escaped, and she'd tear Ashland apart searching for me, not to mention keep terrorizing my friends.

Madeline wanted me dead, so I was going to give her exactly what her black heart desired.

I pulled the strap of the duffel bag up over my head and tossed the whole thing over into the corner, so I could move more quickly and easily. Then I opened the freezer and started tossing out the boxes of frozen peas and bags of ice inside until I had uncovered the maid's body.

She'd been in the freezer for more than twelve hours, long enough to be frozen solid, a life-size icicle with stiff, brittle limbs. It was difficult, since she was dead weight, literally, but I managed to grab hold of her arms, stand her upright in the freezer, and maneuver her over my shoulder like a fireman would. Sweating, and not just from the growing heat of the fire, I carried her over and slung her down so that she was lying on the floor in between the double doors that led into the storefront and the one that opened up into the alley out back, as if she'd been trapped there and overcome by the smoke and flames, just as Madeline wanted me to be.

Then, when that was done, I considered how I might actually survive the fire.

While I'd been working, the sprinklers had come on, spraying water everywhere, but the blaze quickly swallowed up all those precious drops, and they weren't going to be enough to put out the fire. The flames had already reached the far side of the double doors, painting the interior of the restaurant in a bright, flickering, orange-red glow. Thick gray clouds of smoke wisped through the cracks in the doors, making me cough, and I crouched down to keep my head out of the worst of it as I considered my options.

I had no doubt that I could go into one of the walk-in freezers and remain safe from the fire. But I might run out of oxygen and suffocate before the flames died out. Besides, even if I had enough air, part of the restaurant could always collapse in and block the door, trapping me in the freezer until Madeline sent Emery and the cops inside to make sure that I was dead. I had no desire to be captured and taken back to the bull pen. So the walk-in freezers were out, and so was the one I'd hauled the body out of, since it would have far less air.

I could have gone over to one of the brick walls, let loose with my Stone magic, and blasted open a hole big enough to stagger out of, but the cops were still waiting in the alley. At this point, Madeline and Emery had probably told them to watch the walls and be on the lookout for any sign that I was using my power, so I couldn't escape that way.

I might have gone through one of the walls into the storefront next door, but if I were the acid elemental, I would have posted men there too. Besides, I had no way of knowing how fast or far the fire might spread. The sturdy brick walls of the Pork Pit should contain the blaze, but there was no guarantee of that. So nothing doing there.

The drop ceiling wasn't any help either, since it was covered with tiles that would soon succumb to the flames. Besides, smoke was already boiling every which way up there, and I'd die from inhaling it before the flames even had a chance to scorch my skin.

No, I had to stay in the restaurant, and I had to figure out some way to keep myself safe from the fire. My Ice and Stone magic would help with that, but I'd already used up a good chunk of my power escaping from the bull pen. I didn't know that I had the reserves left to wait out a lengthy fire. And my magic still wouldn't save me from the smoke. Even now, it threatened to overwhelm me, and I kept coughing and coughing, drawing treacherous particles of soot and carbon monoxide deep down into my lungs with every ragged breath I took.

My gaze fell to the floor and all those disgusting boxes of frozen peas. I'd tossed them out of the freezer, not caring where they'd landed, but some of them had stacked up together, almost like . . .

Bricks.

Once again, I flashed back to that night with Fletcher and how we'd taken refuge in those metal barrels as the warehouse had exploded around and then collapsed down on top of us. I didn't have a barrel, but in this case I had something better—frozen peas.

I knew what I had to do now.

Time was running out, so I yanked the neck of my bloody T-shirt up over my mouth and nose, blocking out the billowing clouds of smoke as best I could, as I went around to all three of the freezers, throwing the tops open, reaching inside, and grabbing all the bags of ice and the biggest, thickest boxes of frozen food I could find.

I worked as fast as I could, and then, when the freezers were empty, I dragged all the bags of ice and boxes of food to the very back corner of the restaurant and grabbed my duffel bag from where it had landed.

Then I started building my frozen-food fort.

I stacked the bags of ice around the corner, bringing them in as close and tight to my body as I could, then piled the boxes of frozen food all around me, until I had a makeshift wall that was about three feet high. I sank down behind the wall, sitting on my duffel bag, and pulled my knees up to my chest. Already, the flames had eaten through the double doors, and the eerie, orange-red glow had intensified, as had the heat.

My throat burned from the searing, smoky air, and I coughed and coughed, but there was one more thing I needed to do before I shut myself off from the flames. So I turned to the wall pressing against my back.

The bricks had already started to shriek, scream, and shudder from the fire racing through the restaurant, and I couldn't help but wonder if I'd be screaming in the same sort of agony before this was all over with. But I couldn't let myself think about that, so I made my body as small and comfortable as possible, then reached out and put a hand on a single brick, right at the level of my nose and mouth. With a small trickle of power I loosened the brick from the gray mortar and wiggled it out of the wall. I doubted that anyone outside could hear the movements, but the steady *scrape-scrape-scrape* of the stone sliding free sounded as loud as a drum to me, beating out the fact that I was still alive.

I pried the brick loose, set it aside, and peered out the small, narrow opening. The back of a Dumpster stood in front of me, its dull, gray metal hull blocking my view of the alley and anyone who might be lurking in the corridor. I was so desperate for oxygen that I couldn't even force myself to wait a few seconds to see if someone was coming to investigate the noise. Instead, I shoved my nose up to the opening and sucked down gulp after gulp of air. It was foul stuff, reeking of the empty beer cans, cigarette butts, and bags of fast food that had long ago spoiled in the Dumpster, but some of the fog cleared from my mind.

So I breathed in all the fresh air I could and listened. Above the crackling flames, I could hear sharp, excited murmurs echoing back and forth through the alley, although the gunshots had stopped. The cops were still stationed out there, waiting for me to stumble outside and die. Even if they weren't in Madeline's pocket, they'd want revenge for my supposedly killing Dobson, and they'd be all too happy to empty their guns into me until I was dead.

BOOM!

Something exploded inside the storefront, the flames spewing all the way back here and cranking up the heat that much more. I sucked in another lungful of air, then turned back to face my makeshift fort.

There were so many bags of ice and boxes of food that they hadn't started to melt yet, but it was only a matter of time before they did. So I reached out with both hands and touched the closest one—another box of frozen peas—then focused on my Ice magic, on all that cold, cold power buried deep inside me. I concentrated, and silver lights flared in both my palms, centered in my spider rune scars. I drew in a shallow breath, not wanting to inhale too much more smoke, then unleashed my magic.

I sent my power racing through all the bags and boxes stacked around me, filling in all the cracks and crevices between them with my elemental Ice. Slowly, the cold crystals of my power began to spread, until I'd sealed all the bags and boxes into a solid, frozen mass around me. But that wasn't going to be enough to save me from the fire, so I pushed out another wave of Ice, making the crystals spread out from the top of my frozen-food fort and the brick walls all around me at the same time.

It was difficult, especially with the smoke washing over me and the flames creeping closer and closer, but I forced the Ice out in wave after frosty wave, until all the separate sheets met directly over my head, completely sealing me off from the fire, and creating the crudest sort of igloo.

But I didn't stop there. I might be walled off from the fire, but the flames still flickered outside my crystal cage, casting bright, twisting glows in all directions, as though I were staring into the center of a lit candle. Before long the fire would wash over my igloo, cooking the food and me too if I wasn't careful, so I poured all my strength, all my energy, all my power, into making all those sheets and layers and wedges of Ice as thick and cold and hard and solid as I could.

I didn't know how long I did that. It seemed like hours, but it couldn't have been more than a minute, two tops. But all too soon, I exhausted what magic I had, and I slumped back against the wall. This was the choice I'd made, for better or worse, and now all I could do was hope that I'd been clever and strong enough to save myself.

Otherwise, I would soon burn to death, just as my mother and sister had before me, and die in the Pork Pit, just as Fletcher had before me.

So with my frozen-food fort complete, and my magic gone, I put my nose and mouth up against my breathing hole, closed my eyes, and waited for the flames to come.

There was nothing to do but keep breathing, hoping that every lungful of foul, disgusting, garbage-scented air I drew in wouldn't be my last. I didn't know if it was the smoke or my exhaustion, but I found myself thinking back to the fight at the warehouse all those years ago. I didn't think that I was dreaming, but I fell into the memories all the same. . . .

We'd gone from being in trouble to being buried alive.

I didn't know how long the explosions had ripped through the building. It couldn't have been more than a few minutes, but the concussive boom-boom-booms *seemed as though they would never end. Just like my joyride inside the bar-*

rel, which rocked and rattled like a roller coaster as it was pushed every which way by the force of the explosions. All I could do was brace my arms and legs against the inside of the container and hope that it would soon be over.

And it was.

One second, I was listening to the roar of the warehouse shake, quake, fracture, and blow apart, with chunks of concrete, rebar, and more bang-bang-banging against my barrel like it was the centerpiece of a drum set. The next second, everything was quiet—eerily so—the barrel was still, and the only noise was the too-loud thump-thump-thump of my racing heart.

It was so dark that I couldn't even see the clouds of concrete dust that choked me as I sucked down breath after breath. Slowly, my heart fell back down into a slower, more natural rhythm, and my desperate pants for air eased as the dust dissipated. I huddled inside the barrel, straining with my ears, hoping to hear something, anything that would tell me that I was still alive and not just dreaming that I'd survived.

Silence—complete silence.

That hot, sweaty panic rose up in me again, but I ruthlessly squashed it. Breath by breath, the roar of the explosions leaked out of my ears, and small noises bubbled up to fill in the silence. The steady hiss-hiss-hiss of water from busted pipes. The crackle-crackle of a fire burning nearby. Other moans and shrieks and creak-creak-creaks, as if the warehouse were a wounded animal in the last dregs of its death throes.

When I felt steady enough, I stretched my hands out into the waiting blackness. Rocks, pipes, and slabs of concrete covered the opening of the barrel, but they were a loose, jumbled *heap, and it was easy enough for me to claw my way through them, grab hold of the edge of the container, and pull my-self out of it. I slid forward, surfing down another pile of rubble, and lay there panting amid the crushed remains of the cinder-block walls, extremely grateful to have survived something I shouldn't have.*

All of the lights were gone, destroyed by the explosions, but small fires burned here and there in the debris, along with the occasional blue-white spark of a live electrical wire, ripped free from its source. The full moon and sprinkling of stars in the sky added a pale silver glow to the ruins, softening the harsh edges and making it seem as though I were lying in the middle of an exotic lunar landscape and not the utter demolition of a building. Still, as I looked around, there was one thing I didn't see—the barrel the old man had taken refuge in.

"Fletcher!" I hissed. "Fletcher!"

He didn't respond. He might be experiencing the same ringing ears that I had and couldn't hear me. That was what I told myself. Not that he was dead. Not that his barrel had caved in and that he'd been crushed to death by the falling debris. I couldn't let myself think that way. I wouldn't.

So I wrapped my hands around a length of rebar and pulled myself up into a seated position so I could take stock of my injuries. I was in pretty decent shape, all things consid-ered, mostly just bruised, battered, and achingly sore from all the rolling around in the barrel—

A faint whisper of noise about fifteen feet to my left had me reaching for one of the knives still tucked up my sleeves.

"Gin!" The whisper took on a more distinctive, welcome sound. "Gin, where are you?"

I sighed with relief. Fletcher. I rose up into a crouch, ignored my screaming muscles, wobbly legs, and pounding head, and hurried in his direction.

Fletcher had also managed to dig himself out of the debris that had blocked his barrel opening, and he was leaning against the side of the dented container, his face, hair, and clothes streaked with dust, soot, and other grime.

I crouched down beside him, my eyes sweeping over his lean, wiry body. He seemed to be okay, although the way he clutched his arm over his chest told me that he probably had some bruised ribs. Nothing that Jo-Jo couldn't fix, though.

"I'm here," I said, smoothing back his hair, which was almost white from all the concrete dust in it. "I'm all right. You?"

Fletcher smiled, his green eyes bright. "Still holding on—"

"Over here!" a voice called out. "I thought I saw something move!"

Fletcher and I both snapped our heads in that direction. A pair of headlights popped on and crept toward us along the gravel road that ringed the warehouse. Looked like our attackers wanted to make sure we were dead, instead of just assuming that we'd been killed.

"What do you think?" I asked. "Hide or fight?"

Fletcher held up his revolver. "Fight. I don't take too kindly to someone trying to bury me alive, do you?"

My grin was even wider and colder than his was.

I helped him to his feet. Then, keeping low, we made our way through the piles of debris until we found a wall that hadn't completely crumbled. We slid behind the cinder blocks, peered around the edges, and watched the headlights slowly approach.

The yellow beams glowed like two round, giant bug eyes as they pierced the darkness. Fletcher and I ducked down as the lights swept over our hiding spot.

A black SUV coasted to a stop about fifty feet away. The doors opened, and the two men and two women who'd shot up the poker game and blown up the warehouse got out. One of the men had a crossbow perched on his shoulder, while the other guy reached for his Fire magic, the flames of his power flickering in his palm. The two women both clutched guns. All four of them approached the warehouse debris, stopping at the edge of the destruction, not too far away from the barrels that Fletcher and I had crawled out of.

"I heard voices, and I swear that I saw somebody move over here," a man's voice rumbled out into the night. "This is where they were when we blew up the warehouse."

"You're being paranoid, Will," one of the women answered him. "There's no way anyone could have survived that explosion. Is there, Tomas?"

"No way, Valerie," Tomas, the second man, said.

"Yeah," a fourth voice, the other woman, chimed in. "We made sure that all the cops were dead, and we buried the other two alive, whoever they were. So quit worrying, Will. I want to do something fun now. Like count our take."

"Sonya's right," Valerie chimed back in. "Let's look at our loot!"

The two women whooped with joy, skipping back over to their vehicle, and Will and Tomas joined in with their merriment. Tomas opened the back door of the SUV, grabbed a black duffel bag, and hauled it over to the hood to use the glow from the headlights to count their ill-gotten gains.

What they didn't realize was that the headlights made

it that much easier for Fletcher and me to see them as well. I looked at the old man. He gestured with his hand, indicating that I should go left while he went right. I nodded back.

Fletcher and I picked our way through the debris, quietly moving from one rubble pile to the next until we reached the gravel road where the SUV was parked. We crouched down in a ditch that ran alongside the road, but we were still about thirty feet behind the vehicle, and our would-be killers were far too busy cackling and counting their money to care about anything else.

So we both rose up and stepped onto the road. I crossed over to the other side so that I was to the left of the SUV, with Fletcher still on the right. Once we were both in position, we eased forward, weapons ready.

The robbers were so sure we were dead that they hadn't done the smart thing and hightailed it away from the scene of the crime. At the very least, they should have waited until they were somewhere safe to count their money, not spill the stacks of bills all over the hood of their vehicle like it was the poker table they'd shot up inside the warehouse. Kenny Rogers would have been so disappointed in them.

Fletcher and I were about ten feet behind the SUV when I raised my hand and signaled him. Both of us slowed our approach, creeping forward far more cautiously. We had the element of surprise, and we shouldn't have any problems taking the robbers out—

Crunch.

My boot landed on something in the darkness, maybe some glass from a blown-out window that had landed on the road. Whatever it was, the ensuing noise seemed as loud *as a clap of thunder announcing our presence. I cursed and rushed forward, so did Fletcher, but it was already too late.*

"Somebody's here!" Tomas shouted.

Tomas was the one with the crossbow, and he grabbed it off the hood, stepped around the SUV, and held the weapon out in front of him, ready to let loose a barbed metal bolt at whatever moved. He didn't realize that he had moved into the center of one of the headlight beams, making himself the perfect, well-lit target. Idiot. He was already dead.

Crack!

Sure enough, the familiar retort of Fletcher's gun ripped through the air, and Tomas crumpled to the ground, thanks to the bullet that Fletcher had just put into the middle of his forehead. Crossbows were great for snipers. Not so much when you were up against the Tin Man and his trusty revolver.

Will, the Fire elemental, screamed in rage and reared back, ready to throw the ball of flames flickering in his hand at Fletcher.

Crack!

The old man coolly put him down with a headshot as well.

That left the two women, who stood there, mouths gaping open, staring down at Tomas's and Will's still forms like they couldn't believe that the men were dead. Then one of them, Valerie, I thought, shook off her daze and sprang into action, heading for the driver's-side door.

But I didn't give her the chance to get away.

I sprinted for the SUV, and Valerie and I reached the door at the same time. She lunged for the handle, and I punched my knife all the way through her hand, so that the blade scraped into the SUV's shiny black paint. Valerie screamed and then screamed again as I ripped the knife right back out. She dropped her uninjured hand to her waistband, trying to yank free the gun there, but I lashed out with my knife and laid her throat open with the blade. She coughed and coughed, clawing at the deep, fatal wound, even as her legs went out from under her, and she hit the ground.

The last woman, Sonya, didn't even try to get in the car. Instead, she scooped the money back inside the duffel bag, grabbed it off the hood, and started running down the gravel road, even as she held her gun up over her shoulder and fired at us.

Crack! Crack! Crack! Crack!

Her shots went wild, and I moved to the front of the SUV. Fletcher stepped up beside me. I arched my eyebrows at him in a silent question, and he swept his hand out to the side with a gallant flourish.

"Ladies first," he said.

I grinned and flipped my bloody knife over in my hand, so that I was holding it by the blade. Then I drew my arm back, took careful aim, and let the weapon fly.

Thunk.

The knife plunged into the middle of Sonya's back, and she yelped and did a header onto the road, the duffel bag of money tumbling from her hand. She didn't move after that.

"Nice throw," Fletcher said.

"I had a good teacher."

"Yes, you did. Well, then, let's check and make sure that they're all dead." He grinned. "Wouldn't want them coming back to haunt us like we just did to them, now would we?"

I grinned back.

We checked the bodies, but they were all dead, and the dry, dusty earth was soaking up all the blood oozing out of their wounds. I pulled my knife out of the runner's back, grabbed the duffel bag of money, and met Fletcher back in front of the SUV. The headlights were still on, casting their yellow beams out into the night. In the distance, behind the vehicle, something shuffled across the road, a raccoon or maybe a possum. Its eyes flashed crimson for a moment before it scurried off into the shadows.

Fletcher looked out over the rubble of the ruined warehouse. "We should call in a tip about this. Anonymous, of course. I want the Colson family to know that they won't have to worry about Officer Malone and her demands for protection money anymore."

"Speaking of money, what do you want to do with this?" I gestured at the duffel bag. "There's got to be at least fifty thousand dollars in there, maybe more."

Fletcher peered inside at the bloody, crumpled bills. "I say we give it to the Colson family. It won't bring back their boy, but at least they can start rebuilding their store."

I nodded. "Sounds like a plan to me."

The old man stepped forward and zipped up the bag—

That faint rasp drew me out of my memory and penetrated my foggy consciousness, along with something warm and wet *drip-drip-dripp*ing all over my face. I snapped back to the here and now and realized that I was still breathing, still alive, and still curled up in the back corner of the Pork Pit.

16

I pulled my nose and mouth away from my breathing hole, opened my eyes, and surveyed the damage.

My frozen-food fort had completely melted away, leaving nothing behind but singed, shriveled boxes all around me. The fire hadn't touched me, thanks to my Ice magic, but what I could see of the restaurant was a scorched, sooty, ashy mess. It looked as if the fire had swept right up against my elemental Ice igloo, burning everything in its path, before finally running out of fuel and dying down, thanks to the sprinklers in the ceiling.

They were the source of the water on my face, and I tilted my head up, letting the spray wash over me. If nothing else, the warm drops sliding down my skin told me that I was still alive.

So, as the water continued to spew down, I wearily got to my feet to see what remained of the Pork Pit.

* * *

As I staggered away from the wall, the depth of the destruction fully hit me.

Everything was a scorched, blackened, and now soggy mess. All the dish towels, foodstuffs, aprons, and napkins had been reduced to piles of flaky gray ash, while most of the silverware had melted to the floor and was now stuck there, as if someone had glued down all the forks, knives, and spoons as part of some weird abstract-art project.

I was so exhausted that I dragged my feet along the floor, sending up clouds of ash and soot that tickled my nose and made me cough. I clamped my hand over my mouth, muffling the sound as best I could, and moved over to where the double doors had once stood. They'd been completely burned away, and I slowly shuffled through the opening, dreading what I knew I was going to find in the storefront.

Utter destruction.

That was the only way to describe it.

The tables, chairs, and booths were all long gone, incinerated by the fire. All that remained of them were a few spindly metal legs sticking up out of the mounds of soot like crosses marking fresh graves. The patches of floor that I could see beneath the chunky, ashy debris resembled jagged pieces of black molten glass. Most of the appliances had actually survived, although the flames had burned so hot and fast that their edges were smushed and droopy, as though they were candy bars that had melted in the sun. The long counter had caved in on itself, while the ceiling tiles had all been burned away, letting me see the twisted shapes that the flames had scorched onto the brick above. Despite the water still spewing from the sprinklers, a few small fires continued to burn here and there, while exposed wires jutted out from the walls, sparking and cracking with bright blue and white flashes of electricity, just like they had in that warehouse so long ago. Even the bulletproof windows had melted, with thin, brittle-looking bubbles now bulging out of the once-clear panes.

I'd known that the damage would be bad, but to see the Pork Pit, Fletcher's place, my gin joint, reduced to . . . to . . . to . . . *nothing* . . .

My heart seized in my chest, aching, twisting, and sputtering with loss. A strangled sob escaped my cracked, blistered lips, and I bent over double, my hands fisting in the folds of my T-shirt, right over my heart, as if I could ease my terrible hurt. Tears scalded my eyes, even hotter and harsher than the fire had been. I had thought that nothing could be more horrific than seeing the ruined rubble of my family's mansion after it had been destroyed.

But this—this was *worse.*

"Well," a low, male voice drifted inside to me. "That should finally shut off the sprinkler system."

I blinked and looked up. Sure enough, the sprinklers were no longer spouting water. For the first time, I realized that I could see odd, distorted shapes moving outside through the warped bubbles and melted glass of the storefront windows. I didn't know how long the fire had raged, but it was still dark out, except for the steady swirl of blue and white lights on the street. The cops were still outside, and no doubt so were Madeline, Emery, and Jonah.

I wasn't safe. Not here. Not yet.

I ducked down behind what was left of the counter, straining to hear what was going on outside.

"We can't go in just yet," that same male voice rumbled again. "It's still too hot in places, and the structural soundness has probably been compromised."

He laughed at the bad joke he'd made, and his sly chuckles told me he didn't want to come inside and actually hose down what was left of the blaze. Not really. Like the police, the fire department had its share of corruption and took bribes to put out fires . . . or not.

"Of course not, Chief," Madeline answered him. "I trust your judgment. It's already such a terrible tragedy. There's no need to add to it by putting your firefighters in danger."

"I'm glad that you agree," the fire chief replied, the relief apparent in his voice. He knew that Madeline was the one in charge, not him. "Dawn is only a few hours away. I should be able to send my guys in there then. In the meantime, we'll set a watch over the building. No one will go near it, much less get inside."

Silence.

"Oh, I'm not worried about anyone going inside," Madeline said. "Just someone who might come out."

This time the fire chief was the one who paused before answering. "I don't think there's any . . . worry of that. If that gunwoman was in there like you said, there's no way she could have survived. It was one of the worst blazes I've ever seen. You saw how long it took us to put it out. I still can't believe that she set fire to her own restaurant, but you just never know about people, do you?"

"Unfortunately not," Madeline replied in a smug voice.

They must have moved away from the storefront because I didn't hear them say anything else. But one thing was for sure—I couldn't go out the front doors, and the fire chief was probably on his way to set a watch on the back alley right now.

I needed to get out of here before that happened or I was dead.

Still keeping low, I moved away from the remains of the counter and hurried into the back of the restaurant. I must have inhaled more smoke than I'd thought because I felt slow, stupid, awkward, and clumsy, with a dull, languid fog that wouldn't leave my mind no matter how hard I tried to push it away. I kept banging into the scorched walls, knocking free giant chunks of brittle ash, and I tripped over something lying just beyond the obliterated double doors.

I did a face-plant onto the floor. The fall stunned me, as did the charred, ashy thing below me. I slowly lifted my head and realized that I was staring at a charred, blackened skull. It took me a few more seconds to realize that I'd tripped over and was now lying on top of the dead woman I'd dragged out of the freezer earlier. Her body had been burned to a crisp, just like I'd wanted, but that didn't mean I enjoyed the up-close view of what I'd been forced to do to her corpse.

I swallowed down the hot bile in my mouth, rolled off the body, and staggered back up onto my feet. I managed to stumble over to the back corner of the restaurant, where my frozen-food fort had been, and realized that I had another problem. This was the only part of the restaurant that wasn't singed and scorched, as though something had been sitting on the floor that had been removed, showing the smooth, unmarred surface below.

I couldn't let Madeline realize that I was still alive, so I staggered back the way I'd come, scooping up burned bottles and other debris and tossing it all over into the corner. For added measure, I kicked ash, soot, and smoky ruin all over the clear space, until it was as dirty, dingy, and damaged as everything else was.

But now that I'd disguised my hiding spot, a large question remained—how to actually get out of here?

Slipping out the back door was out of the question. I couldn't take a chance that the cops were still stationed outside. But I needed to see exactly what was going on in the alley, so I went back over to the corner, crouched down on my knees on top of my duffel bag, and peered out through my breathing hole.

I still couldn't see anything but the back of the metal Dumpster that was perched in front of this corner of the restaurant, so I put my ear up to the opening, listening. A few soft murmurs of conversation sounded, but they seemed to be at the far ends of the alley, and not right outside the back door. The firefighters must have cleared the cops out of the corridor to make sure that no one got hurt from the flames that had eaten through the restaurant.

I listened another minute, just to be sure, but the murmurs didn't get any louder or come any closer. This was the best chance I had to get out of here. A small portion of my magic had replenished itself while I was waiting out the fire, so I flattened my palms against the wall and let what little Stone power that I had seep into the bricks and chip through the gray mortar that held them together.

If I'd been at full strength, I could have sent out one burst of magic and crumbled the entire wall—the entire restaurant—in seconds. But I was weak and exhausted and still coughing up all the soot, ash, and smoke that had polluted my lungs, so all I could do was loosen one brick at a time, pry it free from the wall, set it aside, and then wearily start on the next one.

Sweat poured down my face and neck, my short nails cracked and bled, and the jagged edges of the stone bit and tore into my skin as I tugged and yanked and pulled each brick free. I made myself work as quickly and quietly as possible, but it still took me the better part of fifteen minutes to make an opening that was wide enough for me to wiggle through. But I managed it, pulling myself through to the other side.

I lay against the cold, dirty, cracked pavement of the alley, panting for breath. Even though all I wanted to do was suck down giant gulps of air, I clamped my lips shut and made myself breathe in slowly through my nose, listening to see if anyone had heard my dig to freedom or had sensed me using my Stone magic. But those voices remained at the same low volume and distance, and I felt safe enough to sit up and slump against the part of the wall that was still intact.

When I had recovered enough of my strength, I took a few moments to take care of my lady business, then reached back inside and dragged my duffel bag out through the opening. Normally, I would have slung the bag over my shoulder, gotten to my feet, and staggered off into the night, but I wasn't done yet. Because I hadn't escaped just to let Madeline realize that I was still alive.

So I gathered up all the bricks that I'd loosened from the wall, including the one from my breathing hole, and put them all back into their proper places. As I placed each stone back into its slot, I reached inside, scooped up a handful of soot, and rubbed the mess all over the part of the brick that would face the interior of the restaurant. Hopefully, the black smears would help disguise that the mortar wasn't as smooth and solid as it should have been.

When I finished, I leaned back, eyeing my work. It wasn't the best job I'd ever done, and if you looked closely enough, you could see the cracks, gaps, and uneven edges between the bricks. But I was hoping that no one would peer too long and hard at this corner of the restaurant. Or, if they did, mistakenly attribute the damage to the fire. Hopefully, they'd be too concerned with the body and the rest of the destruction to even dream that I'd escaped.

When I'd bricked up the wall as best I could, I grabbed the duffel bag and crawled over to the edge of the Dumpster, peering around the corner. Just as I'd suspected, both ends of the alley were blocked off. A mix of cops and firefighters milled around each exit, standing in front of long ribbons of yellow crime-scene tape that had been tacked up between the walls there. The red, white, and blue lights of the fire trucks and the police cars on the side streets beyond highlighted the words on the glossy tape: *Do Not Enter*.

It didn't look like the cops and firefighters were going to come back here anytime soon, but I still needed someplace to hide. I looked longingly at the crack in the opposite alley wall that I used to hunker down in when I was a kid and searching for a safe place to sleep for the night. But my body was far too big to fit in there now, and I didn't have any magic left to help me widen the spot.

But I couldn't stay here forever. There was too great a risk of someone seeing me. If nothing else, the firefighters would eventually examine the back wall of the restaurant to make sure that the structure looked sound enough for them to enter. They would easily spot me in my current location. So where else could I hide? The only thing that was even big enough to conceal my entire body was the Dumpster that I was crouching behind . . .

I sighed.

I really, really didn't want to do it, but I needed someplace to rest and hide while I got my strength back, especially since I was so exhausted that I was in danger of passing out at any second. I knew from my time living on the streets that nobody ever looked in the Dumpsters except the homeless bums searching for food and stuff to salvage. There was too much of a chance of finding a dead body stuffed into one. Nobody wanted to deal with that hassle, not even the cops. I'd be safe enough sleeping in the Dumpster for the rest of the night. And if I wasn't, well, I'd tried my best to survive.

So I waited until one of the cops at the end of the alley closest to me brought over a round of coffee for his men and the firefighters. Then I got to my feet. I stood in the shadows, looking and listening, but now that the fire was out, all the action was on the streets, and no one was peering in my direction. So I stepped up onto a dirty milk crate that someone had left in the alley. I hoisted my duffel bag up and over the side of the Dumpster, holding on to it for as long as I could before letting go. It landed with a soft *thump*. I held my breath, but the sound hadn't carried, and the cops and firefighters didn't even glance in my direction.

So I hooked one leg over the side of the Dumpster, then the other one. I clutched the side of the pitted, pock-marked metal, even as my body sagged against it, my heart racing, sweat trickling down my neck, my breath once again coming in shallow pants. Just that small motion had exhausted what little strength I had left, and I didn't have the energy to move again for several minutes.

I listened over my ragged breathing, but no one entered the alley, and no one had noticed my slithering into the Dumpster. Even if someone had, I didn't have the magic or the strength left to fight off an attack or the energy to try to make a break for it.

When I slid into the Dumpster, I landed on—well, I didn't want to even *think* about what I landed on. All sorts of foul things moved and squished and slopped around beneath my boots and then my body as I sank down into the muck. Trash bags rustled. Plastic cups splintered. Spoiled food slithered this way and that, shifting under my weight. And a small, sharp squeak sounded that could only have been a rat, angry that I'd plopped my ass right down into the middle of its nest.

But the worst part was the smell.

Sticky soda. Rotten banana peels. Blood and snot and vomit and all the other foul, disgusting things that come out of human bodies. And, yes, even spoiled barbecue from the Pork Pit that had baked for far too long out in the autumn sun. The stench invaded my nose and throat, choking me like the smoke had, and I had to swallow down my bile again.

Using small, quiet movements, I grabbed my duffel bag, unzipped the top, and rooted around until I found one of the tins of Jo-Jo's healing ointment. I popped off the top and buried my nose in the sweet, vanilla-scented balm. I inhaled deep, deep lungfuls of the soft aroma, trying to get the scent of the garbage out of my nose and mouth. For added measure, I dipped my grimy fingers into the tin and smeared some of the ointment under my nose. It drowned out the worst of the stench.

I also took the time to smear the ointment over all the cuts, scrapes, and bruises that I could reach on my face, hands, arms, and legs, as well as across my lungs. It wasn't as good as Jo-Jo's healing me herself, but she'd infused plenty of her magic into the ointment, and I felt the soft pins-and-needles of her Air power prick at my skin, stitching together and smoothing out the ragged parts of me that they could.

My movements were slower and more awkward than ever before, and it took me a couple of concentrated tries before I managed to put the lid back on the empty tin of ointment, drop it down into my bag, and zip it all up again.

Then I put my duffel bag underneath my head, made myself as comfortable as possible in my bed of garbage, and drifted off to sleep.

* 17 *

For once, my slumber was peaceful and free of the dreams and memories that so often plagued me.

But the noises woke me all too soon.

Footsteps *slap-slap-slapp*ed back and forth through the alley. Shouts and yells and steady *beep-beep-beep*s bounced off the brick walls. The *rattle-rattle* and *scrape-scrape-scrape* of cars and heavy machinery rumbled at a steady level on the surrounding streets.

I opened my eyes and had to squint against the growing glare of the early-morning sunlight as it slipped in between the buildings and streamed down into the Dumpster, highlighting all of the filth that I was cocooned in. I didn't know what time it was, probably a little after seven, but the fire department was getting an early start dealing with what remained of the Pork Pit, just like the fire chief had promised Madeline. Then again, I imagined that she had paid him or perhaps someone else even higher up on the food chain more than enough to kick everyone into high gear this morning.

One by one, people started trickling into the alley. The Dumpster was high enough to hide me from sight, although I did have a few tense moments when some giants walked by. They were so tall that they could easily have peered over the side of the container, but they strolled on without even looking in my direction. But I remained as quiet and motionless as possible, not wanting to attract anyone's eyes or ears with a stray movement or an unfortunate *squish* of garbage.

More and more *snaps*, *bangs*, and *rattle-rattles* sounded. Even though I burned with curiosity to see what was going on, I didn't dare rise up and peak over the side of the Dumpster. That was a sure way to be spotted. I'd recovered some of my strength and magic, but I had no doubt that Madeline was still lurking around somewhere, along with a large contingent of cops, all of whom would be more than happy to shoot me on sight.

Eventually, I heard enough noises and snatches of conversation to realize that the firefighters were using a metal saw and some crowbars to cut through the locks on the back door of the building. The *banging* got louder and louder, until a loud, violent *screech* sounded, and everyone let out happy cheers of relief and accomplishment.

The door was open.

After that, more and more footsteps sounded, moving back and forth and all around my position in the Dumpster. I held my breath, but once again no one bothered to look inside the container.

Finally, a shout rang out from the back of the restaurant. "We've got a body in here!"

"No!" The sharp, thin scream immediately rose up. "No! It can't be!"

My heart lurched as I recognized Bria's voice. My baby sister was here, and she thought that the body was mine.

She thought that I was dead.

Of course she was here. She'd probably been here all night, along with Finn and Owen and the rest of our friends. They'd probably watched the flames consume the Pork Pit, their hearts twisting just like mine was right now as they realized that I was trapped inside and that there was nothing they could do to help me. I'd been so focused on surviving the fire and finding a place to hide, as well as confused and exhausted from the smoke inhalation, that I hadn't thought to let them know that I was okay.

So I dug into my jeans pocket and pulled out the burner phone that I'd used to call Owen last night. But I must have been clumsier than I'd thought getting out of the Pork Pit and into the Dumpster because the screen was cracked, and the phone was dead.

Damn it! I silently cursed. My hand curled around the phone, and I wanted nothing more than to smash it against the side of the Dumpster, since it was as useless as the rest of the garbage in here. But I couldn't do that.

"You have to let me see her!" Bria's agonized voice rang out through the alley again. "You have to let me in there!"

The scuffle of footsteps sounded, followed by some more shouts.

"Ma'am!" a loud, booming voice called out. "Ma'am!

You need to stay back. You can't be here right now, Detective."

My heart lurched again. Chance of discovery be damned. I had to see what was going on, and I had to try to let Bria and the others know that I was still alive.

Still keeping my head well below the edge of the container and being as quiet as possible, I crawled over to the opposite side of the Dumpster, the one that was the closest to the back door of the Pork Pit. I looked left and right and up and down until I spotted what I wanted—a small hole that had rusted into the side of the metal, close to one of the corners.

I drew in a soft breath, then leaned down and peered through the opening.

The quarter-size hole was about five feet off the ground, and the angle and position of the Dumpster let me see the open back door of the restaurant and the crowd of people milling around the alley beyond it—including Bria, Finn, Silvio, Xavier, and Owen.

Faces tight, eyes red and weary, shoulders slumped. The five of them stood in a row against the wall opposite the Pork Pit, their backs resting against the dirty bricks as if those were the only things holding them upright. Finn had his arms wrapped around Bria, who'd obviously been crying, while Xavier had his hand on Silvio's shoulder. Owen stood a few feet away, his phone clutched in his hand as if he were waiting for me to keep my promise and call him at any second.

My stomach churned with hot, bitter acid at their obvious heartache and suffering. If only I hadn't broken my phone, I could have at least texted Owen and told him where I was hiding and why. But I had no way to communicate with him or the others.

So close, so far away.

Minutes passed, then dragged into more than an hour. And still, cops, firefighters, and other officials kept moving through the alley and all around the Dumpster before going into the restaurant and streaming back out again. Fletcher had taught me to be patient, but it was almost more than even I could bear, knowing that my loved ones thought that I was dead, seeing the doubt, agony, shock, and suffering on their faces, and not being able to tell them that I was alive.

Finally, the coroner arrived and went into the restaurant. Ten more minutes ticked by before he came back out again. He shot Bria a sympathetic look, then turned to the cop in charge of the scene.

"There is definitely a body inside . . ." The coroner's voice trailed off. "And it looks to be female from my preliminary examination."

"No! No! No . . ."

Bria screamed and screamed before burying her face in Finn's chest, her voice trailing off into loud, ugly, heartbreaking sobs. Tears streamed down Finn's face. Xavier's too, and even Silvio dabbed at the corners of his eyes. Owen remained still and stoic, although his fingers curled a little tighter around his phone, almost as if he were willing it to ring to prove everyone wrong.

I closed my eyes, and my heart twisted into cold, hard, guilty, shameful knots. I didn't want to put my friends through the torture of thinking that I was dead, but I couldn't leave my hiding place either. Otherwise, everything that I'd been through inside the Pork Pit would have been for nothing. So as much as it pained me to do so, I held my position and forced myself to open my eyes and keep watching through my peephole.

But even as Bria's screams died down into gut-wrenching sobs, the speculative whispers started, the way I knew they would, and soon everyone in the alley was chattering about the burned body.

"Is it Blanco? Is she really dead?"

"Looks that way."

"Didn't think the Spider would go out like that. . . ."

And on and on it went.

Every muttered comment, every soft word, and every harsh, mocking laugh made me grind my teeth together. Even though I knew that it was crazy, part of me wanted to leap up in the Dumpster and scream *Boo!* as loud as I could. It would serve the gawking, jabbering ghouls right to get the shit scared out of them.

But I swallowed down my anger and held my position, even though the growing heat of the day baked me like a potato inside the Dumpster, as well as intensifying the reek of the garbage. Soon, the sour, putrid stench became so foul that even a thick layer of Jo-Jo's ointment all around my nose couldn't block it out.

While I waited, I planned my revenge.

Madeline had spent weeks setting her grand scheme into motion. Framing Bria and Eva. Causing business problems for Roslyn, Owen, Finn, and Jo-Jo. Coercing her maid into trying to kill me. Getting the Pork Pit shut down with that ridiculous health inspection. Bribing Dobson to put me in the bull pen. That had all taken time, energy, and money to pull off, and I wanted the same time to think and plan and plot.

But most of all, with my supposed death, I wanted to see what Madeline would do next.

Now that I was out of her way, there was nothing to stop her from assuming Mab's position as head of the Ashland underworld, and she would make sure that all of the crime bosses knew that she was the one who'd so thoughtfully, elegantly orchestrated my death. They might grumble about it under their breath, but the other bosses would have no choice but to bow down to their new queen, or she would kill them the same way that she'd supposedly killed me.

So I huddled in the Dumpster and thought through all the implications, wondering how I could stop Madeline's reign of terror once and for all. The acid elemental was smart, clever, and cunning. So far, she'd been three steps ahead of me in our little game, and as soon as she realized that I was still alive, she'd start scheming more than ever before.

But what would she do if I *stayed* dead?

She would gloat and preen and then turn her attention to other matters, like solidifying her hold on the underworld. The more I thought about it, the more I realized that my death was the key to taking her down. I needed to hit Madeline the same way that she had me—completely blindside and bulldoze her until she was buried six feet under.

I wasn't quite sure how I was going to go about doing that yet, but one thing was for certain.

I was sure as hell looking forward to it.

*   *   *

People streamed in and out of the alley the rest of the day as my supposed body was loaded up and carted away, and the Pork Pit was officially condemned as a safety hazard. To help keep my strength up, I guzzled down a bottle of water and ate some of the granola bars that were in the zippered pockets of my duffel bag. Then I made myself as comfortable as possible and dozed on and off through all the noise. That was the only thing I could do.

Finally, night fell, and the clamor and commotion around the restaurant faded away. About an hour after the sun set, I felt safe enough to get to my feet and peer over the side of the Dumpster.

The alley was deserted.

I looked left and right, scanning the shadows, but all of the cops, firefighters, and other officials had vanished, along with all of the curious passersby. Of course they had. Everyone thought that I was dead. There was no reason to stick around and gawk anymore.

So I climbed out of the Dumpster, rotten bits of food and other disgusting garbage dripping off my cold, sweaty, soot-streaked clothes. As soon as my feet touched the cracked pavement, I slid behind the container, out of sight of anyone who might glance down or even enter the alley.

The night was cool, and I was stiff and sore from staying in the same cramped position for so long. So I spent a few minutes bending and stretching to get the blood flowing back to every part of my body. Then I had to take care of the pressing matter of my lady business.

Once that was done, I dug a couple of tins of Jo-Jo's

healing ointment out of my duffel bag and smeared the soothing concoction all over the injuries I hadn't been able to reach before now. I sighed as the soft pins-and-needles of her healing magic traveled up and down my body. I'd never liked the feel of Jo-Jo's power, as her Air magic was the opposite of my Ice and Stone power, but those small stabs reminded me that I was still alive and that this wasn't all some crazy dream.

When I felt like I could actually move without groaning in pain, I dropped to a knee, opened up my bag even wider, and surveyed the items inside. I'd used up all of Jo-Jo's healing ointment, and I only had a bottle of water and one granola bar left. Several of my extra knives glinted in the bag, nestled inside the piles of clothes and money.

I stared at my supplies, thinking about my next move. I didn't have a phone, and it wasn't like I could walk into one of the nearby businesses and ask to use one. Not when I'd been sitting in a Dumpster all day. The owners would think that I was a homeless bum, trying to scrounge around for some free airtime. They wouldn't be too far from the truth. Besides, someone might recognize me, and I couldn't afford to let that happen. Madeline thought that I was dead, and I had to take advantage of her ignorance for as long as and as best I could. If I squandered this opportunity, I'd be right back where I started—waiting for Madeline to strike out at me and mine.

But I desperately needed to let Owen, Bria, Finn, and the others know that I was okay. Since I didn't have a phone and couldn't risk trying to find one, that meant a hike up into Northtown to locate my friends. But where would they be? Jo-Jo's salon, most likely, or maybe Owen's mansion. Someplace where they could all gather and plan what to do next.

Owen would be coldly furious, Bria would want to try to arrest Madeline, and Finn would be demanding that they all load up and let him put a bullet in the acid elemental's head. As tempting as that last thought was, it still wouldn't solve my problems with the underworld bosses, although I thought there was something that would get them and Madeline off my back at the same time. Either way, I had to get to my friends before they went off the rails and declared war on Madeline.

But how to get from here to there without being seen? Oh, I had enough money to take a cab, and I could always steal a car, but I wanted to keep my exposure to a minimum. That meant no cabs, no breaking and entering, no stealing, and no drawing any attention to myself whatsoever. But I couldn't exactly stroll down the streets covered in garbage . . .

Or could I?

I looked at the Dumpster in front of me, then down at my clothes, which were soaked, soiled, and slathered with all sorts of things better left to the imagination. Burning would be too good for the filthy garments, but maybe I could get one more use out of them.

I stripped off all of my dirty clothes, shivering in the cool dark of the alley as I shimmied into clean underwear, jeans, socks, and a long-sleeved black T-shirt. But I didn't stop there. I kept pulling and pulling on clothes, until I was wearing every single item in the bag—all the socks, all the T-shirts, even a silverstone vest—and resembled some sort of marshmallow person. Then, as a final touch,

I put my soiled T-shirt back on top of all the clean layers that I was wearing. I hated to do it, and it almost made me vomit up the granola bars I'd eaten earlier, but no one was going to look too closely at me when I was reeking of so much garbage.

I didn't bother wiping any of the soot and grime off my face, since I wanted my features to be as dirty and hard to recognize as possible. I also had a black knit toboggan in my bag. As a final touch, I stuffed my nasty brown hair up under the toboggan, then pulled the edge down low over my forehead, hiding even more of my face from sight.

When I was satisfied with my grimy disguise, I threw what was left of my dirty clothes into the Dumpster and hefted my duffel bag onto my shoulder. I could have left it behind, but no homeless bum worth his salt went anywhere without what little possessions he'd managed to scrounge up for himself. The bag would add to my cover.

When I was properly attired, the only thing left to do was step out from behind the Dumpster and see if I could escape from the Pork Pit once and for all.

✵ 18 ✵

The alley might have been deserted, but the streets around the restaurant still hummed with activity.

My supposed murder of Captain Dobson, then fiery death in my own gin joint, had caught the attention of all the various news outlets in Ashland. Lights were strung up on the sidewalks in front of the Pork Pit, and I saw more than one reporter clutching a microphone and talking into a camera, with the burned-out remains of the restaurant creating a dramatic backdrop behind them.

The only part of the storefront that seemed to have escaped the fire was the neon sign above the front door, the one of a pig holding a platter of food. But it was as dark and dead as the rest of the restaurant was, with no electricity and light to fill it tonight.

But the reporters didn't bother me as much as the crowd did. In addition to the news crews, people were gathered two and three deep on the sidewalk across the street from the restaurant, their phones held out and up as they snapped photos and shot video. And at least a dozen cops were still on the scene, if not more, each one peering into the crowd, as if they were expecting someone to bust through the yellow crime-scene tape and make a break for the front door in an attempt to loot the restaurant. I snorted. There was nothing left inside to steal, unless someone had a hankering for piles of ash, rubble, and ruin.

But a few folks had gotten close to the restaurant, at least long enough to leave something behind—flowers.

Red roses, white lilies, and other flowers had been placed on the sidewalk outside the Pork Pit, along with stuffed animals—pigs mostly—and even some small, lit candles. Tears stung my eyes at the sight of the makeshift shrine. Apparently, some people were going to miss me after all. It was nice to know that a few folks had come to pay their respects, instead of just gawk.

I put my head down, clutched my bag with both hands, and ambled along. I'd hoped to disappear into the first dark alley that I came to, but the cops had the streets blocked off in such a way that I was forced to shuffle along through the crowd, right under the watchful eyes of the po-po.

"Ugh," someone muttered. "What is that *smell*?"

The wind picked up, and all eyes turned to me as my foul stench spread. Suddenly, I was the center of attention, something that I very much did not want to be right now.

"What did you do?" a nearby cop muttered, his nose crinkling with disgust as he stared me down. "Roll around in garbage all day long?"

I ground my teeth together. That was precisely what I'd done, not that I could tell him that. So I put my head down and hurried along a little faster, before the cop decided to further investigate me and my miserable stench.

As soon as I drew near, those in the crowd shifted back as far as they could and still see the Pork Pit. I started bobbing my head and mumbling nonsense as I shuffled past them. Let them think me some homeless junkie bum, high on blood, drugs, magic, or a combination of all three. At least it made getting through the crush of people easier when they all shied away from me.

I'd circled my way around most of the crowd and was about to cross to the next block over when I spotted a flash of pure white out of the corner of my eye. I stopped and turned my head.

Madeline was here.

She wore one of her expensive white pantsuits that made her trim, toned figure stand out that much more in the darkness. She stood beside Emery at the very back of the crowd, both of them staring across the street at the Pork Pit. Everyone was giving them a wide berth, obviously knowing who Madeline was, except for a couple of folks who were being truly obnoxious with their phones, trying to get the best angle and shot possible for their own ghoulish amusement. But a cold, measured look from Emery soon sent them scurrying away.

Despite the danger, it was too good an opportunity to pass up, so I sidled a little closer to the acid elemental and the giant and slipped into a doorway a few feet away and downwind from them. I sat on the stoop, sprawled my legs out, and slumped my body against the side of the wooden frame as though I were sleeping off a drunk. I held my breath for a moment, but neither of them noticed me or my stench.

"Do you think that she's really dead?" Madeline asked.

"Everything seems to point to it," Emery replied. "The body that the coroner pulled out of the back was definitely female, and Blanco never left the restaurant. The cops made sure of that. Elemental or not, I doubt that even she could have survived a fire like that."

"Perhaps." Madeline's face was thoughtful as she stared at the pig sign over the front door. "And yet, I wonder if she found a way to survive and escape after all. I don't want to make the same mistake that my mother and everyone else has by underestimating Blanco. So far, she's had an annoying habit of surviving the impossible."

"You saw how her family reacted when they rushed over here and saw the fire burning through the restaurant. The only thing that stopped Grayson from going in to try to save her was the gun that cop finally leveled at his head. And you saw her sister this morning after the coroner examined the body. You can't fake grief and anguish like that. Besides, we both know that Blanco would never let her family think that she was dead when she really wasn't."

"True. She's far too weak and soft-hearted for that. Still, I could have sworn that I felt her using her magic during the fire."

Emery shrugged her broad shoulders. "She was probably trying to use her Ice magic to put out the fire, but we all know that didn't happen. Every single part of the restaurant was scorched through and through. Even if she could have somehow fought off the fire, the smoke would have gotten her, thanks to all those sturdy brick walls trapping it inside with her."

"I *suppose* you're right." Madeline's voice was still full of doubt. "Perhaps I'm just being paranoid."

An eerie sense of déjà vu swept over me. Madeline and I were far more alike than I'd realized, if she had spent these last few weeks worrying about me as much as I had about her.

"Regardless," she continued, "we have preparations to make, now that she's finally out of the way. Have you contacted all the underworld bosses yet?"

"Of course. They've been glued to their phones, Twitter, and TVs, watching this all play out. They know you were here when everything went down, and I ordered McAllister to spread the word about what really happened to Blanco. How you trapped her in her own restaurant and then burned it down around her. The other bosses will fall in line. And if they don't . . ." Emery shrugged again. "I'll make sure that they do—one way or another."

So Madeline hadn't been torturing me and mine just for the sake of her own twisted delight. At least, not entirely. Instead, all of this, every single problem, accusation, and misfortune that she'd caused for us, had been part of her plan to take control of the underworld, just as I'd suspected. Now, with her crowning achievement of my murder making the gossip rounds, she was finally ready to consolidate her power.

I was *so* going to enjoy fucking things up for her.

But not tonight. No, tonight I needed to get to my family. Then, together, we could plot our counterstrike against Madeline, Emery, Jonah, and all the rest.

Madeline must have had the same thought that I did because she frowned. "What about Blanco's friends and family? Where are they now? What are they planning? Is there any sign that she's still alive and has made any sort of contact with them?"

Emery sighed. "There you go, being paranoid again. Blanco is dead. Good riddance."

"And her family?" Madeline persisted in a much colder voice. She didn't like having her top lieutenant question her sanity.

Emery grumbled under her breath, pulled out her phone, and started *tap-tap-tapp*ing the screen. "According to my sources, they're all still holed up at Deveraux's so-called beauty salon just like they have been all day long. No sign of Blanco, and no indication that she's alive. See? I told you that you were worrying over nothing. Do you want my men to keep watching the salon?"

Madeline stared at the pig sign for several seconds. "No, they can leave. But I want you to go over to the coroner's office for the autopsy first thing in the morning. I want to be absolutely certain that body is Blanco's before we proceed with anything else."

Emery sighed again, a little louder and deeper this time. "I don't see the point of that. Your plan worked, and she's *dead*. You should be celebrating your victory, not worrying over a ghost that's never going to come back and haunt you again."

Madeline slowly turned her head to stare at the giant, her green eyes glittering in the darkness. "Are you questioning my judgment?" Her voice was soft, but the threat in her words was as hot and caustic as the acid she could so easily create and control.

Despite her giant strength, Emery knew which of them was the more dangerous, and she immediately lowered her head in apology. "Of course not. I'll call my men right now."

"Good. And have the driver bring the car around. I've seen all that I care to here."

The two of them strolled down the sidewalk in the opposite direction, turned the corner, and disappeared from sight.

For a mad, mad moment, I thought about palming one of the knives hidden up my many, many sleeves, charging after them, and burying the blade in Madeline's back. But I resisted the temptation. I didn't know what other deadly webs she might have woven, and I wanted to be sure that I knew each and every one of her schemes before I moved against her. Besides, even if I could have killed her, there were still far too many cops around for me to hope to get away with it.

So Madeline would live through this night, but not too many more.

I'd make sure of that.

When I was certain that Madeline and Emery weren't coming back, I got to my feet and shuffled off in the other direction to start my long, cold trek up to Jo-Jo's house.

So many things in my life had changed since Fletcher had taken me in when I was thirteen. It was strange to be right back where I'd started, so to speak, roaming the streets, looking out for danger, and trying to stay warm for the night. But in many ways, it was all too familiar.

The gang members clustered together at the corners, jeering at everyone who dared to scurry by them. The vampire hookers making their endless rounds up and down the sidewalks before ambling over to the cars that pulled over to the curbs. Their pimps, lounging against the storefront walls or hidden back in the alleys, waiting to take all the cash that their girls and guys earned plying their bodies for the night. The scent of fried food and puffs of warmth that escaped from the restaurants as people moved inside and back out again, greasy sacks of burgers and fries clutched in their hands. The dim glow of lights from the businesses that were still open that couldn't quite banish the darkness on the streets beyond.

Oh, yes. It was all too familiar, and in a way strangely comforting. I almost felt like I'd stepped back in time to a younger version of myself, before Madeline had come to town, before I'd killed Mab, before I'd ever dreamed about becoming the Spider. Back when I was just trying to survive and get through one day at a time without getting murdered in my sleep for my threadbare clothes. Or maybe this was the same-old, same-old version of myself, since I was still just trying to get through one day at a time without getting murdered just for being me.

A few of the gangbangers thought about hassling me, but the stench of the garbage wafting off my body had them wrinkling their noses, cursing, and yelling at me to take a bath already. Normally, I might have flashed a knife at them, telling them exactly what they could do with their suggestions, but I kept my head down and shuffled on. Because Madeline had probably put the word out that she wanted to know about anyone and anything unusual or suspicious happening around the Pork Pit, and a homeless bum brandishing a silverstone weapon would be more than enough to *ping* her radar.

After I made it out of the downtown loop, the people, businesses, and lights got fewer and farther in between, replaced by cars that *whiz-whiz-whizz*ed by me on the highway. I stayed well away from the edge of the road and kept my pace slow and steady. I hated wasting a second in letting everyone know that I was okay, but it couldn't be helped, not without attracting unwanted attention to myself. They would understand. I hoped so, anyway.

It took me more than three hours to walk from the Pork Pit up to Jo-Jo's house in Northtown. It would have taken even longer if I'd stuck to the roads, but I cut through several patches of woods, climbing up ridges and then sliding back down them again, taking the most direct route possible.

Finally, I reached the last leg of my journey. I entered Jo-Jo's subdivision and slid into the trees along the side of the main street, peering out into the night. Just because Emery had told her men to leave their watchers' posts didn't mean that they had yet—or that Madeline hadn't had another hinky feeling and sent them right back out. She seemed to be as paranoid as I was, and with good reason this time.

But I didn't see any cars parked on the street below the hill that led up to Jo-Jo's place, and I didn't spot anyone stationed in the thick patches of trees that ran between the homes, training a pair of night-vision goggles on the three-story, white plantation house.

When I was sure that the watchers had all gone, I climbed the hill, keeping to the trees and low bushes and skulking from shadow to shadow as much as I could. I hadn't come this far just to get spotted by a nosy neighbor.

I paused again outside the house, staring at all the cars clustered in the driveway. Finn, Bria, Owen, Roslyn, Xavier, even Phillip Kincaid, Warren T. Fox, and Cooper Stills. All of their vehicles were here, along with Sophia's classic convertible. Silvio must have been able to bail her out of jail after all.

I let out a long, tired breath because I knew that I was finally safe and shuffled forward, somehow feeling both exhilarated and more bone-weary than ever before.

To my surprise, the front door was unlocked, and the knob turned easily in my hand. I stepped inside and shut the door behind me. The front of the house was dark, but light, sound, and fury emanated from the kitchen, so that's where I headed.

That's where they were all gathered—Finn, Bria, Owen, Eva, Jo-Jo, Sophia, Xavier, Roslyn, Phillip, Cooper, Violet, Warren, Silvio, Catalina. All crammed into Jo-Jo's kitchen, and all talking at the same time.

"I say we go kill that bitch right fucking now," Finn said, his voice the loudest. "What are we waiting for?"

"For once, I second Lane's opinion," Phillip agreed.

Cooper, Warren, Sophia, Roslyn, and Xavier all nodded their heads in grim agreement. Silvio stood by the refrigerator, silent as always. Eva, Violet, and Catalina looked back and forth at everyone with wide eyes, while

Jo-Jo rubbed her head, as though it was aching. Yeah. Mine too, and I'd only been here a few seconds. Judging from the empty pot of chicory coffee and the mugs scattered everywhere, they must have been in here arguing for hours.

Bria let out a brittle laugh. "You know we can't do that. Madeline will be expecting us to retaliate. I'm sure she already has a plan in place for that. It seems like she's had one for everything else so far."

"Forget about Madeline right now," Owen said. "We don't need to do anything except wait for Gin to come home."

He was standing by himself at the back of the kitchen. Everyone quieted at his words, and one by one, they turned to look at him with shocked expressions. Finally, Finn jerked his head at Phillip, who ran a hand over his blond ponytail before stepping forward.

"Listen, man," Phillip said, his blue eyes locked onto his best friend's face. "I know you don't want to believe that she's gone, but you saw the restaurant. There's no way that anyone could have survived that fire, not even someone as tough and strong as Gin."

Owen's violet eyes crinkled, and his lips lifted a fraction. "If you believe that, then you obviously don't know Gin at all. But I *do*. And I know that she'll be here just as soon as she can."

Tears pricked my eyes at the ringing certainty in his soft voice. He hadn't given up on me. Even when everyone else had, even when they all thought that I was dead, Owen had believed that I would find some way to survive.

He had believed in *me*.

I stepped into the kitchen, wanting to rush straight into his arms, despite the furniture and people that separated us. A floorboard creaked under my weight, and everyone whipped around in my direction.

Finn was faster than all the others. In an instant, he'd grabbed the gun under his suit jacket and had it pointed at my head. "Who are you? How did you get in here?"

"The front door was open, so I figured that y'all wouldn't mind if I came right on inside."

Finn's face paled at the familiar sound of my voice, and he did something I'd never seen him do before in all the years I'd known and trained with him—he dropped his gun. The weapon slid from his grasp and clattered to the floor, even as he swayed back and forth, as though he might faint.

Bria clutched his arm, and everyone turned to stare at me again, still wondering who I was and what was going on. I guess my grimy disguise was better than I'd thought.

So I reached up and peeled the black toboggan off my head, letting my dirty, dark brown hair flow down around my shoulders as I used the knit fabric to wipe some of the soot off my face. Then I raised my head.

Everyone let out a collective gasp.

I leaned against the doorjamb, crossed my arms over my chest, and grinned. "What's wrong?" I drawled. "Y'all look like somebody died or something."

❊ 19 ❊

For another long, drawn-out moment, my friends and family regarded me in shocked, absolute silence. They really, truly thought that I'd been dead this time. Yeah. Me too there for a while.

Then Jo-Jo screamed. So did Eva, Violet, and Catalina, and everyone stampeded toward me, or at least tried to, but they all couldn't get around the butcher-block table in the middle of the kitchen. At least, not all of them at the same time.

But even as my friends surrounded me, I looked at Owen, still standing in the back of the kitchen, his hand lying flat over his heart, as though some terrible ache there had abruptly ceased. Yeah. Mine too.

My gray eyes locked with his violet ones, and he winked at me, as if to say, *I told them so*. I smiled and winked back.

Then I was swallowed up by the rest of my loved ones.

Just like before, Finn was the fastest, nimbly zipping past the others and skidding to a stop right in front of me. He started to reach over to hug me but abruptly stopped.

"What is that *smell*?" he asked, wrinkling his nose. "What's on your clothes, Gin? Is that . . . coleslaw in your hair?"

I opened my mouth to tell him that, yes, that was spoiled coleslaw in my hair since I'd been Dumpster-diving for the better part of the day, but his face split into a wide, happy grin before I could speak.

"Aw, fuck it," he declared. "I don't care."

Finn wrapped his arms around me in a fierce bear hug and lifted me off my feet, making me laugh. One by one, the others piled on, until we were all cheering, talking, laughing, yelling, and crying at the same time. Finn put me down.

Bria nudged him out of the way, and her arms went around me just as tightly as his had. "I thought I'd lost you again," she mumbled.

"You'll never lose me," I whispered in her ear, returning her hug with an even fiercer one of my own.

Eva, Violet, and Catalina were next. Then Roslyn and Xavier, and Phillip, Cooper, and Warren. Even Silvio gave me a firm, lengthy pat on the shoulder, which was about as demonstrative as I'd ever seen him be.

Jo-Jo was too choked up to say anything as she hugged me, but so many tears streamed down her face that they made her waterproof mascara run. A hand grabbed my shoulder, turning me to the right, and Sophia pulled me into her tight embrace.

"I . . . can't . . . breathe," I wheezed.

She loosened her grip. "Sorry."

"It's okay. Hug me again so I can really feel it this time."

Her raspy laughter rang out through the kitchen.

One by one, the others fell back, until it was finally Owen's turn. He slowly crossed the kitchen and stopped before me, his eyes sweeping over my body from my dark, matted, coleslaw-dusted hair down to my muck-covered boots and back up again. His relieved sigh was as soft as a whisper, but it made my heart quiver more than a joyous shout.

Owen reached out and cupped my face in his hands, carefully stroking his thumbs down my soot-smeared cheeks and staring at me with ferocious intensity, as though I were a most delicate thing of absolute beauty and wonder, instead of just covered with more dirt, filth, and grime than any person had a right to be. Tears pooled in his eyes, making them gleam like violet stars in his rough, rugged face. Without a word, he drew me into his arms and crushed his lips to mine, even as our friends hooted and hollered and clapped and cheered all around us.

It was one of the best moments of my life.

It took a while—it took a *long* while—but everyone finally calmed down, and we trooped back into the beauty salon. The area looked a bit worse for wear, given all the paint chips and pieces of paneling that littered the floor and all the holes that had been punched through the walls during that phony health inspection. But it was still more or less intact, right down to Rosco, Jo-Jo's basset hound, snoozing in his basket in the corner. The sight cheered me.

I sank down onto one of the padded, cherry-red chairs, with Owen still right beside me, holding my hand. He hadn't let me go since he'd kissed me, and I didn't want him to.

Jo-Jo washed her hands in the sink, then pulled a chair up to me. She reached for her Air magic, and a familiar, milky-white glow filled her clear, colorless eyes, as well as the palm of her hand. She moved her hand back and forth and up and down my body, looking for injuries, and I felt her Air power prick my skin. But the sensation didn't bother me at all tonight. I was far too happy to be alive, to be with the people I loved, to care about anything else.

After a minute, she let go of her magic and dropped her hand. Jo-Jo shook her head, making her white-blond curls fly out before they settled perfectly back into place. "Looks like you already took care of everything, darling. I can't find anything major to repair."

Finn cleared his throat, and we all looked at him. "Well, if you're done with Gin already, I could certainly use a caffeine fix." He waggled his eyebrows at Jo-Jo.

She laughed and got to her feet. "All right, another pot of chicory coffee coming up for you. Gin, everyone else, how about some hot chocolate?"

"That would be great," I said.

The others murmured their agreement. While Jo-Jo went into the kitchen to fix the drinks, I leaned back in the chair and told my friends everything that had happened since I was arrested at the police station and carted off to the bull pen.

I was just finishing up when Jo-Jo returned with a large

tray. She passed out the drinks, handing me a mug of dark hot chocolate piled high with miniature marshmallows and sprinkled with dark-chocolate shavings.

"Just like you like it, darling," she said, winking at me.

I nodded and held the mug between my hands, letting the warmth seep into the spider rune scars in my palms. Then I slowly took a sip, enjoying the decadent richness of the dark chocolate mixed with the frothiness of the melting marshmallows. The sweet concoction slid down my throat, then spread its pleasant heat through my stomach and out into the rest of my body, chasing away the last of the night's lingering chill.

Finn slurped down half his coffee in one gulp, then shook his head. "Only you would think of using boxes of frozen peas to survive a fire. And then hiding in that Dumpster, almost in plain sight, while all the cops and firefighters walked right by you."

"Believe me, it wasn't by choice," I muttered. "So what happened on your end? What's been going on?"

Bria looked at Finn and Owen, then at me. "The three of us were at the station for hours, along with Silvio, Sophia, and Xavier, trying to bail you out, but of course not having any luck. Dobson was nowhere to be found, and Xavier texted me to say that he'd heard a rumor that there was going to be a fight in the bull pen. We all knew it was you. But there was no way that we could get to you, not without getting into a firefight in the middle of the station."

"Which was probably exactly what Madeline wanted," I murmured.

Finn shot his thumb and forefinger at me. "Winner, winner."

"So we were trying to figure out a way around the cops," Bria said. "Then we heard and felt this huge explosion, and I could sense you using your magic."

"After that, everything was a mess," Owen chimed in. "Cops shouting and yelling, and everyone inside the station running everywhere. We'd heard that you escaped, but by the time I got your call, and we drove over to the Pork Pit, the restaurant was on fire, and there was no sign of you."

His voice cracked on the last few words, and his hand tightened around mine. No one said anything for several seconds.

Finn cleared his throat. "After that, it was a lot of running around and screaming at people. We tried to go into the restaurant to find you and get you out of there. But Madeline and Emery were running the show, and they told the cops to keep us back, even if they had to shoot us. So we stayed by the restaurant all night until . . ."

"Until they brought that body out of the back this morning," Bria said, her voice dropping to a ragged whisper. "Madeline was all too happy to let us see *that*."

"I heard you scream," I said. "I was right there the whole time, hiding in that Dumpster next to the back door, watching everything through a hole that had rusted in the side. But my burner phone was broken, so I couldn't text you, and I couldn't get out of the Dumpster and let you know that I was okay. Not with all the cops around. I'm sorry about that—so sorry."

Bria nodded. So did the others. They understood, but guilt still filled me that I hadn't been able to spare them all that pain.

"So what's your next move?" Xavier asked.

"Yeah," Phillip chimed in. "Because from what I've already heard, Madeline hasn't wasted any time letting everyone know that she's the reason why you're dead."

"I had a lot of time to think about that while I was waiting in that Dumpster. And I say we give Madeline exactly what she wants. I say we let her keep right on thinking that I'm good and dead."

"And then?" Silvio asked.

I smiled at my friends. "And then we give that bitch the surprise of her life."

We worked out a few of the details, most of which we'd have to wait until the morning to actually get started on, then I went upstairs, took a long, hot shower, and put on a blue, fluffy robe that was patterned with Jo-Jo's white cloud rune.

Most of my friends had left to go back to their own homes to try to get some sleep during what remained of the night, but Owen was waiting for me in one of the spare bedrooms. He'd taken a shower too, and he was lying on the bed, a robe covering his body, trying to relax and recover his equilibrium after all the seesaw emotions of the day. Yeah. Me too.

Owen got to his feet as I entered and shut the door behind me. We stared at each other, his violet eyes locked onto my gray ones, everything so still and quiet that I could hear the grandfather clock in the hall outside *tick-tock*ing off the seconds.

Then, with one thought, we rushed toward each other. Owen cupped my face in his hands and crushed his lips to mine in a kiss that was even hotter, harder, and more frantic than the one he'd given me in the kitchen earlier. His tongue plunged into my mouth, rough and demanding, while I fumbled with the belt on his robe, yanking it open so that I could touch all of his warm, solid muscles. I raked my nails down his chest, while he sucked at my neck, tearing off my robe as frantically as I had his. I breathed in, letting the rich, faintly metallic smell of him seep deep down into my lungs, imprinting his scent, taste, and touch on my heart.

Given everything that had happened, we were both too impatient to do our usual slow dance of teasing seduction. Owen stopped kissing me long enough to cover himself with a condom, then picked me up, put my back against the nearest wall, and entered me with one long, hard, smooth thrust. I moaned into his mouth, locked my legs around his waist, and rocked against him, desperate to feel every part of him and to mold my body even tighter to his.

He buried his head between my breasts, his breath hot against my skin, and I tangled my fingers in his silky, black hair, urging him on.

"More," I whispered in his ear. "More, more, more . . ."

He growled and kissed me again, our tongues thrusting against each other just as our bodies were. We kept moving together the whole time, so hard that the pictures rattled on the wall next to my head. Everything about it was fast, fierce, furious. The pressure, the pleasure, built and built, and our movements became quicker, harder, longer, until we were both groaning at how good it felt. But we both kept going, trying to drive each other to new heights, trying to give each other more and more pleasure, trying to show just how much we truly cared.

Finally, with one more deep thrust, we both exploded, going over the edge as one, our lips, bodies, and hearts tangled up and bound together more tightly than ever before.

We both shuddered out our release, and Owen slid me down the wall. But instead of grabbing my hand and walking over to the bed, he kept sliding down, down, down, so that we ended up lying on the hardwood floor together.

Owen turned his head to look at me. "I can't feel my legs right now."

I laughed. "That makes two of us."

I leaned in and rested my head on his muscled shoulder. His arms closed around me, and he started stroking his fingers through my still-wet hair, down my neck, across my shoulder, and all the way to my wrist before moving back in the opposite direction, then starting the whole cycle over again. I flexed my hand over his heart, feeling its strong, rapid *thump-thump-thump-thump* deep in his chest.

Finally, Owen spoke. "The others kept telling me that you were gone, but I didn't believe it. I couldn't *let* myself believe it."

"I know," I whispered. "I'm so sorry that I put you through that."

He pressed a kiss to the top of my head, and we both tightened our grips. For a long time we lay there on the floor and just held each other—because it was more than we'd both thought we'd ever have again.

"You know," Owen said, a teasing note creeping into his voice as he propped himself up on his elbow, "I think that I've recovered enough to actually stand up and get in bed, if you want to get under the covers to get warm."

I gently pushed on his shoulders until his back was on the floor. Owen quirked an eyebrow at me, wondering what I was doing, so I hooked my leg over his body so that I was straddling him.

"Really?" I asked, sliding my body against his. "You want to waste all that precious time going over to the bed?"

He laughed and pulled me down on top of him.

We didn't make it to the bed until much, much later.

* 20 *

I left the salon early the next morning to put the first part of my plan into action. After Jo-Jo helped me get ready, I kissed a sleepy Owen good-bye, promising that I'd be careful, then met Bria outside in the driveway.

I slid into the back of her sedan, lying down across the seat, so no one would realize that someone else was in the vehicle. Sophia had already scouted the perimeter, and she hadn't seen anyone watching the house from the woods or noticed any strange cars parked on the streets farther out in the subdivision. But given Madeline's lingering doubts about my demise, I wouldn't have put it past her to send some spies over here this morning or to have them follow my friends around for the next few days, just to make doubly sure that I was as dead as she hoped I was.

"Are you sure that this is the right move?" Bria asked, glancing at me in the rearview mirror. "It's a big risk, going down there, especially right now. If someone sees you, then our advantage is gone."

"It doesn't matter so much if they see me. It's if they recognize me that we'll be in trouble."

In addition to keeping out of sight, I had also taken the extra but necessary precaution of wearing a disguise—a short blond wig, bright blue contacts, and clear glasses with silver frames. Roslyn had been nice enough to bring me the items from her stash at Northern Aggression, since her workers used the wigs and more to satisfy the fantasies of their clients. She'd also brought over the tight black suit jacket, short, fitted skirt, and towering heels that I was wearing, along with a black patent-leather brief-case. Apparently, some folks were really into the whole corporate-raider look, which I found a bit disturbing, but the suit would get me into practically every building in Ashland, including the one where we were going.

Jo-Jo had done my makeup, adding a bit of bronzing powder to my pale skin and slick plum gloss to my lips. The dwarf had even let me borrow a chunky string of her pearls to wear over the black suit. All put together, I looked like a completely different person—and about as far away from Gin Blanco as I could get.

Oh, if someone who knew me well studied my face for any length of time, she would eventually see through my disguise, but I was betting that wouldn't happen. Everyone would be too focused on Bria to pay much attention to me, the office drone drifting along in their wake.

That was my hope, anyway.

Bria steered her sedan out of the subdivision, through Northtown, and into the downtown loop. Thirty minutes later, she pulled up to a familiar location—the Ashland Police Station.

She parked in one of the lots close to the impound yard, and I rose up just enough that I could peer out the backseat window. In the distance, wide sheets of cardboard covered the gaping hole that I'd left in the side of the station. I grinned. Madeline might have her faux dedications to Mab, but I'd left my mark on things around here too.

"You ready for this?" Bria asked.

"I'll be behind you all the way, just like we planned," I said.

"All right, then. Here we go."

She opened her door, got out, and headed toward the station. I waited a minute, then slipped out of the sedan and followed her. It was early, just after seven in the morning, but people were already moving into the station, coffee, cell phones, and briefcases in hand, getting ready for another long day of all the headaches, paperwork, bribes, and bureaucracy that went along with the Ashland legal system.

I made sure that two people were in between us as Bria and I went through the metal detectors. She didn't look back as I collected my briefcase from the cop working the X-ray machine and started walking behind her.

It had only taken us about two minutes to get through security, but that was enough time for folks to realize that Bria was here. Everyone stopped what they were doing to stare at her, but my sister kept her eyes forward and her head up as she moved deeper into the station. Of course, all the cops had heard about what had supposedly happened to me, and a great number of them had been on the scene at the Pork Pit. But what surprised me was how many of them stopped her to say how sorry they were for her loss. Some of them actually seemed to mean it.

Bria gave them all sharp nods and tight smiles before moving on. I followed about fifteen feet behind her, and the only reason the cops looked at me was to leer at my legs. But I fixed my face into a frown, as though I were deep in thought about something, ignored their stares, and hurried on.

Finally, Bria reached an elevator and stepped inside.

"Hold the elevator, please," I called out.

She nodded and held her hand out, so that the doors wouldn't close and I could step inside with her. When the doors slid shut, she murmured out of the side of her mouth.

"Well, that was easier than I'd thought it would be."

"Don't jinx us just yet."

She snorted, and we rode the rest of the way in silence.

After a couple of stops, the doors finally pinged open in the basement. This wasn't the cops' domain, though.

It was the coroner's.

From what Madeline had said last night, the coroner would be doing my supposed autopsy first thing this morning. I wasn't sure how he would try to go about identifying my supposed body. It wasn't like I'd left dental records and DNA samples just lying around for anyone to find. But I definitely didn't want him telling Madeline that the burned body *wasn't* me. That would ruin everything else I had planned.

Bria and I stepped out of the elevator. Unlike the main floor, this one was deserted, so we walked together down the long corridor until we reached the glass door that led into the coroner's office. We entered and found ourselves in a small waiting area with padded chairs along the walls, dusty plastic palm trees in the corners, and several large boxes of tissues lined up on a glass coffee table in the middle of the room.

Bria went to the back of the waiting room and swiped her police ID through a scanner attached to the wall. Another door—this one made out of thick, frosted glass—buzzed open.

We stepped through to the other side and found ourselves in a room made largely out of metal. Stainless-steel vaults fronted with doors lined two of the walls, looking like gym lockers, although they held dead bodies instead of sweatpants and dirty socks. A series of long metal tables took up the center of the room, and several drains were set into the floor. The air was cool against my skin, and the faint antiseptic stench that permeated everything reminded me of Beauregard Benson. My stomach turned over at the memory of the vamp's lab and the torture I'd endured there, but I forced myself to focus on the man standing next to one of the tables.

The coroner was wearing a long-sleeved black T-shirt under bright blue scrubs that brought out his dark hazel eyes and ebony skin. His black hair was cropped close to his skull, and a small black goatee clung to his chin. I'd seen him many times over the past year, the most recently being at the Bone Mountain Nature Preserve, back when his office was dealing with all the bodies that had been found at Harley Grimes's remote camp. The coroner had given me a jaunty wave back then. I hoped that he would be even more accommodating today. But what I'd brought along in my briefcase should help with that.

A badly burned body lay on the metal table before him. It looked exactly as I remembered it from the Pork Pit—a charred husk with dull bits of teeth and bones gleaming here and there. I breathed in, and the scent of smoke and ash drifted over to me, making my chest clench.

The coroner had gotten an even earlier start than I'd expected. I couldn't tell how far along into the autopsy he was, but he'd already started making notes, judging from the clipboard and pen that were lying on another, smaller table.

He looked up at the sound of the door's buzzing open. A faint wince creased his face as he spotted Bria, and he stepped in front of the table, as if he wanted to shield her from the sight of the burned body.

"Oh, Bria," he said in a quiet, sympathetic voice. "I thought that I might see you here today. But . . . later. Much later. After I was . . . finished."

Bria glanced at me, and I nodded. The coroner frowned as he studied me, as if I seemed familiar but he couldn't quite place me. I stared back at him, completely calm, as if I had nothing at all to hide, even though my heart started thumping a little louder and faster in my chest.

But my disguise must have fooled him because he turned back to Bria. "You shouldn't be here. Most people would find it very . . . upsetting. If you'd like, you can wait outside with your friend. I have to warn you that I will probably be quite a while, though. Given the . . . state of the remains."

He kept his voice low and gentle. He was trying to spare her from the horror of seeing the charred body of her supposedly dead sister and then watching as that body was sliced open and examined from head to toe.

"But I'll take good care of her," he continued. "I prom-ise. Just like I always do."

Bria gave him a thin, brittle smile, playing her part well. "Thanks for your concern, Ryan. I appreciate it. Re-ally, I do. But I'm fine. This isn't my first body or autopsy."

"I really don't think that you should be here for this, Bria. There are some things you just can't unsee."

She nodded. "And I agree with you one hundred per-cent. But I needed to talk to you."

He frowned. "About what?"

That was my cue. I stepped forward, put my briefcase on another table, and popped open the top. I reached inside and drew out a fat envelope, which I passed over to Bria.

She put the envelope on the table next to the coroner's clipboard, then stepped back. "We all know that's my sis-ter. Nothing's going to change that, especially not waiting days for the results to come back on all the tests you like to run. Do the autopsy and the tests if you like, but I want you to go ahead, make a positive ID, and declare that that body is my sister, Gin Blanco."

Ryan's eyes narrowed, his face tightened, and he stud-ied my sister in a new light. "I don't take bribes, Bria. Everybody else around here does, but not me. Not for any reason. I didn't think you were like that either."

"And I thought that you might make an exception this one time. Please, Ryan. We're friends. I really need you to do this for me. I just want to bury my sister as quickly as possible. That's all."

That wasn't all, not by a long shot, and he could tell that she was lying. He stared at her, obviously torn between giving in to her plea and telling her where to stick that envelope of cash. From what Bria had told me, the two of them respected each other and had a great working relationship, but he was also an honest man, one of the few good ones in the entire building.

I didn't like using him this way, asking him to do something so underhanded, something that went against his beliefs, but I didn't have a choice. Not if I wanted time to plot against Madeline. But just because I wanted to get her didn't mean that I was going to hurt innocent people to do it. If the coroner wouldn't do what we wanted, then so be it. We'd figure out another way.

"No one will question your findings," Bria continued, trying to convince him. "My sister went into her restaurant, and she never came back out again. Dozens of witnesses support that."

"But she's a powerful elemental. If anyone could have survived the fire, it would have been Gin Blanco . . ." Ryan's voice trailed off, and I could almost see the wheels spinning as he thought about the implication of declaring me dead. "But you actually . . . *want* this body to be your sister. Why would you want something like that to be true?"

Bria must have been taking acting lessons from Finn because she pinched the bridge of her nose, as if she were fighting back tears. "Because it *is* her. You've heard all the rumors about Gin and Dobson and the bull pen."

Ryan winced again.

Bria dropped her hand from her face and stared him down. "I can't do anything about all of that, but I can do this one last thing for my sister. I want you to expedite things so I can bury her as soon as possible. That's what she would have wanted. Not this . . . *circus*. Besides, I know that you're getting . . . pressure to perform the autopsy so you can give your findings to certain . . . interested individuals."

For a moment, I almost thought she had him, but her last, not-so-veiled reference to Madeline hardened his resolve.

He straightened up and crossed his arms over his chest. "I don't hurry my work, and I certainly don't falsify it."

Bria's lips tightened into a thin line. She opened her mouth to argue with him, but he held up his hand, cutting her off.

"But your sister . . . helped me once. Did a . . . favor for my family. At least, I think that she did. So I'll go ahead with the autopsy. I'll say what you want me to, Bria. Giving myself enough wiggle room to backtrack later, of course."

She nodded at him. "Of course."

Bria looked at me, obviously wanting us to leave before he changed his mind, but I wasn't quite ready to go yet.

"Actually, I have something for Dr. Colson," I said. "Something that might answer some of his questions. About Ms. Blanco."

I reached into my briefcase and pulled out several old newspaper articles that I'd had Silvio look up online and print out for me. Puzzled, Bria took the papers from me and handed them over to the coroner.

At first, he frowned, but as he read the sheets and the words sank in, his eyes widened, and his mouth silently dropped open into an O. Then he came to the last sheet, which featured a news photo of a grief-stricken young man clutching the bloodstained body of his kid brother to his chest.

His fingers dug into the paper, crumpling the edges, and his head snapped in my direction. "Where did you get . . . how did you *know* . . ."

"Several years ago, your younger brother Roy was murdered," I said. "Shot by some gangbangers during a robbery of your parents' grocery store. The police did very little to investigate the crime, but the perpetrators were found soon after, all of them with their throats cut."

Bria sucked in a breath. She knew that I'd killed them. And now, so did Dr. Ryan Colson.

"Given your job here, I'm sure that you've seen that particular injury, made with the same sort of blade, more than once over the years," I continued in a calm voice. "Not only that, but the police officer responsible for investigating the crime, the one who had done such a shitty job of it, was also found dead around that same time. Also with her throat cut, although she was buried in a bombed-out warehouse. A few weeks later, your parents received an anonymous donation, enough to help them get their store up and running again."

Colson's fingers tightened on the papers, making them crackle. I wasn't telling him anything that he hadn't already guessed, but he deserved to hear it from me.

"Of course, none of this brought your brother back, and none of it lessened the pain of his loss. There are some things you just can't unsee," I said in a soft voice. "Just like you said. But if it helped at all, well, I think Ms. Blanco would have liked knowing that."

Colson carefully smoothed out the papers in his hand, then raised his eyes to mine. I met his questioning, searching gaze with a steady one of my own. After a moment, his gaze flicked to Bria, then back to me again, as he mentally compared the two of us. He was a smart guy, and I knew that he'd figured out who I really was underneath the blond wig and glasses.

"It did help," he said in a quiet voice. "As much as anything could. Thank you for answering my . . . questions."

I tipped my head at him. "You're welcome."

Bria stepped up and held out her hand. Colson shook it, but he kept looking at me the whole time.

"Thank you, Ryan," she said, dropping her hand back down to her side. "You don't know how much this means to me."

A faint grin lifted his lips. "Oh, I'm sure that I'll find out sooner or later. I usually do when Ms. Blanco is involved." He grabbed the envelope full of cash and tossed it over to her. "You can keep that, though. I don't want it."

Bria opened her mouth to protest, but I shook my head at her. We were still on thin ice, and I didn't want him to change his mind about helping us.

"Well, then," she said. "We'll leave you to it."

Colson moved over to the desk in the corner and started pulling on a pair of latex gloves, purposefully ignoring us. I snapped my briefcase shut and jerked my head at Bria. She slid the envelope full of cash into her back pocket, and we walked over to the door. I pulled it open, letting her step through first as I glanced back over my shoulder.

Colson was still standing at the desk, but he'd put his gloved, fisted hands down on the metal, as if he were propping himself up. His gaze was locked on a framed photo sitting on the corner of the desk—one of two boys laughing and sitting on a stoop in front of a store.

He realized that I was watching him. After a moment, he tipped his head at me. I returned the gesture, then let the door swing shut behind me.

We stepped back out into the front room.

Bria waited until the door had shut behind us before she turned to me. "Ryan told me once about his brother's murder. He said that it was one of the reasons he decided to become a coroner. So he could help find answers for people about what happened to their loved ones. Give them some closure."

"I can understand that."

"I can't believe that he agreed to help us," she said. "I never thought he would, but then I didn't know that you'd killed the people who'd murdered his brother. Was that your backup plan if he'd said no? Reminding him of that?"

I shrugged. "Someone that you helped returned the favor to me when Dobson was searching the Pork Pit. That got me thinking about Colson. He's always been respectful to me whenever we've crossed paths. I wondered why, and then I remembered this particular job that Fletcher had sent me on. That's why I brought the newspaper clippings."

"But he said yes before that. You didn't have to tell him any of that stuff about his brother."

"Yeah. But he deserved to know, regardless of whether he helped us or not."

We left the coroner's office, stepped back out into the hallway, and headed down the corridor. Bria rounded the corner just as the elevator chimed out its arrival. My sister stopped, then lurched back, keeping me from entering the next hallway.

"What—"

"Emery's here," Bria hissed.

"Where is this place?" Emery's voice boomed out.

"It's right up ahead, ma'am," a male voice murmured in response. "This way."

Two sets of footsteps slapped against the floor, heading in our direction.

Bria stabbed her finger at my heels. I slipped off the shoes, then the two of us turned and ran back the way we'd come. Even though I was still wearing my disguise, we couldn't afford to let Emery see us anywhere near the coroner's office. At the very least, she'd report Bria's presence to Madeline, who would realize that my sister had tried to influence the autopsy results and that I was still alive after all.

"Over there!" Bria hissed. "The stairwell!"

We reached the end of the hall and skidded to a stop, but the stairwell door featured the same kind of ID scanner that had been in the coroner's office. Bria fumbled in her jeans pocket for her card.

In the distance, I could see shadows sliding across the floor, growing larger and larger as Emery and her escort headed this way. Another thirty seconds, and they would round the hallway corner and see Bria and me standing at the far end.

Twenty seconds . . .

Bria yanked her card out of her pocket.

Fifteen . . .

She slid it through the scanner, but the light stayed red.

Ten . . . seven . . . five . . .

Bria muttered a curse and ran the card through the reader again. The light turned green, and she yanked the door open.

Three . . . two . . . one . . .

We stepped into the stairwell, the door swinging shut behind us, just as Emery appeared at the other end of the corridor, along with a uniformed officer.

Bria started up the stairs, but I grabbed her arm and yanked her back against the wall with me.

"Wait," I whispered.

Sure enough, a few seconds later, a shadow moved in front of the narrow glass strip in the door, as though someone was peering inside to see if anyone was going up the steps.

"Something wrong?" the officer asked.

Silence. Bria and I flattened ourselves against the wall, holding our positions.

"Nah," Emery finally said. "Must just be all the weird echoes down here."

She moved away from the glass. I waited ten seconds, then looked out through the opening. Emery headed back toward the coroner's office, threw the door open, and stepped inside. The officer followed her, and the two of them disappeared from view.

Bria and I both let out tense breaths.

"Come on," I said, stooping to put my heels back on. "Let's get out of here."

* 21 *

Bria and I slipped out of the police station with no more problems, and she drove me back to Jo-Jo's house. After that, the next few days dragged by in a slow, morbid blur.

It was hard being dead.

Mostly because I couldn't go anywhere. I couldn't go home to Fletcher's, I couldn't go back to the Pork Pit to survey the damage, and I certainly couldn't return to my tree house in the woods outside the Monroe mansion to spy on Madeline.

I couldn't do anything but hide in one of the bedrooms above Jo-Jo's salon and plot my revenge. A pleasant enough pastime to be sure, but once my plans had been laid, all I could do was wait and see if they would come to fruition. The lack of activity tested even my patience.

So did the incessant news coverage. Story after story dominated the newspapers and airwaves about me sup-

posedly murdering Dobson, setting fire to my own restaurant, and perishing in the blaze. That was bad enough,
but the reporters hounded my friends, constantly calling,
texting, and following them around, trying to get exclusive interviews and wanting to know just how shocked
they were that I'd turned out to be a stone-cold killer.
One of them even had the audacity to book an appoint-
ment with Jo-Jo in hopes of picking up a juicy bit of info
at the salon. But the dwarf realized what the reporter was
up to and dyed her hair a lovely shade of pea green. The
reporter never came back after that.

Finally, though, the day of my funeral arrived.

The others protested that it wasn't safe, that it wasn't
smart, going to my own funeral. They were right, but I
was determined to do it all the same. I hadn't been out
of the house in days, but more than that, I wanted to see
Madeline and her reactions for myself and not hear about
them secondhand from my friends.

So I put on the same blond wig, blue contacts, silver
glasses, and black suit that I'd worn to the coroner's office and sat in Jo-Jo's house, waiting for everyone else to
leave. Once my friends were gone, I peered out through
the white lace curtains, but I didn't see anyone watching
the house from the woods or the street outside. There was
no reason to spy, now that it was seemingly empty. So I
went outside, walked two streets over, slid into the silver
BMW that Silvio had rented for me under a fake name,
and drove over to Blue Ridge Cemetery.

I'd thought there would be a crowd, given who I was
and the messy circumstances of my supposed death, but
so many folks had turned out for my funeral that I had to

park my car outside the cemetery entrance and walk the rest of the way in.

More than three hundred people clustered around my gravesite, which was right next to Fletcher's. Given how badly my supposed body had been burned, the silver casket was closed, with a beautiful spray of pink and white roses draped over the top. I wasn't really a pink-and-white sort of girl, but Jo-Jo had enthusiastically planned my funeral, so I'd gone along with what she wanted.

I maneuvered past the gravestones and slipped into the center of the crowd, where I would have a clear view of my family, who were sitting in folding metal chairs in front of the casket. They all wore somber black suits and jackets and were doing their best to seem composed, although Bria and Jo-Jo kept dabbing at their eyes with black silk handkerchiefs. Before they'd left the salon, Finn had insisted that everyone sniff some menthol to give them watery eyes and runny noses and make it seem like they'd all been crying all day long. I had to admit that it was effective. If I hadn't known better, I would have thought that they were all grieving deeply for me.

The rest of the crowd? Not so much.

Most everyone in attendance wore curious but satisfied expressions, since they hadn't come to pay their respects so much as make certain that I was dead. I saw several lower-level underworld minions high-five each other as the minister stepped over to the podium to begin the service. For such a somber occasion, the mood was decidedly cheerful.

At least it was until Madeline arrived.

She swept through the crowd like the queen she

thought she was, and people hurried to get out of her way. Emery and Jonah flanked her, as was their custom. Murmurs of the acid elemental's arrival rippled through the crowd, causing my friends to turn around in their chairs. They all shot her *drop-dead-bitch* looks, but Madeline ignored their heated glares and took up a spot off to the right of my casket so she could have a clear view.

As the minister quieted the crowd and started the service, I studied my enemy. Unlike everyone else, Madeline was not dressed in navy or black but wore her usual white pantsuit. Her only concession to the funeral was her black hat with a matching lace veil and a thin white ribbon around the brim. Through the veil, I could see the bright glitter of her green eyes and the cruel curve of her crimson lips.

She was enjoying this very, very much.

Madeline turned to get a better view of my casket, and the sun caught on her crown-and-flame necklace, as well as the matching ring on her finger. I didn't know if there were any old sayings about wearing something new to a funeral, but Madeline was, since her jewelry was made out of gold now, instead of the silverstone set she'd worn before. I'd noticed the new bling a couple of days ago in some surveillance photos of her that Silvio had taken for me, and I'd found it extremely interesting for a number of reasons.

I focused on her necklace. In many ways, it was the exact same as Mab's sunburst rune had been—a thick gold chain with a large gemstone set in the middle—although Madeline had forgone the gaudy, wavy, ostentatious rays that had radiated out of her mama's necklace.

The longer I looked at Madeline's baubles, the wider I

grinned. I'd been hoping that she would wear them to my funeral. The gold jewelry told me more than anything else that she finally, truly believed that I was dead.

Most of those gathered here might have done everything possible to put me in the ground, but everyone remained quiet, respectful, and solemn during the service. They might all be a bunch of criminals, but even they could behave at a funeral. Us Southerners were quirky like that.

All too soon, though, the minister finished his sermon and called my friends and family forward, each of them taking a rose from the casket spray to supposedly remember me by. Jo-Jo let out a particularly loud bawl when she did so and stumbled, as if she were overcome with grief. Sophia grabbed her sister's arm, supporting and leading her away from my casket.

I raised my hand to my face to hide my grin. Jo-Jo had thoroughly enjoyed this charade, and she had wholeheartedly thrown herself into everything from picking out my casket, to planning the funeral, to selecting the tombstone that would be erected at my grave. I thought that it was a bit morbid, but Jo-Jo had gotten catalogs of various markers and had made me go through them with her while she did my nails in the salon one evening.

Still, I supposed it could be worse. I could actually be in that casket, and I might still end up there. My grin faded away.

Finally, the service concluded, and everyone started drifting away and walking back to their cars.

Everyone except Madeline.

She stayed rooted in her spot and lifted her veil, her

green eyes sweeping back and forth over the crowd, as if she was searching for someone—me.

I ducked my head, not wanting to lock gazes with her, and slowly shuffled away, sticking close to a pair of older men as though I were with them. But I didn't have to worry about Madeline's seeing me because Bria chose that moment to pounce.

"You need to leave," her voice rang through the entire cemetery.

Everyone who'd been leaving stopped and turned around to witness the commotion.

Bria stood a few feet away from Madeline, her eyes narrowed, her body stiff, her hands curled into fists, as though she were about two seconds away from tackling the other woman.

Madeline gave my sister a cool look. "I just came to pay my respects. Same as everyone else."

Bria let out a hard, brittle laugh. "Sure you did. Since you're the reason that my sister's dead in the first place."

Madeline arched an eyebrow. "I know that you're grieving, but I had nothing to do with Gin's unfortunate . . . accident."

Bria surged forward, but Finn grabbed her arm, supposedly holding her back.

"Come on, Bria," he said in a disgusted voice. "She's not worth it."

Bria ostensibly let him march her away, although she kept shooting dark looks back over her shoulder at Madeline. I had to hand it to my baby sister and the rest of my friends. They'd done an excellent job pretending that I was dead.

Still, given the small chance that Madeline hadn't bought our charade, I slipped behind a tree about thirty feet away from my grave, bent down, and started dusting the leaves and twigs off a tombstone, as if I were also visiting that person before leaving the cemetery. But Madeline never even glanced in my direction.

The rest of my friends, family, and legions of adoring enemies headed back to their cars, but Madeline, Emery, and Jonah stayed beside my casket. Madeline stared at Finn and Bria, watching as they walked over to Sophia's classic convertible and slid into the backseat. Sophia and Jo-Jo got into the car as well, and the four of them drove away. Xavier and Roslyn departed, and so did Owen, Eva, Violet, and Warren. Phillip and Cooper left together, and Silvio and Catalina drifted away with the rest of the staff from the Pork Pit.

"What are you going to do about Coolidge?" Emery asked. "She's not going to give up. Now that Dobson's dead, she's already challenging his supposed investigation into her. She has enough friends in the department to get her job back. If that happens, she could make trouble."

"She can try, but she's not nearly as dangerous as Blanco was," Madeline replied. "None of them are. So they get to live—for now. Besides, I'm not done with them yet. Just because their beloved Gin is dead is no reason for them not to suffer even more before they join her. Don't you agree?"

Emery's low, evil laughter matched Madeline's.

"Besides, without Gin around to protect them, it will be all the more amusing to see how they deal with the problems we send their way."

Jonah cleared his throat, finally getting into the conversation. "Needling Blanco's loved ones is all well and good, but we need to focus on the matter at hand—the party tomorrow night."

Madeline and Emery both gave him a flat look. They didn't care to be interrupted when they were plotting someone else's pain and suffering. Jonah took a step back and smoothed down his tie. I wondered if he could see how clearly numbered his days in Madeline's employ were. It wouldn't surprise me if she killed him anytime now, since I was apparently dead and out of the picture. Perhaps Emery would string him up like a piñata, and she and Madeline would take turns whacking him. Now, *that* would be a party.

"Well, Jonah," Madeline drawled, "you are actually right about something—for a change. We do need to focus on the party. I assume that you've handled things on your end?"

Jonah's head snapped up and down as he hurried to reassure her. "Of course. I started sending out the invitations this morning. All the underworld bosses have gotten theirs by now. They will all be too curious and afraid not to come."

"Oh, I'm counting on it," Madeline murmured. "Let's go. I'm done here."

She and Emery both turned their backs to Jonah and strolled away. The lawyer swallowed and followed them, although his steps were much slower than theirs. His obvious misery at his new, tenuous status in life filled me with dark satisfaction.

But I was going to get even more satisfaction when I crashed Madeline's party.

* * *

The rest of the stragglers left, and a couple of guys in blue coveralls appeared, along with another one driving a small tractor with a crane attached to it. I held my position by the tombstone and eyed the men since I'd been attacked by gravediggers at Mab's funeral as part of one of Jonah's many plots to kill me. But the men ignored me, took a couple of swigs from the thermoses full of coffee they'd brought along, grabbed their shovels, and got to work.

An hour later, a car cruised through the cemetery, following the winding path. By that point, the gravediggers and the guy on the tractor had gone, having finished their work. What was left of the casket spray of pink and white roses rested atop the disturbed, black earth. Behind the roses, my tombstone rose up, with my spider rune carved into the center of it. The mark was the same size as the scars on my palms.

I was crouching down in front of the tombstone, staring at the words on the glossy, gray granite surface—*Gin Blanco, beloved daughter, sister, and friend. Gone too soon.*

That last line had been Jo-Jo's idea. Heh. Not everyone would think that, not after what I had planned.

The car stopped, the door opened, and Owen got out. He walked over to my side and stared down at the tombstone, his violet eyes dark and unreadable. Owen hadn't said much these past few days. Pretending that I was dead had been harder on him than anyone else. At night, when we were in bed together, he loved me with furious feeling, as if I might disappear if he didn't hold on to me tightly enough. And I returned the favor.

Because we both knew that I could still die before this was all said and done.

But neither of us mentioned that uncomfortable fact, as if by not talking about it, that wouldn't make it the very real possibility that it was.

"What are you thinking about?" Owen finally asked.

I stared at the tombstone that featured the day of my supposed death for a few more seconds, then rose to my feet. "I'm thinking that this is the second time that I've supposedly been buried in this cemetery, thanks to a Monroe."

I looked up the ridge where the Snow family was buried. A tombstone with my real name—Genevieve Snow—squatted up there, along with one that bore Bria's name as well. Our mother, Eira, and older sister, Annabella, were actually entombed up there, along with our father, Tristan.

"It must be strange," Owen said. "Seeing how the world, how people, just . . . go on without you."

I shrugged. It wasn't strange so much as it was sad, but I wasn't about to confess that to him. Not now, anyway.

"I don't know if I could do that," he said, his voice dropping to a ragged whisper. "Go on without you. I wouldn't know *how* to do that."

"You would find a way, and I would want you to." I stepped into his arms and cradled his face in my hands. "But you don't have to worry about that because I'm not going anywhere. You should know by now that I'm very, very good at surviving. Even when I'm up against someone as dangerous as Madeline."

I pressed my lips to his. Owen returned my kiss, then

shuddered and hugged me tight. I buried my face in his neck, breathing in his rich, metallic scent. We stood like that, wrapped in each other's arms, in front of my grave for a long, long time.

Finally, though, I drew back. Because Madeline was making her plans, and I needed to weave my web as well.

So I kissed Owen one more time, then held out my hand. He threaded his fingers through mine. The warmth of his skin chased away the chill that I hadn't even realized had sunk into my bones until right now. It was a beautiful, crisp fall day, so perhaps the cold had more to do with our standing over my supposed grave than anything else. Then again, I always felt a bit of a chill when I realized that I was still alive when I shouldn't be. The trap that Madeline had set for me had been one of the most dangerous that I'd ever faced. Part of me still couldn't believe that I was standing here in the sunshine, instead of being cold, dead, and buried in the ground.

Owen led me away from the gravesite, but I couldn't help but glance back over my shoulder. The sun was glinting off my tombstone, the bright rays filling in the lines of my spider rune and making it glimmer.

I didn't particularly believe in good omens, but I was going to take the shining silver light as a sign that I wouldn't be back here anytime soon, to be buried for real after my final confrontation with Madeline.

✵22✵

Owen and I drove our respective cars back over to Jo-Jo's, with him going all the way up the driveway, while I parked my rental two streets over, just like before.

By the time I did a sweep of the subdivision to make sure that no one was watching the house, everyone had gathered in the salon, which had been converted into a makeshift war room. Several tables had been crammed in between the cherry-red salon chairs, and papers, blueprints, photos, and more covered all the available surfaces, overtaking the usual stacks of glossy beauty and fashion magazines. Pens, markers, and printouts were piled high in plastic tubs, mixed in with the lipstick, nail polish, and hair curlers that Jo-Jo used on her clients, and Silvio had even stacked some old copies of the *Ashland Municipal Codex* around Rosco's wicker basket in the corner. But the basset hound seemed to be enjoying the makeshift fort, since he'd put his brown-and-black head on top of one of the thick books, snoring and drooling all over the faded yellow pages.

Finn and Silvio were leading the charge, poring over papers and photos while they worked the phones, gathering the final scraps of information I needed to put my plan into action. Bria and Xavier stood in front of a dry-erase board that my sister had brought over from her house, ticking off the names that Owen, Phillip, and Roslyn called out to them off the printouts in their hands. Jo-Jo moved from one side of the room to the other, passing out bottles of water, while Sophia relaxed in one of the salon chairs, bobbing her head and snapping her fingers in time to the golden oldies streaming through her skull-shaped earbuds.

While I'd been hiding out at Jo-Jo's, Finn and Silvio had been looking into things for me, and they'd quickly learned that Madeline's party tomorrow night wasn't just about *ding-dong-the-bitch-Gin-Blanco-is-dead*. Oh, I'm sure there would be some crowing about that, but more important was that the acid elemental had invited every crime lord and lady in Ashland to her exclusive underworld shindig. I could imagine what she was going to do—proclaim herself to be the queen of them all, since she'd finally managed to do what none of them had been able to. Kill me. Or so she thought.

I was *so* going to enjoy ruining her coming-out party.

Since everyone was busy, and I had nothing to add, I slipped away from the noise of the salon and headed into the quiet of the kitchen. Given all the free time I'd had while playing dead, I'd been cooking a lot while I'd been staying with the Deveraux sisters. So it was easy enough for me to pile several platters high with the chocolate chip cookies, dark chocolate-cherry brownies, and a chocolate-mousse pie that I'd made.

But I figured that we might want something a little more substantial to nibble on as the evening wore on, so I started making stacks of grilled-cheese sandwiches. Some plain, some stuffed with sweet, juicy slices of apples and pears, some filled with honey ham and bread-and-butter pickles, and some bulging with thick slices of tomato sprinkled with salt, pepper, and a touch of dill weed. I cut the hot sandwiches into triangles, grabbed some napkins, cups, and pitchers of lemonade and sweet iced tea, and carried everything into the salon.

I slipped inside, and everyone kept right on working, except for Finn. He immediately perked up and sniffed the air a couple of times, just like Rosco did, then turned in my direction, his eyes even bigger and more eager than the basset hound's.

"Do I smell grilled-cheese sandwiches? With cookies? *And* lemonade?"

I laughed, and we all gathered around to nosh on my postfuneral feast, as it were. While we ate, Finn and Silvio updated the rest of us on everything they'd been able to find out so far about Madeline's party.

"Looks like Madeline has invited everyone who's anyone in the underworld," Finn said, stuffing two triangles of the apple-and-pear grilled cheese into his mouth at once.

"No, really?" Phillip snarked. "And here I thought that we were calling out and writing down the names of Ashland's most dangerous criminals just for kicks."

"I agree with Finn," Silvio added, nibbling on one of the chocolate chip cookies. "And we all know why Madeline went with this specific guest list. It's not so much a party as it is a coronation, just like McAllister said."

"At least until someone shows up to assassinate the queen," I chimed in. "A role that I am more than happy to play."

We all chuckled, but our laughter quickly died down. We all knew how dangerous my plan was, but it was the only way to protect my loved ones from Madeline, as well as hopefully get the one other thing I wanted—a little peace and quiet.

So we spent the rest of the afternoon working, dividing up the parts of my master plan into small, manageable sections and tasks, just like Madeline had done when she was targeting us.

Once Bria, Xavier, Roslyn, Owen, and Phillip had finished with the guest list, Finn took over, standing in front of the dry-erase board like a professor, telling us about all the rumors he'd heard about who was moving up in the underworld, who was getting pushed aside, and how many bodyguards they might bring with them to Madeline's party. He even produced a laser pointer from somewhere to help with his lecture. Show-off.

When we had a good idea of how many people were going to be attending the party, Silvio took over, since he'd gotten his hands on the most useful things of all—blueprints of the newly remodeled Monroe mansion, along with the guard rotations.

Jo-Jo cleared off one of the tables, and Silvio unrolled

the blueprints with a slight flourish, then bowed his head to me and stepped back so we could all crowd around them.

Finn pouted. "I've been trying to get my hands on this info ever since Gin fake-died. How did you manage it?"

"A good assistant never reveals his sources." Silvio gave him a small, satisfied smile. "Perhaps people just like me more than they do you."

Finn glared at the vampire, but Silvio kept smiling. He liked needling Finn. Couldn't blame him for that. It was certainly one of my favorite sports, so much so that I thought it should be an official national pastime.

"Madeline doesn't have as many guards as I thought she would," Xavier rumbled, running his finger down a list of names. "Looks like about three dozen total, split three ways—guarding the perimeter, roaming through the mansion, and then at the party itself."

"Yeah, but you're forgetting that she has Emery as the head of them," Bria pointed out. "She's worth at least three giants just by herself."

"Heh," Sophia rasped, cracking her knuckles. "She's not so tough."

We all looked at each other, but nobody argued with the Goth dwarf.

After we'd reviewed the guard rotations and the blueprints, we moved on to the next phase—weapons.

Finn got Xavier to help him carry several large, heavy duffel bags into the salon. A gleeful grin spread across my foster brother's face, as though he were opening up presents on Christmas morning, instead of unzipping bags full of guns, silencers, and ammunition.

"Where did you get all these on such short notice?" Phillip asked, hefting a revolver in his hand.

"Why, they were a gift from Madeline," Finn drawled. "The only good thing she's ever done for us."

"They were the weapons she was going to buy from Harley Grimes to outfit her guards," Owen added. "The ones we intercepted when Sophia and Jo-Jo killed him that night at Gin's."

"They were just gathering dust and cobwebs in that tunnel under Dad's house, so I figured that we might as well bring these babies out of storage and give them a spin." Finn struck a pose with a particularly large rifle. "What do you think? Is gunmetal gray my color?"

We all groaned.

While Finn continued to show off with the weapons, Silvio drifted over and handed me a small sheet of paper.

"What's this?" I asked.

He frowned. "I'm not quite sure, but I thought you should see it, since it's part of the work that Madeline ordered done on the mansion. Most of the renovations were fairly standard stuff. New paint, new ceilings, new floors. But this is different."

"How so?"

He tapped the paper. "From what I can tell, it's a single suite of rooms that she's had remodeled. A bedroom, a bathroom, and some sort of living room."

"What's so unusual about that?"

"This suite is on the bottom floor of the mansion, tucked away in one of the back corners, well away from the rest of the construction." Silvio hesitated. "It almost seems like she's been fixing up a place for someone to stay."

A chill ran through me at his words. "Madeline is going to have a houseguest?"

"That's my speculation."

"Who?"

Silvio shrugged. "Unfortunately, that's something I haven't been able to find out."

He didn't say anything else, but he could see the concern on my face. We were going to have enough problems dealing with Madeline, Emery, and their giant guards. We didn't need to worry about anyone unexpected popping up to throw a wrench in our plans.

"If it helps, the remodeling was only finished this morning," he said. "Madeline's guest probably hasn't arrived yet and might not until after the party."

He was trying to reassure me, but it didn't work. Silvio touched my shoulder, then moved back over to talk to Jo-Jo.

I kept staring at the paper in my hand, not really seeing all the lines, squiggles, and other marks. I wasn't an Air elemental, so I never got glimpses of the future like Jo-Jo did. But for some reason, I felt more concerned about Madeline's mysterious houseguest than I did about anything else.

While my friends talked among themselves, I roused myself out of my worry and stepped back so that I was in the doorway of the salon, my gaze sweeping over the interior. The blueprints, the names scribbled on the dry-erase board, the duffel bags full of guns and ammo, even the old copies of the *Ashland Municipal Codex* that were stacked around Rosco's basket.

As I looked at first one thing, then another, I thought and thought and thought about things, my mind whirring a hundred miles an hour. Trying to picture how it would all go down. Trying to see if there were any holes in or problems with my plan that I hadn't accounted for. Trying to anticipate how Madeline and the underworld bosses might react when they realized that I was still alive.

Trying to figure out if I was dooming myself and my friends to a short, pain-filled night that would end with all our deaths.

But this was how it had to be. I was only going to get one shot at Madeline, and this was it. So I thought about Fletcher and what he might have done in my place. I thought that the old man would have approved of my plan and all the lessons I'd learned that night so long ago when we were trapped in those metal barrels. The ones that I'd largely forgotten about until Madeline had so cruelly reminded me of them.

The others realized that I was staring at them, and they quieted down and looked back at me.

"Well," I said, grinning wide, "I think we're ready to give Madeline and the rest of the Ashland underworld a night that they will never, ever forget. Here's what we're going to do."

* 23 *

The next evening, I got ready for the most important party of my life.

Or at least, what might be left of it.

According to what Jo-Jo had learned, Madeline was going to be wearing some fancy, haute couture gown to her shindig, but I dressed the way I always did—to kill.

Tonight, that meant black boots and thick black coveralls that zipped up to my neck. I also tucked my five knives into their usual slots, since Silvio had returned them to me. My spider rune ring was back on my right index finger where it belonged, with the matching necklace resting in the hollow of my throat underneath my coveralls. Both pieces pulsed with more of my Ice and Stone magic than ever before, since I'd spent a good portion of my time hiding out at Jo-Jo's pouring my power into the silverstone. They were the two most important parts of my plan, even more so than my knives.

Tonight, my jewelry would determine whether I lived or died.

The others geared up in similar style, and we packed the rest of our supplies into black duffel bags. I wanted to hang on to the element of surprise for as long as possible, so weapons weren't the only things we were going to need tonight.

Finally, when we were all ready, we gathered in the salon to check everything one last time. Me, Owen, Bria, Finn, Xavier, Jo-Jo, and Sophia. Phillip, Silvio, and Roslyn were also in on the plan, but they were going in another way. Eva, Violet, and Catalina had wanted to help as well, but we'd voted them down, and the girls were up at Country Daze, with Warren and Cooper watching over them. If things went wrong, the guys would protect them from the fallout.

And things could go so horribly wrong tonight.

Owen came over and slid his arm around my waist. "Are you ready for this?"

I let out a breath. "Yeah. I'm ready, consequences and all. Finally."

He nodded and held me close until it was time to leave.

We grabbed our gear, piled into our various vehicles, and drove over to the Monroe estate.

But we didn't stop and try to ram our vehicles through the closed gate that fronted the mansion. I didn't want to announce our presence until the last possible second, so we cruised on by, although Sophia slowed her convertible down long enough for me to peer in through the gate and take note of the dozens of limos and expensive town cars that were parked in the long driveway that led up to the house. It looked like the party was just getting started. Good.

Sophia drove to the next house over. The gates here opened as the dwarf steered her convertible up to them. Behind us, the others followed in their own cars. We drove up to the mansion, then parked in the driveway in front of the house. The door opened, and Charlotte Vaughn stepped outside.

While the others pulled their gear out of the cars, I strolled over to her. Charlotte eyed my friends for several seconds before turning to me.

"You can imagine how surprised I was to get your call," she said. "Considering that I just went to your funeral yesterday."

I'd seen Charlotte there, and she'd been one of the few folks who seemed genuinely sad that I was gone. Although whatever kindness or affection she felt for me would always be mixed with anger at how I'd killed her father, and rightfully so.

I grinned. "I do like to do the unexpected. What can I say? Coming back from the dead is a specialty of mine."

"What are you planning, Gin?" she asked, suspicion flaring in her brown eyes. "I heard about the party that Madeline Monroe is throwing tonight."

I shrugged. "I'm going to do what I do best."

"And why do you and your friends need access to my estate to do it?"

"Because I don't want Madeline to realize what's happening until it's too late."

Charlotte arched a black eyebrow. "I see. Did you know that I had a visit from Madeline a few days ago? It was right after the fire at the Pork Pit. She wanted to talk about me giving her an interest in Vaughn Construction, the one that Mab used to own."

"Silvio, my assistant, might have mentioned that to me. It shouldn't be a problem, after tonight."

After a moment, Charlotte grinned back at me. "Still looking out for me, Gin?"

"It's another one of those things that I do best."

Charlotte let out a soft laugh. She waved her hand at everyone, then disappeared back into her mansion.

The others were waiting on me, so I grabbed the bag of gear that Owen passed me, and we all headed for the woods on the far side of the estate. We reached the tree line. I took the lead, while the others fell in step behind me.

"Are we there yet?" Finn groused after we'd been walking for all of three minutes.

I rolled my eyes, even though he couldn't see me, and we trudged on.

It took us about forty-five minutes to reach my makeshift tree house. I climbed up into the top, drew a pair of night-vision goggles out of my bag, and focused them on the back of the estate.

The iron lamps that lined the pool and the patio were all lit, casting a soft golden glow over the shimmering surface of the water and the gray stone that surrounded it. The area was quiet, with only three bored-looking guards making their circuits around the lawn. Exactly what I'd expected and hoped for. Now that I was dead, Madeline wasn't worried about anyone's slipping onto the estate or trying to assassinate her from the trees. Why have your guards stationed outside when the folks gathered inside the mansion were the real danger here tonight?

I climbed down from my perch and rejoined the others. "Looks like it's smooth sailing, at least until we get to the lawn. Everybody ready?"

Everyone checked their guns a final time, while I palmed one of my knives.

"Let's do this."

We crept through the woods, still on the lookout for any rune traps, trip-wires, or land mines that Madeline and Emery might have planted. But the area was clean, and we reached the edge of the lawn with no problems.

Now it was time to contact Phillip, Roslyn, and Silvio, who were already here.

Madeline had actually invited the three of them to her party. Phillip was a major power player, given the gambling operations on his *Delta Queen* riverboat, and Roslyn had various dealings with the underworld figures, thanks to all the not-so-legal activities that went on at Northern Aggression. But Silvio's receiving an invite had surprised everyone. Then again, he'd been Beauregard Benson's right-hand man for years. Perhaps Madeline would be in the market for a new assistant, after she finally got rid of Jonah. Or maybe she just wanted to rub Silvio's nose in the fact that I was dead. Either way, he'd merited an invitation as well. So the three of them strolled right in through the front doors with all the other guests, giving me some eyes and ears on the inside.

I pulled my cell phone out of my pocket and texted my friends. *We're here.*

My phone vibrated a second later with a message from Silvio. *Party proceeding as scheduled. Guards sticking to the expected rotations. Go.*

I grinned and sent him back one more message. *Knock, knock.*

"Finn," I whispered, sliding the phone back into my pocket. "You're up."

"With pleasure," he murmured.

Finn drew his sniper rifle and scope out of his duffel bag, attached a silencer to the end of the barrel, and raised the weapon to his shoulder. Then he waited.

Pfft. Pfft. Pfft.

He dropped the three giants patrolling the lawn in quick succession, putting bullets through their skulls with precise, practiced ease. The giants grunted as they went down, but those were the only sounds that broke the hush of the night. In the distance, classical music trilled through the air, but it was soft and muted, almost like the echoes of a dream rather than something that was actually taking place.

I held up my fist, telling my friends to hold their positions. I waited one minute, then two, then three, the others shifting uneasily behind me all the while, but no one came to check on the dead guards. The rest of the giants were too concerned with what was going on inside the mansion to worry about what might be coming at them from the outside. Perfect.

So we left the trees behind, darted across the lawn, and headed up to the stone patio. We hunkered down behind the furniture, weapons up, still looking and listening, but everything was quiet, and no one was up to no good here but us.

Finn, Xavier, and I split off from the others, darted forward, and rounded the corner of the house. Two more giants stood at the bottom of some steps, and Finn shot both of them before they even realized what was happening. We moved to their position, and I kept watch while Xavier dragged the bodies over behind some bushes that ran along this part of the mansion. The three of us repeated the process over and over, until we had killed the dozen giants who served as the perimeter guards, done a full circuit around the entire mansion, and were back at the patio where we'd started.

I nodded at Bria, who nodded back. She reached into a pocket on the front of her black coveralls and drew out a small glass cutter. Bria eased over to one of the patio doors, crouched down, and cut a hole in the glass big enough for her to slide her hand through. A second after that, the door was unlocked.

She looked at me, and I nodded again. Bria tensed, then cracked the door open. We all waited, holding our proverbial breaths, but no alarms sounded. According to what Silvio had uncovered, the security system had been shut off during the remodeling to keep the alarms from blaring every time a worker opened or closed a door or window. Since the construction had just ended, and folks would be moving through the mansion tonight during the party, I'd been willing to bet that no one had gotten around to turning the system back on. And who would be stupid enough to try to rob Madeline now when she was about to seize control of the underworld? Even if someone did have such a foolish notion, Madeline probably thought that Emery and her giant guards were enough to keep any intruders out.

Well, they were enough to keep most folks out—just not me and my friends.

Bria opened the door wide enough for us to slip inside single file. Once we were all in, she shut the door and drew the white lace curtain to hide the hole in the glass.

"Now what?" she whispered.

"Now we take out all the interior guards," I whispered back. "Just like we planned. Let's move."

According to the information that Silvio had gathered, more guards were roaming through the hallways on the ground floor. Of course they were. Madeline didn't think that anyone could get past them and get inside the house, much less sneak up to the upper levels. Even if they did, they'd eventually have to deal with the acid elemental herself. And like her mother before her, Madeline was supremely confident in her skills, magic, and reputation to keep people away.

But I was crazier than most folks were—or maybe I just had more of a death wish.

We moved through the first floor of the mansion, hugging the walls, keeping to the shadows, and staying quiet, although the music and laughter grew louder and louder the deeper in we went. We rounded a corner and came across a giant guard who was leaning against the wall, sipping a glass of champagne he'd swiped from somewhere. He glanced in our direction, then his head snapped back as he did a double take.

Pfft.

Finn put a bullet through his skull just like he had

all the others. While the rest of us kept watch, Xavier grabbed the giant's body, picked it up, and stuffed it into a nearby closet. Meanwhile, Sophia dropped to her knees, reached out with her hand, and used her Air elemental magic to quickly disintegrate the blood and other nasty things that had spewed out of the giant's head wound. In less than a minute, the body was disposed of, and the scene was clean again.

Quick, quiet, effective—just like I'd planned.

We repeated the process, taking out a dozen more guards. The rest of the giants would be serving as waiters in the grand ballroom, where the party was taking place.

When I was certain that we'd eliminated as many of the guards as we could, we all snuck into a large bathroom. Gun in hand, Owen stood by the exit, peering out through the cracked door, while Jo-Jo unzipped the duffel bags we'd brought along for this particular purpose.

I sent another text to Phillip, Roslyn, and Silvio: *Guards down. Changing now.*

Another text back from Silvio: *Everything on schedule here. Go.*

I gave everyone a thumbs-up, then we all stripped.

Zippers were lowered, shoes were toed off, and socks were peeled away as we all quickly shucked our heavy boots and thick coveralls, revealing the elegant evening wear underneath. Owen, Finn, and Xavier all wore classic tuxedos, while Jo-Jo, Bria, and Sophia were dressed in sparkling tops with flowing silk pants. I wore a sleek black satin pantsuit, not unlike the white ones that Madeline always favored, and I also pulled on a pair of black satin gloves that crawled up to my elbows.

We all switched shoes, exchanging our boots for wing tips and heels. We also all donned the items that Roslyn had supplied us with—wigs and glasses. Things that would alter our appearance just enough to keep anyone from immediately recognizing us. I needed to check on one more thing before proceeding with the final part of my plan, and I still wanted to give us all a chance to slip out of the mansion to safety, if things didn't go the way I expected them to.

Finn peered through the silver glasses on his face, looked in the mirror, and fluffed up his wig. "I always thought I'd look good as a blond."

I rolled my eyes and pulled on my own dark red wig, along with a pair of black glasses.

While Jo-Jo fluttered about, fixing my and Bria's makeup and making sure that everyone's wig was on right, the guys stuffed everyone's coveralls and boots into the duffel bags, then stowed the bags in the bottom of the sunken tub that took up one side of the room.

Five minutes later, we were all ready to move on to the next phase of my plan.

I looked from one face to another. "You all know what to do and where to be. So let's go end this once and for all."

Finn held up his hand, and I slapped him a high five, as though we were football players about to storm the field for a big game, instead of trying to take down one of the most dangerous elementals that had ever haunted Ashland. Finn high-fived the others in turn, lightening the tension that had fallen over us.

One by one, my friends slipped out of the bathroom

to take their positions among the party crowd. I was betting that everyone would be so focused on Madeline and whatever speechifying she might do that they wouldn't notice Finn, Owen, and the others, or even me—until it was too late.

Finally, only Bria was left in the bathroom. After me, she was the most visible and well-known among us, and her risk was almost as great as mine, as a cop strolling into a ballroom full of criminals. Her curly black wig and black glasses wouldn't fool people forever, no more than my disguise would. But Bria was more than happy to face the danger with me, and my heart swelled with love for her.

"Well," she said, "this is it. Are you sure you want to do this, Gin? There's no going back, after tonight."

I nodded. "I'm sure. I think we both know that things have been building toward this for a long time now. Besides, Madeline tried to fuck us all over every which way she could. I want to return the favor tonight—in spades."

Bria grinned. "Well, then," she drawled, "far be it for me to keep you from your grand entrance."

I grinned back. "What can I say? Finn has taught me well."

She laughed and slipped out of the room. I gave her three minutes to get into position, then left the bathroom behind myself.

As I moved through the halls, I couldn't help but think of the last time I'd been inside the mansion—the night I'd killed Jake McAllister, Jonah's son. I hadn't said anything to the others, but I'd dumped his body into the sunken tub in the same bathroom that we'd all just changed in. Oh, the irony.

The corridors were quiet, making the trill of music and murmur of conversation coming from the ballroom seem all the louder. All around me, the stone of the mansion whispered of money and power, things that Madeline had in abundance, just like Mab before her. But even more prominent were the sharp, almost gleeful cackles of death, doom, and destruction, all the things that Madeline delighted in causing, even more so than her mother before her.

Even though we'd taken care of most of the guards, I still kept an eye out, in case one was roaming around that we'd missed. But I made it to one of the corridors that led into the ballroom without any problems.

Still hidden in the shadows, I paused, thinking about what lay ahead of me. Not only a confrontation with Madeline, but the things that would happen afterward, should I survive the acid elemental's magic and wrath.

Maybe my words to Bria were truer than I'd realized. Maybe this day had been coming ever since I'd killed Mab back in the winter. Maybe it had even started all those years ago the night she'd murdered my mom and Annabella. Maybe it had been inevitable, even back then, from the very beginning.

Either way, here I was, and now it was time to take the final step, in more ways than one. So I raised my chin, squared my shoulders, and marched into the ballroom— to either my doom or my destiny.

❋24❋

In some ways, the grand ballroom was exactly the same as the last time I'd been here. Since it served as the junction for the three wings of the mansion, the ballroom covered an enormous space and featured a wide staircase that led to the upper floors. An orchestra played off to one side, next to a series of French doors that led out to a terrace, while people danced, drank, and drifted from one clique to another on the marble floor.

But in other ways, things were completely different. Back when Mab was still alive, shades of red had dominated the ballroom, with rubies and garnets burning in the chandeliers overhead and a scarlet carpet stretching up the staircase. But now everything was a cool white or an even colder crystal, from the white marble floor to the diamond-crusted chandeliers to the ivory carpet that covered the stairs. White orchids perched in cut-crystal vases, while others twined up through the columns in the staircase, along with white lights. It all made for a beautiful, elegant display.

The only real splashes of color in the ballroom were the people who'd answered Madeline's summons. The crowd was exactly what I expected it to be. Men and women dressed in their absolute best, the impressive jewels adorning their fingers, wrists, and throats glittering even more than their sequin-studded clothes did. The remainder of Madeline's giant guards circulated through the ballroom, all dressed as waiters and handing out flutes of champagne, along with various bite-size delicacies arranged on silver platters.

The guests all talked and laughed and smiled at each other, but the soft lights couldn't quite smooth out the worry lines in their faces, and the orchestra music couldn't quite drown out the false notes in their forced chuckles. A thick blanket of tension hung in the air, one that all the champagne in the world couldn't dissipate. They'd been summoned here at the queen's request, and they were all anxious to hear what she had to say—and to see if they were going to keep their heads attached to their necks.

I stood in the shadowy corridor, scanning the crowd for my friends, and making sure that everyone was in position before I stepped out into the ballroom. They'd all slipped inside with no problems. Even I might have overlooked them if I hadn't seen their disguises earlier.

Xavier was off to one side of the elemental Ice bar, talking to Silvio. Owen was in the next corner over, along with Phillip, in front of the terrace doors. Bria and Jo-Jo were across the ballroom from them, with the dwarf pretending to sip a glass of champagne, while Bria clutched in her hand her purse and the gun hidden inside. Sophia was lurking in one of the hallways that ran underneath the staircase, steps away from the dance floor. And Finn and Roslyn were among the folks standing next to the railing on the second floor, where they had a view of the entire ballroom, and Finn could pull out his own gun and take care of any problems that might arise when I made my presence known.

Once I was satisfied that everyone was where they should be, I strolled into the ballroom and grabbed a glass of champagne from a passing waiter. He gave me a bored, disinterested look and moved on to the next person. Then again, I wasn't wearing an evening gown cut down and slit up to there or dripping with jewels. In fact, I didn't look at all like myself. Oh, the black pantsuit was a classier version of my regular clothes, but Jo-Jo had rimmed my eyes with smoky-black shadow and added a dark plum gloss to my lips. Add to that the red wig and black glasses, and I looked far more sophisticated and polished than usual. Now I had to hope that no one would recognize me until I wanted them to.

I kept to the perimeter of the crowd, drifting from one group of people to the next, all of whom were more interested in gossiping than keeping an eye on their surroundings.

"I wonder what Madeline wants."

"Can you believe that she killed Blanco?"

"And I hear that she has acid magic too. . . ."

The rumors went on and on, as folks speculated about how harshly their new queen was going to rule them.

Finally, the chandeliers darkened, until the strands of

lights winding through the orchids along the staircase were the only ones still glowing. Someone in the orchestra started a low, rolling drumbeat. A spotlight illuminated the top and center of the staircase on the second floor, and Madeline made her grand entrance.

She wore a white velvet gown that draped around her figure just so, and her thick auburn hair lay in loose waves on top of her creamy shoulders. The slender straps on the gown glittered with gold crystals, while the deep V in the center plummeted down into the swelling valley of her breasts. But I focused on the necklace that glimmered around her throat, along with the matching ring on her finger. They were the same gold versions of her crown-and-flame jewelry that she'd worn to my funeral.

The thick gold chain resembled a snake draped around Madeline's slender neck, with the emerald in the center of the crown its evil eye. The pendant looked so much like Mab's ruby sunburst necklace that I had to blink to remind myself that it wasn't. I'd destroyed that necklace and the woman attached to it—just like I was going to destroy this Monroe too.

Now that I'd seen Madeline for myself, I pulled out my phone and sent a final text to all my friends. *We're a go.*

Madeline paused at the top of the stairs, letting everyone get a good, long look at her. This was her moment, the one she'd planned and plotted and schemed so long for, and she was determined to savor it.

What she didn't realize was that this was my moment too, the one in which my enemy was completely unaware, and I was going to treasure it just as much as she did hers.

Madeline smiled into the spotlight, her white teeth

providing a stark, blinding contrast against her crimson lips. Then the spotlight clicked off, and the rest of the lights brightened again as she glided down the stairs. Appreciative murmurs sprang up in her wake, and even I could admit that she was the picture of beauty on the outside—and completely black, brittle, and rotten on the inside.

Just like me.

Madeline reached the bottom of the stairs and started working her way through the crowd, smiling, shaking hands, and generally making all the underworld lords and ladies feel as welcome as they could be in the heart of enemy territory. I melted back into the shadows a little more, and so did the rest of my friends. According to Silvio, Madeline had some sort of speech planned, and I wanted to hear what she had to say.

As Madeline moved from one cluster of people to the next, and it became apparent that she wasn't going to massacre everyone on sight, the crowd relaxed a bit, at least enough to turn their attention back to their champagne and hors d'oeuvres. Apparently, the thought of being in mortal danger was enough to give most folks the munchies.

It took Madeline about thirty minutes to make a circuit of the room and talk to all the top-tier crime bosses. As she was making her rounds, Emery walked down the staircase and entered the ballroom as well, along with Jonah.

The giant did the responsible thing, going around and checking in with some of the waiters-slash-guards, probably looking for folks who were already drunk and might be potential troublemakers. I held my breath, wondering if Emery might leave the ballroom and check in with the giants who were supposed to be patrolling the rest of the mansion. But after making a much quicker circuit than Madeline was, Emery headed to the bar and got a Scotch, which she sipped with slow, obvious relish. Apparently, it was enough for her peace of mind that the ballroom was secure and that there weren't any problems so far. Even with my wig and glasses, I didn't want to tempt fate, so I made sure to stay out of her line of sight.

The only one who didn't seem to be having a good time was Jonah. He went to the bar and started ordering doubles like there was no tomorrow. Maybe there wasn't going to be, for him. He managed to down three drinks before Emery gave him a cold glare that had him scurrying off to stand in front of the terrace doors, an island of worry in a sea of tension. Jonah kept smoothing down his tie, and I could see the stains from the sweat on his palm that was soaking into the silk.

Now that Madeline had won the crown as the queen of Ashland, she would have little use for Jonah, something that he seemed to realize, since he was eyeing the doors as though he was thinking about slipping out of them and disappearing into the night. That would have been the wisest course of action for him. Actually, leaving Ashland the second that I'd killed Mab was what he should have done. But Jonah might live through this yet. Madeline was my main concern tonight—not him.

Finally, the acid elemental finished with her grand tour. She whispered something to Emery, who nodded. The giant handed Madeline a flute of champagne and then stepped back. Madeline moved to the center of the dance floor and waited while the giants passed out fresh glasses of champagne. When everyone had a drink in hand, the orchestra stopped playing, and a hush slowly fell over the crowd.

Madeline smiled and raised her glass high. "Cheers," she called out, her smooth, silky voice ringing through the entire ballroom.

"Cheers," everyone echoed back to her.

Madeline took a sip of her champagne, but most of the other folks gulped down the golden bubbly in one long, nervous swallow. Everyone knew that the most dangerous part of the evening was beginning.

Madeline waited until the giants had moved through the crowd again, refreshing the many drinks that needed it, before she spoke again.

"I'm sure many of you are curious as to the reason I asked you all here tonight."

Murmurs of agreement rippled through the crowd. Everyone wanted to know why they'd been summoned, and judging by the nervous glances they were shooting each other, they were all wondering which of their enemies might already have made a deal with Madeline and what it might mean for them.

"Tonight is the beginning of a new era in Ashland," she said. "And yet, also a return to the old ways."

More murmurs, the tone a bit more speculative this time. Old ways could be good or bad, depending on your point of view.

"All of you knew my mother," Madeline said. "Many of you worked for her, or paid her to let you go about your business. And for years, the system worked, and everyone got rich. Until one woman came along—Gin Blanco."

This time, the murmurs degenerated into ugly mutters, curses, and sneers. I knew that I hadn't exactly been beloved, but I hadn't expected quite this level of hate. I should have, though. Given how many people here had tried to kill me.

"Blanco thumbed her nose at my mother and killed her men. And for what? To add yet another sad, sordid chapter to an old family feud that Mab had forgotten about years ago."

My eyebrows shot up at the ringing conviction in Madeline's voice. Mab hadn't forgotten about the Snow family and the daughter who would supposedly grow up to kill her one day. It had always been lurking there, in the back of her mind. And when she found out that Bria was still alive, she'd gone after my sister with everything she had, thinking that Bria was the one who had both Ice and Stone magic, instead of me.

But Madeline was twisting the truth around, making me look like more of a villain than I already was. My fingers clenched around my champagne flute, causing the glass to *creak*. Any tighter, and I'd break it with my bare hand. But I didn't need the attention that would bring. Not yet. So I forced myself to rein in my temper and listen to Madeline's version of a bedtime story, as full of lies as it was.

"But Blanco hadn't forgotten about the feud, and she set about terrorizing my mother." Madeline pressed her hand to her heart. "And then Blanco stabbed my mother to death. This woman, this *assassin*, killed my mother. You don't know the pain that caused me, that it still causes me."

Madeline dabbed her finger against the corner of her right eye, as though she were holding back a tear. Please. She had cared even less about her dead mama than I did. At least I'd always respected Mab as a powerful, dangerous enemy. I doubted that Madeline had had even that much regard for her.

"Now, many of you were as outraged by my mother's death as I was," Madeline continued, when she'd seemingly gotten control of her emotions again. "You, her business partners, her friends and confidants, you were the ones who rose up against Blanco and tried to avenge my mother's death."

This time, I couldn't hold back the snort of derision that escaped my lips. But luckily, everyone else around me was too focused on Madeline and her sob story to realize that I wasn't as enraptured as they were.

"But Blanco was a cunning enemy, a powerful elemental, and many of you lost friends and family to her. Brothers and sisters in arms."

Friends and family? Please. What she really meant were the disposable minions the bosses had sent after me, since none of them had had the balls to come down to the Pork Pit and actually face me themselves.

"Still, even though you all suffered great losses, you kept trying to eliminate Blanco. And for that, I thank you."

She bowed her head for a moment, and everyone leaned forward a little more, completely captivated.

"I was away at the time of my mother's death," Madeline said. "Regrettably, my mother and I were not as close as I would have liked. There were also some other matters that delayed my return to Ashland."

Her green eyes slid in Jonah's direction, and he swallowed and clutched his tie again, as if it were strangling him. The cloth couldn't do that, but I imagined that Emery would soon enough, with Madeline gleefully watching.

"I'd heard the rumors about Blanco, but I have to admit that I didn't believe them," Madeline continued. "How could one woman be responsible for so many needless deaths? For spreading so much fear and terror among you all? It seemed incomprehensible, given what I know of the people of Ashland. How brave you are, how strong, how determined."

If she kept this up, I was going to double over with laughter and give myself away. I'd wanted to hear what Madeline had to say, but I'd never thought that she'd bother to tell such outrageous lies. Not to these people who had already realized that she was a younger, stronger, more ruthless version of Mab. Not when they knew that the real reason they'd been called here tonight was so that she could tell them in person just how much she was going to tighten her grip around their throats while her other hand dipped into their wallets and took as much of their money as she could grab.

"When I saw how Blanco was terrorizing you, my heart was heavy. I didn't want to take her on. I'm just a businesswoman, the same as everyone else here. But it became apparent that Blanco was determined to continue with our family feud and her reign of terror throughout Ashland. And I knew that my mother would want me to avenge her, and all of you as well."

Madeline straightened up to her full height. "So I set about planning how to take Blanco down once and for all. And not just her, but everyone who ever helped her murder one of *us*."

Murmurs of agreement and appreciation surged through the crowd, louder than before. They were hanging on to her every word.

"But unlike Blanco, who used the shadows and her knives to terrorize, I decided to do things the right way, through legal means."

That whopper finally caused a few disbelieving titters to sound, since *legal* wasn't a concept that many folks in the ballroom were acquainted with, much less embraced. But a cold glare from Emery silenced the snickering rebels.

"Some of you helped me," Madeline said. "And for that, you have my thanks."

She bowed her head, and several folks puffed up a little taller. Some of them I recognized as people Fletcher had files on in his office, but I made note of all the others too. Silvio was discreetly angling his phone and snapping photos of them, just as I'd asked him to. I'd need the information later on. It wouldn't do me any good to take out Madeline only to have to worry about all the people who'd been loyal to her. Across the room, Bria's expression twisted with disgust as she realized how many cops were here.

"But in the end, Blanco was the instrument of her own

destruction," Madeline continued. "Rather than face justice for her many crimes, she barricaded herself in her own rattrap restaurant and then burned the place down. As far as I'm concerned, she couldn't have met a better, more poetic end."

Satisfaction surged through Madeline's voice, and it matched the growing buoyant mood in the ballroom. Yes, yes, everyone was glad that I was finally dead. I grinned. Which was going to make it all the more fun to see their horror when they realized that I was still alive.

Still, it surprised me that Madeline wasn't taking outright credit for my death. Then again, she didn't need to. Everyone knew that she'd orchestrated the whole thing, right down to starting the fire at the Pork Pit, and I had no doubt that these people both feared and respected her for it. Now here she was, weaving her web over the whole lot of them. They wouldn't even realize that they were trapped in the tangled threads until it was too late.

"So Blanco is finally dead, and I say good riddance." Madeline raised her glass again.

More murmurs of agreement sounded, with more than a few muttering, *I'll drink to that.* Tough crowd here tonight.

"With our number one enemy dead, I say that we return to the old ways," Madeline said. "Because we *are* Ashland, we are the people who haunt its darkest corners, we are the people who meet the deviant demands and dark desires of the so-called good citizens of our fair city. We're the ones they always turn to in the end, no matter how desperate they are to keep all their secret vices hidden."

She glanced around the room, judging the response to her speech, but everyone was still hanging on to her every word, so she continued with her sales pitch.

"So I say that we take what we want, what we had back when my mother was still alive. Who's with me?"

This time, loud, enthusiastic cheers erupted from the crowd, and everyone raised their champagne glasses high again. A few hoots and hollers broke out, which Madeline encouraged with a benevolent smile. Oh, yes. She was a slippery one. Mab would just have stormed into the room, said that she'd murdered me, and that it would be business as usual, with everyone bowing down to and paying tribute to her right then and there. She would probably have already ordered everyone to get out of her mansion so she could enjoy the spoils of her victory in peace.

But Madeline . . . she wanted to be *liked*, as well as feared. It was almost as if she had some desperate *need* deep down inside to bend people to her will without their even realizing that they were kneeling down in front of her. I wondered if it was because she truly delighted in such cruel mind games or that she wanted to be the exact opposite of Mab and make her own scorched mark on Ashland.

"But of course," Madeline continued when the cheers had died down, "this is a business venture like any other. And we all know that any business needs one thing above all others to succeed—a strong leader."

This time, the murmurs were more speculative than happy. This was the heart of Madeline's speech, the thing that would impact every single person here, and they all knew it. She had her hand around their throats, and now all that was left was to see how hard she was going to squeeze. I was willing to bet that it was going to be a death grip.

"I think that we can all agree that *I* am going to be that leader." She paused. "And for my services in that capacity, each one of you will pay me forty percent of everything you earn."

I almost choked on my champagne, and I wasn't the only one. Forty percent? As far as tribute went, that was *outrageous*. Even Mab had never dared to demand that much. Madeline didn't just want to be queen. She wanted to own everyone and everything in the entire city.

For the first time, I wondered if her ambition extended beyond Ashland. If one city wasn't enough for her. If this was just going to be her staging area for bigger and better things, maybe even for a move against someone else, some other boss, although I had no idea who else might be out there for her to conquer next.

Still, as shocking as it was, Madeline's pronouncement was met with uneasy but agreeing silence—at first.

Everyone in the ballroom looked back and forth at each other, thinking furiously. They didn't like an outsider coming in and taking over, especially not at a hefty forty percent, but they didn't want one of their enemies to do it either.

But finally, someone stepped forward to protest. Don Montoya ran a series of sports and other bookies out in the suburbs. He was tall, fit, and handsome, with bronze skin and a shiny black pompadour that made him look like a middle-aged Elvis. "And why should we let *you* just waltz into town and take over?" he demanded.

Madeline's eyes glittered like chips of green ice in her beautiful face. "Because I did what none of you could—I killed Blanco. That earns me the right to be the boss."

"Please," Montoya sneered. "You didn't kill her. Not really. You spun your little lies, and she got caught in them. That's all. You didn't do the honorable thing. You didn't face her down yourself. You didn't stand in the shadows with a gun in your hand and put three bullets in the back of her head."

More than a few mutters of agreement rose up at his words. For as crooked, low-down, dirty, rotten, and double-dealing as the members of the Ashland underworld were, they still respected one thing above all others—strength.

Trapping your enemy with lies, bribes, and other machinations was all well and good. But twisting the knife in your enemy's heart yourself? Well, that was even *better*. It proved that you had the guts to take what you wanted, and damn anyone who tried to show you the error of your ways. That's what Mab had done, and it was one of the reasons she'd held on to her power, position, and influence for so long.

Madeline strolled over to Montoya, her long white gown rippling around her body. The crowd fell back so that the two of them stood alone in the center of the dance floor.

"Just because I didn't kill Blanco with my bare hands or some crude instrument doesn't mean that I wasn't responsible for her death," Madeline said. "She lost *everything* because of me, and her friends are well on their way to doing the same. I've always had a slightly different philosophical approach than my mother. Why merely kill your enemies when you can torture them before you utterly destroy them?"

"Please," Montoya sneered again. "You can spout your pretty words all you want, but we all know the real reason you didn't face down Blanco yourself—because you don't have the magic to do something like that. Your mother, now, she was a *real* elemental, and she showed us all just how much power she had. So many times that we could never, *ever* forget. But you? You're nothing but a spoiled little princess, coming in here, stomping your foot, and telling us all how you think it's going to be."

Madeline arched a delicate eyebrow. "You think that I'm not strong?"

He looked down his nose at her. "Not like your mother."

She let out a soft laugh, but everyone in the ballroom could hear the malice in it loud and clear. Uncertainty filled Montoya's face, finally overpowering his arrogance, but it was already far too late for any apology.

Madeline casually flicked her wrist, as if she were dismissing his harsh words and bitter accusations with a simple wave of her hand. But it was so much more sinister than that. A few small green drops flew out of her fingertips, streaking through the air like emerald comets.

The acid spattered onto Montoya's face.

He screamed, his skin immediately blistering, burning, and smoking as the caustic liquid ate and ate away at it. In an instant, his handsome features had been irrevocably scarred. By the time ten seconds had passed, his bronze skin was melting quicker than candle wax. At the thirty-second mark, the white of his cheekbones was peeking through the bubbling red flesh that was slough-ing off his face bit by gruesome bit.

Montoya went down on his knees, clawing like a wild animal at his own skin in a desperate attempt to gouge the acid out of what remained of his face.

But it was too late.

Montoya collapsed in a heap on the floor, clawing, kicking, thrashing, and screaming all the while. Madeline jerked her head at Emery. The giant drew a gun out from under her black suit jacket, stepped forward, and put three bullets into Montoya's disintegrating skull. Blood, bone, and brain matter flew through the air, landing with wet, sickening *plop-plop-plop*s on the white marble floor.

Madeline stood over his body, delicately dusting off her hands as if they had a bit of unwanted dirt on them. Emery flanked her. The giant holstered her gun, even as her cold hazel gaze swept over the crowd, daring anyone else to challenge her boss.

"Well," Madeline finally drawled, "he wanted three bullets in the head. He got them. Would anyone else like to question my new authority?"

Nobody else dared to step forward. Instead, every-one shifted uneasily on their feet. The nooses had been dropped over their necks. Now Madeline was ready to pull them tight.

"As I said," she continued, stepping over Montoya's burned, bloody body and approaching the crowd again, "I intend to fulfill my mother's role as the head of the underworld. Thanks to Mr. McAllister, I know what each and every one of you was paying her. I know all about your homes, your businesses, your rivals, and everyone that supplies and supports all of your various . . . enterprises."

With every word she said, more and more people turned their hostile glares to Jonah, who gulped down a breath and tiptoed back so that his whole body was pressed up against one of the terrace doors. I'd wondered why Madeline had kept him around this long. She must have spent these past few weeks pumping him for information on how Mab had done things—and all the tribute that she'd been getting from the other crime bosses. Smart. After a few more weeks, once everything was up and running smoothly, she could dispose of him at her leisure. I almost wouldn't have minded letting Madeline live long enough to devise some truly dastardly fate for Jonah. But I was too committed to my plan to back down now.

Madeline glanced back at Montoya's body. "And now, since I had to resort to such an unpleasant display, you will all be paying me an even fifty percent."

Gasps rang out through the crowd, but I studied Madeline with new appreciation. She'd known that someone would call her out, and she was using Montoya's death as a way to get even more than what she'd already demanded. I was willing to bet that fifty percent of everything in town was what she'd really wanted all along.

"So," Madeline said, wrapping up her threats, "you can either accept my terms, or you can dirty up my dance floor, just like your colleague did. The choice is yours."

It wasn't a choice at all, but nervous chatter surged through the crowd, as everyone talked with their neighbors. But all of the sounds were small, hollow, and empty, and they quickly faded away. Madeline might not have her mother's Fire magic, but she'd demonstrated how powerful she was in her own right. She'd already won, and everyone knew it.

Slowly, a hush fell over the crowd. Madeline smiled, looking from one face to another, daring anyone to challenge her, but no one did.

One by one, I looked at my friends, still holding their positions in various corners of the ballroom. Owen. Phillip. Xavier. Silvio. Bria. Jo-Jo. Sophia. Finn. Roslyn. They all nodded back at me and started pulling off their wigs and glasses. This was the moment we'd been waiting for, and it was finally time to make my presence known.

"Well, Maddie," I called out in a loud, sneering drawl, "let me be the first to offer my congratulations on your new position."

Everyone turned to look at the person who'd just committed suicide by speaking to the acid elemental in such a mocking, derisive way. Puzzled frowns filled their faces, and whispers sprang up, as people tried to figure out who I was.

I stepped out of the shadows and strode across the dance floor, stopping in the middle of the ballroom, about ten feet away from Madeline and Emery. Still holding on to my champagne flute, I planted a hand on my hip and turned to one side, so that I could stare out at all the people gathered around. No one had recognized me yet, so I decided to end their confusion.

I reached up, plucked the black glasses off my face, and tossed them aside. Then I did the same thing with the red wig, making my dark brown hair spill around my shoulders.

It took the bosses several seconds to recognize me, but when they did, the entire ballroom went absolutely, completely, deathly quiet, even more so than when Madeline had been killing Montoya with her magic. Faces paled, sweat beaded on temples, and people almost *swooned*. Folks hurried to back away from me, and I gave them all a cold, thin smile before I turned to face Madeline, Emery, and Jonah, who had finally realized who I was—and that I was still alive.

Jonah's mouth gaped open, and he reached for the handle of the terrace door behind him, as if that was all that was keeping him from toppling over in a dead faint.

Emery jerked up to her full, seven-foot height, her hands curling into fists and her body bristling with a mixture of surprise and anger.

But Madeline had the most interesting reaction. Her face whitened with shock, and she blinked and blinked and blinked, her eyes snapping open and shut faster than a camera lens, as if I were some ghost that she could will away if only she focused hard enough.

Despite all her initial suspicions and speculations that I might have survived the fire, she'd lowered her guard and let herself finally, fully believe in the illusion of my supposed death. She'd been so smug, satisfied, and secure in her triumph—a triumph that I had just ripped away during the most important moment of her life.

My grin widened.

"Why, it's so very nice to see y'all again," I said, addressing the crowd. "I thought that my funeral yesterday was festive, but this—*this* is something else."

People shifted on their feet, mouths still gaping open, but everyone kept staring at me, wondering how I could possibly be alive and what I was going to do next.

Finally, when everyone had gotten a good, long look at me, I faced Madeline again. Her shock was rapidly fading, and I could almost see the wheels spinning in her mind as she tried to figure out what I had planned.

"Oh, yes," I said in another loud, sneering drawl, "I say that we all raise a glass and toast to the new queen of Ashland."

❊ 25 ❊

I raised my champagne glass high, but no one in the crowd followed suit. I glanced around, then shook my head and clucked my tongue, as if I were saddened by the sudden lack of support for Madeline.

"Actually, Maddie," I drawled again, "I wouldn't celebrate your victory just yet. It looks to me like there's still some question as to who the biggest, baddest bitch in Ashland actually is. After all, you told everyone that you'd orchestrated my murder. But here I am, just like usual, just like *always*, so I think we can all see that that's simply not the case. I don't want to call you a liar but . . ." I gave a delicate shrug of my shoulders.

Madeline's eyes narrowed to slits. "How the hell did you survive that fire?"

"Frozen peas," I quipped. "Who knew they were so good for you?"

Her face creased into a frown, and confused whispers

trickled through the crowd. No one got the joke but me. Maybe someday I'd explain it to them. Maybe not. A girl should always keep a few secrets to herself.

Madeline kept staring at me, so I decided to answer at least some of her questions.

"I survived because I'm a badass bitch. That's all you need to know."

"But—but—but there was a *body*!" she sputtered, finally losing her composure.

"There was, wasn't there? And I have *you* to thank for that, Maddie. Remember your maid? That poor woman you sent into my restaurant to kill me knowing full well that I would take her out instead? The one whose body you sent Dobson into the Pork Pit to find, but that he never did? Well, she was on ice in one of my freezers. She came in handy when you started tossing Molotov cocktails into my restaurant."

Madeline's frown deepened. "But the coroner confirmed that it was you. And your friends, your family, your funeral . . ." Her voice trailed off as her mind began to whirl at how thoroughly I'd fooled her and everyone else.

"Did you really think that you were the only one who could plan, set, and execute a trap?" I snorted. "Please. You were so sure that you'd won that you never even thought that I could be playing you, that I could be setting you up the same way that you had me. Sloppy, sloppy, sloppy, Maddie. Your mama would certainly have never made such a mistake. Oh, wait. Actually, Mab did make the same exact mistake back when she tried to kill me and my sister when we were kids. She assumed that we were dead, but we escaped her, and we made her pay for what she'd done to our family. And now I'm here to do the same to you. Like mother, like daughter, after all."

I *cluck-cluck-cluck*ed my tongue, mocking her even more. A few laughs sounded at the edges of the crowd, but they dried up when Madeline turned her gaze in that direction. Two red spots bloomed on her pale cheeks, her body trembled with barely restrained fury, and her hands clenched into fists. A drop of green acid squeezed out from between her tight fingers and fell to the floor, causing the white marble to shriek, wail, and start smoking.

But she quickly regained control of herself. She couldn't afford not to. Not with this crowd of sharks gathered around her. She might be the strongest among them, but they could still sense weakness, and weakness would get you killed quicker than anything else in Ashland.

So Madeline unclenched her fists and favored me with a dazzling smile. "Well, Gin, it's all well and good that you survived the fire. Actually, it rather pleases me."

"Really?"

"Really." Her smile widened. "Because it will make killing you now all the better."

She looked past me at the crowd that had now formed a circle around us. "Some of you were questioning my strength. Well, what better way than to kill Blanco right now? Surely, there would be no more unpleasant disputes then. Are we agreed?"

All around me, the bosses nodded, looking back and forth from me to Madeline.

"Well, then, now that that is settled . . ." Madeline glanced at Emery.

Emery waved her hand at the giant waiters. "What are you waiting for? Get her! Now!"

I'd thought something like this might happen, and we'd prepared for it. Before the giants could take one threatening step toward me, my friends erupted from the corners of the room, guns drawn. Xavier drew a bead on the three giants closest to him. Bria did the same to the ones near her corner, as did Phillip and Owen. Jo-Jo pulled a small revolver from her white patent-leather purse, while Sophia stepped out of the crowd, flexing her fists, obviously wanting to use them on someone. Up on the second floor, Roslyn brandished a gun and watched Finn's back while he grabbed his own weapon and put his red sniper laser sight right in the middle of Emery's throat. She froze, as did the rest of her men.

"You didn't really think that I'd come in here without some sort of plan, did you?" I asked Madeline in a soft voice.

She stiffened. "What have you done?"

I ignored her and turned to look at the crowd of people gathered all around us, their eyes on the guns pointed at them.

"My friends and I own this room, along with the rest of the mansion. All the perimeter guards are dead, and, as you can see, we have more than enough firepower to make a serious dent in the lot of you. So if I were you, I'd be good, be quiet, and stay out of the way." I shrugged. "Otherwise, some unfortunate accidents might happen. And wouldn't that just be a shame."

I kept my cold, wintry gaze on the crowd until people started dropping their eyes from mine and lowering their heads. They wouldn't do anything stupid, at least not right now, and they wouldn't try to interfere. Not when they realized what I had in mind.

When I was sure that the ballroom was under our control, I crooked my finger at the closest waiter. He swallowed and stepped forward, clearly nervous, but all I did was place my champagne flute on his tray and give him a dazzling smile. I waited until he had scurried back into the crowd before I turned and faced Madeline again.

Her eyes darted around, no doubt her mind spinning and spinning as she tried to figure out what I was up to—and whether I was going to kill her now.

"So," Madeline said, "you've stooped to taking me hostage in my own home. I'd think that something like that would be beneath you, Gin. After all, don't you prefer to stay hidden in the shadows? Creeping around like that little spider you claim to be? Hmm? Rather cowardly, if you ask me."

I chuckled. "You think that eliminating two dozen guards, taking over your mansion, and holding all of your guests hostage is *cowardly*? I think you need to study up on what that word actually means, Maddie. Then again, we all know what you're doing. Trying to wiggle out of a sticky situation that you've suddenly found yourself trapped in. You've set up so many of your webs for other people, including me. Looks like the black widow doesn't like to get caught up in the very thing she's created. I'd say that's the sort of thing that's truly *cowardly*, wouldn't you?"

That hot, angry blush spotlighted Madeline's cheeks again. She didn't like my mocking her, especially when she didn't have a ready answer or plan of attack. Finally, she just gave up.

"What do you want?" she snapped. "What is the point of this . . . *display?*"

Instead of answering her, I slowly peeled one black satin glove off my arm, then the other one. I clutched them both in one hand, raising them high so that everyone could see them. Speculative murmurs rippled through the crowd.

"The point? The point is that I can get to anyone, anytime, anywhere. Even an elemental as powerful as you. I thought it would be a good idea to remind everyone of that small fact. Just in case they'd forgotten, what with all those silly rumors going around about my death."

Madeline ground her teeth together. "Well, then, you've made your point. Is there anything else?"

"There's *always* something else. You've spent the last few weeks tormenting me and mine. Accusing us of things that we didn't do, causing problems, and in general doing your best to fuck with us all on the sly."

She didn't respond.

"Now, I could have done what I usually do. Set up a sniper's perch out in the woods, put a spray of bullets through your pretty face the next time you stepped outside, then come over and cut your throat just to make sure that you were good and dead." I gave her a thin smile. "But I know how very fond of playing games you are, so I decided to give you a sporting chance."

Unease flickered in Madeline's eyes. "What are you saying?"

I paused a moment for dramatic effect, just like she

always did, then stepped forward and threw my black gloves down onto the dance floor at her feet. "Isn't it obvious? I'm challenging you to an elemental duel, you sadistic bitch."

Madeline's face paled again, and shocked gasps rang out through the crowd, louder than any others that I'd heard all night long. I didn't know if it was because everyone had already seen how strong Madeline was in her magic or the black gloves I'd tossed onto the floor. They knew what the gloves meant, even if she didn't.

"A duel?" Madeline scoffed. "You've got to be kidding me. Nobody fights *duels* anymore."

"If you're going to try to take over an entire city, then you really should read up on your local history," I said. "Elemental duels have been fought in Ashland for more than a hundred and fifty years. They've always been a popular way to settle disputes, especially during the Civil War. A lot of the old family feuds started back then, since whole generations killed each other off one by one by one in various duels. I've always wondered if that was how our families, the Snows and Monroes, started their own blood feud. But I guess we'll never know for sure."

She scoffed again, not appreciating my history lesson. "But you can't challenge me to a duel. I won't *allow* it."

I gestured at the black gloves. "I just did. And we all know what that means."

All the underworld bosses started nodding their heads, realizing exactly what I was talking about, but confusion filled Madeline's face.

"Hey, Jonah," I called out. "Your boss doesn't seem to

understand how things work around here. Why don't you explain it to her, since you're such a legal expert?"

Everyone turned to stare at the lawyer, including Madeline.

Jonah winced. "Once a black glove is thrown down, and the challenge issued, the other person has no choice but to accept the demand for a duel."

Madeline's eyes narrowed. "Or what?"

Jonah cleared his throat. "Or that person immediately forfeits everything that she owns to the challenger—money, jewels, land, homes."

I made a deliberate show of looking around the ballroom. "I always wanted a mansion. I'd have to do some serious redecorating, though. White's not my color—red is."

Madeline stared at me, her mouth gaping open, wearing the same look of horrified shock as I had when the cops shut down the Pork Pit. Like I'd told my friends, Madeline had tried to legalese me to death, so I'd decided to return the favor. That was the reason I'd gotten Silvio to dig up all those old *Ashland Municipal Codex*es. So I could see exactly what antiquated duel laws might be on the books and how I could tiptoe around them. To my surprise and cunning delight, I'd discovered that almost all of the old laws relating to duels still remained on the books in Ashland, even if they hadn't been enforced in years. I'd been particularly happy about the forfeiture clause, knowing that one would upset Madeline the most. She hadn't gone to all this trouble to take over the town just to have everything she owned ripped away from her now.

I beamed at Madeline. "And do you know what the best part about a duel is?"

Jonah opened his mouth, but I held up my hand, cutting him off.

"It's not technically a crime to kill someone during an elemental duel," I purred. "Apparently, there were so many duels back in the old days that the po-po got tired of hauling all the survivors off to jail. Or they knew better than to try to arrest powerful elementals who'd just magicked their enemies to death. So the cops just decided to let them go."

Madeline thought that she'd been so clever with all her little legal maneuvers, but I'd found a way to kill her in front of every underworld boss in the city—and get away with it. Even she couldn't top that trick.

"So it boils down to this," I continued. "You can either give me everything you own and slink out of town like the coward you are, or you can accept my challenge and fight me face-to-face like you should have in the first place. You wanted a return to the old ways. What could be more old-fashioned than a duel?"

Madeline stared and stared at me, her green eyes narrowed, thinking, thinking hard. But the black widow had nothing on this Spider, and I'd trapped her in my own tangled web, as neatly as she had caught me before, and she could do nothing but accept my challenge. Otherwise, the other bosses would see her as weak and start plotting against her. They might even put aside their differences long enough to unite to take down their common enemy. Oh, I had no doubt that Madeline could put all of them in the ground, but it would be an annoyance to do so, and there was always the chance, however small, that one of them could get lucky and kill her instead.

Madeline knew all of this as well as I did, and I saw the moment when she realized that she was going to have to play the game by *my* rules, not hers. Her jaw tightened, her crimson lips flattened out, and her hands balled into fists again, although no more acid drops trickled out from between her clenched fingers. She didn't like how I'd cornered her. She didn't like losing control. Well, that made two of us.

But she recovered quickly, forcing herself to seem unconcerned. Her jaw relaxed, her fists unclenched, and her crimson lips curved up into that cruel, satisfied smile I knew all too well.

"Very well," Madeline purred. "You want a duel? You've got one. But I want this to be a *true* elemental duel. Otherwise, what's the point?"

"Meaning?"

"Meaning that just you and I participate in the actual duel—no one else."

"Agreed."

Madeline's smile widened, as though she'd thought of something that I wasn't expecting. "And we only use our magic—no weapons of any kind. Which, sadly, means no knives for you, Gin."

She waited, expecting me to refuse. She didn't think that I could beat her without my knives. Maybe she was right about that. But I'd made the challenge, and I couldn't back down now. Besides, I had one thing that Madeline didn't, and she wasn't even going to realize it until it was too late.

"Agreed."

Madeline blinked, as if she hadn't thought that I would give in so easily, but she kept that same confident smile plastered on her face. She was strong in her magic, and everyone here knew it, especially given what she'd done to Montoya. But I was strong too, and I was determined to end the Snow-Monroe family feud.

Once and for all.

"So we've set the terms, and the time is now," Madeline said. "I say that we get started, don't you?"

I smiled again. "Nothing would please me more than the pleasure of finally killing you."

☀26☀

While the Ashland underworld looked on, Madeline and I both readied ourselves for our duel.

Sophia stepped out of the crowd, since she'd be watching my back. I picked up my black satin gloves and handed them to her, along with all five of my knives. My fingers lingered on the last knife, the one that I'd killed Mab with, the one that still contained my Ice and Stone magic from that fateful battle. I hated to let it go, but this was the path I'd chosen, and I couldn't turn back now. So I passed that weapon over to the Goth dwarf as well, then stripped off my suit jacket, revealing the tight red tank top underneath. Even though we were going to be fighting with our magic, I didn't want anything to restrict my movements.

"Watch Emery," I said in a low voice. "I wouldn't put it past her to try to take me out during the duel, especially if it looks like I might actually kill Madeline."

Sophia nodded. She stuffed the gloves in her pocket, then secreted my knives on her body much the same way I always hid them on mine. Jo-Jo took my jacket from her.

Meanwhile, my other friends kept their backs to the walls and their guns trained on the crowd. The underworld bosses kept looking from me to Madeline and back again. No doubt some of them were thinking about how they could kill both of us while we were fighting, but my friends and their weapons should discourage the bosses from interfering.

I slipped off my black stilettos and handed them to Jo-Jo. Under my bare feet, the cool white marble muttered at the unease and worry that was slowly sinking into it, along with those drops of acid that were still eating through Montoya's body and the stone beneath one layer at a time.

Across the dance floor, Madeline also stepped out of her white heels and passed them over to Emery. The two of them started whispering, with Madeline's gaze on me the whole time. No doubt she was ordering Emery to kill me no matter what happened. I'd told Finn the same thing—to put a bullet through Madeline's head if I lost the duel. One way or another, she was dying tonight.

But all too soon, we were both ready, and there was nothing to do but get on with things. I stepped out into the middle of the dance floor, and Madeline moved to face me. The crowd circled around once more, the whispers and chatter of conversation getting louder and more excited. I even saw some money exchange hands, just like it had before my fight in the bull pen.

For a moment, I looked at the necklace ringing Madeline's throat. The lights made the gold crown-and-flame rune gleam brighter than ever before. Then I focused my gaze on the acid elemental. The hate glittering in her eyes matched my own hard expression.

"You won't win, Gin," she crowed. "You might have been able to defeat my mother and her Fire magic, but I'm even stronger than she was, thanks to my father and his giant blood. Even if I wasn't, nobody's *ever* been able to withstand my acid magic for more than a few seconds. I don't expect you to be any different."

I crooked an eyebrow. "And that's where you're wrong. Because I *am* different, and I'm certainly stronger than you are. Maybe not when it comes to raw power, but in other ways—the ones that really count."

"Well, then, let's get on with it." She raised her hands.

I did the same. "With pleasure."

Madeline smiled, then threw her acid magic at me.

Even though I was expecting the attack, even though I could see all those green, glistening drops of acid arcing through the air toward me, the hot, caustic feel of Madeline's magic still took my breath away. In the Pork Pit, just picking up the money she'd touched had made me want to scream in agony. But having so much of her power fully directed at me . . . realizing how strong she was . . . knowing that even a few drops of acid hitting my skin in just the right place would kill me instantly . . .

I didn't know if I could survive it or not, despite my plan.

I brought my Ice magic to bear, holding my palms

wide open, and using my power to create a shield to block Madeline's attack. But the drops of acid burned through all my Ice, obliterating it, and I had to use even more of my magic, much more than I wanted to, to freeze the acid in midair before it could touch my skin.

Madeline lowered her hands, and so did I. Wisps of steam curled in the air between us, creating a cold, eerie fog that kissed my cheeks. I could feel the burn of Madeline's acid magic even in the steam, and I had to blink back the tears it brought to my eyes.

All around us, the crowd whispered, debating who was going to win, even as more and more money slipped from one hand to the next.

Madeline shook her head. "One little taste of my magic and you're already crying and playing defense. So sad, Gin."

"You want offense?" I growled. "Well, how about *this*."

I shoved my hands forward and let loose with a cold, bitter burst of Ice magic, trying to take her by surprise. Hundreds of sharp, daggerlike needles erupted from my palms and sliced through the air, heading straight at Madeline.

She laughed, brought up her hand, and flicked her fingers again, sending out another spray of acid. The second that the acid hit my Ice, the deadly needles of my power dissolved into nothingness. A second later, all that remained of them were the few drops of water that had managed to escape Madeline's magic and hiss against the floor.

"Is that really the best you've got?" she asked in a bored tone. "How very weak you are."

My hands clenched into fists. That hadn't been a weak attack. I'd put a good chunk of my magic into it, and so had she. Despite her seemingly effortless defense, I could feel how much energy she'd expended to block my strike. Madeline was strong, but I was right up there with her. Our magic wouldn't determine who killed the other. Not really. How we used our power, who was more clever and resourceful with it—that was what would ultimately decide the winner.

And it was going to be *me*.

We exchanged blow after blow, insult after insult, as the duel raged on. She flung acid balls at me, I tossed Ice daggers back at her. She focused on my face, I went after her knees. She stepped back, I moved in. Ice and acid flew through the air as our attacks and counterattacks grew quicker and more furious, and our voices and taunts dissolved into low, vicious snarls. But neither one of us could get the upper hand in our deadly dance, and neither of us could break through the other's magic to do any real damage.

Stalemate.

The crime bosses scrambled out of the way of our explosive blasts of magic, but they didn't go far, and their faces were cold, eager, and calculating as they *oohed* and *aahed* with every bright burst of power. From the snippets of conversation I'd heard, most of them were hoping that we would kill each other outright and save them the trouble of trying to do it themselves.

My friends watched too, torn between cheering me on and worrying about whether I was going to survive. But they didn't interfere. I'd asked them not to, explained all the many reasons why I needed to face Madeline myself, and they'd reluctantly agreed. Besides, they couldn't have gotten between me and the acid elemental now, not without dying in the cross fire.

But they weren't the only ones who were worried—so was I.

We'd only been fighting a few minutes, but I'd already used up most of my magic, more than I'd wanted to. Plan A had been to kill Madeline outright with my own power, but that wasn't going to work. Time to change tactics.

So when Madeline raised her hands again, I charged at her. She flung a ball of acid at me, but I managed to sidestep it and get in close enough to slam my fist into her jaw. That made the crowd roar.

Me too, since my hand exploded in agony the second that my skin touched hers.

It wasn't any real pain from the punch. I'd thrown more than enough of those in my time to be accustomed to that sharp, smacking sting. No, this was much, much worse. Too late, I realized that not only could Madeline create acid, but that, in a way, her skin was *coated* with the caustic power that she could control. So much for my Plan B of beating and strangling her to death with my bare hands.

I screamed and lurched back, clutching my hand to my chest. That only made the crowd cheer louder.

Madeline's eyes glittered with sly satisfaction. "What's the matter, Gin? Can't use your usual tricks on me? I bet you really wish that you had one of your little knives right now, seeing as how you can't so much as touch me without your flesh melting off your bones."

I shook my hand, as if that would get rid of the burning sensation and the angry red blisters that had formed across my knuckles. "I don't need a knife to kill you—"

She jerked her hand, flinging acid at me in a quick sneak attack, aiming at my eyes and trying to blind me. I whipped my head to the side and reached for my Stone magic, wondering if that would work any better than my Ice power had. The hard shell of my skin kept the acid from destroying my vision, and it even kept the green drops from blistering my skin.

But it didn't keep it from hurting like hell.

The drops were small, little more than a faint spatter of rain against my left cheek, but Madeline's magic slammed into my own like a red-hot sledgehammer, scorching through all the many layers of Stone power that I'd brought to bear. My skin might be hard as a rock, but even acid could corrode a stone, and that's what Madeline's power was doing to my skin. So I sent out a quick blast of Ice magic, freezing the drops and then cracking them off my face. That got rid of the acid, but the caustic feel lingered, the scorching pain so intense that black and white spots winked on and off in my field of vision, even though none of the acid had actually gotten into my eyes.

Madeline surged forward and punched me in the jaw, putting some of her giant strength into the blow. That was bad enough, but the worst part was that her skin touched mine, and her acid magic washed over me again.

Once again, I screamed and staggered away from her—and right into Emery's waiting arms.

Even though she wasn't supposed to interfere, the

giant's arms clamped around me like a vise, squeezing, squeezing tight. Emery knew that a cracked rib could puncture my lung and kill me as easily as Madeline's magic could.

I threw my head back in a desperate, half-assed head-butt, and it surprised Emery enough to get her to loosen her grip. But before I could slither away, the giant twisted my left arm, and I yelped in pain as she dislocated my shoulder with that one great, heaving wrench. More delighted jeers rang out from the crowd. They'd be perfectly happy if Emery tore me to pieces.

Suddenly, Sophia was there, shoving Emery away and making the giant land on her ass on the floor. Sophia grabbed me, holding me up while I tried to focus through the pain.

"Okay?" she rasped. "Your shoulder?"

"Put it back into place," I snarled. "Do it. Now."

Sophia nodded, her black eyes locked with my gray ones. She reached out and wrenched on my shoulder. I yelped, but at least I could feel my arm again. I opened and closed my fingers, making as tight a fist as I could before releasing it, trying to shake off the lingering shock and discomfort of the dislocated joint.

By this point, Emery had gotten back up onto her feet. The giant glared at Sophia, but the dwarf simply stepped in front of me, crossed her arms over her chest, and gave her a flat stare.

"Don't worry," Sophia rasped, still glaring at Emery. "She won't interfere again."

I nodded, staggered back out into the middle of the dance floor, and faced Madeline again.

"What's the matter, Gin?" she crowed. "Feeling a lit-tle . . . out of joint?"

She snickered, and several folks in the crowd howled with laughter.

"Kind of sad, Maddie. You always getting other people to do your dirty work. I'm beginning to think that you just can't kill me yourself."

"You want to see what I'm truly capable of, Gin?" Madeline said, her voice chillingly soft. "Let me show you."

She reared back and tossed a ball of acid at me, larger than any of the ones before. I could feel the corrosive power emanating from the pulsing green mass, so I did the smart thing and ducked out of the way instead of trying to block it with my own magic. The ball of acid sailed through the air over my head and slammed into the middle of the staircase. The ivory carpet disintegrated, and the stone shrieked with agony as the acid spattered all over its slick, glossy surface and began to eat right through the marble.

And the same thing was going to happen to me unless I found a way to stop it.

Madeline threw another ball of acid at me. Then an-other, then another, as though we were playing a game of dodgeball. Acid splattered everywhere. On the dance floor, on the stairs, even on some unlucky folks in the crowd. More than one person ripped off their tuxedo jacket or tore at the skirt of their dress, shucking out of their clothes before the acid started eating into their skin.

I ducked Madeline's attacks again and again, my mind whirring, trying to figure out how I could best block her magic without completely depleting my own power. My thoughts turned back to the one other time I'd been exposed to Madeline's magic—when Beauregard Benson had made me swallow one of the Burn pills that contained her power. Madeline's acid magic had been the secret ingredient in the addictive drug, and it had almost cost me my life, since my inherent power had reacted so badly, so violently, to hers. I'd only survived the drug by using my Ice magic to numb my body from the inside out and block its effects. I could try to do that again now, but I didn't know if it would work. Because the Burn pill— the entire batch of pills—had only contained a few drops of Madeline's blood, and right now, she was unloading on me with everything she had.

I didn't know if I was strong enough to end her outright, but I had to try.

So I reached for my Ice magic, directing it outward, until I could feel the cold crystals of my power coating my skin like a web of snow. I caught a glimpse of my reflection in the terrace doors, and it occurred to me that I looked like the proverbial ice queen come to life. My skin shimmered with an almost silver-blue glow from where my own magic was shielding me. I just hoped that it was enough.

I dodged Madeline's latest blast of acid and stepped forward, determined to tackle her and beat her head against the marble floor until her skull cracked open and she bled out. But she was quicker than I was, and she snapped up her hands again before I could launch myself at her. But she didn't create another ball of acid or fling more drops in my direction.

No, this time her hands erupted into *flames*.

A shocked gasp escaped my lips, and I froze in my tracks, my eyes widening at the flickering green flames dancing across her fingertips. But more disturbing than that, I realized that she'd been sandbagging me this whole time, using just enough of her power to fool me into thinking that we were evenly matched and that I could actually defeat her with my own raw strength. Now she was finally letting me feel the full extent of her magic, and I realized just how much of it she truly had.

Madeline hadn't been lying.

The bitch was even stronger than Mab had been.

More important, she was stronger than *me*.

Once again, I'd underestimated her. Even as I'd sprung my trap by challenging her to a duel, Madeline had already started to outmaneuver me again. She'd only been playing with me before, testing the limits of my power and my response to her acid magic, but now—now she was going in for the kill.

* 27 *

I wasn't the only one who could feel Madeline's power. Everyone could see the acidic green flames burning, burning bright on her hands, and all the other elementals in the room—including Bria, Sophia, Jo-Jo, and Owen—could sense her strength as well. I didn't have to look at my friends' faces to know that they were as shocked as I was.

Madeline let out a delighted peal of laughter at the horrified expression on my face. "What's the matter, Gin? Not quite what you were expecting?"

"You are strong," I admitted. "Probably the strongest elemental I've ever faced. Certainly stronger than Mab was. Why, I imagine that you could burn this entire mansion to the ground with your acid flames, if you wanted to."

Madeline gave a modest shrug, causing the flames to cast an eerie green glow onto her face. "Well, that would have been one way to get the remodeling done a bit quicker, wouldn't it? Maybe I'll take your advice and do that. Just destroy the whole damn thing and start fresh— after I'm finished with you."

She drew her hands back, then shoved the acid flames at me. Once again, she was quicker than I was, and all I could do was stand there and take the full, brute force of her magic.

The flames washed over me, searing through all the Ice crystals that I'd coated my skin with, and forcing me to reach for my Stone power to harden my skin just to keep Madeline from incinerating me on the spot. Even then, the pain was intense, but I gritted my teeth and endured it. I even tried pushing back with my own magic, throwing my Ice power at her time and time again, but the acid flames gobbled it up before the cold could so much as nip at her fingers.

I was losing—badly.

Good thing it was all part of Plan C.

Madeline kept throwing and throwing her magic at me, in wave after hot, caustic wave, and it was all I could do to stay upright. But I held my ground. I might be losing now, but I was going to kill her in the end.

All because of Madeline's vanity.

I looked past the roaring green fire of her magic at her crown-and-flame necklace. The emerald seemed to almost be glowing with the same power that was coating her fingers, and the gold chain glimmered like a strand of sunshine around her throat.

I focused on that shiny band, reminding myself that I'd already won. Because her necklace was made out of *gold*—not silverstone.

Pretty is as pretty does, and as expensive as that necklace was, it might as well have been tinfoil wrapped around her throat for all the good it truly did her, along with her matching ring. Because they were both gold, which meant that they couldn't hold any of Madeline's power, and she wasn't wearing any other jewelry.

But I was—and mine was all *silverstone*.

My spider rune ring rested on my right index finger, while my spider rune necklace was nestled in the hollow of my throat—and both of them were filled to the brim with my Ice and Stone magic.

Madeline didn't have any extra reserves of magic like I did. All the power she had, all the acid she was using, was what was naturally in her body. To be sure, it was impressive, certainly more raw magic than I had, but it wasn't going to be *enough*.

Every time she'd confronted me before, Madeline had been wearing a silverstone necklace and ring. But she'd been so sure that I was dead that she'd lowered her defenses and started wearing gold ones instead. As soon as Silvio had shown me a photo of Madeline sporting her new gold jewelry, I knew that this was how I could finally challenge her to a duel and win. This was how I could finally finish her.

Arrogance will get you, every single time.

I didn't have to beat Madeline with my magic. Didn't have to punch her. Didn't have to touch her at all. Oh, I would have been happy if I'd managed to kill her any of those ways, but those were just the feints I'd used to sucker her into my ultimate trap. My plans within a plan, just like all the ones she'd used on me.

Because the truth was that all I had to do was outsmart her, outlast her, just like I had the fire in the Pork Pit.

Then she'd be mine for the killing.

So I pulled back on my power, using the bare minimum to keep Madeline's acid from melting me where I stood. It was agony, since I could still feel the acid flames licking at my body, could still sense my skin blistering, could still smell my own flesh burning. But I used just enough of my Ice and Stone magic to let me endure the horrid sensations. I even staggered around, then fell to one knee, as though I were finally weakening. Through the green flames, I saw Madeline's crimson smile widen and the white flash of her teeth as she stepped forward, eager to finish me off.

I grinned back, although I doubted that she realized it. If I could have, I would have whispered the age-old adage: *Step into my parlor, said the Spider to the fly.*

Madeline just didn't realize yet that she was the fly.

But she kept coming and coming, completely focused on directing every single scrap of power she had at me. The acid flames intensified. So did my pain, and doubt filled my mind, just as it had in the restaurant when the fire had come for me. I wondered if I'd miscalculated. If she had more power in her body than I did in mine and in all my silverstone jewelry put together.

If she was going to incinerate me with her magic after all.

But this was the path I'd chosen, and there was no turning back now. Even if I'd wanted to try to fight her with my own power, there was no point. Not anymore. Her acid was so hot, so caustic and corrosive, that it would eat right through whatever Ice and Stone magic I could summon up, other than what was keeping me alive at the moment.

So I huddled there on the floor and concentrated on my own magic and the low, urgent whispers of the stone around me. The marble had experienced the cruelty of Madeline's power, just as I was feeling it now, and they wanted me to end it and her just as badly as I did. I thought that the crowd was screaming for my death—and my friends were just screaming—but I couldn't tell. The world had reduced to a solid wall of acid green fire, creeping closer and closer with every passing breath.

I don't know how long I crouched there on my knee with one hand braced on the floor, steadying myself. It could have been a minute, it could have been an hour. There was just pain and the stench of my burning flesh and then more pain. So I concentrated on the feel of my power. On that hardness deep down inside me that was Stone, perfectly matched and married to the bitter cold that was Ice. Two complementary elements brought together in one person, and now, in the one protective shell of my magic.

Madeline towered over me, more and more acid flames erupting from her hands, like fireworks exploding in my face over and over. But I maintained my control, and I held on.

And eventually, finally, *at last*, she started to falter.

It was just a small tremor, just the faintest hiccup of her power. As though one gas tank were empty, and she was plugging herself into another one for round two. Maybe that's exactly what she was doing.

But that's the moment I knew that I'd finally won—once and for all.

I drew in a breath, careful not to suck in any of the green flames, and let loose with a bloodcurdling scream, as if I were mere seconds away from fully succumbing to Madeline's unending waves of acid. I screamed again and again, then let my voice choke off, as if I were suddenly overcome with more pain than any person had a right to bear.

I tried to rise up. I could have made it if I'd really wanted to, but it was all part of my plan. I tried again. Then, on my third try, I let my feet slip out from under me and crumpled to the floor, as though I were on my deathbed.

I wasn't, but Madeline was—she just didn't know it yet.

But she was so eager to finish me off that she never even thought that I might be playing possum. She took another step forward, then another, then another, coming closer and closer.

I let her come.

I *wanted* her to come.

Then she did the one thing that was most important of all—she started pushing even more and more of her acid into the flames, thinking that my end was near and that all she needed to finish me off was a big enough dose of magic, one that would finally blast through the protective shell of my Ice and Stone power.

I lay there on the floor and let the world burn around me.

Finally, there was another little hiccup in Madeline's

magic. Another faint tremor. I waited, wondering if she might have guessed my plan, if she might be trying to sucker me in the same way that I was her. But the hiccup came again, and again, and again, like a car that was out of gas and sputtering along as far as it could before it ran out of juice completely.

Good thing, since I was almost out of magic myself.

My own natural power was long gone. So was what had been housed in my ring. One by one, I'd emptied all the links in my necklace, and all the magic that I had left was what was still stored in the spider rune pendant.

Finally, just when I thought that I couldn't last another minute, Madeline let out a great, heaving breath, as though she was as exhausted as I was. The flames on her hands died down, and she staggered back a few steps before she was able to regain her footing.

I huddled there on the floor, which had long ago been burned all the way down to the foundation. Slowly, the black and white and green stars faded from my vision, the roaring in my ears ceased, and I could hear the whispers of the crowd.

"Is it over?"

"Is Blanco dead?"

"She's burned, but it doesn't seem too bad to me."

Madeline stood there in front of me, panting with exhaustion. But still, I didn't move, didn't speak. All I did was breathe and breathe and gather up what was left of my magic.

Finally, I lifted my head. Gasps rippled through the entire room, and Madeline's face paled as I managed to lurch up and onto my feet.

"You—you—you should be *dead*!" she sputtered. "I heard you scream. I saw you fall to your knees, to the fucking *floor*. I used all my magic on you! How can you possibly still be alive?"

I grinned. "Because sometimes, to win, it's better to play defense than offense. At least, until the final horn is about to blow."

Madeline frowned, wondering what I was talking about. Then she reached for her magic, still determined to kill me. But she'd burned through all of her power, and all she could muster up were some weak drops of acid that flickered like sparklers on her fingers. I looked at her, as tired and bone-weary as she was.

"This isn't over," she hissed. "You're not dead, but you haven't won either. Not while I'm still alive. You can't possibly have any more magic left than I do."

I shrugged. "I don't. Not in my own body, anyway. But do you know what the difference is between you and me?"

I reached for my spider rune pendant, holding it away from my neck and out to her. "I came prepared to *win*."

Madeline's eyebrows knit together in confusion, her green gaze locked onto the pendant as I let it go. The spider rune swung back and settled into the hollow of my throat, the silverstone rune a cool balm against the red burns and blisters that marred my skin.

Madeline's fingers crept up to her own necklace, and she finally realized what I meant. She sucked down a breath to scream, probably for Emery to come finish me off, or save her, but it was already too late.

"Good-bye, Madeline."

Before she could move, before she could react, before she could fight back, I reached out and clasped her hands with my own.

The flames of her acid magic licked at my skin, but I ignored the pain, even though it felt as though my fingers were melting, melting off. Madeline gritted her teeth and brought what was left of her magic to bear.

But it wasn't enough.

Oh, her acid still burned me terribly, and the silver-stone branded into my palms heated up, as the magical metal absorbed as much of her power as it could to try to protect me.

Madeline was right. I'd exhausted all of my natural magic fending her off, but I still had the reserves tucked away inside my spider rune. When Owen had given me the necklace for my birthday, I'd appreciated its beauty and the thought and sentiment he'd put into crafting something so exquisite for me. But I'd also seen it as the weapon that it truly was.

One that I finally put to good use.

I reached for the magic that was stored in my pendant. I gathered and gathered and gathered up all that cold, hard, chilling power, imagining cupping it in the palms of my hands.

Then I shot it out at Madeline.

Her hands froze first, since that's where I let loose with the power. In an instant, my Ice and Stone magic had turned her delicate fingers a cold, bitter blue, and I knew that her skin and bones would shatter if I so much as blew a breath of air onto them.

In the next second, the Ice and Stone had traveled up

her arms and started spreading across her chest before zipping down her torso, pooling in her legs, and spreading out through her bare feet onto what remained of the marble floor. In another second, she was anchored in place, even as she desperately struggled to move.

I could feel her pushing back with her own power, forcing more and more acid magic out of her hands, but this time, it wasn't enough to overcome the elemental Ice that I was encasing her with. Still, I added another three inches of it around her hands, just to be sure.

Madeline opened her mouth. Maybe to scream at Emery to help her and kill me, or maybe just at the unfairness of how I'd used her own tricks to beat her. But I sent out another wave of Ice magic, more powerful than all the rest. A bright silver light flared, so intense that I had to shut my eyes against the cold burn of it.

When I opened them, it was done, and Madeline Magda Monroe was fully encased in my elemental Ice.

My hands were still clasping Madeline's frozen ones, and I could see her green eyes darting back and forth behind the Ice as she tried to think of some way to escape. But there was none. I'd made sure of that.

So I held hands with my mortal enemy and watched as the frantic movements of her lips, nose, and eyes grew slower and slower, and weaker and weaker, until she finally died, frozen in place by the cold, hard fury of my Ice and Stone magic.

❊ 28 ❊

When I was sure that it was done, and that Madeline was dead, I drew in a breath and finally let go of what little magic was left in my spider rune.

It was harder than it should have been to pry my burned, blistered hands out of her cold, dead, frozen ones, almost as if she were still somehow desperately clinging to me, but I managed it, even though I left a fair amount of skin behind.

This time I stumbled back for real and fell to my knees in the center of the ballroom. All around me, pools of bright green acid smoked, bubbled, and burned, but they were slowly losing strength, their flames sputtering, as if their hot, caustic power had somehow been tied to Madeline's life, her very existence. Maybe they had been. Either way, she was dead, and I wasn't, and I didn't care about what remained of her magic or how it corroded everything it touched.

"No!" an angry shout rose up behind me. "No! Impossible! She can't be dead! She can't be!"

Emery darted forward. I grimaced, ducked, and braced my hands on the floor, thinking that she was going to tackle me, but instead she hurried over to Madeline's side, drew back her fists, and started pounding at the Ice that coated the acid elemental's body. But I'd mixed my Stone magic in with all the cold, frosty layers, making the Ice hard and thick, and she couldn't so much as chip the façade, despite all her giant strength.

"No!" Emery kept screaming. "No! No! No!"

While the giant kept trying to free Madeline, Jonah had a much smarter thought—he turned and sprinted for the terrace doors. He would have made it too, if Owen hadn't stepped up, stuck his foot out, and tripped the lawyer.

Jonah stumbled forward and cracked his head against one of the glass doors, splintering a pane, before collapsing into an unconscious heap on the floor. Owen grinned and flashed me a thumbs-up. I managed to grin back at him.

But the rest of the crowd had an entirely different reaction. I thought that they might try to flee, along with McAllister, but instead, several loud cries ripped out.

"Let's get them!"

"Yeah!"

"Now's our chance!"

I wasn't sure if they were talking about me and my friends or all the collective enemies who were gathered in the ballroom. Either way, a brawl erupted. Madeline hadn't allowed anyone to bring weapons inside her mansion, but the shattered end of a champagne flute made for a good enough knife. Fire and Ice flashed, blood and bodies flew through the air, people tackled each other, and folks rolled around on the floor, kicking and clawing and stabbing and biting for all they were worth. By killing Madeline, I'd shattered the fragile peace among all the underworld bosses and their followers, all of whom were doing everything they could to stick it to all their enemies within arm's reach.

Despite the fights rampaging through the ballroom, no one approached me, and none of the bodies even came close to hitting me. I supposed that they were all too afraid of me to openly attack me. Or perhaps they just didn't want to navigate the pools of acid that were still burning and flaming on the marble floor all around me.

I looked at the crowd, too tired to do anything to break up the massive free-for-all. Maybe if I was lucky, they would all take each other out, and I could quit worrying about the whole troublesome lot of them.

One woman stumbled forward, clutching her stomach and bleeding out from the jagged wound in her belly. Sandra Smyth, a socialite who paid for her lavish lifestyle by dealing in prescription drugs. She fell to her knees, right onto one of the pools of acid that was still flaming, and she screamed and bucked violently before her body suddenly went slack. The flames crawled up into her hair and down the back of her dress, the acid burning a little brighter now that it had something new to chew on.

Her gruesome death was enough to snap me out of my daze, and I realized that if I didn't stop this, no one would get out of here alive—including me and my friends.

So I forced myself to get up onto my knees, although I wobbled back and forth, burned, bruised, and utterly exhausted from my duel with Madeline.

"Enough!" I yelled. "That's enough!"

But the brawl continued, despite my friends' firing their guns up into the air, and my hoarse voice was lost in the cacophony of snarls, shouts, shrieks, and screams. Since I was still closer to the floor than I was to standing, I leaned forward and laid my hands flat on the marble, or what was left of it, careful to keep my fingers out of the pools of acid.

I must have had a bit more power left than I'd realized because I was able to send out a strong enough blast of magic to make the entire ballroom floor ripple like water. That wasn't enough to get everyone's attention, so I let loose with another burst of magic, this time making the walls quiver and even the chandeliers above our heads tremble and shake.

Everyone froze, their hands clenched into fists, their fingers curled around their champagne-flute shivs, their thumbs digging into the windpipes of their enemies.

It took me a moment, but I managed to get up onto my feet, then straighten up to my full height.

"That is *enough*." My voice was cold and dangerous. "Unless you want me to tear this entire mansion apart and bring the whole thing down on top of your idiotic heads."

My threat was enough to get everyone to drop their fists and hands and shuffle away from me. I walked forward, and they pressed back even more, as though the air in the room were somehow propelling them toward the terrace doors, and they were about to pop right out through the glass. Or maybe that was just the cold chill blasting off my body.

I stopped and placed my hands on my hips. I knew that I looked a fright, my body bruised, my face battered, and my skin red, blistered, and burned from Madeline's magic. But I was still standing, which is more than any of them could have said had they gone up against the acid elemental.

"Good," I said. "Now that I have your attention, let me tell you how it's going to be."

At my words, everyone's eyes sharpened, and their mouths flattened out into hard, knowing lines. No doubt they thought that I was going to give them the same exact speech Madeline had and announce that I was taking over the underworld. But I didn't want that.

I'd *never* wanted that.

"Now, unlike some people, I don't give a fuck about being the big boss," I snarled.

Snorts, scoffs, and disbelieving murmurs rippled through the ballroom just like my Stone magic had a few seconds before.

"I *don't*," I snapped again, my voice even colder than before. "If it were up to me, I'd walk out of here and never think about or see any of you ever again. But we all know that's not going to happen. Because, like it or not, Ashland is your home as much as it is mine. We've all done bad things here, and we'll all keep doing bad things. Because, like it or not, the corruption isn't just going to disappear overnight. Neither are the drug dealers or the gangs."

"What is this? A plea for the downtrodden?" Lorelei Parker snickered. "An after-school special?"

I glared at the crime boss, and her laughter quickly died down, although she lifted her chin and glared right back at me.

"Now," I growled, "most of you have spent the last several months trying to kill me. As Madeline oh-so-eloquently described it, you sent your brothers and sisters in arms after me. She said it was for revenge, but we all know that's bullshit. You all just wanted to prove your worth. You thought that by killing me, you could get everyone else to anoint you as the head of the underworld."

Most everyone in the crowd shrugged, and I caught a few snatches of conversation.

"Can't blame us for that."

"It's just business."

"Too bad we didn't succeed."

That last snide comment came from Lorelei.

"I'm talking about you, Parker. And you, Ron Donaldson. And you, Dmitri Barkov." One by one, I stabbed my finger at the underworld bosses I'd named before throwing my hands out wide. "Well, here I am, standing in front of all of you. I've frozen Madeline in her tracks—literally—and I'm willing to take on anyone else brave or stupid enough to try. Please, if you want me dead so very badly, make yourselves known. I've fought one duel tonight. Trust me when I tell you that I've got enough magic left for plenty more."

A blatant lie on my part, but now was not the time to look weak or indecisive. No, now was the time to finally get what I'd wanted, what I'd *always* wanted ever since

I'd killed Mab—a little peace and quiet. Even if I knew that it wouldn't last long. Not in a place like this. Never in Ashland. But it was my home, for better or worse, and these hills and mountains were as much a part of me as my Ice and Stone magic and the spider runes branded into my palms.

But no one stepped forward to call me on my bluff, so I moved on to what I really wanted to say.

"As of this moment, you will all stop being so damn *stupid*," I snarled. "Every single one of you will stop trying to kill me. You'll stop sending men to my restaurant, my home, and everywhere else. And if *any* of you black-hearted sons of bitches even *think* about hurting one of my friends, then I will rain my cold wrath down on you and yours like you have never seen before."

I looked from one face to another, making sure that they all got my message loud and clear. "Madeline wanted fifty percent. Well, this is what *I* want. Consider yourselves lucky that you're getting off so light."

"And if we don't stop?" Lorelei Parker piped up again. "If we all keep trying? What will you do about it then, Blanco?"

I stared her down. "Then I will keep eliminating you—all of you—until I've made my point. I'd thought it would have sunk in by now, given everyone I've killed over the past few months, but apparently, y'all are slow learners."

Lorelei opened her mouth, but I held up a finger, and she swallowed whatever she'd been about to say.

"I don't care what you do," I said. "If y'all want to get in a pissing contest to determine who rules Ashland, that's fine. Paint the streets red with each other's blood. Doesn't much matter to me. I can't stop all the crime in Ashland. No one ever could. And it's not like I'm any better than the lot of you, with all the bad things I've done. But don't involve me in your power struggles anymore, and don't think that killing me is the answer to being king or queen of the mountain. All it's going to get you is dead. Trust me on that."

I didn't point to Madeline's still-frozen body. I didn't have to. Silence descended over the ballroom as everyone shifted on their feet, wondering what came next. It suddenly occurred to me what they were all waiting for.

I sighed. "Y'all can leave now."

But no one made a move to actually open any of the terrace doors, even though they were all still pressed up against them.

"Leave!" I barked out. "Now! Before I change my mind!"

That got the lot of them moving. Oh, they tried to maintain some semblance of dignity, but their movements became faster and faster. Doors were wrenched open, and they all practically trampled each other in their desperate desire to get away from me as quickly as possible. In less than two minutes, my friends and I were the only ones left in the ballroom.

As soon as the last of them were gone, I shuffled over to the marble stairs and collapsed on the lowest one. I groaned at how good it felt to sit still and not have to try to appear tough and strong and pretend that Madeline hadn't done a number on me with her acid magic.

Jo-Jo rushed over to my side and took my hand in

hers. The milky-white glow of her magic flashed in her eyes, and I welcomed the pins-and-needles sensation of her Air magic sweeping over me, repairing all my burned, blistered skin and healing the worst of my wounds. But my injuries weren't as bad as this hollow feeling deep in the pit of my stomach. The one that told me that I'd used up all of my magic, more than ever before. I had no idea when it might return to me or how many days that could take.

Or how many plots might be hatched against me in the meantime.

Just because the underworld bosses had seen me kill Madeline didn't mean that they wouldn't keep coming after me. Oh, it might take them a while, but they all still wanted to be the top dog, and I was still standing in their way. So I would try to enjoy my respite for as long as it lasted.

"Well," Finn drawled, coming down the acid-splattered stairs to stand beside me, "I think that went rather well, all things considered."

Owen hurried over as well, crouching down in front of me, his violet eyes full of concern. "Are you okay, Gin?"

I waited until Jo-Jo had finished with her latest wave of healing magic. "Right as rain, now that Madeline is dead. I just didn't think that there would be so many other casualties."

More than a dozen still, crumpled bodies littered the ballroom. The bosses hadn't been brawling all that long, no more than a few minutes, but they'd gotten their licks in, and they'd made them count. Bria, Xavier, and Sophia were already busy going from body to body to see if anyone was still breathing underneath all that blood. Roslyn walked down the stairs and joined Phillip, who was trailing along behind the others and cataloging the bodies as well, to see which of his competition might have been eliminated.

Owen pushed a bit of loose hair back from my face. His fingers fell away, and I tried not to notice the clump of hair that they dragged along with them. Madeline's magic had eaten into me a little more deeply than I'd thought, but I wasn't worried. Jo-Jo could fix the parts of me that were broken, even if she could never touch or heal the scars that would continue to smoke and burn in my heart, just like the pockets of acid on the floor.

"So now what?" Owen asked.

I scanned the ballroom again. Jonah was still out cold next to the terrace doors, but there was one body that I didn't see among all the others.

"Where's Emery?" I asked.

Finn shook his head. "Gone. Out one of the doors with the rest of the crowd. I tried to get a bead on her, but there were too many people in the way."

A cold finger of unease crept up my spine at the news of the giant's escape. She wouldn't let this go. Madeline had been her boss, her cousin, her friend, and she'd want revenge. Emery would find some way to make me pay for Madeline's death. It was as certain as the sun coming up in the morning. But there was nothing I could do about it tonight. Even if the giant had been standing right in front of me, I barely had the energy to blink at the moment, much less take her on.

"Don't worry, Gin," Silvio piped up, texting on his

phone. "I'm already reaching out to my contacts to track her."

Finn slapped his hands on his hips. "*Your* contacts? And what makes you think that *your* contacts will find her faster than *my* contacts will?"

Silvio gave him a patronizing look. Finn glowered back at the vampire. I was too tired to even roll my eyes, much less snicker at their rivalry—

"Who are you people?"

Every single one of us froze. Me. Owen. Finn. Silvio. Jo-Jo. Even Bria, Xavier, Sophia, Roslyn, and Phillip on the other side of the ballroom.

Then, with one thought, we all whirled around, fists and weapons raised, looking for the source of that soft, hesitant voice.

A little girl stood at the edge of the dance floor.

She was dressed in soft, pale blue footie pajamas patterned with penguins and clutched an even softer-looking blue rabbit to her chest. Her hair was mussed with sleep, but I could see the auburn highlights glinting in the dark brown strands.

She looked at all of us in turn, not really afraid, but her green eyes were big and curious.

"Who are you?" she asked again. "And where's my mommy?"

❋ 29 ❋

All the air left my lungs in a ragged rush. I blinked and blinked and blinked, as if that would change who and what was before me.

But it didn't.

A little girl. In the Monroe mansion. Staring at me with Madeline's eyes. Wondering where her mommy was.

I didn't have to look at the others to know that they were just as shocked and surprised as I was. In all the intel that Finn and Silvio had gathered on Madeline, in all my spying on her, in all my confrontations with her, there had never been so much as a whisper that she had a child. Then again, I'd never known that Mab had had a daughter either. But now here I was, confronted by the next little girl in the Monroe family. I couldn't help but wonder if she had the same kind of acid magic that her mother did, or perhaps even her grandmother's Fire power.

Jo-Jo was quicker and kinder than the rest of us. The dwarf got to her feet, plastered a smile on her face, and slowly approached the girl.

"Hi, there, darling," Jo-Jo crooned in a soft, easy voice. "What's your name?"

"Moira. Moira Monroe."

She held out her hand. "Nice to meet you, Moira. I'm Jo-Jo."

The two of them shook hands, the little girl as serious as she could be. Jo-Jo gestured over her shoulder at the rest of us.

"And these are my friends."

Moira looked us over, her green gaze moving from one of us to the next, even as my friends shuffled forward and sidled sideways, trying to hide as much of the blood and as many of the bodies as they could from her.

Finally, her eyes met mine. Her tiny face creased in thought, and I realized that she was staring at my spider rune necklace.

"Oh," she said, her face clearing. "You're the spider lady, the one that my mommy doesn't like. What are you doing here? I thought that you were dead."

I heard her words, even though they all sounded like gibberish at the moment. But I forced myself to get to my feet and slowly walk over to her, not wanting to scare her. It was a good thing Jo-Jo had healed all the burns and blisters on my skin already, or I would have looked like even more of a monster than I already did.

Up close, Moira was as pretty as a picture. She couldn't have been more than three or four, but I could already tell that she would grow up to look just like Madeline.

I imagined that she'd be even more beautiful than her mother had been.

I opened my mouth, but no words came out. I didn't know what to even *think* right now, much less say to her. I wet my lips and tried again, but I still couldn't utter so much as a single sound. My silence must have scared Moira, because she backed away from me. A pale green light began to flicker around her fingers.

And the stuffed rabbit began to smoke and burn in her hands.

Small drops of acid spattered onto the rabbit's face, melting it in an instant, as Moira looked up at me with round, scared eyes. I sucked in another breath, and I finally managed to plaster a tight, miserable smile on my face. Well, that answered my question about what kind of magic she might have. As for her power level, it was hard to tell since she was still so young, but if she had even half of Madeline's strength, then she would be an elemental to be reckoned with.

Still, as I looked at the girl, trying to seem as non-threatening as possible, I almost felt as if I were . . . *Mab*.

I could see it all so clearly, just the way that she no doubt had all those years ago. How this one innocent girl could one day grow up to be a threat to me. How she could destroy everything I'd built. How she could kill everyone I loved, before she finally murdered me herself.

In that moment, I could almost . . . *understand* why Mab had murdered my mother and Annabelle and had tried to do the same to me and Bria all those years ago. How, in her mind, she'd simply been trying to protect herself and her empire. How she'd wanted to nip this potential threat in the bud, since it was by far the most dangerous one that she would ever encounter. And how all she had done was set in motion her own destruction with her attack on my family.

Yes, I could almost understand Mab's reasoning back then, but that didn't mean that I could do what she had done. Because no matter how ruthless I was, no matter how cold or tough or brutal of an assassin, Fletcher had taught me a few simple rules, ones that held firm even now, when I was confronted by the next generation of the Snow-Monroe family feud in the making.

No kids—*ever*.

So I cleared my throat, plastered a more genuine smile on my face, and crouched down on my knees so that my face was level with hers.

"Hi, there, sweetheart. My name is Gin."

I held out my hand to her. Moira stared at me, still frightened, but I had soothed her enough to get her to release her acid magic. The pale green sparks flickering around her fingers vanished, although her rabbit continued to burn against her chest. She gingerly took my hand in hers. I gritted my teeth, expecting to feel the invisible waves of her magic burning my skin, but her hand was small, warm, and soft, with no trace of her power pulsing on her delicate skin—yet.

"Hey," she said, perking up for no apparent reason the way that kids so often do. "Would you like to see my room? It's this way!"

Instead of letting go of my hand, Moira started tugging me out of the ballroom. I looked back over my shoulder at my friends. Most of them gave me helpless shrugs, but Bria stepped forward, following us.

Moira led me down the hallway like a general directing a soldier. She didn't let go of my hand until she reached a door that was cracked open at the end of one of the corridors. The door was painted blue, and as soon as she saw it, she barreled ahead into the room. I drew in a breath and followed her, bracing myself for what I knew I was going to find.

An enormous playroom lay before me.

A child-size, white wicker table with four matching seats stood in the center of the room, covered with a white china tea set patterned with delicate blue roses. Real pitchers of lemonade sat on the table, along with a plate of half-eaten sugar cookies and apple slices that had already turned brown. Picture books, dolls, and stuffed animals lined wooden shelves built into one of the walls near a white, padded window seat, while large, open cedar chests in the corners held even more toys. Any little girl could spend hours in this sort of fantasy playground, happily drinking lemonade, eating cookies, and reading books to all her stuffed-animal friends.

At the far side, an archway led to a large bedroom, and I could see a bathroom branching off that area. This was the suite of rooms that Silvio had shown me yesterday, the ones that he'd thought Madeline was remodeling for some guest. Well, now I knew exactly who'd been staying in them.

I just didn't know what to do about it.

Beside me, Bria stood in the doorway and stared at the playroom, memories, heartache, and longing etched in the tight lines around her mouth.

"We used to have a room just like this," she said in a low voice. "Full of toys and games and dolls and tea sets.

Do you remember, Gin? What it was like, what *we* were like, before . . . Mab?"

I nodded and gripped her hand tight.

Moira plopped her half-melted bunny down in one of the chairs, then skipped over and grabbed my hand again, pulling me forward.

"C'mon, Gin. Let's have a tea party!" Moira stopped, giving Bria a shy look. "The pretty princess lady can come too."

I looked at Bria, who looked just as stunned as I did. I shrugged at my sister, and she shrugged back. Moira tugged on our hands and led us both over to the white wicker table in the center of the playroom.

Why not. It would be better than the party we'd just been at.

Bria and I sat on the floor next to the table while Moira ran around the playroom, introducing us to all her dolls and stuffed animals. My sister and I made the appropriate noises, but we were both still too stunned to really hear what the little girl was chattering on about.

Jo-Jo came to the playroom a few minutes later, and the dwarf somehow managed to get Moira settled in bed and started reading a book to her. So Bria and I slipped away and went back out to the ballroom.

The rest of my friends were still there, checking the bodies, but I ignored them and marched over to where Jonah McAllister lay in front of the terrace doors. He was still out cold, so I started kicking him in the ribs until the weasely bastard woke up. It didn't take long before he groaned and rolled over onto his side. I kicked him one more time, then leaned down, grabbed the lapels of his tuxedo, hoisted him upright, and slammed his body back against the closest door. It took his brown eyes a moment to focus on me, but I was pleased to note the fear that filled them the second he realized that I was looming over him.

"The girl," I ground out. "Moira. Madeline's daughter. Start talking. How old is she? Where is she from? Who is her father?"

Jonah just stared at me, more and more fear filling his eyes and blocking out everything else, including my pointed questions.

I shook him once, roughly, then leaned forward a little more so that my face was inches away from his. "I'm not going to ask you again."

His tongue darted out to wet his lips. "I don't know much."

I leaned forward even more.

"I don't! I swear!" Jonah cried out. "Just that the girl is almost four years old. Madeline had her, but she wanted to focus on building her own business empire, so she left the girl with her father."

"And who might that be?"

He shrugged. "Some Stone elemental, I think. Apparently, he really loved Moira and was happy to raise her by himself. Then Madeline came around again and told him that she was taking her daughter to Ashland. The father tried to run, tried to take the girl with him, but Madeline had Emery track him down."

My heart sank. I could imagine exactly what the giant had done to the runaway father. "Is he still alive?"

"I think so. But you know Emery. She could have easily killed him just for spite."

I dropped McAllister. His head cracked against the marble floor, but he shook off his daze enough to flip over onto his belly like the snake he was and start crawling away from me. For once, I let him. I was too busy thinking about Moira.

Xavier and Bria moved toward McAllister, probably to ask him more questions about Moira and her father, but I stalked back across the ballroom until I was standing in front of Madeline.

"You sly Monroes," I growled to the acid elemental's still-frozen corpse. "You do delight in fucking with me from beyond the grave, don't you?"

Madeline didn't answer, of course, but I could have sworn that I saw the curve of her crimson lips and the gleam of her white teeth through the Ice, almost as if the black widow were laughing at me one final time.

At my request, Bria and Xavier called the cops to the mansion so we could put our own spin on how everything had gone down here tonight. Instead of leaving the scene of my crime like I had so many times before, I stayed and faced the po-po with my friends.

Most of the officers seemed more shocked at my having actually killed Madeline than anything else, even that I was still alive, but none of them approached me, and none of them dared to arrest me. Even if they'd tried, they couldn't have so much as touched me, thanks to all those old, antiquated laws I'd found on the books. I'd challenged Madeline to a duel, she'd accepted, and she'd lost. Perfectly legal, and perfectly deadly. For her at least.

I'd thought that the cops might try to take me in

for supposedly killing Captain Dobson, but Silvio had already laid the groundwork to get me out of that too. He had a quiet, but rather pointed, discussion with the commanding officer on the scene about the bull pen, how I could identify many of the cops who'd been there that night and, worst of all, sue the department for every dime it had. So all the charges against me were summarily dropped. Silvio even got the commanding officer to promise to issue me a public apology.

As for the other dead bodies, Bria and Xavier claimed that the crowd watching the duel had panicked and that several folks had been trampled to death as a result. It wasn't plausible, not at all, but none of the surviving underworld bosses were going to speak up and tell the police what had really happened.

Dr. Ryan Colson arrived soon after that, along with several of his assistants. I hadn't seen the coroner since my visit to his office, but he didn't seem surprised or upset by my presence here. Colson gave me a respectful nod, which I returned, then went about his business of seeing to the bodies. He would know that they hadn't died from being trampled, not given all the stab wounds, snapped necks, and bruised throats on them, but I doubted he would make an issue of it.

Eventually, I settled myself on part of the marble staircase that had escaped Madeline's acid. Owen drifted over and sat down next to me. Together, the two of us watched the cops work.

"Now what?" he asked. "What are you thinking about, Gin?"

I looked around the ballroom. Two hours ago, it had

been a beautiful spot, glittering, pristine, and perfect with its diamond chandeliers, creamy orchids, and soft white lights. Now it looked like a bomb had gone off inside the once-elegant space.

I felt the exact same way inside with the revelation that Madeline had a daughter—and that perhaps our family feud wasn't as finished as I'd thought.

Mab had killed my mother and older sister and had tried to do the same to me and Bria. Because of all that, I'd grown up with one thought on my mind—revenge. I wondered if Moira would be the same way. If she'd grow up with that same obsessive desire, that same driving ambition, that same unending thirst for blood.

My blood.

"Gin?" Owen asked again. "Bria says that there's nothing more we can do here. Are you ready to go?"

I glanced around the ballroom a final time, at all the blood and the bodies and the still-burning pools of green acid, and me sitting smack-dab in the center of it all. Part of me wondered how I'd ever wound up here, in this time, in this place. A larger part of me wondered what would happen next—what all the consequences of my actions here tonight would be.

But those were questions and worries for another day. Madeline Magda Monroe was finished, and her schemes as dead as she was, and that was all that mattered tonight.

"Yeah, I'm done here."

Owen got to his feet and held out his hand. I threaded my fingers through his, and he pulled me up. Together, arm in arm, we walked past Madeline's frozen corpse and out of the ballroom.

❆ 30 ❆

The next few weeks flew by in a whirlwind of activity.

Several stories popped up in the media about Madeline's death, Dobson's too, but given Silvio's not-so-subtle threats that I could still sue the department, the po-po decided to pretty much sweep everything under the proverbial rug. Par for the course in Ashland.

With Madeline dead, her schemes against my friends all unraveled as well. Roslyn's liquor distributor backed down, Owen's business deal finally went through, Eva's name was cleared and she was reinstated at the community college, Jo-Jo's salon was declared to be mold-free, and Bria and Xavier got their jobs back on the police force. Even Finn's lawsuit got dropped for lack of evidence.

But there was still the not-so-small matter of the Pork Pit.

The interior of the restaurant had been a total loss, thanks to the fire, although the brick walls were still intact, along with the pig sign hanging over the front door. By some stroke of luck, the fire hadn't so much as touched the sign, although I'd hired a crew to clean off all the residue left behind from all the smoke and ash that had boiled out of the restaurant.

After that, another crew came in—this one from Vaughn Construction—to gut what was left of the interior, clear out all the debris, and start again. I'd thought that Charlotte might refuse the job, given our tangled, troubled history, but she accepted it. In fact, she'd come down to the restaurant to personally oversee the construction, along with a few new features that I was adding— including a hidden door in one of the brick walls that would give me a secret way outside, should I ever have need of such a thing again.

Given my luck, I was betting that would happen sooner rather than later.

But the days and weeks passed by, and before I knew it, I was standing on the sidewalk outside the restaurant on a cool November day, staring up at the freshly cleaned sign with the pig holding a platter of food. Maybe I should change the logo to a phoenix. After all, the restaurant had risen from the ashes, just like I had. I grinned. Nah. I liked things just the way they were.

Still, as I slid my key into the front-door lock, I couldn't help but look around, searching for rune traps and any other nasty surprises that someone might have left for me. But things had been shockingly, amazingly quiet since I killed Madeline. None of the underworld bosses had sent any more of their men after me. No one had tried to kill me at all. Perhaps they'd taken my words to heart. Or perhaps they were lying in wait like Madeline had, spinning their black-widow webs and hoping to ensnare me in them. Either way, I'd finally gotten my peace and quiet, and I was going to enjoy it while it lasted.

There were no runes or traps, so I stepped inside the restaurant and locked the front door behind me. It was early, just after nine, and today was the first day that I was going to open the restaurant since the night it had burned.

I looked out over the storefront, which was brand spanking new, yet so familiar at the same time. Everything inside was new, shiny, and polished, from the blue-and-pink vinyl booths that lined my improved bulletproof windows, to the sturdy metal tables and chairs in the middle of the storefront, to the padded, swivel stools that fronted the long counter that ran along the back wall.

I'd even had an artist come in and redo the blue and pink pig tracks on the floor. They curved over to the restrooms as usual, but the artist had taken the extra step of having the tracks lead to other places too—the cash register, the double doors, the back of the restaurant, and even up onto the walls and all the way across the ceiling. To me, the tracks were almost like Fletcher's footsteps, marking his paths through the restaurant and all the memories I had of him here over the years. Mine too. I liked them, and I knew that he would have too.

I moved over to the counter and ran my hand along the slick surface. Since I'd had to remodel the entire restaurant, I'd upgraded everything inside and now had fancy new appliances, dishes, and silverware that would put the most expensive, highfalutin, and uppity restaurant to shame. Underwood's didn't have stoves, pots, and pans as nice as I did now. Even the dish towels were all new, fresh, and clean.

I moved over to the cash register. It was just about the only thing that I hadn't modernized. Oh, it was new to me, but Jo-Jo had found it in one of the antique shops a few blocks over. It wasn't exactly the same as the one that Fletcher had had for so many years, but it was close enough and made a similar *ring-ring-ring* whenever I opened the cash drawer.

But there were two important things that were missing. I unzipped the black duffel bag hanging off my shoulder and reached inside. I drew out some paneling nails, along with a small hammer. A few *tack-tack-tack*s later, and I had put two nails in the wall close to the cash register, right where I wanted them.

When that was done, I put the nails and hammer away and reached back into the bag. The photo of a young Fletcher with an equally young Warren T. Fox went up on one nail. On the other, I carefully hung the framed copy of *Where the Red Fern Grows*, the one that was spattered with the old man's blood. I looked at the two framed items, the counter, the old-fashioned cash register, and the pig tracks curving every which way through the restaurant. Things that were old, new, borrowed, and blue. I took them all as a sign of good luck. I had finally reclaimed the last thing that Madeline had tried to take away from me, and it felt damn good.

The Pork Pit was back in business.

* * *

I admired the restaurant for a few more minutes before getting to work. Turning on the appliances, tying a new blue work apron on over my jeans and long-sleeve T-shirt, pulling out vegetables and other foodstuffs to get everything ready for the day.

The first thing I put together was a vat of Fletcher's secret barbecue sauce. As soon as it started simmering away with its rich, smoky mix of cumin, black pepper, and other spices, the restaurant felt like home again. I quickly fell into the usual routines and lost myself in the welcome familiarity of cooking. Sophia, Catalina, and the rest of the waitstaff came in, and I went over and flipped the sign on the front door over to *Open*.

My first customer of the day was Moira Monroe.

The bright, shiny silver bell over the front door chimed, and the little girl skipped inside, followed by Jo-Jo. Moira was the only thing that we hadn't told the cops about, and she'd been staying with the Deveraux sisters ever since we found her. But today, she was leaving Ashland—I hoped for good.

It had taken them more than two weeks, but together Finn and Silvio had managed to find her father, Connor Dupree. Apparently, in the middle of the night, Emery had stormed into the hotel room where he'd been hiding with Moira and had taken his daughter away from him, almost beating him to death. I'd had Finn and Silvio thoroughly vet the dad, digging into every part of his life and background, but he seemed to be a genuinely good guy who loved his daughter.

Jo-Jo led Moira over to the counter and helped her sit up on the stool closest to the cash register.

"Hi, Gin," the little girl said in a bright voice.

"Hi, sweetheart," I murmured. "Are you having fun with Jo-Jo?"

A grin spread across Moira's face. "She painted my nails this morning. See? I can't wait to show them to my daddy when he gets here."

She held out her hand so I could see the pale pink polish and silver sparkles that glittered on her tiny nails.

"They're so pretty," I said. "Just like you."

Moira giggled and started spinning around and around on her stool. I fixed her a cheeseburger and some sweet-potato fries, and a barbecue-chicken sandwich and some coleslaw for Jo-Jo.

People came and went, and we had a much larger crowd than I'd thought we would, everyone from my friends and family to folks who had heard about the fire and had come to gawk at how the Pork Pit was open for business again—and that I was still standing when I should have been cold, dead, and buried in the ground.

Eventually, Jo-Jo moved Moira over to one of the booths so the little girl could color on a paper place mat printed with the Pork Pit's pig logo.

Bria came into the restaurant a few minutes later. She stopped to say hello to Jo-Jo and Moira, her eyes lingering on the little girl, her face creasing with sadness and just a touch of anger.

Bria had had a much harder time coming to terms with Moira than I had. Then again, Bria had been younger when our family was torn apart, and Mab had stolen more of her childhood than she had mine. Still, Bria managed to smile at Moira before walking over and sliding onto a nearby stool.

"Her dad's still coming to get her, right?" Bria asked.

"Yep. He should be here any second. He's driving down from Cypress Mountain."

My sister kept staring at Moira. "Do you think that she'll be all right? Is she still asking where Madeline is?"

I grimaced. That had been the hardest part about this whole thing. Even though Madeline had taken her away from her father by force, Moira still knew that the acid elemental was her mother, and she kept asking where she'd gone. Jo-Jo had tried to explain to her that Madeline had passed away, but I didn't know if Moira understood it. The little girl had asked me one time if Madeline was up in heaven, and I'd told her yes, even if I didn't think that was where Madeline had ended up. But who was I to judge? I wasn't going to end up there either. Not by a long shot.

But maybe Moira could. Maybe she'd finally break free of the vicious cycle of the Snow-Monroe family blood feud. Maybe she'd leave it all behind. Maybe she'd have a long, happy, worry-free life.

That was my hope for her.

Moira kept coloring, but Jo-Jo kept glancing at her watch, then at the door. The dwarf had just looked over a third time when someone yanked it back, and a man hurried inside, his blue eyes frantically darting around the restaurant. I recognized him from the photos Finn and Silvio had shown me.

Connor Dupree was right at six feet tall, and I could feel the worry pulsing off him, along with his magic—Stone magic, just like Jonah McAllister had said. I suddenly wondered just how many areas Moira might be gifted in herself. If she could be a duel elemental like me—or something even more powerful.

Dupree's face was thin, and his steps were slow, almost as if it hurt him to walk, even though he didn't have any visible injuries. From what Bria had found in the police reports, Emery had beaten him to within an inch of his life. Even then, he'd tried to stop her from taking his daughter away from him. Maybe he was still feeling the psychological effects of that beating, of having someone he loved so cruelly ripped away from him.

"Daddy!" Moira shouted, throwing her colored pencil down, getting up out of the booth, and running over to her father.

Dupree bent down and gathered her in his arms, tears streaming down his face as he whispered something in his daughter's ear. Jo-Jo went over to talk to them, but Dupree kept hugging and hugging Moira to his chest, as if she might disappear if he let her go for so much as a second. But Moira giggled and wiggled away from him, running around the restaurant. She grabbed her place-mat coloring, marched back over, and proudly showed it to him. Dupree smiled, more tears streaming down his face, and pulled her close to him again.

It took him a few more minutes before he was able to wipe his tears away, straighten up, and speak to Jo-Jo. He didn't look at me, and I didn't go over and talk to him. Thanks to Finn and his penchant for creating fake IDs, as far as Dupree knew, Jo-Jo was from social services and had been watching after Moira until he could come get her.

Jo-Jo gave Dupree a phony business card that Finn

had had printed up with one of my burner phone numbers and anonymous e-mails on it, just in case he ever needed anything. Dupree took it, then held out his hand. Moira skipped over to her father and threaded her fingers through his. He opened the door for the two of them.

"Are you sure this is the right thing to do, Gin?" Bria asked.

Moira looked at me, then raised her arm in a cheery good-bye wave, her colored place mat and the bag of cookies that I'd given her earlier dangling from her other hand. Her father opened the door, and Moira kept waving until it swung shut behind them.

"I guess we'll see in about twenty years or so," I said, finally answering Bria's question. "When Moira grows up, comes into her magic, and decides how she wants to use it—and if she wants revenge for her mother's death."

"And if she does?"

I shrugged. "Then we'll see if she can get it. I tried to set her free the best way that I know how. The rest is up to her."

Just like every person's life was their own to lead. I'd tried to make the most of mine. Only time would tell what Moira Madeline Monroe would do with hers.

Bria left, and the rest of the day passed by in the usual fashion of cooking, cleaning, and cashing out customers. But more than once, I found myself staring out the storefront windows, wondering about Moira. I hoped that she recovered from the trauma of being taken away from her father. I hoped that he found some way to explain to her what had happened to Madeline. I hoped that she had a better childhood and a happier and more carefree life than I ever had. I hoped so many good things for her. But like I'd told Bria, only time would tell if they came true.

So I went about my business and the rest of the day. A few folks wandered in who clearly had more on their minds than just barbecue. Gangbangers, underworld bosses, and the like. But they sat in their seats and ate their food, and no one was waiting in the back alley to try to kill me when I took out the trash after the lunch rush ended. It seemed that at least some of them were heeding my warning to leave me alone. I wondered how long their good sense would overpower their ambition and greed.

But that didn't mean that I hadn't just created a whole new passel of problems for myself.

Around four o'clock, during one of the few lulls in the restaurant today, the door opened, and a blond woman came inside wearing oversize sunglasses and a red suit jacket and matching skirt that were both so tight that they looked like they'd been painted onto her porcelain skin. She looked around the storefront, obviously searching for someone. After a few seconds, she spotted Silvio sitting at his usual spot at the counter and headed in his direction.

I looked at the vampire. Someone had been blowing up his phone ever since he'd come into the restaurant an hour ago. Perhaps even several someones, judging from how Silvio had been texting like his life depended on it ever since he sat down.

The woman slid onto the stool next to Silvio, four down from where I was sitting behind the cash register, reading a copy of *The Bourne Identity* by Robert Ludlum for my spy-literature class.

"Sorry I'm late," she murmured to him. "You wouldn't believe the parking outside. You can't even get within three blocks of this place right now."

"That's quite all right, Ms. Jamison," Silvio said. "Ms. Blanco was taking a brief break."

"Call me Jade." She stared at me. "But she's going to help me with my problem, right? I mean, that's what she does now."

My eyebrows shot up in my face as I looked at Silvio, but he ignored me and sent out one more text before he set his phone aside. "You can explain your situation to Ms. Blanco. It's up to her to decide if she wants to help you or not."

Jade Jamison sighed, then slid the sunglasses up so that they swept her blond hair away from her face . . . and revealed the truly spectacular black eye that she was sporting. Somebody had ground his fist into her face—repeatedly.

"So look, I run some girls out in the suburbs," she started. "A couple of guys too. For the last year, I've had a mutually profitable arrangement where all the pimps up there leave me and my folks alone as long as we don't poach clients from their territory. Only now, one of them, Leroy, says that I have to start paying him protection money. You can see the *what else* on my face that he gave me when I told him no way."

"And what do you expect me to do about it?"

Jade rolled her eyes. "You're Gin Blanco," she said as if the answer should be obvious. "You kill people."

I looked at Silvio, but he shrugged. "I've been getting calls and texts like this for days now. I thought that I would at least wait until you had reopened the restaurant before we started addressing them."

"How considerate of you."

"Listen," Jade said, leaning forward against the counter, her suit jacket straining to keep from popping open. "People say that you're the big boss in town, now that Madeline Monroe is dead. I was dealing with her before, trying to get Leroy off my back, but she wasn't exactly doing anything, you know? So Silvio told me to come on down here, and you'd help me out. I don't want to make any trouble. I just want Leroy to hold up his end of our agreement. He'd have to do that if you told him to. . . ."

She kept talking about the specifics of their deal, but I was focused on the two most important words she'd said.

Big boss.

Big boss? I wasn't anybody's boss, except for the folks who worked at the restaurant. But it sounded like some people had made it seem otherwise. My eyes cut to Silvio, who gave me another *what-can-you-do?* shrug of his thin shoulders.

I had told everyone in the underworld not to mess with me, and it looked like they'd finally decided to listen. But an entirely different consequence had arisen, one that I hadn't even seen coming, much less dreamed would ever happen.

My hand crept up to the spider rune necklace around my throat. I'd been wearing it openly, over my T-shirts and other clothes, ever since my duel with Madeline. More than a few folks had stared at the pendant, but no one had dared to comment on it, and I hadn't thought much about it—or the message others might think that I was sending.

As my fingers curled around the familiar symbol, my gaze locked on the blood-spattered copy of *Where the Red Fern Grows* up on the wall, and I thought of Fletcher. I wondered if the old man had ever imagined that this would happen. If he'd ever dreamed that it would come to pass. If he'd known all along that this was where the road would take me. That, in a way, I'd set myself up to become the very thing that I'd hated for so long.

Mab fucking Monroe.

The thought punched me in the gut, but that didn't make it any less true. Mab had been the queen of the underworld, and now it looked like I was too. It wasn't something that I'd wanted or had strived for or had ever even hoped for. I had enough worries of my own. I didn't need to mediate others' problems too. Or whatever Mab had done to solve disputes.

But this wasn't the time for such philosophical musings, so I forced myself to relax my fingers, let go of my spider rune, and drop my hand back down to the counter.

"So are you going to help me or not?" Jade snapped, realizing that I wasn't paying attention to her.

I didn't respond. I didn't know what to say right now.

She looked back and forth between me and Silvio, let out a disgusted snort, and hopped to her feet. "Terrific," she snarled. "So I drove all the way down here for nothing and left my folks alone and defenseless. You're just as useless as Madeline was."

Jade whirled around to stomp away.

Silvio arched his eyebrows at me. "Somebody has to step up," he said in a soft voice. "Or things will get worse. People will die."

And you've been elected. He didn't say the words, but we both knew that they were true. Just like I knew that if Jade Jamison confronted Leroy again, he would most likely beat her to death, when all she was trying to do was protect the people she cared about. And that made my decision for me, the way it always did.

"Wait," I called out. "Come back, sit down, and tell me what happened."

Jade stopped and gave me a suspicious look.

I pointed at the stool she'd just left. "Please."

That made her eyes narrow a little more, but she slowly walked back over and resumed her seat. I touched my spider rune pendant one more time, then leaned my elbows down on the counter, giving her my full attention.

As she started telling me about her problem, I realized that the Pork Pit wasn't the only thing open for business again.

The Spider was too.

Turn the page for a sneak peek at the
next book in the Elemental Assassin series

Spider's Trap

by Jennifer Estep

Coming soon from Pocket Books

1

"I really want to stab someone right now."

Silvio Sanchez, my personal assistant, glanced at me out of the corner of his eye. "I would advise against that," he murmured. "It might send the wrong message."

"Yeah," Phillip Kincaid chimed in. "Namely that you've reverted back to your deadly assassin ways and are going to start killing people again instead of hearing them out like you're supposed to."

"I don't think I ever really left those ways behind," I replied. "Considering that I could kill everyone here and sleep like a baby tonight."

Phillip snickered, while Silvio rolled his eyes.

The three of us were sitting at a long conference table that had been dragged out onto the deck of the *Delta Queen*, the luxe riverboat casino that Phillip owned. Normally, slot machines, poker tables, and roulette wheels would have been set up on the deck in preparation for the night's gambling, but today the riverboat was serving as the site of a meeting between some of Ashland's many underworld bosses.

Supposedly, this meeting was to be a peaceful mediation of an ongoing dispute between Dimitri Barkov and Luiz Ramos, two of the city's crime lords, who were currently disagreeing about who had the right to buy a series of coin laundries to, well, launder the money that they made from their gambling operations. Not that there was anything peaceful about the way that Dimitri and Luiz had been standing nose-to-nose and screaming at each other for the last five minutes. Their respective guards stood behind them, fists clenched tight and shooting dirty looks at each other, as though they would all love nothing more than to start brawling right in the middle of the deck.

Now, *that* would be entertaining. I grinned. Maybe I should just let them have at each other. Winner take all. That would be one way to settle things.

Silvio nudged me with his elbow and narrowed his gray eyes at me, as if he knew exactly what I was thinking.

"Pay attention," he murmured. "You're supposed to be listening to the facts so you can be fair and impartial, remember?"

"I could be fair and impartial in stabbing them *both*."

Silvio gave me a chiding look.

I sighed. "You always ruin my fun."

"That's my job," the vampire replied.

I palmed one of the silverstone knives hidden up my sleeves and flashed it at my friends under the table, out of sight of the other bosses and their men.

"C'mon," I whispered. "Just let me stab one of them. Surely, that will shut the other one up too."

Phillip snickered again, while Silvio let out a small, sad sigh. He wasn't crazy about my managerial style. Couldn't imagine why.

My friends turned their attention back to Dimitri and Luiz, who were still yelling and pointing fingers at each other, each trying to shout the other man down. But instead of listening to them, I looked at the third boss who had shown up for the meeting—Lorelei Parker.

Unlike Dimitri and Luiz, who were both dressed in slick business suits, Lorelei was sporting black stiletto boots, dark jeans, and a black leather jacket, just like I was. Her black hair was in a French braid, and her blue eyes were focused on her phone, since she was busy texting. Only a single guard stood off to her side: Jack Corbin, her right-hand man. He too was dressed in boots, jeans, and a leather jacket, but his cold blue eyes continually scanned the deck and everyone and everything on it.

Corbin realized I was watching him and tipped his head at me before sidling a little closer to his boss, ready to protect her from everyone on the deck, including me. I nodded back at him. My deceased mentor, Fletcher Lane, had a thick file on Corbin in his office, so I knew that he was far more dangerous than he appeared to be.

Then again, so was I.

Lorelei was here because she actually owned the coin laundries in question and was more than willing to sell them—to the highest bidder, of course. I didn't know if she'd approached Dimitri and Luiz about buying the front businesses or if they'd come to her, and I hadn't had the chance to ask any questions, since the gangsters had been screaming at each other the entire six minutes that I'd been on the riverboat. Either way, the men just couldn't agree on who was getting what, and things had escalated to the point that Dimitri and Luiz were about to declare war on each other. That would mean shootings, stabbings, kneecappings, and lots of other messy crimes.

Don't get me wrong. As the Spider, I'd made plenty of bloody messes in my time. It was sort of my specialty.

But a few weeks ago, I'd taken down Madeline Magda Monroe, an acid elemental who'd declared herself the new queen of the Ashland underworld, following in the footsteps of her mother, Mab.

Just as I had done to her mother several months ago, I managed to kill Madeline with my Ice and Stone magic, and with no more Monroes left to try to take control of the underworld, the other bosses had made me their de facto leader. At least until they started plotting how they could murder me and one of them could seize the throne that they all coveted so very much.

I almost wished that one of them would succeed in putting me out of my misery.

Contrary to popular belief, being the head of the Ashland underworld was not a bed of roses. It wasn't even a bed of thorns. It was just a giant *headache*—like the one throbbing in my temples right now. I'd thought I'd been a popular target before, but now the bosses sought me out more than ever before. And they actually wanted to *talk* to me. *Incessantly*. About business deals and treaties and who was letting their gang members spray-paint rune graffiti in someone else's territory. As if I actually *cared* about any of those things. But being the big boss now, it was apparently my job to listen. At least, according to Silvio.

I would have been happy to stab people until they got the message to shut up, solve their own problems, and leave me alone already.

Lorelei was the one who'd requested this meeting, although she'd actually approached Phillip about settling the dispute instead of me. Apparently, Lorelei didn't want to acknowledge my new authority or involve me in her affairs. That, or she just hated me for some reason. Didn't much matter either way, since I had as little regard for her as she did for me.

But Phillip was my friend, and he'd told me about the meeting. So here I was, about to mediate my first big dispute as Gin Blanco, the Spider, new queen of the Ashland underworld. Yeah, me.

Still, I would have been perfectly happy to skip the meeting and let Dimitri and Luiz duke it out until one of them killed the other, but Silvio had correctly pointed out that if I resolved their feud today, they wouldn't show up at my restaurant, the Pork Pit, tomorrow. Since I didn't want the criminals scaring my customers, I'd decided to be a good boss and show up at the meeting.

Everyone had been sitting at the conference table when I walked on board with Silvio. But at the sight of me, Dimitri and Luiz had immediately shot to their feet and started shouting accusations at each other, as if they thought that I would side with whoever yelled the longest and the loudest.

Now Dimitri was cursing at Luiz in Russian, and Luiz was returning the favor in Spanish. Since it didn't look like they were going to stop anytime soon, not even to take a breath, I tuned them out as best I could and looked out over the brass railing.

The Aneirin River flowed by the white riverboat, the swift current causing the enormous vessel to sway ever so slightly. The November sun glinted off the surface of the blue-gray water, making it sparkle like a sheet of diamonds, while a faint breeze brought the smell of fish along with it. I wrinkled my nose at the wet stench. A few crimson and burnt-orange leaves clung to the trees that lined the far side of the river, although the breeze would soon send them spiraling down to the ground—

Something flashed in the trees directly across from me.

I frowned, leaned to the side, and focused on that spot. Sure enough, a second later, a small flash of light caught my eye, the sun reflecting off something hidden back in the trees—

Silvio nudged me with his elbow again, and I realized that Dimitri and Luiz had stopped their shouting and were staring at me with expectant faces, their arms crossed over their chests. On either side of the deck, their guards wore similarly hostile expressions, their hands still clenched into fists.

"Well, Blanco?" Dimitri demanded in a low, gravelly voice. "What is your decision?"

"Yeah," Luiz chimed in, his tone much higher. "Who gets the laundries?"

I looked back and forth between the two of them. "Um . . ."

Dimitri frowned, and anger sparked in his dark eyes. "You weren't even listening to us!"

"Well, it was kind of hard to follow," I admitted. "Especially since I don't speak Russian, and my Spanish is rudimentary, at best."

Dimitri threw his hands up in the air and let loose with a string of Russian words, many of which sounded like curses.

Phillip leaned over. "I think he just insulted your mother."

I groaned, but I held my hands up, trying to placate the Russian mobster. "Okay, okay. That's enough. Stop. Please."

Dimitri finally finished his cursing, but he still gave me a disgusted look. "I knew this would be a waste of time. I should have just killed Lorelei and taken the laundries for myself. Just like I should have put a bullet in your head the night of Madeline's party and taken control of the underworld myself. Just like I should do right now."

Silence descended over the deck, and the only sound was the steady *rush-rush-rush* of the water flowing alongside the riverboat.

I put my hands flat on the table, then slowly got to my feet. The *scrape-scrape-scrape* of my chair against the deck was as loud as a machine gun.

I stared at Dimitri. "That was exactly the wrong thing to say."

Everyone could hear the chill in my words and see the ice in my wintry gray eyes.

Dimitri swallowed, knowing that he'd made a mistake, but he wasn't about to back down in front of everyone else, so he raised his chin and squared his shoulders. "I don't think so. There's only one of you. I have three men with me."

I smiled, but there was no warmth in my expression. "That's because you need guards. I don't. I never have. So if I were you, I'd start apologizing to me. Pronto."

Dimitri wet his lips. "Or else?"

I shrugged. "Or else your men will be dragging what's left of you off this boat, and Phillip will be sending me the cleaning bill."

Dimitri sucked in a ragged breath, but anger stained his cheeks a bloody red. "Nobody threatens me."

"Oh, sugar," I drawled. "It's not a threat."

Dimitri kept staring at me, his breath puffing out of his open mouth like he was a bull about to charge me. Beside me, Phillip and Silvio both got to their feet.

"Try to show a little restraint," Silvio whispered as he passed me.

Restraint wasn't a popular word in my vocabulary, but I nodded, acknowledging his point. If I killed Dimitri and Luiz, it would just convince the other bosses that I wanted them all dead and they would probably start trying to murder me again. I'd fought hard for my relative peace and quiet, and I wasn't going to throw it away on a couple of minor mobsters.

Even if I did feel like stabbing both of them. Violently. Viciously. Repeatedly.

Phillip and Silvio moved over to where Lorelei Parker was still sitting at the far end of the table. Lorelei had quit texting and was now staring at me, but she remained in her seat, with Jack Corbin still standing by her side.

The two of them weren't dumb enough to take me on, at least not face-to-face, but the same couldn't be said for the other two bosses.

Dimitri wasn't brave enough to fight me on his own, so he turned to Luiz. "You help me with Blanco, and I'll let you have the coin laundries. All of them."

Luiz narrowed his eyes. "I want the laundries *and* that deli you own on Carver Street."

Dimitri sighed and nodded his head.

I rolled my eyes. A minute ago, they would have been happy to murder each other, and now they were going to work together to try to kill me. Well, at least Luiz had the good sense to try to squeeze everything he could out of the other gangster. Had to admire him for that. Even if he'd picked the wrong side.

Dimitri and Luiz shook hands, sealing their hasty deal, then they both turned to face me, with their guards standing behind them, glaring at me and cracking their knuckles in anticipation of the beat-down they thought they were going to give me. Fools.

"Now what are you going to do?" Dimitri sneered. "Against all of us?"

"Me? I'm finally going to have some *fun*. I certainly deserve it, after listening to you two whine like a couple of kids fighting over the same ice-cream cone."

Apparently, my insult was the last straw, because Dimitri's cheeks burned even hotter, and he stabbed his finger at me.

"Get her!" Dimitri roared.

"Kill Blanco!" Luiz yelled out.

The two bosses and their guards surged toward me,

with Dimitri leaning over the conference table and reaching out with his hands, as though he wanted to strangle me to death.

I kicked my foot into the table leg, making the whole thing slam forward, right into the Russian's potbelly. He gasped and doubled over, causing his very bad, very obvious, very shaggy black toupee to almost slide off his head.

But I was already moving on to the next threat. I leaned down, snatched up the metal chair I'd been sitting in, and slammed it into the face of the closest giant guard. He yelped and staggered away, clasping his hands over his bloody broken nose. He lurched past Silvio, and the vampire stuck his foot out and tripped him. The giant's head hit the top part of the railing, and the brass let out a loud, pealing note, as if it were a bell that had just been rung. The giant slumped to the deck unconscious. *Ding*. Down for the count already.

Silvio flashed me a smile and a thumbs-up. I grinned back at him, then turned to the next guard.

Phillip had had the good sense to make sure that no one had come onto the riverboat armed, except for me, so I wasn't worried about getting shot. Even if someone had managed to sneak a gun or knife on board, I could always use my Stone magic to harden my skin and protect myself from any bullets or blades.

Using that same chair, I whacked my way through two more guards, opening up cuts and bruises on their faces, necks, and arms. By the time I got done with those giants, the plastic seat had cracked apart in my hands, so I ripped two of the metal legs off the chair and swung them around like batons.

Whack-whack-whack-whack.

I slammed the metal poles into every guard I could reach, cracking the chair legs into knees and throats and temples and groins. Moans and groans blasted out like fog horns across the deck, and more than a little blood arced through the air and spattered onto the glossy wood and gleaming brass rails.

"Restraint!" Silvio called out after I jabbed the end of one of the poles into the face of the giant closest to me. "Restraint, please, Gin!"

"What?" I yelled back. "I'm not stabbing them to death . . . yet!"

At my words, the giant I'd been fighting froze, his fists drawn back to punch me. But apparently, he took my warning seriously, because instead of hitting me, he whirled around and made a beeline for the gangplank on the other side of the boat. I let him go, since he was the last guard standing. All the others were huddled on the deck, trying to find the strength to hoist themselves upright and will their eyes to stop spinning around in their heads.

"You!" Dimitri roared, having finally gotten his breath back, and shoved his toupee up onto his head where it belonged. "I'm going to kill you if it's the last thing I do!"

With a loud roar, the crime boss charged at me. But instead of hitting him with the chair legs like I had all the guards, I simply squatted down. Then, when he was right on top of me, I surged up and tossed him over the side of the railing.

"Ahhh . . ." Dimitri screamed on the way down.

Splash!

Footsteps pounded on the deck, and I saw Luiz rushing at me out of the corner of my eye. I squatted down again quickly and then, when he was right on top of me, surged up and tossed him over the side as well.

Another loud scream, another satisfying *splash!*

My eyes cut left and right, but there were no more enemies to fight. So I looked at Lorelei Parker and Jack Corbin, who were in the same positions as before.

"You two don't want to join in the fun?" I drawled, twirling the metal chair legs around in my hands again. "I was just getting warmed up."

Lorelei let out a disgusted snort and shook her head, while Corbin held up his hands in mock surrender.

Faint cries sounded—"Help! Help! Help!"—and I went over to the railing. Phillip and Silvio came to stand on either side of me, and we all looked   down.

In the river, Dimitri and Luiz were clinging to each other, both of them thrashing around and trying to stay afloat by drowning the other man. Dimitri had somehow held on to to his toupee, which he was now beating against Luiz's face. They both looked like the wet, slimy rats that they were.

I grinned at Phillip. "You were absolutely right. Throwing people overboard is *tons* of fun. I feel better already."

"Told you so," Phillip said in a smug voice, his blue eyes bright with mischief and merriment.

Silvio sighed. "Don't encourage her."

More moans and groans came from the fallen giants on the deck. I tossed my metal poles aside, turned around, and leaned back against the railing. All the guards stopped and looked at me, wondering what I was going to do next.

"So," I called out, and jerked my thumb over my shoulder. "Anyone else want to go for a swim?"

Strangely enough, no one stepped forward to take me up on my offer.